THE SARANTOS
BABY BARGAIN

BY
OLIVIA GATES

Published in Great Britain 2014
by Mills & Boon, an imprint of Harlequin (UK) Limited,
Eton House, 18-24 Paradise Road, Richmond, Surrey, TW9 1SR

© 2014 Olivia Gates

ISBN: 978 0 263 91465 8

51-0514

Harlequin (UK) Limited's policy is to use papers that are natural, renewable and recyclable products and made from wood grown in sustainable forests. The logging and manufacturing processes conform to the legal environmental regulations of the country of origin.

Printed and bound in Spain
by Blackprint CPI, Barcelona

Olivia Gates has always pursued creative passions such as singing and handicrafts. She still does, but only one of her passions grew gratifying enough, consuming enough, to become an ongoing career—writing.

She is most fulfilled when she is creating worlds and conflicts for her characters, then exploring and untangling them bit by bit, sharing her protagonists' every heart-wrenching heartache and hope, their every heart-pounding doubt and trial, until she leads them to an indisputably earned and gloriously satisfying happy ending.

When she's not writing, she is a doctor, a wife to her own alpha male and a mother to one brilliant girl and one demanding Angora cat. Visit Olivia at www.oliviagates. com.

To all my readers. Thanks so much for all your support and enthusiasm. It's for you that I keep writing.

<u>One</u>

Naomi Sinclair stared at the face filling the TV screen in her partner's office, an avalanche of memories swamping her. Memories of a time when she'd known exactly how the *Titanic* had felt.

She'd crashed into her own iceberg, after all. A colossal one by the name of Andreas Sarantos. The one whose ice now reached out from the screen to freeze her marrow… and simultaneously spill lava into her bloodstream.

Despite all the cautionary tales of what befell those who approached him, she'd steamed ahead on an intercept course. When she'd collided with him, it hadn't been for a catastrophic but brief encounter. Oh, no. She'd smashed herself against his frozen annihilation for two tumultuous years. Total wreckage had been the only possible outcome.

Now her whole being quivered at seeing Andreas again, after four long years. With the sound off, and with him looking right at her so fiercely, she could imagine him saying what he'd said that first day she'd pursued him.

You don't want to get mixed up with me, Ms. Sinclair. Walk away. While you still can.

She could still hear his voice, dark and pulsing with sensual menace, that slight Greek accent making it more compelling. Could still feel his eyes burning her with their inimitable brand of aloof yet searing lust.

She hadn't heeded his warning. Not before she'd had a protracted demonstration of how right he'd been. His words had not been a cautioning, but a promise. Of destruction. One he'd carried out. And she'd had no one to blame but herself.

"What do you know! He's back in town."

The comment, laced with surprise and not a little excitement, pulled Naomi back to reality with a thud.

Tearing her gaze from the gorgeous yet forbidding face still filling the screen, she blinked at her partner.

Malcolm Ulrich's comment made her realize where Andreas was. In front of his Fifth Avenue headquarters. He *was* "back in town." Where he hadn't been for four years.

Though she knew he could be in the next room and make no effort to see her, her heart hammered at the realization.

Malcolm turned his gaze to her, his green eyes eager. "I'd just about given up on doing business with him, since he deals only in person, and only when he's here." Her partner looked at the TV again. "But here he is."

She unwillingly followed suit, found Andreas's eyes drilling into hers as he glowered at the camera with all the tolerance of a wolf regarding a rabbit.

Malcolm sighed. "I still can't believe I didn't manage to pin him down to something when he pulled our fat out of the fire back in Crete, then came here personally to discuss how he resolved our problem with Stephanides. But it's never too late, and that guy is bigger than ever. This time I'll do whatever it takes to nail down his elusive hide long enough for him to give our expansion plans serious consideration."

A scoff almost escaped her. She hadn't gotten "serious consideration" from Andreas when she'd been in his bed every night. Not even mind-blowing sex had swayed him to get involved in something he hadn't considered "financially feasible." He'd said their sustainable development methods posed too many logistical problems and promised too little profit for him to bother with. That had been the sum total of the business talk they'd had during their...liaison.

But she doubted telling Malcolm that would dissuade him from continuing his pursuit of Andreas. And it might make him suspect there'd been more between her and Andreas than he, and the world, knew. Only Nadine, her only sister, and Petros, his only friend, had known the truth. To the world, she and Andreas had been two professionals who'd crossed paths sporadically, he as the Greek multibillionaire venture capitalist whose magic touch every business in the world craved, and she as a partner in a real estate development company struggling to make its mark in an increasingly competitive field.

When it had been over, she'd been endlessly grateful for that fact. No one knew of her folly, making it possible for her to pretend the ordeal had never happened. And she wanted to keep it that way. As much as it pained her, she had to let Malcolm butt his head against the wall that was Andreas Sarantos.

But it wasn't as if Malcolm didn't know it was probably futile, anyway. He'd been after Andreas's transformative financing even before they'd become partners seven years ago. It was when Andreas finally answered one of Malcolm's persistent invitations that she'd first met him, a year after she, Malcolm and Ken had set up Sinclair, Ulrich & Newman, or SUN Developments.

Andreas had come to inspect one of their first projects, with Malcolm hoping to tempt him to finance their ambitious offshore expansion plans.

From photos, Naomi had already thought him the most incredible looking man she'd ever seen. But it had taken that face-to-face encounter to turn her inside out.

His gaze and handshake had been cool, detached, yet an all-out invasion at the same time. Throughout his fifteen-minute presence, he'd fascinated and intimidated her as no one had ever done. He'd made few comments, but those had been so ruthlessly denuding, they'd uncovered weaknesses neither she nor her partners had realized had been inherent in their system. Then he'd abruptly taken his leave, giving no indication if he'd been interested or not in their business plan—or in her.

That hadn't stopped her from thinking of him to distraction afterward....

The images on the screen changed, interrupting her reminiscing. Her gaze clung to his figure as he strode away to his limo. Even from the back, he looked every inch the indifferent raider who conquered without trying, devastated without effort and cared nothing about the damage he left in his wake. The reporter, a woman evidently unnerved by her close encounter with the Greek god, regretted that she hadn't been able to get enough from Mr. Sarantos.

Enough from, or of? a voice inside Naomi scoffed.

But if she could have given the woman a word of advice, she would have told her that no one got a thing from Andreas Sarantos. Nothing but hurt, heartache and humiliation.

Malcolm reached for his cell phone. "I'd better call him right away, reserve the first free hour he has while he's here, before the whole city starts hounding him."

Feeling as if she'd run a mile, Naomi rose unsteadily to her feet. "I'll leave you to it."

"Hey..." Malcolm stood, too, his expression dismayed. "We haven't even started our meeting."

"There's always tomorrow." Naomi stopped at the door, mainly to lean on it until she regained her balance. "And I'd probably be useless to you, worrying about Dora, anyway."

Which was, incidentally, true. Leaving Dora with a slight fever had made her unable to focus on anything all day. She'd spent most of it checking back with Hannah obsessively, though her nanny kept insisting everything was fine. Now Andreas's unexpected return—even when Naomi was certain that the news spot would be her only exposure to him—had finished off any possibility for coherent thinking today. Might as well head home early.

She attempted a smile. "Just as well you found a more important thing to pursue today."

"Nothing is more important than you!"

Naomi's smile remained unchanged at his protest, and she made no response as she closed his office door behind her.

Malcolm had always made such gallant statements, but lately she'd been detecting something more in his courteous remarks. Something she hoped she was wrong about. She'd hate it if anything spoiled their friction-free working relationship and friendship. She'd started the partnership with him and Ken in the first place because both men had been happily married. But after Malcolm's wife died from cancer three years ago, she'd started picking up different vibes from him. They'd become more noticeable since Nadine's and Petros's deaths three months ago. Naomi dreaded thinking Malcolm might be rebooting his program with her as the object of his monogamy.

Her mind was overflowing with this disturbing possibility and with Andreas's out-of-the-blue return when she entered her apartment in Manhattan's Upper East Side.

She'd thrown her purse on the foyer table and was hastily hanging up her coat when she heard footsteps rushing toward her. She swung around to find Hannah, once her nanny and now Dora's, looking anxious.

The heart that had been thudding all the way here now pounded with alarm. "Is Dora's fever up again? Why didn't you call me? I would have come back at once, taken her to the doctor!"

Hannah looked momentarily taken aback before waving her hand. "Oh, I told you countless times today that her temperature went down after you gave her medicine, and hasn't come up again. We had a wonderful day and she went down for the night a couple of hours early."

Naomi leaned against the wall as tension deflated abruptly. She exhaled. "When you came rushing like that— God, my mind's been all over the place, more than usual today."

Sympathy overflowed in Hannah's shrewd hazel eyes. "After what you've been through, it's natural for you to be jumpy. It's amazing you've held up this well. But you don't have to worry about Dora. Robust little tykes like her can weather far more than a temperature. After raising four kids of my own, and you and Nadine, with Dora my seventh baby, I should know."

"While I feel I know nothing," Naomi lamented. "Next week Dora will be ten months old and I still feel like a total novice. I keep worrying every minute she's out of my sight. Accidents do happen...." Like the accident that had taken Nadine's and Petros's lives.

The words clogged in her throat, the wound that had never stopped bleeding for the past three months opening yet again.

Hannah reached for her, gave her one of those hugs that, as far back as she could remember, had always made things better even at the worst of times. "Being paranoid is part of being a parent, sweetie. And you have more reason than usual for your anxieties. But we won't let anything happen to our Dora, ever, and she'll grow up safe and loved, and become a beautiful, exceptional woman like her mom and aunt."

Agony swelled all over again as her sister's exuberant face filled Naomi's mind. Before tears flowed, she nodded into Hannah's ample shoulder, letting her touch and scent soothe her. Hannah had always been an integral part of her life, filling the void her mother had left behind when she'd died when Naomi was only thirteen.

Sniffling and attempting a smile, she pulled away. "So why did you come rushing to the door like that? Did you think I was an intruder or something, since I'm a bit early? Shouldn't you have come armed?" Her smile wobbled as another alarm sent her hair-trigger nerves into an uproar again. "If you ever suspect anything of the sort, lock yourself in a room with Dora and call the police—"

Hannah raised both hands. "You really *are* extra jumpy today. This apartment building is intruder-proof, and you've certainly padlocked all entrances against an invading army. Anyone who comes in here has to be invited." She stopped, hesitated, unease creeping over her genial face again. "Which brings me to the reason I rushed out to intercept you."

"Intercept me...before what?"

"Before you walked into your family room and found *me*."

Naomi lurched, a spear of shock lodging in her heart.

That voice. The voice that had never stopped whispering its insidious spell inside her mind.

Andreas.

A bolt of stupefaction wrenched her around.

And there he was, filling the archway of her foyer.

Andreas Sarantos. The man she'd barely escaped four years ago, with her soul and psyche in tatters.

It was impossible, preposterous for him to be here. In her apartment, where he'd never even dropped her off, let alone set foot inside, during the years they'd been together... though not really together.

But there he was. His presence reached out and enveloped her, drowned her. Elemental, primal. Bigger than she remembered, broader, more ominous. He stared at her across the dozen feet of barely breathable air that was all that stood between them. Then he started obliterating them.

He approached like advancing darkness, and his aura eclipsed her, made her insides quiver with a mess of reactions she'd never thought she'd experience again. If anything, time had faded her memories of his impact. Or had he grown more overwhelming?

But he can't be here, her mind screamed, as her heartbeats spiraled into the danger zone.

The chips of steel he had for eyes captured hers, freezing her to the spot. Then they swept her from head to toe, engulfing her in simmering ice.

Her gaze careered down his body in return. From sun-gilded hair, to skin the texture and color of polished teak, to the slashes and planes and hollows of a face assembled with ruthless perfection. His body was shrouded in a suit that looked molded on him. She knew from extensive experience that the flesh beneath had been carved by a divine hand. But all that physical flawlessness would have never affected her if it hadn't been imbued with a charisma and character that bent masses to his merest whim. This man, this force of darkness, commanded thousands, his every decision and action impacting millions. And he'd once had her completely in his power, to do with as he pleased. As she'd once begged him to.

She'd also once begged him to let her go. Because even then she'd feared she wouldn't have the strength to walk away. What he'd done next, to spite her, to torment her, had had her swearing *never again.*

But she'd believed she had nothing to worry about. That he'd disappeared from her life forever. After his latest and most terrible transgression, she'd been certain she would never lay eyes on him again.

But there he was. Why? *Why?*

"What the hell are you doing here?"

She barely recognized the alien rasp that hissed out of her. Then she heard Hannah's agitated voice.

"When I found him at the door, I assumed you instructed the concierge to send him up. And since you do know him, I let him in." Even Hannah thought the extent of Naomi's acquaintance with Andreas had merely been a few encounters when her sister had married his friend. "He led me to believe you *did* invite him, said he had to arrive early, but insisted I didn't disturb you at work, and that he'd wait for you."

Naomi turned to Hannah, barely processing her apologetic account, only one thing registering within the mass of shock her brain had become. Fury.

Before she could assure her the fault had all been Andreas's, he spoke again, addressing the older woman. "Thank you for being the perfect hostess, Mrs. McCarthy. Tea was lovely. But now that Naomi is here, you can tend to your other business."

He was dismissing her!

And Hannah, one of the strongest characters Naomi had ever known, was already obeying him without hesitation, not even pausing to catch her eye to check if that was okay with her.

This tipped her still reverberating shock over the edge into pure outrage.

She ground her teeth as she turned to him, pulling herself to her full height, even though it still left her almost a foot shorter than his six foot five. "Now that I am here, *you* can go."

Andreas waited until Hannah disappeared, no doubt to the farthest recess of the apartment, then cocked his head at Naomi. "I will go…back to your family room. Or would you prefer we conduct this meeting in some other room?"

Some other room.

His words dripped with nuance. Not that he necessarily

meant the bedroom. He'd once turned every square foot of wherever they'd met into a setting for intimacy. The sexual variety only, of course.

That he could imply any such thing now added another layer of blackness to his already dark-as-sin character.

"The only place you'll go is out," she gritted. "Whatever you're here for, it's way too late. Everything—*everyone*— is long dead and buried."

The Andreas she once knew would have met her rebuke with nothing but blankness in his eyes. The one actual reaction she'd seen, apart from incinerating passion, had been the last time they'd been together. He'd shocked her with his anger then. It had infuriated him that she'd mustered the will to end whatever it was between them. She'd been his handy outlet and it had enraged him that she'd been the one to end it all, probably only before he'd been ready with a replacement.

But now she could read some response in his gaze. Within the unfathomable steel-gray of his eyes, there was the stirring of surprise, of calculation, of…amusement?

He found death and burials amusing? Probably. He must also be marveling at the puny human who dared defy the god that he was. If so, she'd give him some serious entertainment.

Turning on her heel, only rage holding her together, Naomi reached for her purse and phone. She punched three numbers.

With a finger hovering over the call button, she turned to him. "Get out right now, or I'm contacting the police and reporting that you conned your way in here, and are staying against my will."

Looking totally unconcerned by her threat, he calmly said, "Once you hear why I'm here, you'll beg me to stay."

"I'd sooner beg a shark to devour me."

Those lethal lips twisted so offhandedly that frustration

expanded inside her. "Speaking of devouring… The last time I ate was that horrid meal on my flight here."

"Whatever happened? Have you now joined mere mortals in suffering commercial flights?"

He gave a shrug of dismissal, since of course multibillionaire Andreas Sarantos had his own fleet of jets.

"Even food on private jets can be bad. At least it seemed that way as I sat for the past thirty minutes being tormented by Mrs. McCarthy's mouthwatering cooking aromas. I bet she made enough to accommodate my presence. Let's honor her efforts and have this conversation over dinner."

Naomi shook her head, as if that might make this nightmare fade away. But it was really happening. He truly was here, disregarding her anger and threats, and inviting himself to dinner. It was so atrociously arrogant, it numbed her.

She shook her head again. "I know you believe everyone is a chess piece in the game you perpetually play. But if you think you can still move me around, you've progressed from being detached from humanity to detached from reality."

He met her low-voiced tirade with a cool-eyed stare. She snapped her fingers in front of his face. "See this? I really exist and I'm done playing my role in an act where you have the only lines. Now for the last time—get out."

She could almost see her wrath shattering against the indifference he wore like impenetrable armor. If a fallen angel did exist, he had to look and feel exactly like Andreas. Terribly beautiful, sinister and sublime at once, impossible to withstand or to look away from.

He tilted his head, causing his now collar-length hair to sift to the side with a sigh. She suppressed a shudder at the sound, her hands fisting at the memory of threading through those layers of silk.

Then he tsked in mock reproach. "After four years of separation, is this any way to talk to your beloved husband?"

Two

Husband.

The word—the *lie*—detonated inside Naomi's head.

"*Ex*-husband!"

Her barked qualification had no impact on him whatsoever.

He only shrugged. "Technicality."

His nonchalance as he reduced some of her life's worst times to nothing exacerbated her fury.

"That 'technicality' is called *divorce*."

And it hadn't been the easy, quick one she'd believed it would be when she'd demanded it. He'd put her through hell before he'd allowed her to conclude the "technicality" that had ended the empty charade they'd called a marriage.

He gave another shrug, even more careless, more provocative. "Why all the drama? Anyone hearing you would think you're a woman scorned, when in fact you were the one who left me."

"This self-centered affliction of yours has reached its terminal stages, hasn't it? You really are incapable of considering anything but your own concerns or anyone but yourself."

"Is there a point you're getting at, or did you just have a bad day and are in need of some venting?"

Her mouth opened, closed. Being a normal human with regular emotions had always caused her severe frustration and disappointment in the face of his total detachment. But this was beyond anything he'd exposed her to. He *had* reached the nirvana of indifference.

He went on. "If you've nurtured some imaginary grievances against me in the years we've been apart, I wouldn't mind standing here until you have your fill of verbal abuse."

"It's only abuse if it isn't true. And I don't have vocabulary enough to describe the awfulness of your truth."

"I don't have any experience with the practice, but I hear some people find bashing others very cathartic."

She finally realized how "some people" had apoplectic fits. "That's it. I won't tolerate your presence a minute longer."

"You mean that up till now that was you being tolerant?"

"Get. Out. Andreas."

He leveled those arctic eyes on hers for fraught moments, until she felt he'd given her a cold burn. Then he turned on his heel…and headed inside.

She stared at his receding figure until he disappeared. Then she was flying after him, with nothing left in her but the need to stop him from invading her life again.

Her fingers turned into talons as they sank into his arm. It was so thick, so hard she had to grab it with both hands and wrench with her full strength. That still didn't make him turn around. She bet he finally stopped of his own accord. He was showing her how she had no effect on him and no say in his actions or decisions. As if she didn't already know that.

Another wave of fury crashed within her when he turned in utmost tranquility. That snapped her last viable nerve.

She hit him. With both fists. Pounded on his formidable chest with all the bitterness that had long been bottled up inside her. Struck him again and again.

He just stood there, bearing her aggression without a change of expression, letting her "vent," watching her intently, as if documenting the reactions of a strange and unstable entity. His lack of reaction cracked her open, had every loss and grief she'd ever suffered spewing out, swamping her in agony now that the leash of control had snapped.

Then suddenly, both hands were behind her back, held in the shackle of one of his, and she was pressed between the cold wall and his hot body. Before she could snatch in another ragged breath, one of his knees drove between her legs, splaying them, his other hand at her nape, tangling in her hair, securing her head, completing her imprisonment.

After one last glance into her eyes, a declaration of intent that had her choking on déjà vu, he bore down on her and crushed his lips to hers. And poisonous memories flooded her, plunging her into the past.

It had been exactly like this, when she'd gone to his hotel suite that first time, demanding he take her up on her insistent offer of herself. She'd instinctively known the edge of roughness was integral to his nature. But she'd felt he'd pushed the envelope, trying to scare her away. When that didn't work, sending her wild with desire instead, he'd pushed some more, testing how much she would allow.

She'd allowed him everything, had reveled in the unbridled power of his passion. From that first night, he'd given her physical pleasure beyond imagining. He'd mined her body for responses and ecstasies she hadn't known it capable of. With every encounter, he'd escalated the wildness of his possession and the ferocity of her satisfaction. But without the development of any emotional response on his part, even intense sexual gratification had started leaving her feeling drained, used up, like an addict who experienced indescribable highs, followed by crashes to dismal depths.

His conquering rumbles filled her now as he angled his

hard lips against hers for a deeper invasion. He plucked at her trembling flesh with his teeth, plunged into her recesses, his tongue a slide of sex and silk against hers, inundating her in sensations, each acutely remembered and longed for.

Her surrender, even if it was with shock, not willingness as it had been before, made him take his sensual assault to the next level. His hand twisted in a fistful of her hair, sending a thousand arrows of pleasure to her core. Then he ground his arousal into her quivering belly, making that core spasm, then melt.

But it was his growl of enjoyment that caused her legs to buckle. "You taste even more intoxicating than I remember."

And you taste exactly as I remember. Overwhelming... indispensable...

No. She'd already fallen into that abyss. Twice.

Never again.

Feeling as if she was being dragged under, drowning, she tried to squirm out of his hold, fighting not only his hunger, but hers, too. She only managed to grind herself harder into his potency. Her only hope of escape would be if he decided to let her go.

He only eased his grip by degrees, dragged his lips from her gasping mouth and across her cheek, nipping her earlobe on the way to her throat. For heart-thundering moments he sucked at her pulse point, as if he wanted to draw her heartbeats out of her. Then with a final groan, he set her hands free and raised his head.

He didn't step away, kept their bodies fused. She remained still, not even breathing as that only pressed her closer to him. Not that she could move. It was all she could do to contain the tremors that threatened to shake her apart. It was his body's support that kept her upright. And it was he who finally backed away from her, with such care, as if his flesh had melded to hers and sudden separation would tear off a layer of their skin.

It wasn't far from the truth. Every inch he'd imprinted felt raw, every nerve he'd strummed exposed. His scent and feel still pounded in her core, his brooding eyes leaving her no place to hide, no chance to regain her composure.

Finally he stepped back, putting just a foot of charged space between them. She drew in a tremulous breath, hoping oxygen would kick-start her volition.

"I won't apologize for hitting you," she murmured. "I bet it's the response you were after, so you'd have an excuse to do what you just did. You manipulated me into doing exactly what you want, as you always did. Good for you. Now leave. Or it won't be your chest my next blows target."

His eyes narrowed to steel slits, the flames of lust still flickering in their depths. "I like this new fire. You were always too…accommodating before."

"You mean submissive."

His gaze grew contemplative as he pursed lips fuller in the aftermath of the devouring he'd subjected her to. "Is that how you saw yourself?"

"It was how I was."

"Not from my point of view. But then you made it clear you think I invent my own convenient, totally inaccurate version of reality. But for what it's worth, I thought you were…pliant, yet never truly submissive." His hand suddenly rose to her face, then he lowered it oh so slowly, running the back of his forefinger down her temple, cheek, neck and collarbone before pausing at the top of her cleavage. His voice dipped an octave into the darkest reaches of hypnosis. "You not only found pleasure in submitting to my demands and desires, but you demanded and took what you wanted as well."

Heat surged in her loins with every recollection of those

countless times she'd demanded and taken, when he'd let her feast on him until she'd lost herself in the delight.

She shrank back from his touch, which felt as if it had burned a hole right through her. That wouldn't have been enough to sever the contact if he hadn't dropped his hand.

She hated him for being the only one who'd ever been able to toy with her so effortlessly, hated herself more for allowing him to, for being so susceptible to him still.

She forced out a thick whisper. "I don't think you're here to discuss our defunct liaison…."

His slanting eyebrow arched at the word.

"You're right," she continued. "If I could find a word that's more trivial and impersonal than *liaison,* I would have used it. Anyway, I'm not interested in dredging up a past I've left behind, with a person I should have never gotten mixed up with, as you so kindly pointed out to me at the beginning."

He shoved his hands into his pockets, drawing her gaze to his daunting and unabated arousal. It had just been pressed against her flesh, reminding her of all the times it had invaded her, driven her beyond all sense of self and self-preservation with urgency and ecstasy.

She snatched her gaze up, found him watching her with that cool assessment that made her want to scream.

No doubt satisfied that he'd again provoked her, in every way, he half turned. "I am going to sit down. Coming?"

Without waiting, he continued to her family room, as if those explosive minutes that had thrown the precarious stability of her world back into chaos hadn't occurred.

This time she managed not to pursue and attack him. Not because her anger had lessened, but because she knew he'd respond the same way. She couldn't withstand another assault on her senses. Knowing him, he might even take it further, press on until he made her beg him not to stop. Even now she feared he'd make her do whatever he wanted her to.

Feeling as if her legs had turned to soggy sandbags, she followed him into her family room.

She'd not only childproofed recently, but also redecorated the space, to make it cheery for Dora and to counter the melancholy that permeated her and the place since Nadine's and Petros's deaths. Now Andreas walked into it and his presence made the room darken and shrink, as he'd always done to her whole world.

He headed to the high-backed red armchair beside the gleefully floral L-shaped couch, which he must have occupied as he'd waited for her. The tea tray on the coffee table and the briefcase on the floor affirmed her deduction.

After he'd resumed sitting, he swept back the hair that had fallen over his forehead during their tussle, drawing her aching gaze again to its luxuriousness. If anything, the longer tresses made him appear even more masculine, made every slash and hollow of his face more rugged. Each change in him did. His every line and feature had been honed to a fiercer virility. And she'd thought he'd already been the epitome of manhood.

Damn him.

But that was only a facade. He was as monstrous on the inside as he was divine on the outside.

He cocked his head at her when she remained standing several feet away. "Your reaction to seeing me wasn't spur-of-the-moment. Seems your animosity has been brewing for a long time."

Those statements made her scoff incredulously. "If I didn't know you have a family somewhere, I'd have thought you were grown in a lab, an experiment in producing a frighteningly efficient humanoid devoid of feelings or scruples."

His expression showed no offense, no amusement, no

challenge. Nothing at all, as usual. "If this is how you see me, it's your prerogative. But don't you think the impervious entity you describe wouldn't have tried to keep you from leaving him?"

"I think you would do nothing else, to assert your dominance. You were being a dog in the manger when you refused to finalize the divorce. You never really married me, just signed a bunch of papers to stop me from ending our ill-advised affair, only to continue it under the false label of marriage, on the same barren grounds."

"And I tried to stop you from leaving me, twice, just to 'assert my dominance'? Don't you think it was too much trouble for just that?"

"Not at all. I believe you'd go to any lengths to maintain your record."

That eyebrow arched again. "What record is that?"

"Your perfect one of having everyone at your disposal and everything done according to your rules and at your command."

"Interesting." He scratched the stubble she still felt burning her cheeks, looking as if he was considering a new perspective, before leveling his gaze on her. "That is me to a tee, but none of that was among my motives at the time. I was only trying to wait out your tantrum until you came back to me."

"Tantrum? Is this how you saw it? And if so, what made you decide to let go of the tug-of-war? Did you wake up one day and say to yourself, 'To hell with it, who needs a brat?' It wasn't as if you could have gotten fed up, after all. You weren't even involved in plaguing and pestering me. You just sicced your lawyer on me and went about your business, not once appearing in the picture."

"You must have a theory why I finally let go."

"Probably because even such hassle-free vindictiveness eventually got old."

He made no corroboration of her explanation, nor did he provide his own of why after six months he'd suddenly decided to sign the divorce papers.

Not that she would have accepted any reason he gave. Her analysis made the most sense. He'd gotten bored. Or he'd found a satisfactory replacement. Or many.

"You were right." That made her blink. He was admitting it? But he went on, "I'm not here to recycle past conflicts. But though you claim to have no desire to do that, it seems you're pretty hung up on them."

"My disgust with you has nothing to do with our past."

"What then?"

"You really have no clue, huh?"

"None. Enlighten me."

"Petros called you on his deathbed." The words seethed through gritted teeth. "You didn't bother coming back. You let him die without making the effort to see him one last time. You didn't even attend his funeral."

All the response she got was a slow blink. Then those lasers he had for eyes resumed regarding her with the same steady appraisal, waiting for her to continue.

The emotional bile backed up in her system poured out, swerving from outrage on Petros's behalf to hers. "*Everyone* came. Even business rivals, even *enemies*. Everyone knew Nadine was my world. And that Petros had become the brother I never had. Everyone put everything aside and came or at least called to console me. *You* didn't."

Another slow blink allowed her bitterness to gain momentum, as she finally understood why his absence had hurt so much. "Somehow your disregard made everything that happened between us even worse. I was always ashamed I threw myself at you, blamed myself for everything that happened afterward, but that day I *despised* myself for it, for pursuing, then staying with someone so... warped. When you didn't answer your only friend's dying plea, and didn't grant me even a few empty words of sympathy, I finally realized the magnitude of the crime I'd committed against myself. I never hated anyone in my life. I never hated you even after all you put me through. But when you proved you were worse than a stranger, worse than an enemy...I finally hated you that day."

His lashes lowered again, giving the momentary impression of him being moved, disturbed.

Then he raised his eyes, and they were their usual unfathomable chips of steel. "I didn't realize you'd appreciate seeing or hearing from me at the time."

Her jaw dropped. "Are you pretending you didn't come or call, in deference to my feelings? Play another one."

"I'm stating what I believed. But that wasn't why I didn't come or call."

She waited for him to tell her the reason. A heartbeat later she realized she'd fallen into the trap of expectation all over again. He wouldn't be giving her anything to quench her curiosity or indignation, would never justify his actions or seek understanding or even tolerance for them.

At least she could always count on him for that. No excuses. Everyone invariably lied, or pulled their punches to observe decorum or butter others up, or at least spare their feelings. Not Andreas.

And it would continue to sink in. The magnitude of what she'd risked when she'd thrown herself, body and soul, into his void. Even now he realized she'd been in need of support from any familiar face at the time—he still didn't bother to say he was sorry.

It seemed disappointment and disillusion had no end with Andreas.

Suddenly, she was tired. So very tired. She'd been struggling to act strong, to appear intact, for so long now. First for her mother, then for Nadine, then for Dora and Hannah. But she could no longer pretend she was on Andreas's level, when no one was, and when she was at her most brittle. He was a disturbance she couldn't afford, a battle she couldn't fight. She needed whatever strength she had left for Dora.

All fight gone out of her, she walked to him, no longer minding if he saw how fragile she was, how she was no match for him. "Whatever your reasons for not coming to the funeral, it was for the best, Andreas. Your presence would have only made me feel worse. It's the worst thing you could have done, coming back now. Whatever brought you here, it doesn't matter. Just go. Please."

In response, his hand reached for hers, cradled it in its warmth. Then, with an effortless tug, he had her spilling into his lap, sinking in his power and heat.

Before another neuron fired, a buzz went through her. Seconds stretched out before she realized what it was. His phone.

That galvanized her to push out of his arms. He only tightened them and groaned, "Don't, *omorfiá mou.*"

She shivered at the way his magnificent voice vibrated as he called her "my beauty," just as she always had when a Greek endearment flowed from those spectacular lips.

Keeping her wrapped in one arm, he got his phone out, evidently to silence it, then groaned again when he saw the caller's name.

He dragged in a harsh breath. "I have to take this." He clasped her closer as she squirmed again, immobilizing her with his mesmerizing gaze. "I'm picking up right where I left off afterward."

She somehow managed to rise from his embrace, making it to the couch opposite before collapsing on it. "No, you won't."

His eyes smoldered, running over her with his intention to do just as he'd promised. Then he answered the call, and the name he said...Stephanides. Could it be...?

Next moment he said Christos. So it *was* him. The man who'd once threatened to smash her kneecaps…and worse.

It was how everything had started between her and Andreas, six years ago. She'd been in Crete with Malcolm to set up a branch of their company. They'd been about to close a deal when one day, thugs had accosted them, delivering a threat from Christos Stephanides, *the* local real estate development tycoon. The message had been succinct. Either they took their business elsewhere or they wouldn't leave Crete in one piece.

But before the thugs could give them a taste of what awaited them if they didn't comply, Andreas had materialized out of nowhere and spoken one word: "Leave." The ruffians had almost vanished into thin air in their rush to do just that.

In his usual concise way, Andreas had said he'd deal with the thugs' boss, and had advised them to leave Crete until he told them it was safe to come back. They'd done so, unquestioningly.

Once home, though still shaken, Naomi had been more disappointed. That the one man she'd ever been interested in remained the only man who hadn't tried to approach her.

Nadine had thought his appearance at the moment they'd needed him had to mean something. She'd insisted that next time they met, if he didn't make a move, Naomi should take matters into her own hands.

Having no faith in her sister's romantic notions, Naomi had been surprised and delighted when she'd found Andreas in Malcolm's office days later. He'd seared her in his focus again, but had made no move. And she'd ended up taking Nadine's advice, inviting him to dinner. It was then that Andreas had issued his famous warning, turning her down.

Mortified at his rejection, she'd told Nadine that her advice had backfired. Her sister had still insisted that maybe he'd truly believed it wasn't good for her to know him.

Maybe he was being kind, letting her down easy. What had Naomi known about Andreas anyway?

But she'd known what should have been enough. Everybody said he was an iceberg, a man with no feelings, relationships or friendships, who lived only to accumulate more success and money. The presence of females in his life had consisted of abundant one-nights stands.

Not that any of that had discouraged her in the least. She'd still wanted nothing more than to be with him, to appease the unstoppable hunger she'd felt for him, come what may. So she'd approached him again.

This time, Andreas had agreed to her invitation. But as if to test her limits, he'd insisted she come to his hotel suite. Certain that he'd posed no danger beyond the emotional—and she'd had no intention of getting emotionally involved—she'd gone to him.

Bluntly, he'd told her he'd never wanted anything the way he wanted her. But he'd left her alone, knowing she wouldn't be able to withstand him. His ominous words had been blatant with the implication of his insatiability, as well as what she'd realized only later. His total disregard and insensitivity.

But she couldn't blame him for any of that. He'd made his terms brutally clear. If she stayed, he would devour her. But he was nothing she might want in a man. Beyond passion and pleasure, he had nothing to offer her.

Drunk with desire and recklessness, she'd told him that was exactly what she wanted, too. Since her mother had died, she'd taken care of her four-years-younger sister, becoming an adult prematurely. Naomi hadn't made one step since before taking every possible ramification into consideration. Even her professional life was steeped in feasibility studies and risk calculations. But she'd wanted Andreas as she'd never wanted anything else. She couldn't approach that desire with caution.

And starting that night, she'd let him sweep her like a tornado into a tempestuously passionate affair that had been beyond anything she'd dreamed of. Sex between them had been, even according to him, unparalleled, the pleasure escalating and the lust unquenchable.

But soon she'd found her emotions becoming involved—or they had been all along, and she'd lied to herself so that she'd accept his noninvolvement terms. Apart from his inability to feel, Andreas had been everything she could have admired and loved in a man. Brilliant, driven, disciplined, enterprising and a hundred other things that appealed to everything in her. Being a phenomenal lover had ended any hope that her emotions would remain unscathed for long. As he'd made love to her, it had been impossible not to delude herself that his ferocious passion, his meticulous catering to her needs, hadn't been signs of caring. That was, until he'd stepped out of bed and reverted to iceberg mode.

It had taken only four months for the lack of an emotional dimension to make her confess she'd been wrong to think she could handle the terms of their involvement. She couldn't wait for things to deteriorate between them, and it was best to part when they had only the fantastic memories.

In answer, he'd only brooded as she'd walked away, not trying to stop her....

"Christos sends his regards."

Her heart fired as his calm voice yanked her from the past, landing her in the present with a thud.

Her glower was equally for him and for the hoodlum who paraded as a businessman and dared pretend they were on a cordial footing. Though it surprised her Andreas had told him he was with her. He'd never acknowledged her before.

"Tell him I'm sending them back as undeliverable. And when he gets them, he knows where to put them."

Andreas's eyebrows rose slightly, his closest expression

to amusement. "He will be shocked a lady like you could be so…harsh. Especially since he's taken such a shine to you."

Yeah, and he had tried to "acquire" her "golden beauty" as if she were part of their business deal. "The feeling is certainly not mutual."

"That would only make you even more enticing in his eyes. Mere men expect the goddess that you are wouldn't reciprocate their interest, expect you to be haughty and out of reach."

Was he speaking as a fellow god who knew how he affected mere women? Not that she could accuse him of exaggerating when he called her a goddess. He'd always lavished praise on her that had surpassed poetry. It had been what had kept her with him for two years through the alienation on all other fronts. That and the sheer perfection of their chemistry.

He put his phone away. "I now understand the source of your current antipathy toward me. But why is Christos still in the bull's-eye of your wrath? Your conflict has long been resolved."

Strange that he wasn't taking credit for that, when it had been he who'd gotten Stephanides to relent and then to even do business with her company. They'd done a couple of very lucrative projects together before things had fallen through again, if amicably this time. Not that she was about to thank Andreas for that right now, or for anything else.

Gathering what felt like her last spark of energy, she sat forward. "Listen, I'm sure you didn't come here to chat about your money- and image-laundering business buddies, or to exercise your irresistible sexual prowess on me—"

"I didn't intend to touch you…not during this meeting. But it seems nothing has changed. It remains impossible for us to be around each other and not ignite."

His quiet response shuddered through her. That he claimed she affected him as he did her tipped her beyond endurance.

"Enough, Andreas," she groaned. "Whatever you came here for, just spit it out."

He gazed at her in silence until she felt her every cell begin to crackle.

Then, in absolute tranquility, he inclined his head. "As you wish. I'm here to claim Dorothea."

Three

Naomi found herself on her feet, looking down at Andreas. He only tipped his head back as he met her flabbergasted stare, his gaze steady and earnest.

And she exploded. "What kind of *sick* joke is this?"

He rose with the utmost economy and composure, was towering over her before she could take a breath or a step back.

"It isn't a joke. When Petros called me—"

"You didn't come back."

"I didn't need to. He was calling me to—"

"I don't give a damn why he called you, or about anything you're going to say. Dora is mine."

"Dorothea is Petros's."

Naomi's heart pounded until it felt like a wrecking ball inside her chest. "*And* my sister's."

But she'd lost Nadine so recently, the loss so overwhelming and fresh, she hadn't yet started Dora's adoption process. But she'd been sure there was no rush, that her claim to Dora was uncontestable.

She said so. "With Petros being an only child, and with his parents dead, Dora has no other family but me. That makes her *mine*."

"Petros wanted her to be mine."

Naomi shook her head, trying to stop the world that was suddenly spinning, feeling as if he'd punched her square in the face. "God...every time I think I know what depths you can sink to, I discover there's no limit to your callousness. But this...this is a new depth, even for you. This is...evil."

He moved past her, giving her a sideways glance that froze her blood and started it boiling all at once. "As I said, what you think of me is your prerogative. That doesn't change the fact that Petros, Dora's father, wished me to have her."

Afraid she'd keel over if she moved too fast, Naomi turned to face him, found him across the coffee table, both hands back in his pockets, staring at her broodingly.

He wasn't joking. He meant it. This was real.

A hysterical giggle burst out of her.

He only inclined his head in what looked like a nod. "I can understand your shock. I'd hoped I could introduce the subject in a better way, at least gradually. But we couldn't even establish any semblance of a conversation, with you being so hostile and uncooperative."

"Sure, I'm to blame for that. I'm the one who tormented you for six months for laughs, before granting you your freedom. I'm the one who disregarded my dying friend's plea for me to be there for him in his last hours. I'm the one who's standing right there pretending I'm willing to take on a baby, when I made it cuttingly clear I never wanted a child."

"It doesn't matter what I want anymore."

"But it matters what you can or can't do. And I'd sooner believe you'd give birth to a baby rather than take one on."

He had the temerity to huff in what sounded like amusement.

But even if all she wanted was to scratch his eyes out, she had to summon all her diplomacy and end this. This was too...huge for her to let it go any further.

"Listen, Andreas, if you're suffering from belated guilt,

for not being there for Petros when he needed you, and you think you should do something for his daughter when you never did a thing for him, don't bother. Petros is dead and gone, and nothing you do or don't do can hurt or help him anymore. If some anomalous sense of duty regarding Dora has been roused inside you, just steer it away until it dies down, as I'm sure it will as soon as this misguided mission is over and you walk out of here. Dora doesn't need your guardianship and is perfectly safe and happy and provided for with me."

"I have no doubt you are an exemplary aunt—"

"I am more than Dora's aunt. *I gave birth to her!*"

At her cry, it was as if all the air was sucked out of the room. Something fierce reverberated from him in shock waves.

He didn't know?

She rushed to explain. "Nadine and Petros wanted a baby so much, but it was impossible for her to get pregnant or to carry her own baby to term. So I became their surrogate for the baby they made together." She'd wanted to help them, and also thought it would be the only way she'd ever have a baby. "Dora is my flesh and blood in *every* way."

"I know."

His quiet words lurched through her.

So what had caused that fierce reaction? Or had she imagined it? Probably. Andreas experienced no such reactions.

He went on. "Not that it makes a difference what you are to her. It's what Petros wanted me to be to her that's the issue here."

Hanging on to control with all she had, she asked, "When did he even make that so-called last wish? Over the phone? In that call you now claim wasn't to ask you to come back before he died?"

"That's what I tried to say when you interrupted me. He didn't ask me to come back for him, but for Dorothea."

"Wow, this keeps getting better. He asked you that three months ago, and you just got around to it now? If Dora had you to count on, she would have been lost somewhere in the system by the time you deemed it convenient to come for her."

"I knew she was safe with you."

"So there was no rush, huh? And there will never be one, so you can return to wherever you've disappeared for the past four years, and just never come back again."

"I can't and won't do that."

"Don't posture. It was just something Petros said."

"It was something he wrote. In his will."

That felt like a resounding slap across her face.

A minute passed before she stammered, "I—I can't believe Petros wrote such a will. If he did, he must have been panicking after the accident, when he suspected from everyone's evasions that Nadine was dead, and realized he'd die, too." Naomi shook her head. "And it still doesn't make sense he'd think you'd make Dora a better guardian than me."

"He didn't ask for me to be her guardian. He wanted me to give her my name."

She gaped at him. He looked deadly serious. And she found herself staggering back and collapsing on the armchair he'd just vacated.

Then denial surged, pitching her forward. "This is preposterous. I know Petros loved me, but he loved you way more—God only knows why, or how he could love you at all. But how could he think that Dora would be better off with you rather than with me, who's been her other mother all along? How could he believe you'd make a better parent for her? I could have understood it if he wanted you to be her guardian, financially, though he also knew I'd need no help in that area."

She gulped down the agitation that threatened to suffocate her. "Though he never cared about money beyond being comfortable, maybe it was different when it came to his daughter. Maybe he wanted you to secure her future beyond anything I could afford. But to ask you to be her *father?* You of all people? Who never nurtured a living thing, not even a pet or a plant? You, who *hates* children?"

"I don't hate children. I never said I did. I said I would never have any. If it had been my choice, I wouldn't have. But this is no longer a matter of choice. Petros was specific in his will in what he needed me to be to Dorothea. And I will fulfill the terms of his will to the letter."

"And I say again, don't bother. I will have his will overturned. He was on death's door and not of sound mind when he had it written."

"He drew up his will seven months before the accident. As soon as Dorothea was born, in fact."

Naomi slumped back, the world collapsing around her like a burning building. "I don't believe you! If there is such a will at all, his attorney should have informed me of it, should have let me know of your alleged claim, since it directly clashes with mine."

"Petros used my attorney to draw up the will, and had it delivered directly to me. He told me not to inform you of it until it was possible for me to come do it in person."

Andreas approached her as he spoke, and she felt as if she was waiting for a tidal wave to crash on top of her and crush her.

Once in front of her, he bent smoothly. She lurched backward, unable to bear his physical closeness now, feeling she'd lose all control if he touched her.

He didn't. He just reached for the briefcase at her feet. Straightening, he opened it, produced a file. Bending once more, he placed it, opened, on her lap.

She tore her gaze from his, dragged it to what felt like a slab of ice on her legs, freezing every spark of warmth and life. Her vision blurred on the lines, as if to escape registering the evidence of his claims.

Then her focus sharpened, and every word she read struck her to her marrow with horror.

It was true. Every word he'd said. Apart from the framework of legalese, this was a letter from Petros, in his inimitable voice. Dated two days after Dora's birth. Signed unequivocally by him.

Suddenly, she felt she'd been stabbed through the heart. That Petros would bypass her in favor of Andreas, giving him Dora…Dora…*her baby*.

She closed the file with a trembling hand, shoved it to the table as if it burned her, and looked up at him, red-hot needles prickling at the back of her eyes.

Andreas was watching her intently, analyzing her reaction, documenting its every nuance. Didn't he already know how hard this blow would hit her?

He finally exhaled. "You're welcome to verify the will's authenticity."

"You mean if you wanted to fake a document, I'd have a prayer of proving it was a forgery?"

His head tilted, as if he was accepting praise. "I know for a fact no one would."

"Spoken like an expert counterfeiter. Forge anything major lately?"

"Not lately, no."

How blasé he was as he admitted to past and no doubt frequent fraud. But then, why not, when he was certain there was no possibility of exposure?

"But there's no forgery this time," he said. "This is authentic."

She gritted her teeth. "Why should I believe you?"

"What reason do I have for doing this, if it wasn't?"

"How should I know? No one in this world has any idea what goes on inside your mind, what drives you. For all I know you might be doing this to spite me."

"Contrary to what you seem to believe, I never wished to spite you. If anything, I only ever wished to do the opposite. I have clearly failed."

"Gee, I wonder why? Just *how* did Petros not only love and trust you, but will his daughter to you?"

"So you believe this is his will."

"I'd give anything for it not to be, but yes, I believe it." She dropped her head in her hands, feeling it would snap off her neck if she didn't. "The only reason I can think why Petros might have done this is that he thought it a precaution that would never come into play. He was your age, had every reason to think he'd live another fifty years."

"Actually, Petros discovered he had an inoperable heart condition two years after he married Nadine."

Naomi jerked her head up. "What?"

"Once he was diagnosed, he believed his father and grandfather had it, and it was why they died at around forty. Fearing the condition ran in his father's family, afflicting males only, when he and Nadine decided to resort to IVF through surrogacy, they ensured the gender of the baby to avoid the possibility of passing on the problem. He actually didn't want to have a child at all after he discovered his condition, hating to think he'd die and leave Nadine and his baby prematurely. But she wanted one so much, he had to do everything in his power to give her one. You know how impossible it was not to give Nadine what she wanted."

"But…but he never told her of his condition. If he did, she might have never persisted in having a baby."

"He did tell her. She just didn't tell *you*. She insisted that his condition might never threaten his life, and she wasn't letting it stop them from living their shared life to the fullest. She turned out to be right. It wasn't his condition that ended up killing him, but a drunk driver."

Naomi found herself on her feet again, mortification at being left in the dark tightening her every muscle until she felt they'd snap. "I can't believe she kept this from me!"

Andreas took a step closer. "Don't feel bad that the kid sister you believed shared everything with you kept something of this magnitude from you. I believe she made the right choice. By not telling you, she was refusing to acknowledge the whole thing, refusing to let it poison their daily lives. She felt she'd imposed on you enough to solve their conception problems, didn't want to burden you with a dread she'd decided to ignore. And she was right again. By pretending his condition didn't exist, she managed to give them that full life they craved together. While they lived."

Naomi stared at him, feeling as if she were plummeting into an alternate universe. She'd never heard Andreas talk so much. That was a week's worth of words in his book.

But it was the words themselves that bewildered her. And that there was an actual expression on his face, in his voice, as he'd said them. As if he was concerned, was trying to ameliorate her shock. Which was the most improbable thing in this whole situation.

"Is there more?" she finally whispered. "I'd rather you hit me over the head with it all at once and get it done with, rather than prolong the ordeal."

His shrug said he had nothing more to relate. She didn't believe that. There was more, and he knew it all, but would tell her only what suited him.

But even in what he'd deemed to tell her, there were too many question marks. "So Petros believed he might not live long enough to be Dora's father, but there was no reason he'd fear for Nadine's life, too. How could he think of willing you to be Dora's father when her mother was around?"

"He wanted Dorothea to have more than just her mother. He wanted her to have a family."

"He didn't consider *me* family?"

"He thought it would be too much for you, being all the family Nadine and Dorothea had."

"I was *always* all the family Nadine had. And she was all my family, too, as Dora is now. How could he have thought I'd find it too much? What the hell did he think he was doing, deciding what I'm capable of, and making decisions for me?"

Andreas's gaze grew more serene, as if to counteract her rising agitation, and she wanted to hit him over the head with something. That file, preferably.

"Petros knew his wife, knew how dependent she was on you all your lives, the dependence she only partially transferred to him when they got married. He feared if he died, Nadine would be too destroyed to care for Dorothea properly. He believed she couldn't bring up a baby alone and would lean on you completely. He also knew you would have let her, would have supported her and Dorothea fully, at the expense of your own life. He didn't think it fair to you."

"Did he tell you all that?"

"Yes."

Naomi pressed trembling hands to her eyes as her voice quavered. "And he considered you the one qualified to carry Nadine's and Dora's burden? He thought you were equipped to deal with a bereaved woman and a fatherless baby? That you can become the first's pillar of strength and the second's stand-in father? Are you sure it was his heart that had something wrong with it and not his brain?"

"I didn't argue with him about my eligibility for the role he wanted me to play in the event of his death. I always did, and will always do, whatever he wanted, no questions asked."

"Are *you* out of your mind then, thinking you can do what he asked you to do? You're not equipped to feel anything for anyone, let alone a baby, and a girl at that. And wait a minute! He wanted you to be her father, so she would have a family? How are you supposed to provide her with *that*?"

"As you pointed out earlier, I wasn't grown in a lab. I do have a family. A big one."

"A family you have nothing to do with, and have never been a part of. A family in name, but never in reality. A family you didn't even inform that you got married and divorced."

"For Petros's sake, for his daughter's, I'm willing to change that."

Feeling his calm, ready answers singeing her insides with oppression and frustration, she raised both hands, needing to abort this conversation and its possible catastrophic outcomes. "You don't have to go to the trouble of establishing a relationship with your family to give Dora one. Dora already has a family. Me, Hannah, Hannah's family, my friends and colleagues. She will grow up surrounded by people who love her, and she certainly doesn't need someone like you in her life, someone who knows nothing about emotions, nor cares anything about other people, let alone children."

As her last words rang in the room, he exhaled. "Are you done? I can stand here and listen to you enumerating my fatal flaws as long as you wish."

"How kind of you. Your every word is just another display of the depth of your insensitivity. But I'm done. And you're gone. Take that will with you and forget that Petros ever wrote it. Forget all about us."

"I can't. And I won't. Petros was my only friend, and his wishes are sacred to me. I will carry out his last will and testament, Naomi. There's nothing you can do to stop me."

"Don't be too sure about that. I don't care if that will is authentic. I will contest it. I will contest Petros's mental state at the time he made it. He thought he would die, and the validity of his decisions while under that conviction is questionable. And you can bet I will contest *you*. Any court would take one look at you and realize you're not father material. No judge would give you custody of Dora over me."

"Then you have no idea how family courts work. I am far richer and more powerful than you, than almost anyone. There's no contest. Any court would give me custody."

"We'll just have to see if they'll consider money and status over the proof of existing emotional bonds and stability and previous healthy relationships."

"If it comes down to comparing pros and cons, I have what would tip the scale in my favor. Dorothea's father's direct endorsement. Do you have any such thing from your sister?"

That had Naomi's heart stopping for a terrible beat, before it detonated with a gush of dread. They'd never even *thought* of any provisions for a situation like this.

Even after Nadine was gone in the blink of an eye, Naomi had never thought her claim to Dora would ever be contested, let alone in jeopardy. And for the rival claim to be Andreas's! It was so preposterous she could almost believe this whole visit was a vivid nightmare.

But she would fight him to her last breath. Not because he would be snatching away the one thing she had to live for, but for Dora herself.

She told him so. "You might be able to trump my claim to Dora, but did you think what you'll do once she's yours? You, the ultimate example of emotional dysfunction? Dora would be better off in an orphanage than with you."

In answer, he bent, swept the file off the table, and calmly put it back into the briefcase. "Again, Naomi, your opinion of me is irrelevant. As far as I am concerned, Dorothea is a Sarantos already. The rest is just formalities. Ones we can conclude with minimum conflict, for Dorothea's sake. Though she's very young, I'm sure she'd sense the discord if you turn this into a needless struggle."

Pivoting, he walked away now that it suited him, leaving destruction in his wake, as he always did.

Before he disappeared from the room that now felt like a battlefield, he drove icicles into her heart. "If you choose to do it the hard way, I'm ready for as long and as costly a battle as it would take. One you'll end up losing, anyway."

Four

"There's no doubt, Ms. Sinclair."

Naomi stared at the immaculate man, the regret on his face and in his voice making her heart give another painful thud against her ribs, before spiraling into her gut.

"Are you absolutely certain, Mr. Davidson?"

"Positive. Mr. Sarantos's claim is far stronger. He has a bona fide will from Dorothea's father, and you have nothing of equal strength in your favor. With his being who he is, no matter what you cite as your superior qualification as a parent or that you are her surrogate mother, his claim will have precedence. The one thing we could do is petition for you to remain a regular presence in the child's life, but that would also be at Mr. Sarantos's and the judge's discretion. Though I have no doubt we would get you generous visitation rights, as I don't see why Mr. Sarantos would contest them, since there's no dispute as there would be in a custody case after a divorce."

A scoff almost escaped Naomi. If only Mr. Davidson knew that with Andreas, anything was a dispute. He shredded his opponents on principle, even if he had nothing to gain by it. She had their divorce as solid proof of how vicious he could be, just because he could.

But her attorney had no idea, because he hadn't handled her divorce battle with Andreas. His daughter, Amara, had. Amara had been a good friend before becoming an attorney, and Naomi had trusted her to keep the divorce proceedings a total secret. As Andreas's own attorney had, since there hadn't been a word about their marriage or its dissolution in any media outlet. Not that she was about to enlighten Mr. Davidson now. At this point she felt any more information might be fuel that would burn any bridges to having Dora in her life at all.

She let out a shaky exhalation. "So in a fight, I don't stand a chance of keeping Dora?"

"As only her aunt, and with the will you describe, and with Mr. Sarantos's enormous influence, regretfully, no."

She'd already more than half known that, was here hoping against hope. Hearing the words still felt like a burning coal sliding down her throat.

Feeling she was pushing the lump of agony back out, she whispered, "Any advice?"

"Just this. Keep this out of court if you possibly can. Your best hope is not to antagonize Mr. Sarantos, but to appeal to him. His goodwill is all you can count on."

In an hour's time, she was staring in the mirror in her building's elevator.

Her reflection looked worse than what had looked back at her after she'd left Andreas four years ago. Or even after Nadine's death. Her complexion was mottled, the blue of her eyes was muddy, even the luster in her blond hair was gone. Two people who'd met her on the way from her attorney had been so alarmed they'd both thought she was ill. One had tried to convince her to let him take her to the emergency room.

The ping announcing her floor lurched through her, had

her stumbling out of the elevator. At her apartment door, she stopped, her hand clenching the keys until it ached.

The delightful baby sounds coming from inside, which always lifted her heart even at its most leaden, only sank talons of misery in it now. It was unimaginable, unbearable, unsurvivable—the thought of losing Dora. A life without her constantly there, hers to love, to take care of and to worry about, wasn't worth living.

Leaning her clammy forehead on the cool wood, Naomi drew in a ragged breath, trying to suppress the tears that threatened to pour. She had to get her act together, couldn't walk in looking as if her world had ended. It had disturbed Dora when Naomi had been unable to control her anguish after Nadine's death, and she'd been only seven months old then. Now she was much more aware, and supremely sensitive to moods. Whenever a wave of desolation swept Naomi, it got to Dora bad. She couldn't expose her baby to her current condition.

God, this was all her fault. Everything had snowballed from the moment she'd allowed her desire for Andreas to overrule her logic and self-respect. And again, when she hadn't escaped with minimum damage that first time she'd walked away.

But when he'd eventually come after her and offered what she'd thought impossible with him, marriage, she'd fallen back into his arms.

Unable to break her addiction to him, she'd accepted his stunted proposal. She'd convinced herself it had been as close to a confession of involvement as she could expect from him, and consented to his abnormal terms. She hadn't even contested it when he'd stipulated their marriage would be a secret known only to them and Nadine and Petros, so his complicated business life wouldn't invade his private one. Their so-called wedding day had consisted of signing a few papers, then a meal with her sister and his friend, which Andreas hadn't even attended, having to leave before it started. Naomi hadn't let herself mind, especially when the wedding *night* had dragged her back into the depths of delirium.

Afterward, he'd remained insatiable, but true to his terms. He'd kept their marriage a secret he guarded to the point of obsession. Rationalizing his behavior had become the basis of her thinking, believing that it was natural for him to protect his private life at all costs. But that would have made sense if said life actually included her. And it hadn't.

Just like when they'd been only lovers, he hadn't let her enter his inner world. He'd never taken her to his home. She'd never even found out if he'd *had* a place he called home. They'd met in hotels or rentals, he'd never joined her in her personal places or endeavors, and they'd never even gone out together. He'd kept her strictly out of everything he'd done, personal or professional, told her nothing of his past and never mentioned the future.

The sum total of mentioning his family had been to admit that *the* Aristedes Sarantos was his brother. It had been how she'd found out—from *Aristedes's* scarce online info—that Andreas had a large family that included four sisters, with an assortment of nephews and nieces. He'd closed the subject of his family forever by claiming he had no relations with them whatsoever. While that seemed plausible, he might have said that just to end any possibility of her asking to meet them. Whatever the truth had been, she'd been certain of one thing. His family hadn't known she existed. She'd been right.

But while she and Andreas had continued leading separate lives, except during the constant sex sessions he'd seemed as addicted to as she'd been, Nadine and Petros had become inseparable and had soon gotten married.

It had been the up-close example of their true intimacy

and intense emotional bond that had broken the trance Naomi had placed herself in so she'd accept the conditions of her non-marriage to Andreas. Not that she'd given in easily. Whenever the need to share with Andreas something approaching what Nadine and Petros shared became unbearable, she'd reminded herself how different she and her sister were, how Andreas and Petros were opposites, and that their relationships were bound to be as dissimilar.

Then one day Nadine had told her of her and Petros's failed efforts to conceive, and that they'd seek professional help. Later that night, Naomi had mentioned that to Andreas. She would never forget his reaction. He'd turned to her, colder than she'd ever seen him and said that if she thought relating that to imply it was time *they* had a baby, she could forget it. He was *never* having children.

His icy declaration had finally forced her to face the pathetic emptiness of their relationship. He'd underscored the fact that if she remained with him, she'd have nothing to look forward to but more of the same nothingness. And it *had* been her fault yet again. She should have known she wouldn't be able to withstand that unnatural arrangement with the emotionally aberrant man that he was for long, let alone forever. Not only hadn't there been any hope for anything more between them, they'd never had *anything* to start with. She'd never felt like his wife, and he'd certainly been no husband to her. Apart from being his "sexual habit," she hadn't existed to him.

Next day she'd asked him for a divorce. Thinking he'd be as nonreactive as he'd been the first time she'd tried to end their liaison, she'd been shocked by his fury. He'd seethed, saying that he wouldn't be coerced into giving her what she wanted. Her anger had risen to match his. What had he thought she wanted? A real marriage, God forbid? He'd retorted that she'd known exactly what to expect, and she'd agreed. She wouldn't make him the villain.

Heart breaking, she'd asked for one thing, the first and last thing she'd ever ask from him. A quick and hassle-free divorce, to end what they should never have started.

When he'd again watched her leave in silence, she'd been certain he wouldn't come after her this time. And he hadn't. He'd just sent his legal hound to snap at her feet and drag her through six months of struggle and anxiety before he'd deigned to let her go.

If it weren't for her pursuing Andreas in the first place, then going back for more when she should have run, Nadine wouldn't have met Petros. None of the chain reaction of catastrophes ending in the current one would have occurred.

But then, Dora wouldn't have come into existence, either. And for her alone, Naomi would never wish anything different.

Now she had to figure out how to keep her from Andreas's cold grasp.

Straightening, she filled her lungs with air. The plunge into the past, as mortifying and self-condemning as it had been, had had a good side effect. It had driven away her desperation, dried her eyes and steadied her nerves.

After another bracing breath, she walked into her apartment.

Entering the family room where Andreas's echoes still lingered, she found Dora sitting on the floor by her playpen, playing catch-whatever-I-throw-to-you with Hannah. Loki and Thor, their mink and flame point Ragdoll cats, were curled up on the couch, watching them.

Though Naomi's feet made no sound on the plush carpeting she'd installed throughout the apartment in time for Dora's very active crawling phase, the baby turned around as soon as she walked in. And Naomi's lungs emptied once again.

Meeting Dora's sky-blue eyes across the distance, imagining again she was looking into Nadine's, would have been enough to knock the breath out of her. But the instant delight, the total trust and dependence she saw in them overwhelmed her barely restored control. Tears stung her eyes as Dora let out a squeal, threw down her toys and scooted on all fours toward her. The cats followed at a slower strut.

"Darling, oh my darling…"

The all-encompassing love she felt for Dora, the baby she'd carried for nine months in her womb, whose heartbeats and kicks she'd felt inside her own body, who'd been the focus of her life since her first wail, and who was all that remained of her beloved Nadine, came pouring out. She rushed to snatch her up, fiercely hugging her precious body.

Dora squealed as her plump arms grasped her neck, her face mashing into her shoulder.

Naomi buried her own face in the raven silk of Dora's hair, inhaling the sweetness of her baby scent, her heart trembling with the totality of emotions she felt for her.

After giving them time to enjoy their tête-à-tête, Hannah rose from the floor, her smile wide…until she met Naomi's eyes.

Her smile faltering, Hannah injected her voice with brightness for Dora's sensitive ears, even when her words were anxious. "What's wrong, Naomi? Did something happen at work?" Then she seemed to make the connection. "Is it something to do with Mr. Sarantos's visit yesterday?"

Naomi debated telling her the truth, and decided against it. No point upsetting Hannah, too, when there was nothing she could do about it but fret sooner than she had to.

Trying to clear the anguish from her expression, she attempted a smile. "It's just that seeing him seemed to rewind everything…the accident, their deaths. Made me feel it all just happened."

Hannah sighed, caressing Naomi's back soothingly. "It will keep creeping up on you, for years. Sometimes it will come out of the blue, but mostly it will be seeing people or things or places that you associate with Nadine or Petros that will trigger it. But from my experience with losing loved ones, especially after my Ralph's death, I can assure you it will get better with time. And one day the good memories will become stronger, will be what come to you when you think of Nadine, making you happy to remember."

Naomi's smile almost shattered as she nodded, fondling and cooing to Dora. Dora cooperated for a minute more before she started wriggling, demanding to be put down. With one last kiss and nuzzle of her downy cheek, Naomi obliged.

Once on the ground, Dora zoomed away with the utmost zeal and determination, the cats in tow. She stopped after a few feet, sat back to check that Naomi was following, too, her chubby hand opening and closing, demanding she hurry.

A laugh bubbled out of Naomi at the baby's earnest expression. Dora took playing very seriously indeed.

She rushed to obey her imperative demand, and for the next two hours, she reveled in all the things that were now the center of her universe, its emotional glue—the play, feeding and bath time with Dora.

After putting her down to sleep at eight, Naomi declined Hannah's offer of watching a movie on the grounds that she had work to finish, and entered her study. She sat at her desk, staring into nothingness for what felt like an hour, her attorney's words echoing in her head.

Your best hope is not to antagonize Mr. Sarantos, but to appeal to him. His goodwill is all you can count on.

It was way too late for that advice. She'd already antagonized Andreas and then some. And appeal to his goodwill? If this was all she could count on, then she was doomed.

An unstoppable impulse had her reaching for her cell phone, keying in his number. It might not be working after all these years, but it was the only one she'd ever had for him.

"Naomi."

His deep, electrifying voice poured right into her brain after a single ring.

How did he know it was her? Her number was new, and only the people closest to her knew it.

But why was she even wondering? There was probably nothing about her that he didn't know.

God. Why had she called him? She should hang up, bundle up Dora and Hannah and board the first flight to anywhere. Disappear until he got bored again, and just let them be.

Yeah, right. As if he ever let anything go without first sucking it dry of whatever he wanted. Only then would he let go. He'd move on, like a hurricane always did, only after it had destroyed everything.

"You can call back when you're ready to talk."

His patient suggestion zapped through her, sparking her ire. "Sorry if I'm interrupting something important."

As soon as she said that, the malignant images assailed her again, as they had since she'd left him. Images of Andreas with other women...

"I am actually between important things."

Which could mean he was between a brunette and a redhead.

After all, he'd once admitted that, before her, he'd never been attracted to blondes.

Not that she thought he was in a babe sandwich right now. He would have told her if he were. He was just being himself, the man who'd never offer gallantries, such as claiming that nothing was more important than her.

But knowing he'd always hit her with the truth in its most unadorned form was what made her despair. He said nothing he didn't mean. If he said he'd take Dora away, he would.

"I was heading for the shower," he explained.

"Then by all means." She barely stopped from suggesting he instead fill the tub…and drown in it.

Another patient sound poured into her ear, something that resembled a sigh. "I can stay on the line until you decide to tell me why you called."

The forbearance in his voice snapped the last thread of control. "I called to tell you that you are a monster, Andreas. And don't tell me it's my prerogative to see you as I please. This is not a point of view, this is a fact."

She could almost see him incline his head in assent. "As you wish. Anything else?"

So much crowded inside her, protests, pleas, scalding invective. Out loud she found herself saying, "So where are you holed up on your victorious return to New York?"

"You know where I am."

Suddenly, she was certain she did know. The Plaza.

Their first night had been all over the royal suite there. The memories of that transfiguring night had been why she'd once intimated she preferred its ambience to all hotels. They'd met there whenever he was in downtown New York from then on, even when she'd insisted the place was too expensive, too *much* for only them. He'd disregarded her protests. Later, she'd found he owned a big chunk of the hotel and paid nothing. She would have appreciated the explanation, so she wouldn't have felt so wasteful. As always, she hadn't warranted one.

Not that he could be there for sentimental reasons. It was most probably for the anonymity the establishment had always been eager to provide him.

"Still there as Thomas Adler or Jared Mathis or one of the other aliases you parade under?" she asked.

When she'd discovered his pseudonymous activities, he'd briefly explained that while people unavoidably recognized him in public, he made sure no one could trace his whereabouts. Such meticulous evasions had never made sense to her. She would have understood his obsessive security measures, if he didn't walk around *without* any.

"I'm here as myself."

The unexpected response skewered through her heart.

If security had ever been the motive, he was an even bigger target now, being so much richer and more successful and having far more enemies. That left her old suspicions as the only explanation. All that secrecy *had* been on her account. So no one would associate him with her. He'd never wanted a wife or even a steady lover, and he'd gone the extra thousand miles so it wouldn't be known he'd had either, keeping his image as an icy womanizer untarnished.

Without one more word, she ended the call.

There was nothing more to be said, anyway.

It was time for action.

Fifteen minutes later, she was staring at the achingly familiar door of the Plaza's royal suite.

It felt as if she'd been here only yesterday for yet another rendezvous with Andreas. The concierge had rushed to receive her, the same man from her visits four years ago. The one Andreas had entrusted with keeping his stays and their meetings a secret. With a gushing welcome that seemed genuine, he'd given her a key card to access the exclusive floor and suite. It seemed Andreas had never bothered to rescind his orders to extend to her the same privileges he commanded.

Putting the key card away, she rang the bell.

In a minute, the door opened. And all her systems almost suffered an instantaneous shutdown.

Andreas stood there, hair gleaming, white shirt wide-open and faded jeans hanging dangerously low on his hips. Everything she'd seen encased in his suit yesterday, then felt against her body, was on display. He seemed even taller barefoot, his shoulders so wide they blocked out her world.

His torso and abdomen were a sleek, mouthwatering sculpture of muscle sheathed in polished skin dusted with the perfect amount of bronze silk. Everything else was a composite of pure power and masculinity molded to perfection.

His steel eyes penetrated her as he stood aside, his motion like a magnet pulling her across the threshold. He stalked barely a foot behind as she walked into the oval foyer that led to an array of social and private rooms. Soon she was walking into the living room, barely noticing its rich decorations, sumptuous textiles and exquisite furnishings that she vaguely remembered were inspired by the royal court of Louis XV. All she knew was that every inch of this place echoed with memories, of when he'd taken her and pleasured her, in its every nook, in every way.

Just inside the huge room, she turned around to face him, found him watching her with that intensity that had always melted her. It now made her feel besieged, fenced in, even in the almost five thousand square foot suite.

"I calculated you'd let a day pass before you came," he said, his voice thrumming every inflamed nerve. "When you called, I adjusted that to an hour. You're earlier than all my estimates. It's a good thing I decided not to shower before—"

She slapped him. So hard her palm went numb with pain.

Horrified at her action, she watched the imprint of her hand form then evaporate on his chiseled cheek.

His only response was a calm "Don't hit me again, Naomi."

"Or what?"

His eyes told her exactly what.

Feeling as if it wasn't her doing this, in slow motion, announcing her intention with absolute clarity, she raised her other hand and slapped his right cheek.

His eyes remained open, roasting her alive. "I'll step

out of your reach now, Naomi. Just in case you don't know what you're inviting."

Her hands bunched in his open shirt, all her agony and dread and yearning boiling over. His gaze devoured her, but his body remained inert, refusing to respond to her fury, leaving it up to her to slam into him.

She did, and it was as if she'd hit a wall, one that buzzed with a million volts of magnetism and maleness. She yanked on his shirt, trying to get him to respond. He just looked down at her, doing everything to her with his eyes, but letting her know he wouldn't give her what she was after...yet.

Taking her incursion further, she groped for his hair, sank her fingers in its silky depths and tugged. A hiss escaped his thinned lips, a testament to her roughness and his enjoyment of it. Surging on tiptoes, she dragged his head down, her lips gasping for his, parched, unable to withstand those last seconds before he quenched years' worth of thirst.

But it seemed he still needed more. He would not accept any demonstration that would have him meet her halfway. Her offer wasn't total enough yet for his liking, what would later make her fully accountable for her actions and decisions. By holding back, he was letting her know he would share none of the responsibility for them...as usual. His role was to tempt and inflame. It was up to her to throw herself into his inferno. Like that first time...and from then on.

Mind gone, body ablaze, she was ready to go to any lengths, whatever the consequences, just so he'd take her over, expose her to the full power of his passion. Not knowing what would satisfy him, she rubbed breasts aching for his possession against his chest, undulated the core weeping for his invasion against his hardness.

Suddenly, it felt as if his whole body expanded when he dragged her head back by her hair, and his breath, fresh and potent, filled her tight lungs as his snarl scorched her lips.

"That's it, Naomi, that's *exactly* it."

Then he smashed his lips down on hers.

It was like a dam had burst, flooding her with what she'd never experienced except with him. Oneness. Need that sliced her open, left her begging for everything...*everything*.

Her senses went off like fireworks with the delight of reconnection as he gave her the ravaging she'd been starving for. Her whimpers became incessant as his teeth sank into her lips, as his tongue drove inside her mouth, occupying her, draining her.

Then he snatched his lips away. The letdown buckled her legs, but he was only taking his onslaught to the next level. Pressing her to the wall, his hands roamed all over her, tearing every stitch of clothes from her burning body, his every move loaded with the precise ruthlessness of a starving predator unleashed on a prey long kept out of reach.

His pupils flared, turning his eyes black as her breasts spilled into his palms. His homage to them was brief but devastating before he was on his knees, dragging her panties off, burying his lips in her core, diving into her flowing readiness. She hovered on the edge of orgasm; one more sweep of his hot tongue or graze of his teeth would finish her. But she didn't want release. She wanted *him*.

"Please..."

He understood her need, as he always had. He heaved up, caught her plea in his savage mouth. He ravaged her lips as he lifted her, his large hands locking her feet around his buttocks, sending her heartbeat stampeding at his effortless strength. Then he freed his erection.

Another plea choked out of her depths as his length teased her swollen flesh, sending a million arrows of pleasure to her womb. He glided his incredible heat and hardness through the molten lips of her core, from her bud to her opening, just once. On the next sweep, he rammed inside her, sinking in her to the hilt.

The savagery and abruptness of his invasion was a shock so acute, her heart faltered and she collapsed in his hold.

He growled something ferocious, what she thought was "Too long…too damn long…" His teeth sank into her shoulder, like a lion tethering his mate for a jarring ride. Then he withdrew.

It felt as if he was dragging her life force out with him, and her arms tightened around his neck, her hands clawing at him, begging for his return. He complied, responding with an even harder, deeper plunge, blacking out all her senses with the searing fullness, the beyond-her-limits expansion around his girth and length. Then he set her on fire as his thrusts picked up the tempo.

Every withdrawal was maddening loss, every plunge excruciating ecstasy. Her cries blurred into wails, her flesh yielding fully to his invasion. He muttered her name in a litany, each thrust accentuated by the carnal sounds of their flesh slapping together. The scents of sex and abandon were like an aphrodisiac, the glide and burn of his hard flesh inside her stoking the inferno of pleasure until she felt she'd combust. She needed…needed… Please…please…*please*…

As always, realizing what she needed, when and how hard and fast she needed it, he hammered his hips between her splayed thighs, his erection pounding inside her with the cadence and force to unleash the conflagration that would consume her, until one thrust breached her womb and shattered the coil of need.

Her body detonated, from where he was buried deepest outward, merciless currents of release crashing through her, squeezing her around him, choking her shrieks.

Roaring her name, he fed her convulsions with his own climax, jetting the burning fuel of his pleasure on hers, filling her to overflowing, sharpening the throes of release, until she slumped in his arms, sated, replete, complete.

Before consciousness fully returned, she heard him groan, "Not enough, *agápi mou…*"

Boneless in his hold, like a marionette with all her strings cut, her head spun as his endearment echoed inside her. My love…or my darling. What he only ever said during sex.

Then the world was thudding with the urgency of his strides. She drifted off for what might have been seconds or an hour, jerking out of the sensual stupor as she felt him laying her down on the bed where he'd once owned her. His scent rose from the silk sheets to wrap around her, compensating her for his loss as he left her body.

He retreated only to rid himself of his clothes, before coming back over her, impacting her with his demand.

Spreading her quivering thighs, bending her knees, he braced his at the bed's edge and bore down on her, pinning her by the shoulders. Then, bending to thrust his tongue inside her panting mouth, he reentered her in a long, burning plunge.

She'd thought he'd drained her of every need, that she'd want nothing ever again. But as he forged inside her, and her sore, swollen tissues expanded around his daunting girth, urgency slammed into her once more, her awakened flesh clamoring harder, louder.

After that first frenzied coupling, he took her in a deliberate yet even more gloriously raw possession. Throughout, he exploited every inch of her body with hands and lips and teeth. And he watched her. Oh, the way he watched her.

His feral focus made it all more primal and mind-blowing, making every touch a bolt of ecstasy, every bite and dig and thrust a howling pleasure.

Soon, unable to stand any more stimulation, she climaxed again, four years of deprivation exploding into torrents of sensation, even fiercer than the first firestorm. At her peak, he rode her harder, faster, till he rammed himself into her recesses, roaring as he hurled himself after her into the abyss of abandon. Her whole body shook with ecstasy as his hardness pulsed inside her, shooting his essence, her over-sensitized muscles fluttering around him, greedily milking him for every drop of satisfaction.

This time, as her consciousness flickered, he sank on top of her, his breathing as labored as hers, his heart thundering against her sputtering one, completing her domination.

At last, he rose off her, swept her enervated form up to the pillows and contained her in the cloak of his great body.

After long minutes of lying there, savoring the descent, painting her savagely pleasured body with indolent caresses, he pulled himself up on one elbow and looked down at her, his gaze one of supreme male triumph and possession.

"Now that I've gulped you down twice, it's time to savor you."

She blinked dazedly up at him, shocked to find her body readying itself for him again. This sickness had never been cured. If anything, it had intensified.

He reached over her to his cell on the bedside table, suckled one marvelously sore nipple soothingly as he offered the phone to her. "Tell Mrs. McCarthy you won't be home tonight."

Naomi's throat tightened. "I have to go home."

"No, you don't. And won't. I'm just getting started."

She pushed against him feebly, drowning as he resumed suckling and fondling her. "Andreas, stop. We have to talk."

"Talking is definitely not on my to-do list tonight. I might consider it tomorrow. Or the day after."

"Andreas...please, we must talk first."

He lifted his head from her breast, smile indulgent. "About this?"

"About Dora."

The heat in his eyes drained away. In two seconds, they

were as cold as she'd ever seen them. Then without one more word or look, he released her and rose from the bed.

Every muscle feeling like jelly, she scrambled for the bedcovers as she watched him pull on his jeans.

Then he turned his unfathomable eyes to her. "Was that what this was all about? Dorothea? What did you think you were achieving here? Bribing me?"

"I gave you what you came blackmailing me for."

"I don't remember any blackmail."

"It was implied, loud and clear."

"Then you forgot all about me. Or never knew much about me at all. I never imply anything. If I wanted to blackmail you, I would have spelled out my ultimatum 'loud and clear.'"

Feeling hope for a way out quickly fading, she gasped, "It was, to me. You made your sexual interest patent, then told me you'd take Dora. When you *know* I'd do anything to keep her."

"Even throw yourself in the shark's bed, eh? So what was your scenario? That I was here to extort you for vengeance sex, and once you gave me a mind-blowing send-off, I'd walk away and forget all about Petros's will, which I never considered seriously, anyway, but was only holding to your head?"

"What else could I think? You *can't* be considering taking on Dora for real," Naomi cried, feeling her world being ripped from under her as his stony glance told her he considered nothing else. "For God's sake, Andreas, you *know* you don't want a baby, and won't be able to give her the home and family life she needs and deserves."

He shrugged. "Probably. Even definitely. That's why I don't intend to take Dorothea from you."

Her heart surged with hope. "Y-you don't?"

He moved then, coming back to where she sat stiff and tangled in his covers. Leaning down on one knee, he made the mattress dip, tumbling her toward him, and murmured, "I don't."

Before she collapsed back with relief, his hand slipped beneath the sheets and cupped her breast, giving it a delicious squeeze. "I do intend to take you, though."

Her breast swelling in his large, warm palm, she moaned, "Don't you have it in reverse? I already slept with you."

He removed the sheet, engulfed the nipple that had been envying its twin in his hot mouth and pulled hard, making her moan and arch up. "You thought a couple of rolls in the royal suite would be all it took?"

Resigned that she'd end up giving in to his conditions, and temptation, she asked, "How many 'rolls' would it take?"

He raised his head and one eyebrow. "I can name any number?" At her grudging nod, his lips twisted. "How many would do it, do you think? Considering my record of insatiability with you? I must have had you over a thousand times during our time together, and it failed to sate me."

"It sure won't be anywhere near as many as that!"

"You won't consider an unlimited usage arrangement? Pity."

"Oh, fine. Whatever you want."

At her sullen capitulation, he withdrew, rose from the bed and stood over her, studying her molten pose.

Then, thumbs hooked into his jeans, eyes enigmatic, he exhaled. "The thing is, Naomi, what I want is something a bit more significant than even your limitless sexual services."

She struggled up, numb with dread, cold with outrage and flaming with desire all at once. "What could that be? My soul?"

He waved his hand. "You can keep your soul. I only want everything else. What you'll give me when you remarry me."

Five

Where the hell was her other shoe?

Naomi limped around, frantically looking for the damned thing. Where *had* that *damned* man tossed it?

She might be looking right at it and not seeing it. And that wouldn't be strange. Everything had been a blur since Andreas had made his outrageous proposition.

Following an interminable period of gaping at him, she'd exploded from the bed and run out to retrieve her clothes. She was one shoe away from fleeing this place, and hurtling in search of any way to keep that tormentor at bay.

Remarry him, indeed!

Her sanity and self-respect had barely survived marrying him the first time.

What shocked her most was that he'd never wanted to marry her at all. He'd wed her only as a means to keep an "accommodating" sexual partner placated so she wouldn't leave. He didn't view marriage as other human beings did. So why would he—

"It's beneath the divan. The three-seater."

Whirling around at the sound of his calm voice, she found him still in only his jeans, leaning one formidable shoulder against the archway into the expansive room.

A stifled imprecation escaped her as she lunged for the shoe she only saw when he'd told her where to look. She *had* looked there before and hadn't seen it.

In seconds she had it on, then snatched her purse off the same divan, where he'd thrown it what felt like a lifetime ago. Cursing under her breath again, she headed toward the escape route he was blocking.

He let her come within a foot before he uncoiled and filled the archway. It would be impossible to pass him without physical contact. She knew full well where that would lead.

She raised her eyes to his. "Move aside, please, and let's not turn this into a worse mess than it already is."

"I take it all this flouncing about is your way of saying 'hell, no'?"

"Flouncing!" She reined back her indignation. This man was turning out to be an expert provocateur, a quality he'd never demonstrated before, but seemed to be taking much pleasure in now. Since it was so unexpected, she'd been an easy mark, letting his every yank pull her wherever he wanted. But this stopped now.

Exhaling, she tried to access her control, as fractured as it was, and attempt to do what she hadn't done so far— take her emotions out of the equation and talk pure sense.

"Listen, Andreas, we do share an unhealthy level of sexual affinity, as we just proved...." Her gaze flicked to the wall a few feet away, where he'd taken her the first time tonight. "And that was why 'our past' happened. I take full responsibility for how it turned out, as I was young, more in experience than in actual age, and you were my first adventure, my first passion. You were as clear as possible about what you expected, and I still mixed up my intense lust for you with expectations that had no place between us."

His focus was total as she talked, as if he was memorizing her words. But then he did that with everything. His retentive powers were phenomenal, and it had nothing to do with interest in her or what she said specifically.

She inhaled. "But since you made *your* expectations clear from the start, you didn't accept it when I walked out. You no doubt thought you were justified in trying to stop me, as I was reneging on the terms of our agreement. I'm the first to admit I did, and that was why I ended it. Now you have a card to pressure me into rectifying my transgression and resuming the arrangement you found so convenient, but I can't 'accommodate' you anymore. I *am* ready, though, to have as much no-strings sex with you as you want, in return for you not disrupting Dora's life. We both have the obvious to gain from that kind of arrangement. Anything else is out of the question."

"Why?"

That was all he had to say? After all she'd said?

Holding on to her temper, she forced herself to answer. "Because I won't enter another charade with you. Certainly never with Dora caught in the middle."

"There was no charade tonight. That was all too real."

"As real as these things get. You know it was just sex."

"There's nothing 'just' about it. That after all these years I still want you."

"And you can have me. Just not like *that*."

"Again I ask, why? If you want me as much as I want you?"

"Because desire never made a difference. I wanted you at times more than I wanted to breathe, and yet being with you was the worst chapter of my life. Considering that I lived through the horror and desolation of losing my mother when I was so young, then losing Nadine, that gives you an idea of just how miserable I was with you."

That emptiness in his eyes intensified. And suddenly she realized something.

That blankness was a unique indicator of his emotions.

The more surprised or dismayed he was, the emptier his gaze became.

Which made no difference now. Or ever. Only one thing mattered. Making him take back his demand.

Struggling to keep her voice level, she continued. "Agreeing to something as disruptive to me as what you're demanding would damage me and undermine my ability to mother Dora. And that's what I will never let happen."

After looking at her as if he wouldn't answer, he let out a forcible exhalation. "If you're willing to sleep with me as frequently and for as long as I want, why is calling it marriage any more disruptive?"

"Because it would be. Labels and legalities and the life adjustments stemming from them complicate everything. No-strings sex is all I can offer you. It's all you want, anyway."

"I already told you what I want. Marriage."

Now it was her turn to ask. "Why?"

He shrugged. "Because I'm not in the market for no-strings sex anymore. I have Dorothea now."

"No, you *don't*. Dora isn't yours, she's mine."

"Not according to Petros's will."

Anxiety and aggression almost overpowered her. She reeled them back with all she had.

Andreas *was* a shark, and the scent of blood—her vulnerability and desperation now—would only make him more vicious.

But appealing to his compassion, as her attorney had advised, would get her nowhere, either, as he had none.

Only one thing remained. Appealing to his paramount sense of self-service, what had seen him to the top in his cutthroat field.

She drew in a steadying breath. "It's clear you haven't thought this through, Andreas. You might assume that having a child, with your power and wealth, would be easy. But there's nothing more disruptive and consuming than having a little one in your life, even with others handling the daily caretaking. If you consider it without the influence of duty or pride…" She swallowed the words *"or challenge."* Not prudent to provoke his cold-blooded killer instinct. "…you'd know you can't take on the responsibility of a child."

"I know I can't. I already admitted that."

"Then what do you think you'd do if you take Dora? Toss her to a nanny and a string of private tutors, then send her off to an exclusive boarding school once she's old enough, and go about your business as if she doesn't exist?"

"I already told you this isn't what I intend. I never factored in that I won't have you both."

She gaped at him. He'd intended this remarriage thing all along? A "convenience package" that would allow him to have her cake and eat Dora's, too?

She swallowed the outrage, emptied her voice of expression. "Well, start factoring it in now. You have my offer."

He inclined his head, as if he accepted her refusal.

Then he stepped aside to let her pass.

Feeling as if her prison door had opened, she hurried away. He followed at a slower pace, his longer strides keeping him a step away, making her struggle not to break into a run.

She was almost out the door when he said, "I'll have my chauffeur follow you home."

She shook her head without turning. "The area is safe, and it's only a five-minute drive."

"Still."

Something in his solitary word made her turn. And she regretted it at once. Getting another eyeful of his half-naked grandeur, and remembering what he'd done to her with it, wasn't conducive to her ability to breathe.

He took the door from her hand. "I would have done it myself, but we've had enough arguments tonight."

Suddenly she was clasped to his hot hardness, and his lips were pulling her heartbeats right out of her pulse point. Her blood surged with need, and she was on the verge of begging him to take her again when he muttered into her flesh.

Once his words sank in, she tore out of his arms. "You *are* a monster."

This time she ran away, as if she were really escaping from one.

After a night that was one of her life's worst, Naomi arrived at her office next morning, the last words Andreas had said still echoing in her head in a maddening loop.

Whatever you felt about our marriage, or think you feel about me now, you'll end up agreeing to my terms. I'm not letting you go again.

The first thing she did was call her attorney. He assured her again that she had no leverage, that Andreas would be the one to call the shots. She bet if she told him about Andreas's ultimatum, he would have thought it a fantastic offer she should snap up before Andreas changed his mind.

Not that she thought he would. Once Andreas set his mind to something, he never let go. But she was damned if she'd let him steamroll over her. There *had* to be another way out.

After an hour of frantic thinking, an idea burst into her mind. The more she thought about it, the more it felt like her only hope. Gaining an ally who was as powerful as Andreas, one who had power over him.

Only one man on earth met both criteria.

Andreas's older brother, Aristedes Sarantos.

An hour later, Naomi entered Sarantos Shipping headquarters, suffering from whiplash at the speed with which this meeting had been arranged.

After failing to find a personal number for Aristedes, she'd settled for his headquarters, gone through the automated menu until finally a live person, a man named Dennis, had regretted there was no way she'd get hold of Aristedes himself. Some collected voice in her churning mind had inspired her to say it was a matter of paramount urgency, concerning Aristedes's brother. At the silence her claim had been met with, she'd thought the man had hung up. Then Dennis had said that Mr. Sarantos's brother was long dead.

That had stunned her, that Aristedes might not know that his brother was alive.

But Dennis had rushed to apologize. She must have meant Mr. *Andreas*, not Mr. Leonidas. He hadn't heard of him in so long, he didn't remember him right away.

That had been news to Naomi, that Andreas had a brother named Leonidas, who was dead. He'd never volunteered the fact, and she'd never heard it from Petros, the only other source of information on him. Petros had clearly been under strict instructions not to share anything about Andreas, even with his wife. The only way she'd known anything about his family life had been through investigating Aristedes. But beyond a fleeting internet search once, she hadn't been about to dig any deeper into what Andreas hadn't wanted her to know.

Once Andreas's name had been introduced, she'd been put through to Aristedes's personal assistant. Within minutes, the woman had come back to her. Aristedes could meet her in half an hour. Would that be soon enough for her?

She'd almost blurted out it was too soon. Thinking that securing an audience with Aristedes would be an arduous endeavor, she'd thought she'd have time to prepare for meeting the man. If Andreas was anything to go by, she cringed to think what his big brother might be like, the man everyone mentioned in whispers of awe and called "the raw material of ruthlessness."

But she couldn't postpone meeting the only man in existence who might be able to hold Andreas at bay.

And here she was, in his imposing skyscraper's lobby, not knowing where to go or what to do.

As she swept her uncertain gaze around, a gorgeous dark-eyed brunette in her early twenties, a little shorter than her five foot seven, in an exquisite navy blue skirt suit, came rushing toward her.

"Ms. Sinclair?" Naomi nodded dumbly in answer to the woman's inquiring smile, noticing that she was older than she'd first surmised. Maybe thirty, like her, but untouched by tragedy. The woman's smile widened, showing off a stunning set of teeth as she held out her hand. "I'm Cora Delaney, Mr. Sarantos's junior PA. Please come with me. He is waiting for you."

Cora steered Naomi through security, then to a private elevator, seeming in a hurry.

Oh, God, was she late? What if this started the whole thing off on the wrong foot? How *could* she start this on the right one? What was she doing here, anyway? What *would* she tell Aristedes?

"Relax."

Her gaze jerked to Cora, and only then realized she was clutching the railing in the elevator car, her white knuckles stark against the mahogany walls.

Sympathy filled the secretary's eyes. "Mr. Sarantos can be really scary when he wants to, I'll admit, but he rarely wants to nowadays. Today is certainly not one of the days anyone is in danger of being shredded by him."

"What makes today special?" Naomi croaked.

Cora's smile widened. "He's expecting Mrs. Sarantos, his wife."

Mrs. Sarantos. Naomi had once been that. Not that anyone had ever known. Now she was here in hope of never becoming that again, whether people knew about it this time or not.

The elevator door whirred open smoothly. They were there. In the lion's den. Or was it the devil's domain? She'd once heard it would be bad-mouthing the devil, calling Aristedes Sarantos that.

A minute later, Cora ushered her to what had to be Aristedes's inner sanctum, clearly not intending to accompany her, and Naomi's knees almost gave out. She was used to interacting with moguls, but this man, from what she'd heard about him and especially because of who he was to Andreas, unnerved her as nothing had before. And she hadn't even seen him yet.

Then she did.

Rounding the corner of the waiting room, she spotted him at the far end of the austerely elegant office, rising from a spaceship-like desk. Even across the distance, his impact almost made her feet gnarl.

She'd seen him in photos, had thought him photogenic, but in reality, he was far, far more incredible. Like Andreas, nothing but in-person exposure could do him justice. He wasn't handsome. It would be an insult to call him, or Andreas for that matter, that. They were beautiful in a way that transcended good looks, were the embodiment of unadulterated power and raw maleness in human form.

Beyond that, they had the same color of eyes and skin, but Aristedes's hair was darker, with silver-shot temples, whereas the highlights in Andreas's hair were the gilded touch of the sun.

There was no doubt those two juggernauts were brothers. Even with eight years between them, the differences were slight, physically speaking. On another level, there was a major difference that she sensed, but couldn't put her finger on. And probably wouldn't.

As Aristedes unfurled to his full height, which appeared equal to Andreas's, her observations stalled. He was unsmiling as he walked around his desk, his steel eyes as penetrating and unsettling as Andreas's, even if their disturbance had a different texture. She could feel him reaching inside her to extract the truth about her and about her claim that she had urgent business concerning his estranged brother.

Before he came within hand-shaking distance, she heard a soft knock. It was followed by a gently opening door, rustling clothes and light feet on the plush carpet.

It had to be his wife.

Feeling like an intruder, Naomi kept her eyes fixed on Aristedes. And got a direct hit of the spectacular change that came over his face.

It was as if his deepest recesses opened, every passion and emotion blazing in his eyes. His delight at the sight of his wife was blinding.

"Selene, *agápi mou…*"

Agápi mou. One of the empty endearments Andreas had lavished on her…only at the height of arousal or the pinnacle of satisfaction. But from the ragged edge in Aristedes's bass voice, she had no doubt *he* meant it. His wife, the lucky Selene, *was* his love.

With a brief excuse, he strode past Naomi.

She didn't want to witness the greeting of this man who'd probably left his wife's side this morning, and yet was already elated and eager to see her. But standing there with her back to the woman might be construed as rude. So she forced herself to turn around…and caught the tail end of the passionate kiss the couple exchanged.

Aristedes's lips relinquished his wife's, only to return immediately for another brief but profound taste. Then, after one last look full of all the secrets and trials and certainties that constituted their intimacy, he turned his attention to Naomi.

And she realized what the major difference between him and Andreas was. Even though she felt the demons of his harsh beginnings on the quays of Crete lurking within his psyche, to be unleashed when needed, she felt Aristedes had mastered them and relegated them to the deepest corner of his being. This man had reclaimed himself from the darkness. He was something Andreas had never been and would never be. He was serene, content. Happy.

And it was clear this hadn't happened only *for* Selene, but with her help, and was maintained by her unstinting support. A man of Aristedes's caliber didn't develop that level of emotional involvement and dependence without total trust in an equal, who offered him a commitment of matching depth, scope and strength. From the fleeting yet unequivocal demonstration she'd witnessed, Naomi had no doubt Aristedes would lay down his life for his wife, and that his devotion was reciprocated in full.

Her instincts had once told her she could share that level of allegiance with Andreas. Even against all evidence to the contrary, her senses had insisted they'd turn out to be right. But he'd proved to be exactly what he himself had warned her he was—a man incapable of emotional commitment and unworthy of it.

So how could two brothers who were so alike in genetics, in background, even in intelligence, determination and achievement, be such opposites? How was it possible for one to have the capacity to feel so much, while the other was incapable of feeling anything?

Aristedes was tugging his wife ahead, to be the one to meet Naomi first. "Ms. Sinclair, please meet my wife, Selene."

Selene Sarantos was the embodiment of her name. A moon goddess, tall and voluptuous, with a waterfall of ebony silk hair and the most vivid, midnight-blue eyes Naomi had ever seen. But she was more than beautiful, she was…ripened. By the passionate worship of the virile, powerful Aristedes.

Selene extended her hand to Naomi with the smile of someone who had no idea who she was meeting, but was very open to making the new acquaintance. It was clear she didn't mind finding her incredible husband with an unknown woman. That she was okay with that, and with having women like the gorgeous Cora working so close to him, was a testament to her security in his fidelity and her hold over his heart.

Naomi shook her hand with a smile she hoped wasn't brittle. "Pleased to meet you, Mrs. Sarantos."

Selene let out a crystalline laugh. "Selene, please. I'm Mrs. Sarantos everywhere. In private, I want to revert to being Selene only."

"You're *Louvardis*-Sarantos everywhere," Aristedes mock griped.

Selene laughed again, her eyes crinkling at Naomi. "Would you drop a name like Louvardis if you can possibly keep it?"

Naomi shook her head, making the connection. "If you mean Louvardis of Louvardis Enterprises fame, I certainly wouldn't. I wouldn't anyway, based on the chicness and uniqueness of the name alone."

Selene turned her face up to her husband's, her eyes teasing and caressing him, and telling him so, so much. "You see?"

"Oh, I do see." His eyes caressed her back, and Naomi doubted that this was ever an actual issue with him.

Aristedes would be happy with anything that made Selene happy. Keeping her maiden name in combination with his was evidently important to her, maintaining her identity and paying tribute to her father and family. And that was exactly what Aristedes would want her to do.

And *Naomi* had to go fixate on the one man incapable of giving her a look like that, of valuing her or needing her or considering her anywhere near the way Aristedes did Selene…or at all.

The familiar sense of futility twisted her insides again as Aristedes turned to her. "Shall we sit down, Ms. Sinclair?"

"Naomi, please, Mr. Sarantos." He opened his mouth, and she rushed to preempt him. "But please don't expect me to call *you* anything else."

"We'll see, *Ms. Sinclair*," he drawled, renewed shrewdness invading his gaze as they sat down, she in an armchair, he and Selene on the couch. "Once we find out what you want to see me about." After a minute of silence, he added, "Please relax."

A nervous giggle escaped her. "Ms. Delaney advised me the same on the way up here. She assured me I have nothing to fear from you, if only on account of Mrs. Sarantos being here today."

The next moment a gust of wind could have blown her away. She was, anyway. By Aristedes's smile. And what a smile it was. Especially as he turned to share the joke with Selene.

"You sure came at the best time, Ms. Sinclair. Selene is so busy with our kids and her own firm that she rarely visits me at work. Her arrival has me in a celebratory mood, so you'll find me most receptive to whatever you need to say. Though if it's about Andreas, I'm sure I won't like hearing it. But it seems you dislike having to tell it even more. The best way around that is to just spit it out. So let's have it."

Naomi looked uncertainly at Selene.

Aristedes waved. "You can say anything in front of my wife. I'll tell her everything, anyway, and this saves me having to recount it to her later."

Selene gave him a chiding glance, then turned reassuring eyes on her. "You don't have to say anything in front of me. I'll leave if it will make you more comfortable."

Naomi lunged forward and stopped Selene as she rose. "Oh, no, please, stay. I was only uncertain how Mr. Sarantos would prefer this. I would actually like you to stay."

"As a buffer against any crankiness, no doubt." Selene smiled at her, then at her husband as she sat back. He reached for her hand with an answering smile, caressing it as if compelled, clearly finding extreme pleasure and comfort in the action.

The sight of them as they sat unconsciously entwined even as they focused on someone else was exquisite. Two powerful entities who'd come together in a far bigger and stronger new whole. This was more than love. This was… unity.

But every second in their company underlined ever more painfully how stunted Andreas was, how hopeless it had always been with him, and what a terrible future awaited her and Dora if Aristedes couldn't help her.

Drawing in a steadying breath, she told them everything.

They both listened attentively, even if their reactions to her account were diametrically different.

Selene looked increasingly pained, as if imagining herself in Naomi's place, being forced into such an emotionally traumatic choice, with her children's future hanging in the balance. Aristedes only looked progressively more angry. Enraged.

He was evidently a protector, had severe issues with the coercion of anyone weaker, especially a woman. That the one guilty of such a transgression was his brother, the brother he evidently thought very little of, exacerbated his outrage. It was as if it tarnished his own honor that this intimidation was originating from someone who shared his blood.

By the time she finished, Aristedes looked as cold as his brother always did, but she could feel the volcano beneath. It was so scary she almost blurted out a defense of Andreas. But she stopped herself. She couldn't ruin her own petition in order to protect Andreas from his brother's wrath now that she was certain she'd managed to unleash it.

But she only wanted her and Dora's salvation, she didn't want Andreas hurt in the process. Even if he wasn't bothered in the least by the idea of hurting her.

Before she could say anything, Aristedes squeezed Selene's hands, which were now clinging to his, and disengaged from her to rise to his feet. Naomi staggered up to hers, explanations and excuses crowding on her tongue.

Aristedes gave her no chance to voice them, taking her hand in both of his, giving it a reassuring squeeze. "Ms. Sinclair…Naomi…you don't have to worry. Petros was like a younger brother to me back in Crete, to us all. Once he got here, we never reestablished relationships, as his friendship with Andreas took him wherever Andreas was—away from any of us. I can't begin to tell you how much I regret that we didn't know of you all, of his marriage or his death. But now I know of his daughter, I assure you she is as precious to me as any of my nephews and nieces. I would never let anyone disrupt her life, or yours, least of all Andreas. Leave him to me."

After she thanked him and received further bolstering from Selene, Naomi left in a state of imbalance.

All she hoped was that she hadn't set up an impending clash that would lead to an unbridgeable rift between the brothers. Not that they had much of a relationship to preserve, but still. She couldn't bear to think it would be severed totally on her account.

But it was already done. Aristedes would order Andreas to back off, might even pressure him. She doubted Andreas would buckle easily. Or at all. He was too powerful and established, and he didn't care about losses. It was how he'd grown so big. By being fearless and holding nothing dear.

Still, Aristedes was now an ally. He would buy her time, or manage to negotiate terms she could live with. Such as making Andreas take her offer instead of insisting on his terms.

Or it could all go horribly wrong.

Unable to think about the consequences of the events she'd set in motion, she only hoped this would be resolved with the least damage possible. And that she and Dora would be saved from plummeting into Andreas's void.

Six

Andreas stopped in front of the building he'd passed so many times during the past years and never entered. His older brother's office building.

The brother who'd called him an hour ago and ordered him to report to his office. Aristedes's growled "now" was still a dull pain in his left ear.

His first reaction was to tell him what to do with his imperious summons. He *would* have ignored him, if he didn't realize with near certainty what this was all about.

Naomi.

There was no other explanation. Aristedes had called him only four times in as many years. For Leonidas's funeral, for his own wedding, and for their youngest sister's son's first birthday, which had also become her wedding. Andreas had gone only to Caliope's wedding, because the situation had allowed it.

Another major event in the family would be too much of a coincidence a day after Naomi had fled from him, calling him a monster. No, Aristedes's aggressive, out-of-the-blue call had to be at her instigation and on her behalf. She must have thought her last resort was to sic Aristedes on him. Not because he was his older brother. She must know that would have no influence on him. But because he was Aristedes.

Aristedes *was* formidable. If anyone could stand up to Andreas, it would be him. She must have calculated Aristedes would at least slow him down while she kept searching for a way out that didn't include surrender. The wily, fiery lioness.

But she *had* surrendered last night. She'd come to him gloriously furious and taken all her aggression and passion out on him. She'd hit and bit and rubbed against him until he'd given her what she'd come demanding. And it had been as mind-blowing as it had always been. More, as if the time apart had boosted everything they'd shared, the intimacy more searing, the pleasure more excruciating.

But as soon as he'd realized what had driven her into his arms, he'd grown cold. If only for minutes. He'd always been certain Naomi suffered his same affliction. He knew she'd do anything to end up beneath him, as he would to have her there.

She might have a legitimate excuse in Dorothea, but it *had* been only an excuse. She'd wanted him. That was why she'd offered herself to him. Whether for Dorothea or anything else, she certainly would have never gone to another man's bed....

The idea caused an instant boiling in his blood.

A whack against his arm brought the surge of ferocity to a jarring end.

Great. He'd literally gone blind with possessiveness. He'd knocked a man over as he entered the building like a charging bull.

Helping the man to his feet, Andreas apologized, ignoring his curiosity and that of everyone around as he walked into the huge, ultramodern lobby.

It was clear everyone had recognized him, whether as himself or on account of his unmistakable likeness to Aristedes. They must be wondering what tremendous incident could have brought the prodigal brother back.

Last night had been tremendous indeed.

What had happened between them until Naomi had come out of the fugue of passion had been overwhelming. And *real*. What he shared with her was the only thing that he was certain *was* real. The unstoppable chemistry, the explosive satisfaction.

What had she called it? An unhealthy level of sexual affinity? Substituting "unhealthy" for "addictive" and "enslaving" was more like it. Whether that was unhealthy or not, he'd never cared. Not when it was that magnificent.

He'd cared only after she'd left him, when he could no longer wallow in his addiction and enslavement. Through the years, his body had hardened just reliving being buried inside her, his nerves constantly buzzing with the memorized feel of her velvet skin and resilient flesh, his nostrils always filled with echoes of the distillation of her essence and overpowering femininity. Relief, deficient and short-lived, he'd only achieved by replaying their countless encounters of abandon.

After the years of torment, he'd been as angry as Naomi, though for a different reason. At her hold over him. He'd come back intending to reclaim her, but had been hoping it would be different, that he'd be cured of addiction. He'd hoped he'd still be attracted, but not compelled.

But then he had seen her, touched her, and his fever had spiked to its previous power….and exceeded it, too.

Everything about her—the texture of her skin, the sound of her gasps, the melody of her voice, the taste of her kiss, the scent of her breath, the magic of her glances and gestures—it was as if her every nuance was his very own designer drug, a mind-altering high and an aphrodisiac in one, specifically formulated for him by a merciless god of compulsion.

Then had come last night. *Theós*…last night.

He'd thought bingeing on her pleasures would break starvation's hold over his senses. It had only fractured the leash on his cravings. Now they ran rampant, would consume him if he didn't have her again. And a thousand times more.

And there he was, standing in the lobby of one of the busiest buildings on Fifth Avenue, fielding dozens of curious stares and about to tussle with his older brother. And all he could think of was her, beneath him, hot and wet and incoherent with lust, her petal-soft arms clasped around him, her velvet inferno core gripping him as he drove into her, inundating her with pleasure and pouring his seed inside her.

His heart thundered, all blood rushing to his erection, forcing him to come to a full stop.

Dekára. Dammit. He was so hard he'd hurt himself if he moved.

At least being crammed so unbearably in his jeans had an upside. They were tight enough to obscure his arousal. If not according to the stares of the men. They had this male empathy in their eyes acknowledging his predicament, before they looked around to check out who was causing it.

They'd realize his condition was more advanced than it looked if they knew the instigator of his libido crisis not only wasn't around, but had also laid the trap he was walking into.

And he had to walk into it and get it over with, so he could resume her pursuit. He'd go into serious withdrawal soon....

"Mr. Sarantos."

Turning his head, he found a woman rushing toward him. He deflated in the time it took her to reach him.

With a tentative smile, she extended a hand to him. "Cora Delaney. Mr. Sarantos sent me to escort you to his office without delay."

Giving her a brief handshake, he absently noted how her gaze flickered. He was certain she didn't look at Aristedes that way. Then a slightly wider smile and direct eye contact let him know she was *very* interested, if he was.

Glancing ahead without returning her smile, he started walking, a clear message that he wasn't.

She was pretty. Beautiful, even. Years ago she'd have been his type. Dark and vivid and svelte. He would have let her know his interest was fleeting, to take it or leave it. Once she'd agreed to his terms, he would have let himself be picked up, for an evening.

Then Naomi had happened. A voluptuous angel with sunlight spun in her hair and turquoise shores trapped in her eyes, vulnerable and valiant, innocent and insatiable. And that had been it for him. Ever since, it had been her... or nothing.

Women, on the other hand, remained interested, made advances everywhere he went. Whenever a passive dismissal like the one he'd given Ms. Delaney wasn't enough, he ended the situation by saying he was already taken.

And he was. Naomi had taken his libido prisoner from that first look, a genie in a bottle that only she could unleash.

She was unleashing something else now. Aristedes's wrath. Andreas had better start gearing his mind to that.

As he did, he finally noticed his surroundings. Everything in the building was stamped with Aristedes's character, at least his professional side, austere, oozing with class and power, unflinchingly distinctive and cutting edge.

In minutes, they'd arrived at their destination and Ms. Delaney left him to enter his brother's den alone.

Walking in without slowing down, he crossed what had to be a waiting room, rounded a corner...and saw Aristedes.

He was standing like a monolith in the middle of the expansive room, his reflection in the polished hardwood floor giving the illusion of him rising from another world, like a god of vengeance. He sure looked the part.

Something shifted deep inside Andreas at the sight of his brother. Something elemental. Unreasoning and over-powering.

Because of his choices, he'd never truly known Leoni-das, his younger brother. He'd been better with Petros. He hoped. But the feeling of being too late, doing too little for either of them, never stopped creeping up on him and gar-roting him with regrets. Now they were both gone, so tragi-cally, so prematurely, both to car accidents. Leonidas's had been ruled as his fault, but at least no one else had been hurt by his tragic mistake. Now Aristedes was the only brother Andreas had left. The only *male* in this world who was close to him.

Granted, they were not close in reality, which was also his doing. But there was this fundamental bond, this in-exorable tug in his blood that recognized Aristedes's, its kindred nature soothing and bolstering him by its purity and power.

And though said kindred entity was now glaring at him as if he wanted nothing but to flay him, Andreas reached out and pulled him into a hug.

Aristedes went stone still in his embrace, made no move at all, even to breathe. His heart might have stopped. He was that shocked.

Not that Andreas could have expected a different re-action. He'd never showed Aristedes or anyone else any spontaneous demonstration of affection, physical, verbal or otherwise.

Sighing, he stepped away, releasing him. He didn't want his brother to suffocate or have a heart attack, after all.

Aristedes stared ahead as if in a trance. Then he shook his head as if to exit one, and his vacant gaze panned to Andreas.

"What was that all about?" he rasped.

Andreas shrugged. "I'm almost certain that was what people refer to as a brotherly hug."

"Since when are brotherly hugs applicable to your species, Andreas?"

He gave another shrug, more dismissing. "I felt like it, I did it. Let it go."

"How can I let it go? You *hugged* me, Andreas. This is right up there with...with the sky raining fish."

"I'm sure *that* happened in some historically obscure event. And no doubt won't again. As this hug won't."

"If it happened, then a set of bizarre circumstances came together to make the impossible occur. What happened to make you hug me?"

Exhaling, Andreas pulled Aristedes into another hug, a rougher, briefer one, then pushed him away. "There. I took it back. Or put it back. Or whatever returns you to your former state before the anomaly occurred. Better now?"

"If you think I can be the same, that *anything* can be the same after this, you've got another think coming. What's going on with you, Andreas? Are you...sick?"

A mirthless laugh escaped him. "You think I'm dying or something? And what? I'm overcome with regret for all the things I've missed, all the things I haven't done or said, and I've come to make amends before it's too late?"

His sarcasm was evidently lost on Aristedes, who scanned him in anxiety-tinged exasperation. "*Are* you okay, dammit? If there's something wrong with you, tell me *now*."

Andreas winced, pressing his hand over the still aching eardrum that his brother's previous "now" had almost ruptured. "It was just a damn hug, Aristedes, and I took it back. What else can I do to restore our peaceful, subzero-expectations status quo?"

The emotions in Aristedes's gaze evaporated, the void

Andreas had seen in the mirror for as long as he could remember filling their place.

Andreas had long perfected this unreadable stare as a weapon and a defense mechanism, until it had become a part of him. He lost his grip on it only when he was too stimulated or disturbed. In other words, with Naomi.

Born into the same hell before him, Aristedes had developed his own array of disturbingly blank stares long before life had taught Andreas the need for them. Being an expert in all their brands, he recognized the significance of this one. It was his brother's substitute for putting him over his knee.

After making sure he'd hit him with its full brunt, Aristedes turned and strode to the sitting area.

As soon as Andreas joined him, he said, "Do you want to restore it?"

"Our status quo? You mean we really exited it? We now have Pre-Hug and Post-Hug status quos?"

Another look. "Just. Answer. Do you?"

Did he? What if he didn't? He was so used to his segregation he had no idea if he could handle anything else, or if he was even equipped for it.

Andreas exhaled. "Nothing needs to change."

"I think everything needs to change. *You* need to change."

"And you know that because you're my big brother who knows best?"

"I know that because I *was* you until a few years ago."

"Until Selene came along and saved you from yourself."

It still seemed unreal to Andreas that Aristedes, of all men, had fallen in love, and with the daughter of his worst enemy. Of course, it had started out bumpy and their initial tryst had ended in separation, during which she'd had his baby, but thought he didn't deserve to be told. Once he'd gone back, she'd made him jump through hoops for the privilege of another chance with her and of knowing his son. Being an overachiever, Aristedes had gone overboard proving himself, and would clearly never stop doing so. They were now married, with another child, a daughter, living a happily-ever-after that was far more perfect than any fairy tale.

It was all too nauseating, really.

"Ridiculing it doesn't make it any less true," Aristedes said. "Selene did save me. She dragged every worthwhile thing out of me, and gave me a second and real chance at life."

"Then I'm doomed, since according to you I have no such worthy stuff lurking inside me to be excavated."

"I was as bad as you and worse. Turns out it's not important if *you* think you are worthy of redemption. What's important is that *someone* thinks you are, and you're not too stupid to let them reach out to you."

"You were never as bad as me, Aristedes. I'm in a class of my own, remember?" He shook his head. "I can't believe the conversation we're having. And over a hug, too. It's not as if this was the first time I hugged you."

"The last time you hugged me you were seven, Andreas."

"Ne." Thirty years ago.

He looked away, and into the past. He remembered how he'd felt about Aristedes then. His brother had been his anchor, the only beacon of hope and strength in a dark and turbulent existence. He'd loved his mother and older sisters, as a child would those who cared for him. But he'd recognized them as fellow victims, to be despised for their helplessness just as he'd despised himself. It was only Aristedes he'd admired, whose determination had set his own course, whose drive had imbued him with the will to fight.

Andreas exhaled. "I never told you, but I idolized the hell out of you back then. You were my role model."

"That I believe. Your role model in detachment. But in my case it was a tool, what I needed to survive, then to get ahead. For you, it seems to be a fundamental component. Or rather, the absence of one. It seems the entity responsible for putting you together in the cosmic factory left your emotional package on the conveyor belt."

"You are the second one in as many days to tell me I lack such an essential building block. I can only be grateful for its absence, since I can't imagine what it would have been like having it when I was around our father. Or the other pieces of shit who littered my path. I would have wasted so much time and energy *feeling* stuff about them when they're not worth a second thought. *You,* on the other hand, always warranted an actual response from me."

"I never had any idea you even noticed I was alive. Not when you looked at me with the same lack of concern you bestowed on everything and everyone else."

"Oh, I noticed you, and looked up to you…when you were around to be looked up to."

Aristedes frowned, as if in remembered pain. "You know I couldn't be around when I had to provide for you all."

Andreas waved away his justification. "I was there, re-member?"

And he'd been there in a way Aristedes had no idea about. When his brother was working twenty-hour days to put food on the table, Andreas had been left behind, the "man of the house." And the things he'd had to do to fill that role…

"Is this about Petros?"

Andreas blinked at Aristedes's question, Petros's name skewering his heart.

"I always thought you felt nothing for anyone except Petros. His death, though you didn't deem to inform us of it, must have hit you hard, even if you wouldn't admit it."

"Why wouldn't I? I admit it. I'm still reeling."

It was Aristedes's turn to blink in surprise at the ready admission. "You are? I mean, it's only natural anyone would be, but it's just that you are…"

"Not natural? Probably. But he was as close to me as anyone ever was. Closer than any of you."

"Which wouldn't be saying much, since you weren't close to any of us in any way. It seemed you turned thirteen and just…shut down, turned away from everyone."

"This, coming from the man who gave his family money and services in lieu of human interaction. Mother used to say you sold your soul for a Midas touch. And speaking of hugs, she said she'd gladly exchange everything you gave her for one hug."

Aristedes's frown turned thunderous. "We're not discussing which of us was the colder bastard, Andreas."

Andreas grimaced. "*Theos*…listen, I'm sorry. That was a cheap shot. Too cheap. I didn't condone what she said or felt. In fact, I actually despised her for it. You supported us in an impossible situation, then got us all out of Crete, made us new lives in the States, which she didn't live to see because she killed herself with a broken heart over our scum-of-the-earth father. Our mother was sick, with toxic emotionalism that caused her to make every wrong choice possible, and scarred us all for life. She worshiped our father, who told her sweet lies while he swindled her out of her whole life, and she didn't appreciate the miracles you were achieving for all of us, because you didn't do them with a smile and a hug. Is it any wonder we grew up despising such poisonous sentimentalities?"

Aristedes's gaze sharpened, as if he was viewing their lives in a new light, seeing Andreas from an unexpected angle.

At last he said, "Our mother was damaged, for too many reasons, as was our father, and their relationship was pathological. But we left them and their legacy far behind, and shouldn't let their mistakes and shortcomings poison *our* inclinations. You don't need to go that far in the opposite direction to having no emotions, because you saw what losing herself to them did to her. There is a huge range of balanced feelings you can experience without having them overpower you."

"Like those you feel for Selene and your kids? I think you're way beyond overpowered by those."

"And that's bad only if such emotions are damaging or degrading or depressing. My feelings for Selene and our children resuscitated me and now sustain and rejuvenate me." Aristedes suddenly gave a growl of impatience. "You've taken us on another tangent."

"It's you who started reminiscing about my shutdown."

"What I asked," Aristedes barked, "was if your strange behavior is on account of Petros's loss—"

"I'll never hear the end of this hug, will I?" Andreas interrupted. "Next I'll find Caliope texting me to discuss my unfurling emotional potential." He sat forward, the idea actually making him anxious. Caliope had been trying to reel him into the family circle since he'd made the mistake of attending her wedding. "Whatever you do, *don't* tell Caliope about this. I'll do anything if you promise not to."

"How about you leave Naomi alone?"

So. Moment of truth. The point of all this.

Andreas sat back, cocked his head at his brother. "So she enlisted your services in deterring me, eh? What did she tell you? I should hear her list of charges before we go on."

And for the next ten minutes, Aristedes let him hear, in very colorful language, his own version of Naomi's "charges" and what he thought of him and his actions.

His rebukes were still echoing like rolling thunder when Andreas finally inhaled. "You done?"

"Yes, and so are you, *agóri*," Aristedes growled.

He huffed. "Been a while since anyone called me boy."

"Don't make me demonstrate that in comparison to me, you *are* still a boy."

"We're comparing sizes now?"

Aristedes sat forward. Andreas was certain any other man would have cowered. "You *will* leave Naomi alone. And that's my last word."

"I wasn't aware this was a bid. But here's *my* last word, so we can wrap this up. There's no way in hell I'm doing that."

"Andreas—"

His raised hand interrupted Aristedes's threat. "I spent the past four years thinking of nothing but getting her back, and now that I can have her again, I'm not letting her go."

"You'd use your friend's will and his baby to coerce her back into your bed? You care nothing about the fact that she doesn't want to be with you again?"

"She wants nothing more. Trust me on that."

"I trust her word…and the turmoil I saw and felt in her. If you think she wants you, and that's how you're justifying this to yourself, you're self-deluding."

"You know nothing about our history, Aristedes."

"I know everything. She told me."

That surprised him. And intrigued him. He hadn't thought she'd go that far. But what had she said, exactly, to get Aristedes within a hairbreadth of getting physical?

"It might be impossible for you to consider anyone but yourself," his brother said, keeping his temper under control with obvious effort. "But consider this. This is a woman who recently lost her only sister and is still barely dealing with the loss. She inherited the responsibility of her niece—"

"Which she won't shoulder alone when she remarries me."

"She *didn't* ask for help, least of all yours. I get the impression Dora is all she lives for."

"Which isn't right. Her life shouldn't revolve around the child. That's bad for both of them."

"And what's good? You? The man who failed to give Naomi the minimum of consideration and respect in your so-called sham of a marriage? You want to force more heartache on her by holding her daughter hostage? And Dora *is* her daughter in all the ways that count. Are you so without feelings or honor?"

"I'll do what I have to do. Wouldn't you do anything to get Selene back if you ever lost her?"

"I would never coerce Selene and override her choices like you're doing to Naomi."

"I'm not coercing her, I'm pursuing her. She needs me to, before she can allow herself to do what she really wants to do, which is come back to me."

Aristedes's look was incredulous. "You think she's playing hard to get?"

"Not exactly. It seems she's ashamed that she pursued me in the past. And it seems she took particular exception that I kept our marriage a secret from you all. I believe that's one of the main reasons she came to you, to right this wrong retroactively. I'm restoring her dignity by pursuing her this time. And if she hadn't preempted me, I would have told you about us the moment I got her to agree. So no, I'm not coercing her, I'm giving her the tussle she needs so she can have whatever pound of flesh she feels I owe her. But her reasons for resisting me don't include not wanting me. She does want me, as much as I want her. *Do* trust me on this."

Aristedes got the implication this time—that Andreas had obtained unquestionable proof of his claim, very recently.

Aristedes still plowed on. "You're talking about physical lust, and that's never enough to overcome mental and emotional aversion. If you manage to make her remarry you, a woman who can't bear you out of bed, what do you think you'll do when you're not making love? What kind of dysfunctional battlefield would you have dragged her onto?"

Andreas waved as if to swat away his brother's concerns. "This initial conflict will end soon."

"What if it doesn't? According to her it will only escalate. You'd risk that kind of personal and domestic hell? Just because you want to get her out of your system?"

"I *can't* get her out of my system. And I don't want to."

"That's still just sex."

A mirthless laugh escaped Andreas as he remembered Naomi's exact words last night. And his response. *Just sex, indeed.*

Aristedes went on. "And for that, the arrangement she suggested is the perfect catharsis for both of you."

"I don't want 'an arrangement.' I want a permanent situation."

"Do you even have a concept what permanence is, Andreas? The only pseudo relationship you ever had was with her. You think that's what marriage is? That farce you're asking her to repeat? Even if you're completely detached from the way other people experience emotions, you never waste time on something that doesn't work. Why are you insisting on repeating what failed as absolutely as your first so-called marriage did?"

"I don't think it failed."

"Sure, because divorce is an indication a marriage was a resounding success."

"It indicates…a problem. She must have told you about it. It doesn't apply anymore, so it won't be the same this time."

Aristedes's growl would have made anyone else run for cover. "Why don't you admit you're after her because she dared to walk away? I wouldn't put it past you that you'd make her bow to your will, only so you'd be the one to walk out, in your own good time."

"I see you've adopted her analysis of my actions and motivations."

"It does suit what I know about you."

Andreas pushed himself to his feet. He'd had enough of this. "I'm done. I won't repeat myself."

Aristedes stood and grabbed his shoulder. "Even if I adopt *your* analysis, you'd still be tussling with her in another passionate if pathological relationship. I might have sanctioned this if it was about the two of you alone. But it isn't. There's a child involved. Didn't you think of that little girl at all? If you get Naomi back in this dishonorable way, life between you will be an even worse hell than it was, and Dora will be caught in the middle."

Andreas frowned. "Who said life between us was hell?"

Aristedes huffed in ridicule. "Naomi, of course."

"It *wasn't* hell," he hissed. "And it wouldn't be."

"That's your word and prediction against hers. And even if you're right, what happens when you get enough of Naomi? Did you think how Dora will feel when you toss her aside along with Naomi after she comes to consider you her father?"

He hadn't thought of any such possibility, since it would never happen. He'd never get enough of Naomi. And he'd never toss Petros's child aside.

But that wasn't what he objected to in Aristedes's conjecture. "I will make it clear to Dorothea from the start that I'm not her father. I have no illusions I could be that."

The flare of disgust in Aristedes's eyes hit him harder than a punch. "I always knew you were cold, but I never dreamed you were heartless." He grasped his arm roughly. "I warn you, Andreas, pursue this and I will stop you, no matter how much I have to damage you to make you back off."

He held his brother's gaze. "You done now?" Aristedes's hand tightened. Andreas removed it with utmost calmness.

"Here's how it will be. I will fulfill Petros's will. He wanted Dorothea to be a Sarantos, and that's what I'm making her. I want to make Naomi my wife again, and that is what she'll become."

"Andreas—"

He raised both hands to stem his brother's explosion. "*If* during this process you have any indication that any of Naomi's fears are coming to pass, that I am harming either of them, you can use any deterrent you see fit."

"You think I'll wait until you cause them harm?"

"Why are you so certain I will? Aren't you the advocate of second chances? Didn't you just lecture me on redemption? Or do you believe those are possible for everyone else but me?"

Uncertainty entered Aristedes's eyes and his aggression dissipated in the span of a heartbeat. "If I thought for a moment this is what you're after…"

Andreas reached a hand to his brother's shoulder, held it and his gaze with his pledge. "It is."

An hour later, sitting on the bed where he'd taken Naomi last night, Andreas closed his eyes and let the echoes of the magnificence they'd shared reverberate inside him.

Groaning, he fell back among the covers she'd wrapped around her hot, fragrant body, turned his face to inhale deeper her bouquet, letting her lingering scent and sensuality cloak him.

His arousal had been so hair-trigger after she'd left, he'd dragged himself off to sleep in another room. He was still in agony, but his other disturbance was canceling the worst of it.

This disturbance had nothing to do with his meeting with Aristedes. In fact, he felt…contented that they'd had that confrontation. Even if his brother had spent 90 percent of the time scolding him like the father he'd—*they'd*—

never had, and expressing his disappointment in him, it had only…pleased him. More than that. It had appeased him.

Amid all the disapproval and dressing-down, one thing had become clear. One thing he hadn't thought possible. Aristedes cared.

While his brother had become the epitome of caring in his private life, remaining a bulldozer only professionally, Andreas had never thought that this thawing would extend to him. Not when he'd done everything to warrant being frozen out for good.

Not that Aristedes had cut him any slack. He'd pledged to hurt Andreas, badly, if his alleged second-chance bid showed a hint of exploitative cracks.

But far from being bothered by Aristedes's threats, he was actually amused by his father-bear tactics, even warmed that Naomi and Dorothea now had yet another fierce protector. Besides, Aristedes couldn't hurt him. He couldn't be hurt. There'd been one way he could be, and *that* he'd finally resolved.

What disturbed him was what Naomi had told Aristedes. That their marriage had been hell. True, she'd told him that she'd never been more miserable than when she'd been with him. But initially he'd dismissed that statement, thinking she'd made it out of spite, in the heat of the moment. He'd always believed that their marriage, while unorthodox, had been fantastic. Well, as fantastic as possible given the constraints he'd placed on it. Things between them had gone smoothly in general, and explosively in bed—up till that night he'd told her he never wanted children. That had been the established reason he'd believed she'd left him. She had asked for a divorce the very next day, after all.

Now he was no longer sure.

His head told him she'd made those claims of misery to him to make him back off, then to Aristedes to ignite his protectiveness. If said claims weren't total fabrications, she'd probably worked herself up into believing she'd been unhappy with him all along. She could have resented him retroactively for not having a child of her own, something he'd intended to deprive her of as long as she remained with him. Resentment had a way of warping memories and rewriting history.

But his senses told him a different story. Her fierce resistance to any commitment again, even after their mindmelting lovemaking, had felt too real, too distraught. Now he replayed everything she'd said, the way she'd looked and sounded.... Could it be that had been how she'd really felt at the time, not something she'd constructed after the fact?

He'd be the first to admit their relationship had been irregular. When he'd asked her to marry him, he'd wanted a continuation on the same terms of their affair, only with the assurance that he was hers, and that it wouldn't end. He'd thought that would resolve her discontent and uncertainty, since he'd believed her need for permanence and exclusivity had been why she'd walked out in the first place.

He'd known he wasn't husband material in the accepted ways, and his life situation couldn't have accommodated anything different from what he'd offered her. But he'd thought she'd been content with what they shared, that their passion compensated for anything that had been missing. He'd never suspected she'd been unhappy with him, let alone miserable.

It had been why he'd clung so hard when she'd walked away, believing she'd come back to negotiate her needs. Once she did, he'd intended to argue that they had plenty of time before children became an issue, counting on their phenomenal sex life to satisfy her for years before that maternal need became pressing.

But if their sex life had only made her feel worse about herself for putting up with a situation she'd found so awful, what had made her stay that long? And if expecting the same unhappiness was why she was so adamant about not remarrying him, what could he do now?

He *could* coerce her. Easily.

But he wouldn't. It would defeat his purpose. He wanted—*needed* her unpressured eagerness again.

To get that, she had to agree to his proposal of her own free will. But how could he achieve that?

He'd come back believing that Naomi's need for a child had already been fulfilled, eliminating the one obstacle in the way of her return to him. But it seemed she'd needed things from him beside children, things he hadn't been able to give her. And though his situation had changed, he had no idea if he could.

What if he didn't have it in him?

What if Aristedes was right in distrusting him, and the best thing for her, and for Dorothea, was for him to leave them alone? If so, could he do it?

Could he walk away? Forever this time?

Seven

Naomi stared at the schematics on her laptop screen.

They could have been alien runes for all the sense they made to her.

Not that there was anything wrong with them. It was the perpetual shortage of oxygen to her brain that was causing the malfunction. She'd been bating her breath to find out if Aristedes had succeeded in his mission. But he'd told her only that he'd confronted Andreas, and that things were under control. What *that* meant, she had no idea.

Only one thing would make her breathe easy. For Andreas to say he'd forget about Petros's will. Or at least that he'd negotiate a middle ground. Maybe that when Naomi officially adopted Dora, he'd be her godfather…or something.

And that she didn't have to remarry him.

Whenever she'd come to that part, voices inside her kept adding feverishly that he would instead take her up on her offer of unlimited sexual services.

She hadn't had much luck stifling those.

But for three days after Aristedes had summoned his brother, there'd been absolute silence on Andreas's part. No news didn't feel like good news. Not knowing was driving her insane.

She was also suffering from another problem.

Her body, which he'd savagely reawakened, had been tormenting her. It wasn't leaving her a waking or sleeping moment without demanding his.

Turning off her laptop with a huff of exasperation, she snatched her purse and headed out of her office. No use trying to work when she could barely sit or think straight.

Fifteen minutes later she was entering her apartment, to hear Dora's usual jabbering issuing from the family room. The adorable sounds wrung a smile from her tight lips.

Halfway there, she felt as if she'd bumped into an invisible wall when she heard what emanated from her destination. A deep, deep voice.

Swallowing the heart that seemed to have vaulted into her throat, she forced herself to continue on shaking legs. It might be Aristedes. It probably was. He'd said he'd come to meet Dora, and she'd told him to drop by whenever he could, no advance call necessary. He did sound a lot like Andreas. From a distance their voices could be mistaken for—

She groaned. Who was she fooling? That dark baritone thrummed her already inflamed nerves, itched behind her breastbone and pooled in her loins. Even if her ears and brain couldn't make a positive ID, the rest of her body knew.

That *was* Andreas.

He was here. Uninvited and unannounced again. And with Dora.

Naomi shook off the initial surge of fright. After all, he was still here, hadn't absconded with Dora.

But she'd left herself wide open to his incursion again. She should have made it clear to Hannah that he wasn't welcome here. Should have left strict instructions with the concierge to bar his entrance.

Reaching the family room, she scoped out the situation

before making an entrance, no expectations forming in her mind. What she saw sent her thundering heart sputtering.

Andreas was sitting on the couch, looking even more vital than usual in a light beige suit that made his hair and skin glow in contrast. Her cats flanked his sides, Hannah was sitting across from him in the armchair, and Dora played at his feet.

To anyone looking in on the scene, it would have appeared as though this huge man who dwarfed his companions and darkened the whole room was a regular guest here. Hannah seemed so pleased and animated as she talked to him, Loki and Thor were grooming themselves in utmost relaxation, and Dora was handing him her prized toys to inspect, babbling her brand of baby explanations and inquiries nonstop. They all behaved as if being with him was an accustomed and favorite pastime.

And while he looked totally out of place in this scene of domesticity, his demeanor as he matter-of-factly accepted the attention and familiarity her household extended him, belied the fact that this was an unprecedented situation in his experience, and one alien to his nature.

Which mattered not at all right now. The need to charge in, grab Dora and Hannah and get them the hell away from Andreas was so fierce it paralyzed Naomi.

Which was a good thing. She couldn't expose the reality of the situation to Hannah or Dora. Inertia was giving her the chance to get herself together before she walked in.

One other thing held her back: the fact that Andreas knew she was there. The way he lowered his lashes as his eyes shifted in her direction made her certain. He'd always had an uncanny radar where she was concerned. She bet he wasn't acknowledging her presence on purpose. To goad her into some uncalculated response. One she wasn't giving him, even though she felt his magnetic pull tugging at her every instinct and craving.

Cursing under her breath, she straightened and walked into the room.

As soon as she did, Andreas inched to the edge of the couch, still holding Dora's latest offerings, his gaze opaque as usual. Her body nearly roared its demand for his. Having him within reach was sending it bucking like a wild horse against the reins of decorum and prudence.

Gritting her teeth against the hammering urges, she dragged her gaze to Hannah, who was rising with a bright smile.

"Darling, you're home early! Everything all right?"

Failing to return her smile, Naomi felt her heat rising with each step she took closer to Andreas. "Just wrapped things up earlier than expected."

"Great. Now Mr. Sarantos won't have to put up with our company for as long as he'd resigned himself to."

"It's I who had my doubts you'd bear my company that long, Mrs. McCarthy." Andreas's calm self-denunciation dragged Naomi's gaze back to him. She found him looking at Hannah. "And again, it's Andreas. Every time you say Mr. Sarantos I have the urge to look around for my older brother."

"But you must be used to being called Mr. Sarantos, too!"

"I've been suffering this condition since I came back on his turf. New York can't handle more than one Mr. Sarantos, and that's definitely him around here."

Hannah chuckled. "Fine, but only if you call me Hannah."

"That's a relief…Hannah."

And there Hannah went, totally submerged under Andreas's spell.

His gaze turned to Naomi, and suddenly her clothes felt like sandpaper against her skin, and the air felt like the blast of a furnace.

His cool appraisal made it all worse. "In case you're preparing another rebuke for my being here uninvited again, this time I thought you'd be here when I showed up on your doorstep."

As if he didn't know she worked afternoons on Saturdays.

"You could have called ahead." Her attempt at a smile was all for Hannah's sake. "Saved yourself the wait."

"If I did, I wouldn't have had the chance to sample the fantastic walnut-and-spice cake Hannah had just baked when I arrived. And I wouldn't have met the rest of your household."

He turned his gaze to those who'd come to welcome her. Loki and Thor were rubbing against her legs, while Dora clasped her knees, asking to be picked up.

Feeling she'd keel over if she bent too quickly, Naomi petted her cats, then swung Dora up, moving away from Andreas for some breathable air.

She still couldn't stop watching him as he took in the sight of her and Dora smooching each other, his gaze enigmatic and heavy-lidded. She'd never seen this specific look in his eyes before. And it elicited a whole new level of disturbance.

"You must be hungry."

His remark set off firecrackers in her blood. He should know. But she also knew he wasn't making an innuendo. Though he was terminally blunt, he wasn't blatant. Being so came with the need to provoke people, and Andreas didn't consider others at all. And though he'd been provoking her of late, she doubted he'd make a lewd remark in front of Hannah. Those weren't his style, anyway.

"Hannah said you come home famished," he elaborated. "Since you don't eat or snack at work."

Putting Dora down when she squirmed, Naomi shook her head. "I'm not today."

Because I'm only famished for a juggernaut with a body made for sin and a touch that turns me into a mindless mess.

"Which is a relief," Hannah said. "I forgot all about starting dinner, what with Andreas's entertaining company."

Naomi blinked at her. Andreas? *Entertaining* company?

Hannah pulled herself energetically to her feet. "But no matter. Dinner will be ready in half an hour." She turned to him, eyes hopeful. "And of course you're staying?"

"On one condition."

Sure. Andreas always had one. Something that entailed soul forfeiting.

"I won't sit here waiting to be served. I'm simply incapable of being waited on."

Naomi couldn't accuse him of telling a lie here. Andreas was self-sufficient to the point of aggravation. Though they'd always had room service or catering when they'd been together, he'd never let her as much as serve that food. He'd never even let her make him a cup of coffee. Nor had he ever offered to make her one, either.

"So what did you have in mind for dinner, Hannah?" he asked.

"Oh, just baked salmon, mashed potatoes and stir-fry. The crème brûlée for dessert is ready. But I can put together another menu if any of this isn't to your liking."

"You just mentioned some of my favorite foods."

He wasn't being polite, as he never bothered to be. This was true.

He rose, falling in step with Hannah on her way to the kitchen. She was clearly overjoyed to have him, touching him the way she did David, her only son among her four children, whenever he came visiting. The rest of Naomi's "household" followed in his wake, cats twining between his legs and Dora determinedly crawling after him.

And since she hadn't even been consulted in his dinner

invitation, and unable to make a scene in the others' presence, Naomi grudgingly followed.

Once in the kitchen, Dora climbed his leg, demanding he be the one to put her in her high chair. He looked down at her as if one of the cats had started talking to him.

Expecting him to ignore her, Naomi was surprised when he bent and, with perfect efficiency devoid of an emotional element, did as asked. Seemingly satisfied with his handling, Dora pointed to her feeding-time toys that were lined on the marble island. He didn't comply this time, just pinned her with one of his mesmerizing glances. In a moment, the baby's face scrunched up in its most endearing expression.

Naomi couldn't believe it. This was Dora asking nicely!

Only then did Andreas give her what she wanted. Then he bent and looked her straight in the eyes. "And *now* I cook with your mommy and nanny. *You* play until we're done."

Naomi bet Dora understood his refusal to be at her disposal when he had other things to do, and that it was non-negotiable. Giving him another wide grin, she got busy with her toys.

He moved next to Hannah. "I'll take care of that salmon. I think you'll be impressed with my seasoning."

With a smile that split her face, Hannah offered him the fish and all the ingredients he asked for.

Shaking herself out of the trance she'd fallen into at the impossible sight of Andreas in her kitchen, sharing dinner preparation, Naomi said, "I'll do the potatoes."

Andreas extended her one of those multi-meaning glances before turning his attention to his chore. "That's a perfect cut of salmon. Kudos to whoever chose it. And you must have felt I'd be coming, Hannah, since there's enough for all of us. For Dorothea, too, if she eats that kind of food now."

Glowing from his praise, the older woman said, "Dora

eats most of what we eat. She is the least fussy eater of all the babies I've ever dealt with, and I've dealt with six beside her."

"Naomi was one of those, I hear. How was she?"

Hannah looked at her apologetically. "From one to ten, one being Dora? She was an eleven. Nothing pleased her, and it was over two years before we managed to get her to eat anything not specifically prepared for her."

"I eat anything you put before me now, Hannah."

At her mumbled response, Hannah smiled lovingly at her. "Oh, you've long made up and then some, in every way possible, for any aggravation you ever caused."

Andreas's eyes were on her, contemplative. It must be difficult for him to imagine her being particular about anything. She'd bet she'd been the most accommodating person he'd ever known. Life had punched and wrung any demanding tendencies and expectations out of her.

After he removed the salmon skin, he spoke again. "I grew up on Crete, and most of our food was seafood we caught ourselves, but we never had salmon, since it doesn't exist in the Mediterranean. Once I was introduced to it here, I got addicted. I now eat no other animal protein."

"Is it a moral or health stance?" Hannah asked.

"I can't claim either, no. We could never afford meat or poultry. And when I tried them for the first time here, at age sixteen, I just couldn't develop a taste for them."

Naomi's hands shook as she peeled the potatoes. She'd noticed he'd never eaten those things, but had never asked why. He'd never given her straight answers to anything, so she'd stopped asking. But there he was, volunteering information about his past for the first time.

She'd known, from Aristedes's background and from Andreas's slight Greek accent, that he'd spent his formative years in Crete. She'd had no idea exactly when he'd come to the States. Now she knew. And that they'd been *that* destitute. That must have entailed endless difficulties and uncertainties.

It was impossible to imagine Andreas as a boy, poor and powerless. But maybe that had been responsible for turning him into this self-contained, invulnerable entity.

She suppressed a wave of sympathy with all she had, kept her distance as she prepared her part of the meal. He didn't try to invade her space, either. He took no opportunity to brush against her or touch her, though as they moved around the kitchen, there were plenty of those. Every time one presented itself, she held her breath, every nerve ending in a rage of anticipation. But he took advantage of none.

Even though his aloofness kept pushing her frustration higher, she was amazed at how easily and efficiently they worked together. It was as if they did this every day.

When the meal was ready, he set the table while she fed Dora and Hannah cleaned up. They sat down in the kitchen, as he'd insisted on observing their everyday practices.

Naomi sampled the salmon and was once again amazed. It was the best she'd ever had. His seasoning brought out the fish's natural taste, and made her eager for the next bite of complex and incredible flavors. When she and Hannah said so, he merely accepted their praise, without a show of either pleasure or modesty. He *knew* he was good.

He had to be superlative in everything, didn't he?

But what flabbergasted Naomi was that he was entertaining.

Now that he was actually talking, and not only brooding and distilling his responses to absolute minimums, he was witty, sometimes even funny. The strangeness of the situation was the only thing that kept her from engaging him fully, from demonstrating the effect his wit and drollness had on her.

At one point, as he related anecdotes about his early childhood, he said, "I barely saw my father, growing up, and I considered Aristedes an entity unto himself, whom I didn't consider in the simple terms of a male or female role model. My brother Leonidas was still a work-in-progress at the time. Then one day I demanded a dress like my sisters. I felt discriminated against, wearing only shorts and pants. It was only then that my mother broke the news that I couldn't wear a dress because I was a boy. You can't imagine my shock at that disclosure."

Naomi couldn't hold back anymore; she burst out laughing.

For this overwhelmingly masculine man to be sitting here admitting he'd thought he was a girl, had been happy thinking it, and crestfallen when he'd found out the truth, was just…hilarious.

He slanted her a long-suffering glance. "Go ahead and laugh. My sisters howled for days. And with every stage I passed through after that earthshaking revelation, their amusement escalated."

"What stages were those?" she spluttered.

"The usual. Denial, then anger then bargaining…"

She snorted. "Bargaining?"

"I was certain there must be something that could be done to stop this condition in its tracks, or to reverse it." At her renewed peals of laughter he sighed in mock despair. "You can laugh now, but I was grief-stricken. I felt so betrayed when I found out this condition was permanent."

Thankfully, for her. Or maybe not so thankfully. His overriding maleness had cost her six years, and would probably be *the* source of torment for the rest of her life.

But even this thought couldn't dampen her mirth right now. "You must have been very young."

"Six. It took me a year to accept my terrible fate."

After that, the conversation flowed, so spontaneously, so enjoyably. Hannah made few contributions, watching them with evident pleasure and keeping Dora entertained all through the meal.

It felt so natural having him there, talking to him that way, that Naomi had to keep reminding herself this was indeed Andreas, the man who'd shut her out all through their relationship, who'd never showed her any of the ease and unaffectedness he offered so freely now. By the end of the meal, it was difficult to accept that her dinner companion and that other Andreas were one and the same man.

Was this the real him? If so, what had kept this wonderful person locked up in ice all these years? What had happened now to thaw him out? It couldn't be her, since she'd never succeeded in unleashing these facets of him before.

But being exposed to said facets only caused her condition to worsen. She had to fight the urge to drag his hands to her burning cheeks or aching breasts, or to lean into him and rest her head on his chest. From the look in his eyes, she surmised that he saw it all—and chose not to respond with the merest touch or even an acknowledgment.

After a brief lull as Hannah rose to fetch dessert, Naomi said, "I thought you left town."

This came out too much like an accusation for her liking.

But the contrary emotions he wrung from her were tearing her in two opposite directions. She did want him to leave. For Dora's sake. But when she'd thought he'd left without a word, after the night they'd had, the thought had been a hot poker in her middle.

He thanked Hannah as she placed his crème brûlée in front of him, then said, "I'm here to stay...for a while."

Conscious of Hannah's piqued attention, Naomi emptied her voice of expression. "For how long?"

"It depends."

"On what?"

"On when I'll conclude the business I have here."

"What if you don't, or can't?"

One formidable shoulder rose in an indolent shrug. "I'll deal with the possibilities as they arise. My plans are fluid."

Just as her insides were, being this close to him.

After that, she let him draw her back into their bantering, though it was more difficult to keep up her end, since thoughts of him leaving and her fluid-with-desire state had put a damper on her mood.

Then they moved back to the family room for coffee.

The cats rushed to climb on his lap as soon as he sat down, but Dora insisted on evicting and replacing them. Since they considered her the baby of the family, while they were old and wise felines, they moved on, in obvious displeasure. They didn't go far, though, and sat flanking him again, grooming the fur messed by the tussle with Dora.

Andreas let the baby explore him, not helping or hindering her. Soon she made it impossible for him to continue his conversation with Naomi, demanding his attention by grabbing for his phone, belt buckle and anything he held. She whined when he refused to bow to her will.

He did that without a trace of irritation. Naomi wondered how, since Dora was being *very* irritating. Which was probably a good thing, she reasoned, since it would give him a taste of what it would be like if he took on responsibility for her, even if not as her main caretaker.

But if he showed no irritation, neither did he exhibit any indulgence, not in the way he regarded Dora, not in his refusal to let her use him and his articles for her new take-apart or teething toys.

At Dora's latest antic, trying to find out if the silky bronze hair on his chest was attached, things took a turn for the confrontational.

When he stopped her, if not gently, at least carefully, the baby's lip curled downward.

"You're a demanding little tyke, aren't you?"

For good measure, Dora's chin shook and her eyes filled with tears.

"And a grade A manipulator, too."

Dora lunged again at his open shirt in pursuit of her interrupted experiment, making Naomi rush to take her away.

Andreas raised a hand, staying her movement. Sitting back down, she itched to end this, since Dora began to sob with frustration as he held her chubby little hands at bay. Short of snatching her from him, and making this even worse, there was nothing Naomi could do but wait and see how he would handle it. She had no hope it would be in any way suited to a baby.

With both of them ignoring her presence completely, they locked horns, Dora's eyes indignant and swimming in tears of frustration, his contemplative yet unyielding.

Then in a very quiet voice, as if he was whispering in confidence, he said, "Here's how it will be, Dorothea. These are my hairs, and they stay on my chest. You don't get to feel bad about not getting something you shouldn't ask for. But I promise, when you want something you can have, I'll let you have it. How about that?"

And wonder of wonders, the willful, tearful expression on Dora's face dissipated as he calmly discussed the situation with her as he would with an adult. Then, seeming to accept his nonnegotiable terms, she gave a yell of glee, as if she hadn't been agitated a moment ago, and threw herself on the chest she'd been keen on attacking, and rubbed her face in it. Andreas made no attempt to hug her, as anyone else would have. Which didn't deter Dora in the least. Moments later, she raised her head with a smile that Naomi could swear was deferential, then she scrambled off him and went about her business.

Although the situation had been calmly resolved without her intervention, Naomi felt compelled to say something.

"Sorry about that. She's not usually so demanding. It

must be the novelty of having someone other than Hannah and me around. And a man, at that."

His gaze acknowledged that the one man who'd been a constant presence in her life, Petros, had been taken from her when she'd been too young. She had either forgotten him or hadn't really formed any memories of him.

Andreas's eyes grew thoughtful. "She doesn't see any men?"

"None like you."

He made no comment on that, her placing him in a category of his own, but his stare made Naomi's every cell start to sizzle like popcorn.

To break the tension she muttered, "I guess she was exploring her boundaries with you, since you're a new and totally different person. She already knows her boundaries with us."

"Are you sure she has any? You and Hannah anticipate all her needs and whims. That's the reason she's undemanding. You leave her nothing to demand."

"Are you saying we're overindulging her?"

"Claws back into your paws, mother lioness. I'm not criticizing your upbringing methods, I'm observing. As someone new around here, I might be able to see what you can't, because you're too used to the dynamics in your family and too settled in its rules. But I do think there's a definite risk of overindulgence here. If only from her growing up realizing she's the center of your and Hannah's universe."

"I'm sure you have a suggestion how to rectify this."

"None. It must be next to impossible to look at someone this size, someone so totally dependent on you, and be objective. Considering the situation, too, it's understandable you're trying to compensate her, and perhaps ending up overcompensating."

"So what you're really saying is that I'm a bad mother."

She was expecting him to say "you're not a mother at

all" or something to that effect, but he again surprised her. "I have no idea what kind of mother you are, Naomi. I've been here a few hours and Dorothea spent those focusing on me. I had only fleeting impressions of your relationship—which could turn out to be totally off the mark on closer inspection. But I expect you'd be as efficient in this role as you are in everything else. I'm only wondering if your overachieving tendencies might not be best applied in this field."

"*I'm* an overachiever?"

"You most definitely are, and that is something to be proud of. In your professional life. With Dorothea, on the other hand, it could lead to…"

"…overindulging her."

"It's likely, and it would be understandable. That said, if you say she's undemanding in general, I'll take your word for it. She did respond promptly to my refusal to indulge her whim, after all."

Naomi bit her tongue so she wouldn't admit that it was his handling and influence that had resolved the situation so amicably, not the baby's responsiveness.

Still, she felt the urge to explain Dora's character more. "She is overly inquisitive sometimes, but it's not whims that make her demanding. She just gets very interested in things, in how they work, what they're made of. Demanding brats often lose interest as soon as you give them what they fussed for. But once you give Dora what she asked for, she sits aside and examines it for hours. All her favorite toys are articles from around the house that she demanded, and she never lost interest in them. In fact, she keeps finding new uses for them, alone or together."

"Seems we have an inventor on our hands. But it's too bad she got interested in things I couldn't let her have. My phone and belt *could* have been negotiated, but my chest hair…that would have to remain taboo."

Naomi's smile broke out, wiping away her defensive tension. Though he didn't smile back, there was an unknown warmth in his eyes that felt better than any smile could have.

Moments of silence ensued as Hannah came back from the kitchen and Dora and the cats came asking permission to climb over him again. With a nod of consent, he let them, sat back like a lion letting the kids of the pride have free range of his great body. Dora was now on her best behavior, imitating the cats in their sinuous grace as they showed him acceptance and affection with rubs and head butts. Andreas let them have their fill of exploring the body that was twice as big as the females they were used to, and must feel very different, too.

In the middle of playing, on cue at eight, Dora curled over his chest and promptly fell asleep.

Andreas sat there looking down at her as if he'd had a live grenade tossed in his lap.

Naomi rose to take her, and his whisper, dark and hushed, stopped her in her tracks. "She looks exactly like Petros."

Swallowing the immediate lump in her throat, Naomi nodded. "Yeah, only with Nadine's eyes."

He made no response, his gaze pinned on Dora's peaceful face as she surrendered to slumber in the security of his presence.

Long moments passed before he finally spoke. "If she's anything like him on the inside, she'll turn out to be an angel."

Her heart felt too full to make an answer, so Naomi merely reached for Dora. He made no move to help as she carried her away, nor offered to accompany her as she put her in bed.

Once Naomi came back, Andreas turned his gaze from Hannah to her. "You must be tired, too. Hannah said you wake up early with Dora, and that makes your days even longer."

"I don't know about Naomi, but that's definitely it for me." Hannah stood, stifling a yawn.

Andreas rose to his feet at once, making Naomi blink.

He'd never stood when she did, at least not out of gentlemanly politeness.

But she hadn't observed him around others much, certainly never with an older lady. Maybe it was his old-world Greek blood kicking in or something.

He shook Hannah's hand with what passed for warmth in his book, and again thanked her for her hospitality and for sharing her evening and kitchen with him.

Hannah fairly swooned with delight as she assured him the pleasure had definitely been hers. She met Naomi's eyes briefly as she rose to kiss her good-night. It was clear the woman thought Andreas was a god and that it would be Naomi's phenomenal luck if he was interested in her. It was clear Hannah would do anything to facilitate that interest. Such as pretending to be unable to keep her eyes open so Andreas would have time alone with Naomi, if only minutes before he left.

As soon as she'd disappeared, Naomi turned to Andreas.

Having him alone for the first time tonight, she couldn't wait anymore for all the things she was dying to know.

Why had he come? Why had he been this way all evening? What did he decide? And most important of all… what would he do now? Right this second?

He strolled past the coffee table, approaching her. "Thank you for this evening, Naomi."

She stood rooted, waiting for him to reach her.

He didn't. He headed in the other direction, and was halfway out of the room when she realized he was leaving.

Did he want her to run after him, ask him to stay? Was this to make up for when she'd told him to get out?

Though he'd better not get used to it, she had no choice but to bow to his wishes now. He'd yet to tell her what he'd decided.

Rushing after him, she caught up with him at the door.

He turned after he opened it, and it felt like a reversal of those last moments in his suite. His gaze was at its most unfathomable as he looked at her. Her blood surged to every inch of skin nearest to him, seeking his touch, begging his assuagement.

If he kissed her now, what would she do? Just let him, or meet him halfway?

He only said, "*Kalinychta*, Naomi," and walked out.

Unable to believe he'd just said good-night and left, she staggered forward, gripping the door for support. Her aching eyes clung to him as he walked away, willing him to turn so she could show him she wanted him to come back, to carry her to bed and end this gnawing hunger.

He just kept going, bypassed the elevator and headed for the stairwell. In seconds she heard his footfalls, sure and steady on the marble steps, receding until they were no more.

With her heart clanging in her chest, she shakily closed the door and leaned on it, disbelief expanding inside her.

He'd gone.

But…had he really gone, or would he come back?

If he didn't tonight, when would he?

Andreas didn't come back.

After a couple days of absence and silence, suspicion had started to gel in her mind. Then more days passed, and she could no longer find any other explanation.

That evening he'd spent with them must have been a test, to see if he could bear having them around. And he'd found he couldn't.

He might have also been trying to decide if he still wanted her, and had discovered that he didn't.

It seemed that night they'd shared, what had reignited her need for him, had only managed to purge her from his system. He'd had the closure sex she'd deprived him of when she'd walked away so abruptly. Now he had no more use for her. And he'd decided to leave her and Dora alone.

Mentally, she knew she should be feeling relieved, that Dora was safe. But she wasn't. She was only disappointed.

No, she wasn't disappointed.

She was crushed.

It felt as if she'd lost him all over again.

But it was even worse this time.

This time he'd shown her a glimpse of what she'd dreamed of from the moment she'd first seen him. A taste of Andreas the man, the companion, not only the lover and devourer.

And it had been ambrosia. She craved more of the closeness and fun and spontaneity that he'd given her during that magical evening.

And he'd just walked away. After he'd released the slow poison of longing all over again in her blood. A more potent one this time, since he'd shown her that what she'd longed for wasn't a mirage. It could be real. It *was* real. But it would never be hers.

As he never would be.

Eight

"I was beginning to think you'd never come."

Naomi winced at Selene's brightness. She couldn't tell her she was late because she had been debating not coming. It had taken her all morning to summon the guts to bundle up Hannah and Dora and drive to Manhattan Beach.

Not that Andreas had factored in her dread of attending the Sarantos family gathering Selene and Aristedes had invited her to. It was a "family" gathering, and he was the man who had no relations with his.

She'd ended up coming because she wanted a relationship with them, for Dora's sake. Aristedes had said they'd all considered Petros a brother, and no matter how Naomi felt, she'd do anything to give Dora uncles and aunts who cared about her, and kids her age to grow up among.

Selene linked her arm through hers after she'd kissed and welcomed Hannah and Dora. "No more wasting time, ladies. Everybody is dying to meet you all."

Walking into the waterfront villa was like stepping through a wormhole and landing in Crete. The Greek influences in design were prevalent throughout, even if the traditional touches were imbued with the latest in modernity. It stood to reason that would be the Sarantoses' choice, since both Aristedes and Selene were of Greek origin.

It was sumptuous yet unpretentious, spacious yet not massive, a testament to the taste and priorities of those who'd built it. While the man of the house could afford something a hundred times more luxurious, he and his wife cared only about comfort, privacy, safety…and each other.

Naomi's observations ended when she found the Sarantos family coming to meet them en masse. What with the four sisters, their husbands and children, and a few more people who were close friends or distant relatives, she could barely keep up with the introductions and the new faces. The only ones who stood out were Caliope, Andreas's youngest sibling, and her Russian husband, Maksim Volkov, one of the world's biggest steel magnates. With brothers like Aristedes and Andreas, Caliope could have fallen only for someone as overwhelming.

Suddenly, Naomi's heart rammed the base of her throat.

Strolling in from the terrace, framed by the breathtaking vista of the Atlantic, was Andreas.

Everyone's voices rose as he came to stand at the periphery of the gathering, ignoring everyone who scolded him for being late in welcoming Naomi and the others.

"Naomi, Hannah." That was the sum total of his acknowledgment of their presence before he turned his gaze down to Dora, who'd left her newfound friends and was crawling toward him at high speed.

He let her reach him, pull herself up his leg, and only when she gave him the most endearing grin in history did he relent and pick her up.

Voices rose again, some laughingly claiming it had to be the end of the world, others complaining that he hadn't given *their* kids that unprecedented privilege.

Andreas gave them all a serene look as Dora nuzzled his neck. "I didn't pick Dorothea up. She compelled me. Didn't you see that glance and grin? Ask Naomi. This child is an expert in getting whatever she sets her sights on, and she must have wanted to see what it's like being at this altitude. I don't volunteer pickup services, but when *your* kids lay claim to them like Dorothea did, I will comply."

Everyone laughed and ribbed him about turning out to be a huge rattle toy just like everyone else. But Naomi knew it wasn't true. If Dora had resorted to her demanding ways, he wouldn't have picked her up. But he'd had her trained from just their one encounter.

Andreas would never take the first step, or respond to approaches, until they were made to his strict specifications.

After making the connection with Andreas, Dora asked to be let down so she could rejoin the kids, who ranged in age from one to seven. Then everyone started drifting into smaller groups.

They all seemed to be leaving Naomi with Andreas on purpose. The moment they were alone, he said he was going back out on the terrace. She followed, only because she wanted to blast him apart.

He was braced with outstretched arms on the balustrade, his hair ruffling in the breeze, his gaze searching the horizon by the time she was at his side.

Snatching a glance back, to make sure they were out of earshot of the others, she fixed her eyes to the same point in the distance. "What are you doing here?"

"Right this second?" The voice that was as deep as that ocean, as alluring and merciless, washed over her. "I'm looking at the ocean."

She turned to him, found him regarding her in amusement, which he seemed to think she'd reciprocate.

She didn't find turmoil amusing. Nothing had explained the past ten days other than that he'd come, seen, conquered, then left. And just as she'd resigned herself that she would never see him again, she found him here. And could think of no good reason for that.

"How about a real answer?"

His lips twisted quizzically. "What's your theory about my presence? You must have come up with a few."

"Just one. You're toying with me."

He frowned. "How and why would I do that?"

The sudden seriousness in his eyes, that tinge of confusion, of dismay, deflated the bubbling accusations.

Had she gotten it all wrong, again? Could it be he'd just decided to visit his family and it had nothing to do with her?

The terrible thing was, that made sense. To go to the effort of toying with her, he'd have to think about her first. And he seemed to have dropped her from his consideration.

Without another word or look, she turned and walked back inside, wishing she could just take Hannah and Dora and leave.

God, why had she come? She should have never wished for more, even for Dora, just protected what they had. Now every exposure to his family—and him, now that he'd gotten it into his mind to start seeing them—would chip away at her. He'd already damaged her. More injuries might cripple her for good.

All her senses screamed a warning that Andreas was approaching. She lengthened her stride, reaching for the sanctuary of company.

Before he caught up with her, she fell into step with Caliope, who'd just left one of her older sisters.

Caliope turned with a radiant smile, stopping and forcing her to, as well. "Back already? Is it as nippy outside as it looks?" Her turquoise eyes went over Naomi's head. "Or is it another temperature-compromised reason that sent you back so soon?"

"All this creativeness to call me cold, Cali?" Andreas tutted.

"Not cold, my dearest brother, cool. Maddeningly so."

"Another lie, since I'm not your 'dearest' brother. We all know I'm at the end of the list of dearness around here."

Caliope laughed, not contradicting him, but clearly very fond of him. Andreas made people love him without doing a thing. Or while doing everything to make them hate him.

"It's just lack of exposure. Let us see you and you'd climb the list and share the top spots in no time."

"Hmm. That's all it takes? That might be arranged."

Caliope's eyes widened. "Really?" Without warning, she jumped forward and wrapped her arms around his neck. "Oh, yes, please, Andreas."

He looked as if he'd been hit by lightning.

This probably was the first time Caliope had hugged him.

Naomi could only hope he wouldn't rebuff her eagerness.

Then, as if approaching an abandoned package that might explode, he slowly wrapped his arms around his sister.

Yelping in delight, Caliope surged up to kiss him exuberantly.

Evidently thinking things had gone far enough, Andreas eased his hold on her and straightened to his full height.

No doubt knowing she'd gotten more than she could have expected, Caliope let him go with a sigh of contentment. "Man, I can't believe I have your promise we'll be seeing more of you. After you attended my wedding, too. Have I told you how much that meant to me?"

His lips twisted. "Only thirty-four times."

"Oh, I thought it was thirty-*five*."

"Four. It's how many times you've called me since."

Caliope's mouth dropped open. "You count people's calls?"

"Only yours…and Aristedes's. He always has something earth-shattering to tell me, while you, *mikrá* Cali, I dread even more."

Caliope laughed again, turning to Naomi. "Do I look tiny to you? But that gives you an idea when the last time Andreas *really* saw me was." She turned back to her brother. "And what was so dreadful about my calls? I only updated you about where each of us was, to see if you could drop by."

"It's your efforts to 'remodel' me that I dread."

Caliope looked back at Naomi with a conspiring grin. "I think I can abandon all my efforts now, don't you think?"

Meaning that Naomi would be the one doing the remodeling? If only Caliope knew.

But she wasn't about to correct her assumptions. All she wanted was to escape this scene of familial reacquaintance, and Andreas, until she could leave. She would never come within a mile of any Sarantos ever again.

Andreas's eyes had turned to her, as if expecting her to respond to his sister, before being drawn back to Caliope when she winced and started stroking her belly.

He frowned. "You all right?"

"Oh, it's just Tatjana's daily acrobatic exercises."

His eyebrows rose. "You already named her?"

Caliope chuckled. "We decided on Tatjana Anastasia, after Maksim's mother and late sister, before we found out the sex. Then we did, and that was it."

Something like indulgence hovered over his lips. "I thought you looked your most beautiful at your wedding, but you've…blossomed since. Cliché, I know, but nothing else would do. Married life has been good to you. After a few bumps, that is."

"Maksim has been good to me. Phenomenal wouldn't even cut it. And those bumps only made things better."

Andreas whistled. "Better than phenomenal? Maksim must be some kind of supernatural being."

Caliope's grin was so bright, it nearly blinded Naomi. "He is."

"Glad to know I'm related through marriage to a superhero. He might come in handy."

Caliope poked him. "You should try them, you know."

"Maksim or bumps?"

Poking him harder with an unfettered laugh, Caliope flashed a devouring glance at her husband, who was watching her in the same way even as he talked to her sister Melina.

It was impossible to see those two together, just like Selene and Aristedes, and not be buffeted by the force of emotions they shared. But there seemed something extra between Caliope and Maksim. According to Selene, they'd been through hell and back together, and it had clearly fused them in ways that the most sublime happiness couldn't have. Maksim looked at their child, Leo, and Caliope's advanced bump as if he were watching his own beating heart. As for how he looked at Caliope…it made Naomi's hair stand on end. It was almost too much love to witness.

Still chuckling, Caliope said, "Sorry, Maksim is taken, for this life and whatever comes next. You go get your own bumps with your own soul mate."

Naomi escaped Caliope's glance, which swerved to her, only to find her eyes colliding with Andreas's.

Slowly releasing her gaze, he turned to his sister. "Don't I require a soul first?"

"Oh, you have one somewhere. Even if it's buried under decades of dust. All we need to do is unearth it."

"As long as you leave the unearthing to me and don't try to precipitate it with your drilling methods."

After that, Caliope's direct comments forced Naomi to participate in the conversation, until Hannah called her away, thankfully, to inform her that she was taking Dora to the pool.

Afterward, counting the seconds until she could leave, Naomi tried to respond to everyone's welcome and reciprocate their interest. It was as if all present considered her and her family theirs already. Which only made her decision not to see them anymore harder.

But one thing made it easier to forget her turmoil: the rich family spectacle unfolding before her eyes. Everyone weaved such a complex tapestry of relationships and emotions, it was fascinating to watch them interact. With her own father dying when she was five, only a year after Nadine was born, and growing up with just her mother, an only child, and Hannah for family, Naomi had never known what an extended one was like.

The most interesting part to her was when their reactions and interactions involved Andreas. It was clear they loved him, not that even they seemed to know why. And it was equally clear they didn't know what to make of him or of his unaccustomed presence among them today.

But her real fascination was in watching Andreas. Though there was nothing too overt, she started to believe that he actually cared about them, especially Aristedes and Caliope.

At one point, Naomi found herself with Caliope again. This time she told her the story of their early life in Crete, mainly about their parents' dysfunctional relationship.

Their father had been a charmer and a user who'd drifted in and out of their mother's life, each time coming back to add another child to his brood and take all she had, before disappearing again. He'd vanished from their lives for good when Caliope was not yet born, leaving their mother heartbroken and unwilling to go on.

This made Naomi look at Andreas in a new light.

Had he inherited his lack of emotion from their father? The others seemed unscathed by the man's genes. Aristedes seemed to have emotions in abundance, while Caliope had said her late brother, Leonidas, had been the most loving man on earth. So had Andreas been the only one who'd won the lottery of their father's terrible legacy?

From then on, Naomi watched him even more closely. Whenever she could find him. He disappeared for stretches of time before reappearing again at random.

She wondered if she had only imagined that he cared for his family. Had she merely seen what she'd wanted to see, still hoping to find something redeemable about him?

But whatever he felt or didn't feel for them, it wasn't relevant where she was concerned. Though he did talk to her during the evening, it was in conversations involving others. Like that evening in her apartment, he made no effort to be alone with her. If she'd needed any reinforcement of her previous analysis, that gave it to her in spades.

He no longer wanted her.

While it hurt like she hadn't thought anything could ever again, at least it meant Dora was safe.

At the end of the evening, as everyone kissed her and she made promises that she knew she wouldn't keep, Andreas stood apart, watching her and his family. Just watching.

Hannah went ahead to put the sleeping Dora in her car seat before catching a ride to her daughter's house. While she did that occasionally on weekends, Naomi suspected she was doing it tonight hoping for something to develop in her absence. Turning away with a generalized good-night and thanks to everyone, Naomi rushed after her.

She wanted this over with...*now*.

She was almost outside the door when she found Andreas beside her. "Did you enjoy yourself today?"

Feeling seconds away from tears, she nodded without raising her gaze to his.

"Dorothea and Hannah seemed to enjoy themselves, too."

God, now she knew what a mouse felt like being tormented by a majestic, indifferent feline.

"Everyone loved having you all here."

She almost rounded on him and screamed, *"Everyone but you. And just what do you want now? It's sure not me."*

Out loud she said nothing, concentrating on counting the steps till she reached her car and escape.

He kept up with her until she got into it, kept the door open before she could slam it.

Bending, he seared her with his steady gaze. "I was coming to your place tomorrow, but I thought I'd give you a heads-up, since you're not big on surprises."

Fury at his presumption burned away her misery. "Or on people deciding to drop by without consulting me."

"I am consulting you now."

"You're *informing* me, only so graciously ahead of time."

There was this confusion in his eyes again, as if he had no idea why she was so agitated. And why would he?

"May I come over tomorrow, Naomi?"

So we can start this maddening merry-go-round again? Out loud she only managed a terse, "No."

Then she pulled the door from his hand. He stood there as she turned the car on and drove away slowly.

She arrived at home an hour later, put Dora in bed and did all her nightly rituals. Then she slipped between the covers…and finally let the tears fall.

Nine

Naomi woke up to find her pillow soaked.

The first thing she did was punch it.

As she should have Andreas. Long ago.

And when the opportunity presented itself, what had she done? A few chest thumps and a couple slaps. The huge lout must still be laughing his head off.

Jumping from bed, determined to leave him and any thoughts of him behind, she rushed about her morning routine before Dora woke up. Though judging from the sounds of deep breathing over the baby intercom, she was too soundly asleep to wake up soon. Playing nonstop with so many kids yesterday had wiped her out.

Naomi had just finished making coffee when the bell rang. Thinking it must be the super, she rushed to the door.

She took a look through the peephole…and lurched back.

Andreas.

She took another look. Because it wasn't *only* Andreas. Another Peek confirmed the absurdity of the first one.

It was him. And flowers.

Andreas? Bringing her *flowers*?

And not just any flowers. A bouquet half her size, with

every type of gold blossom, with the stems and leaves tinted turquoise.

Her head spun. Was he exhibiting his father's condition? He'd return, then leave, then return and so on, in an endless loop, until he wrecked her?

She didn't think so. She might have been a victim of her craving for him so far, but no longer.

She spoke loudly enough for him to hear her through the thick door. "Go away, Andreas."

His answer was immediate. "No, I won't."

"Then you'll stand there until you have to leave."

"I'll stand here until *you* have to leave."

"I'm not leaving for the whole weekend."

"Then that is how long I'll stand here."

And the worst thing? She believed he would.

"I still won't talk to you when you finally ambush me."

"You're talking to me now. Might as well make it about something constructive."

"Here's something constructive. I'm allergic to flowers."

"No, you're not."

"I'm allergic to *you*."

He gave a long-suffering exhalation. "Apparently I do elicit inexplicable reactions in you."

"Oh, those reactions are very explicable."

"Not to me. Enlighten me."

"Listen, this is just silly."

"First thing we agree on today."

It was her turn to sigh. "Did Aristedes put you up to this? Or was it Selene or Caliope who advised the flowers? It was probably a committee decision, especially with this over-the-top bouquet that mirrors my coloring."

"I can understand your skepticism. But no, the flowers and their color connotations are my own initiative. I bet the others wouldn't have suggested something you found so aggravating. But as ridiculous as it sounds now, I thought flowers would provide an opening in the impasse we inexplicably reached last night, or a peace offering in this one-sided war you've resumed for no discernible reason."

"You're that lost in your own world? You see no reason?"

"None."

"How about that I'm not at your disposal to disappear and then return, pretending nothing happened?"

"I didn't disappear."

"What do you call what you did for the three days after you met Aristedes?"

"After you had Aristedes issue me a cease and desist, you mean. And I call it 'giving you time to calm down.'"

"Calm down? When I was going out of my mind needing to know what the meeting achieved, what you decided?"

"I thought you wouldn't want to hear from me directly, and that Aristedes would tell you how things went."

"How could he? He didn't know what you'd decided, either, which left me even more agitated until I heard from you. Then you came, spent the whole evening with us and didn't say a word. After which you disappeared again for a week. And the next time I saw you it was by accident. And you still said nothing!"

"It wasn't by accident."

That stopped her ready volley. Then she huffed a harsh laugh. "And to think I believed you weren't toying with me."

"Why would you think I was? When did I ever 'toy' with you?"

"That's the euphemism I came up with for the manipulation you've been exposing me to since you came back."

"How was it manipulation, when I said I would claim Dorothea, not take her from you?"

He had said "claim" not "take." But the rest...

Suddenly everything inside her was like one of Hannah's knitting balls after Loki and Thor had had their way with it.

"As for the second instance of disappearance you claim, it took me that long to put together that family event."

She snatched the door open. "What?"

Everything seemed to spin around her as the sight of him impacted her senses. He stood there, legs braced apart, as if preparing for a grueling fight, the gigantic bouquet gripped in one hand beside a long, powerful thigh. He looked a few light-years beyond fantastic. Though on closer inspection he had a haggard look about him. And was that the same suit he'd had on last night?

"Can I come in now?"

"Did you just say this so you can come in?"

"I have plenty of vices, Naomi. Lying isn't one of them."

He was right. And since he never lied, in light of all he'd said, had she jumped to conclusions about everything?

Oh, she didn't know anything anymore.

Exasperated, with herself more than anything, she stepped aside with an ill-tempered huff.

His raised eyebrow as he brushed past her made her bristle more. "No comments about my lack of graciousness?"

"I wouldn't dream of it. I now know how sharp your claws are, and I need my eyes where they are."

He headed to the family room, put down the bouquet, then turned to her with an expression that looked like disappointment, then morphed at once into anxiety. "Why isn't Dorothea up yet?"

Wondering if she'd read him right, Naomi said, "She's just sleeping off yesterday's unusual exertion."

He seemed unconvinced. "Hannah said she wakes up no later than six. It's nine. And she spent a lot of time in the sun and the pool. Maybe too much. Maybe she's not well."

"How do you know that?"

"I was with her most of that time."

So that was where he'd kept disappearing yesterday. Then anxiety burst inside her as his words sank in. She'd left Dora to Hannah's care, never doubting that she'd know what was enough. But… Had Dora's breathing been too deep? Could she be suffering from sunstroke? She could be burning up….

Naomi bolted to her room, feeling Andreas hot on her heels. Braking at the door, she opened it with all the control she had left, turning to Andreas to signal *quiet*. He nodded, followed her soundlessly to Dora's crib.

Naomi's heart hammered as she bent to press her cheek to her forehead…and all tension deflated. It was cooler than her own hectic flesh.

Before she could turn to Andreas, he bent, spooning her. Her breath caught even as she realized he was just unable to wait to find out if Dora was okay, was reaching out to check her temperature, too.

As soon as his large palm cupped the baby's cheek, she gurgled something contented and caught his hand and swept it with her as she turned noisily to her side.

They ended up standing there, with him bent over her, both trapped with his hand held beneath Dora's cheek.

"Will she wake up if I withdraw my hand?" His whisper tickled Naomi's ear, poured right into her brain.

Turning her head, she found her lips in his neck, and somehow managed to whisper back, "She's bound to wake up soon, anyway."

"I'd rather it's not me who woke her up."

"It's actually better if you do. Oversleeping will throw her whole pattern out of whack."

"In that case, go ahead and wake her."

"Withdraw your hand first and let's see if that does it."

He tried, but Dora only whimpered and clung to it.

"So much for that. Let's go for a more direct approach," Naomi murmured. His other hand came around her, stopping hers as she reached for Dora, enveloping her whole body in his.

Everything inside her fell apart as she turned to him and found him gazing at Dora, his face gripped in some fierce…emotion?

"She looks so content sleeping."

His whisper was the deepest Naomi had ever heard, almost reverent. There was no doubt anymore what this was about.

He didn't have the heart to wake Dora up.

Andreas now had a heart?

From all signs so far with the baby, it seemed he was sprouting one where there'd been none before.

Shaken by the idea, Naomi let her voice get louder, since she'd decided Dora should wake up. "You won't remember those moments when she's cranky and whining later because she's tired and can't fall asleep…because you let her oversleep."

He grimaced, gave an apology in Greek then withdrew his hand from Dora's grip, firmly but still gently. There *was* gentleness this time, not only the clinical care he'd demonstrated before.

Dora protested and turned on her back, her eyes fluttering open. Naomi heard Andreas catch his breath.

Shutting out the disturbing observations, she stroked Dora's head. "Enough charging, darling. It's time to wake up."

As always, Dora woke up with no disorientation. Her eyes crinkled in pleasure at seeing Naomi, before bypassing her and rounding with surprise at finding Andreas there.

Naomi felt man and baby lock gazes, and held her breath. Then Dora squealed in excitement, rolled to her side and climbed up the rails of her crib. Once propped up, she bobbed up and down, eyes luminous with glee, her grin showing every tooth she'd sprouted.

Andreas reached out a tentative hand to stroke Dora's cheek. "Does she always wake up excited like this?"

Naomi's throat tightened. "She is sunny most of the time, and wakes up in a great mood. But this is extra."

"She must be too used to you to make such a fuss every morning. I must be a novelty."

Acute honesty forced Naomi to correct his assumption. "She never greets new people with this fanfare."

His eyes widened. "Really?"

"Really. We got her a wonderful stand-in nanny, and she vetoed her. Our neighbors, a really nice couple, had dinner with us a few weeks ago and she ignored them completely."

Andreas looked so pleased, Naomi almost had to rub her eyes. But there was no doubt about it. He was thrilled Dora was treating him preferentially.

What the hell. Let him have more proof of his supreme influence on any being that breathed.

Naomi sighed. "Are you waiting for her to ask to be picked up in the exact way you trained her to?"

Andreas blinked. "That was when she was being bratty. Now she's being..."

"Delightful?" Naomi suggested when he couldn't find the right word, and he nodded. "So what are you waiting for? All these squats mean she can't wait for you to pick her up."

He reached down for Dora, his large palms spanning her rib cage as she kicked and gurgled in delight. "*Sygnómi*, Dorothea. Climbing my leg was much more understandable."

Hearing him apologizing so earnestly to Dora had a weird effect on Naomi. She burst out laughing.

Both man and baby turned to her in astonishment.

"Don't mind me. Carry on," she spluttered as she headed to the changing table. Andreas followed her when she beckoned, relinquishing Dora to her with utmost reluctance. He stood watching intently, showing no signs of distaste, as she changed the baby.

Then she stood aside and let him pick her up again. When he apologized for not being the one to change her, as he had to learn first, Naomi laughed again and headed out to the kitchen.

Andreas followed, Dora in his arms, cats around his legs, that famous eyebrow raised.

Naomi didn't press the issue of his reason for being here as she got things out for breakfast, while he put Dora in her high chair as if this was his morning routine, and Dora asked adorably for her toys.

He joined Naomi in preparing breakfast, admitting that he'd had none. As they worked in tandem, there was again a pervasive ease and companionship. This time she was certain it wasn't something he did on purpose. It was simply…there.

As if by agreement, they didn't bring up anything during breakfast.

Afterward, once in the family room, after she'd distributed his bouquet into four vases, with Dora and the cats busy together, he explained that tidbit that had made her open the door.

"After I left that evening, I knew I needed to get my family together to meet you and Dora. I had to get a place first."

"What? You mean that house in Manhattan Beach wasn't Aristedes's and Selene's?"

"No. Their home is a couple miles away, though."

That stunned her. Though…thinking back, she recalled they'd invited her to a "family gathering," not to "our place," and no one had implied the home was theirs. Had they all been in it together, leaving it vague, so she wouldn't realize? But why?

"It took a week to finalize the deal, get the place ready to receive people and to gather everyone."

He'd gone to all this expense and effort to put that day

together? Which would have been wonderful for her, had she known all that, but…

"You went to these lengths, just to end up ignoring me?"

His eyes widened. "Where do you keep getting those interpretations for my actions? I was giving you a chance to get to know the zillion members of my family. I thought we could talk some other time. Not that you seemed to want to see me at all. Though I now realize why."

So she'd gotten that wrong, too.

"You could have told me any of that," she mumbled.

"You mean alert you to my plans beforehand, so you'd surprise me by not attending? Didn't even occur to me."

"You could have called."

He shook his head. "To say what? I was still taking the steps to try to reach the decision you wanted to hear."

It was her turn to shake her head. He had no clue, did he? But he had gone to all this trouble for Dora. It proved he'd had powerful feelings for Petros, even if Naomi hadn't understood the connection or seen its evidence. Now, from the times he'd seen Dora, that first reconnaissance evening, his vigilant day yesterday, and this morning, it was clear he'd already developed an attachment to her, and she to him.

So had his emotions been dormant, and it had taken what he'd viciously said he'd never have—a child—to awaken them?

This made sense. Perfect sense. It also explained why he hadn't tried to touch Naomi in over ten days.

This was no longer about her in any way.

"I never told you about me and Petros."

His solemn tone brought her focus back to him. "You never told me anything, Andreas."

He nodded. Acknowledging, making no excuses.

But from the way his steely eyes smoldered, it seemed he'd tell her something now. Something seriously important.

"Before I do, you have to know about my family. My

father was a useless, selfish son of a bitch we scarcely saw, and my mother was a silly, sentimental pushover he used up, with us scrambling in the middle. Aristedes, being the oldest, was the one who bore the main brunt of it all, dropping out of school to work four jobs to support us when he was only thirteen."

Wanting to spare him retelling this part, Naomi interrupted. "Caliope told me all that yesterday."

He exhaled. "But what she couldn't tell you, since neither she nor anyone else knows it, is that by the time I was that age, as the 'man of the house' in my elders' absence, I had to fend for my family of women and babies in different ways. There was this gang who 'ruled' the area, and the only way any household could be safe from them was if they 'volunteered' a son to their service. I volunteered myself, for my family and Petros's."

Naomi sat forward, her heart racing. She'd never expected anything like that. Which was naive, to think such poverty hadn't exposed him to crime and criminals.

But his had been more than simple exposure. "You volunteered yourself in Petros's place?"

"There was no choice, really. He'd always been the gentle soul you knew. He wouldn't have survived a day as a gang member, while I was already almost six feet tall, and I oozed aggression and fearlessness. The gang leader took a shine to me, trained me himself, then put me to work."

The way he'd said that. Work. She saw a world of pain and ugliness and fear in it, of danger and damage and degradation.

She couldn't ask for specifics. Whatever he'd done, he'd been a minor and he'd been coerced, with his family and Petros's held as hostages.

"Then, three years later, Aristedes took us to the States. I kept it a secret or they wouldn't have let me go—or worse. But I promised Petros I'd take care of him. I worked while studying, and sent him all the money I made to support his sick parents and pay the protection money the gang demanded in lieu of my services. But when I went back for him as soon as I finished college, I found them in abject poverty. The gang had been taking every dollar I sent. Then they asked for three million dollars to let me take Petros and his parents with me. They wanted me to ask Aristedes for the money, but I refused to drag him into this. So they gave me another option. To be 'theirs' for five years. I agreed."

Naomi's heart squeezed until she felt it would rupture.

He'd entered into indentured slavery for his friend!

"And for the next five years, they put my 'talents' to use, defrauding and embezzling countless millions for them."

God. If hearing about this oppressed and enraged her that much, how had it felt living through it?

"But as the fifth year drew to an end, it became clear I was too lucrative for them to ever let me go. So I confronted the boss, my original recruiter and 'mentor.' It enraged him that after all he'd done for me, I wanted to leave him."

"He destroyed your life!" she cried out. "He *enslaved* you! Was he insane as well as a monster?"

"He wasn't exactly sane in the way he viewed me. He considered me his firstborn, as none of his sons had followed in his footsteps, and he'd bestowed his 'fatherly' pride on me. From my uncomplaining efficiency, he'd thought I'd become fully engaged in his way of life, and he'd planned to surprise me at the end of that five-year test of his. Instead of cutting me loose, he would have made me his heir, bypassing his own sons. I had one father who didn't know I was alive, and when I stumbled on another, he became obsessed with me."

"And he thought you should love him for it and be grateful, huh? I can't even imagine how you felt, but just hearing about it makes me so mad I could kill that man."

"Don't bother. I already did."

Her jaw dropped. "Y-you…?"

"I killed him. In self-defense…I guess."

Beyond shocked, she could barely articulate the question. "W-what do you mean?"

"He said I was destroying all his hopes, but I wasn't walking away with all his secrets. In one of the rare times I ever got angry, I told him what I thought of him, I guess breaking whatever he had for a heart that morbidly loved me. Bad mistake, since he came after me with his favorite machete. Then he was lying at my feet…dead."

"So why do you say you 'guess' it was self-defense? It was!"

"I say so because he was much older and I had long surpassed him in expertise with weapons. It was crystal clear to me during that explosive fight that it was him or me. But I don't know if I thought that because I was in danger in those moments, or because I knew that if I only stopped him then, he would still have me killed eventually. Then what was to become of Petros and his folks? To this day I don't know what is true."

"Then it was self-defense and in defense of others, too."

His eyes thanked her for her fierceness, but didn't concede that verdict. "Whatever it was, I got away with it. I turned myself in, but the Cretan police were so thrilled someone had finally rid them of that kingpin, and seemed extra glad that it was me who'd done it. Seemed they knew exactly what he'd done to me. Their official report said it was a hired assassin from a rival gang, and they even helped me take Petros and his family out of Crete. I'd just gotten them settled here, thinking I had finally escaped this nightmare, when I discovered that it wasn't over, not by a long shot."

When he paused, Naomi grabbed his forearm. "Just say everything at once!"

He looked surprised at her agitation, but pleased by the evidence of her involvement in his story.

Then his gaze looked into the past again. "The man's wife, who became the new kingpin in her husband's place, called me. She somehow knew it was me who'd killed her husband. And she pledged that as I'd deprived her of the love of her life, she would strike at my loved ones. I scoffed at her threat, told her I didn't have any, thanks to her late husband. I lost all contact with my family during the years of servitude to him. As for Petros, he wasn't a loved one but more of a…pet."

Naomi knew he'd had to say this to make that bitch lay off. It must have galled him having to do so. "Did she buy it?"

"I guess, about Petros. But she said that one day I would resume relationships with my family or make a new one. And that's when she'd strike."

All the missing shards hurtled together so fast, so hard in her mind, Naomi collapsed back on the couch under the barrage.

This…this was monstrous. And explained so much….

"I knew she was capable of keeping me under surveillance forever, having laid their networks and provided their financing myself. But I didn't think it was such a big problem. I doubted my family wanted me back. But as the years passed, they tried to reconnect with me and I started feeling that ax hanging over my head more every day. Then I met you."

Every wisp of air left her in a rush.

"I suddenly couldn't let this go on anymore. So I went to Crete to negotiate an alliance with a rival cartel, to help me neutralize the threat from I Kyría, as she'd come to be known."

"W-was that the time you saved me and Malcolm from Christos Stephanides's thugs?"

"Yes. I knew Malcolm was courting my favor by planning to do business in my homeland. When I found out you were going with him, it brought things to a head and I decided it was time to seek that alliance."

"Were you following us that day?"

"I was following *you*."

So Nadine had been right.

He went on. "I know you think I saved you, but I don't believe Christos would have seen his threat through. He's not that bad. Nothing like the people I was mixed up with. That's why I succeeded in negotiating with him on your behalf, but failed in my own negotiations, since I couldn't offer my prospective allies full disclosure about why I needed their help."

"And money didn't work?"

"It doesn't work that way in these areas. It's people throwing their lots together and depending on each other to have each other's back, and it was a price I couldn't pay. I was never again becoming vulnerable to anyone."

"What happened then?" She could barely choke out the question.

"I did the stupidest thing I'd ever done in my life. I went back to the States and straight to Malcolm's office. I had an excuse to see you and I took it. And you approached me... and you know how that went. You were the first one I ever *wanted*, but I knew this was what I Kyría was waiting for. I knew you'd be her target if anyone ever found out about us."

So that was it. Why he'd so obsessively kept their relationship, then their marriage a total secret.

Only one question was left. "Why didn't you tell me?"

He huffed. "That I was a criminal and a murderer, and associating with me might make you target to a vengeful mob boss?"

Naomi found herself on her feet. "You're no such things!

You were forced into whatever crimes you perpetrated. As for her, I would have understood the need for secrecy."

He seemed stunned by her reaction. "I didn't think you'd understand. I thought you'd just run away." He barked a harsh, ugly laugh. "But in the end, you ran because I *didn't* tell you, it seems. But I had hopes I could end this, and this was why I stalled you in that divorce. I'd been going all out to negotiate with I Kyría and she'd suddenly seemed amenable, had me doing things for her to 'atone.' Then after six months, she told me that she'd been only stringing me along, giving me hope before taking it away, and that I'd have to live like her forever, without having anyone close. Because the moment I came near to someone, anyone, she'd deprive me of them. She'd moved from bereaved to deranged, and her hatred of me had become what fueled her existence. I knew then that I'd gotten away with the time we had together, but we'd entered a whole new level, and no amount of secrecy or precautions would prove enough from then on. I signed the divorce papers then and just cut myself off from everyone, including Petros."

And everything finally made sense. Horrific sense.

"I couldn't come back even for Leonidas's funeral or Aristedes's wedding. I only went to Caliope's wedding because it was in the depths of Russia and a spur-of-the-moment affair that no one could have known about. But Petros and Nadine's funeral was announced, and you were there. I couldn't risk alerting her to your and Dorothea's existence."

This was atrocious. He'd been living in fear that he'd act as a bull's eye to whomever he was close to.

"Then how did you end up coming back?" she whispered.

"How do you think?"

"Y-you…?"

At her choking horror, his lips twisted. "Don't you think she deserved it?"

"Actually, yes, but…"

He ended her stammering. "Much as I had long wished to send her to her husband's side, I'm no killer. She just died. Thankfully. Not that I thought this would change anything. I was sure she left instructions to hound me into the next life. But I went to her funeral, anyway. No matter that she'd turned my life into hell, I did kill her husband and it was what sent her off the deep end. I wanted to make my peace with her."

Naomi exploded to her feet. "And what? Has she risen up from her grave and is after you as a zombie now?"

He tugged her back to the couch. "You managed all that, and now you flake out on me?"

"Dammit, Andreas," she shouted. "What happened?"

He exhaled. "Her oldest son approached me, said that whatever vendetta existed between me and his mother had died with her. He condemned his parents' criminal activities, and what they'd done to me. The man said he bore me no ill will, even begged my pardon."

"That was it? For real?"

"I know what you mean. I could hardly believe it myself. That no one was in danger because of me anymore. That I was free. For the first time since I was thirteen."

Naomi didn't know how she held back from throwing herself at him. Probably because she was paralyzed with so many realizations and emotions.

"I came back that same day. With the time difference, I arrived here to wait for you to come home."

Suddenly, she felt her consciousness begin to flicker.

He was…was…*smiling*.

Sinking back on the couch, she moaned, "What a time for you to crack your first real smile."

His grin widened even more. "It's just…phew, what a load off. I never told anyone any of this. Only Petros knew.

And not everything. I never told him about my suspicion that I didn't kill that man in pure self-defense."

But you haven't told me *everything.* So many questions still clamored inside her.

Before she could ask any, he continued. "But I can't blame everything I am on these events. Even without this hanging over my head, I wasn't relationship material, not with my background."

"Your father, you mean?"

"And myself. With the kind of life I led, I never felt much for anyone."

She gaped at him. He really thought so.

She surged toward him, needing to put him straight. "You felt far more than most people ever could. You sacrificed yourself for your family's and Petros's safety."

He frowned at her. "I never looked at it that way, or that I did anything because of feelings. I thought I was responsible as the one who could do something about it all. So I did it."

"And to do it, you wouldn't let yourself feel, so you'd operate on maximum efficiency unclouded by emotion."

He mulled over her statement, which he seemed to have never considered. "You might be right. I didn't let anything surface, not even anger. I got so used to being this way, I no longer knew if I had emotions lurking beneath or not. But then I was free of the threat that has defined my life, and free to honor Petros's will." Andreas suddenly took her hands in his. "And that was before I saw Dorothea. But now that I have, I want to far more than I ever thought I could. You might think it too soon for me to be saying this, and I know I'd never be the father Petros would have been, but I'll do my damnedest to be there for Dorothea in every possible way."

His impassioned pledge lodged right into Naomi's heart. For she now knew without a doubt he meant it. And he would fulfill it. The Andreas who'd borne all that for the father would do even more for the daughter.

Holding back tears with difficulty, Naomi nodded. "You'd succeed in anything you put your mind to, Andreas."

"But I can only if I'm part of her daily life."

What about being part of *hers*, too?

But he'd just admitted she wasn't why he'd come back. She'd been incidental to his main objective.

An hour ago, *Naomi's* main objective had been to defend Dora and herself. But now, with their history rewritten, all she wanted was to give Andreas whatever he needed, to try to erase the pain and injustice he'd suffered, even at the expense of her own needs. There was only one answer she could give him.

"I'll agree to anything you want."

His eyes flared with relief, his hands squeezing hers in supplication. "Then move in with me."

Ten

"Move over, world, here comes super Dorothea!"

Naomi's eyes jerked up, the newspaper she'd been reading already forgotten.

But then this sight regularly made her forget the whole world. The sight of Andreas with Dora.

In workout pants and a tank top that showed off the poetry of his physique, Andreas was holding Dora up high in one hand. Clad in a bright red-and-blue jumpsuit, Dora was shrieking in delight as she held herself in a tight upward bow and spread out her arms and legs like a flying superhero.

It was his turn today to handle Dora's morning routine. She was one happy baby in general, but she reserved that extra edge of glee for her daddy. And there was no doubt anymore *that* was what Andreas was becoming, or had already become, in the month since they'd moved with him into the house in Manhattan Beach.

A month when he'd been performing all possible fatherly chores for Dora, been the perfect host and housemate to them all and a great companion and friend to Naomi…and nothing more.

Not one single look or touch more.

Andreas approached the chuckling Hannah, swept Dora

down for a smacking kiss, then did the same with Naomi, to Dora's raucous delight. He ended the aerial show by flipping her into her high chair, and when she yelled for more, he only raised an eyebrow and she at once changed her tone, pretended to clap, asking for her toys with utmost courteousness.

After he prepared her breakfast and poured himself a cup of coffee, Andreas came to sit across from Naomi at the huge kitchen island. "Doing anything special today?"

Hannah was the one who answered him. "I'm heading for Connecticut as soon as one of you comes home from work."

Andreas turned to Hannah. "You can go now so you can have the whole day with Susan. I'll do all my meetings on-line. Call Steve the moment you're ready to go."

Hannah, who never stopped being awed by Andreas's pampering, smiled with grateful pleasure. "That would be great to get a head start, even if I'm staying with Susan and the kids till the weekend. And I'll take Spiros if he's available. He's so entertaining to drive with."

Andreas gave her one of those smiles that progressively came easier to him. "Spiros it is." Then he turned to Naomi. "It's you and me, then. If you don't have something else planned, that is."

She was only glad she had. "Actually, I'm going out with Malcolm after work. We're meeting a couple of potential clients for dinner. What was this all about?"

His gaze betrayed nothing but mild if good-natured disappointment as he turned around to Dora. "Seems we'll celebrate alone, *mikri prinkipissa mou.*"

Naomi's heart trembled at the way he called Dora my little princess. "Celebrate what?"

"A milestone. You've all been here a month today."

"If only you'd given us a heads-up," Hannah lamented.

Andreas waved a hand. "There'll be other milestones." He rose to clean the mess Dora had made while attempting to eat alone, then started feeding her another portion to make up for what had ended up on the tray and floor. "Like Dorothea's first birthday in a month. We'll do something big then. How about that?"

After the two women approved of his plan, Hannah excused herself, giving Naomi a look that clearly meant: *Are you mad? Going out with Malcolm when you could be celebrating with Andreas? When I've left you two alone, too?*

Naomi escaped her gaze, pretended she had to run, kissed Dora and said a few vague things to Andreas before striding out.

She had to settle this with Hannah soon, so she'd stop trying to give her time alone with Andreas. To him, Naomi was now merely Dora's mother or caretaker…or whatever she was.

The irony never ceased to torment her. Now that he was free to feel, he couldn't feel even passion for her anymore.

But she knew this situation was the only logical solution. Even if it meant she would now have him constantly in her life…yet never have him at all.

All she could wish for was that one day, she'd be free of her feelings for him, too.

"I think this contract is ours, Naomi."

She smiled at Malcolm across the table. "We did give a damn irresistible pitch."

"We make an unstoppable team." Malcolm's eyes twinkled at her with their usual geniality, before an edge of seriousness entered them. "And I think it's a great time for us to take our teamwork and friendship further."

Oh, no. Please, God, *no…*

Malcolm went on, oblivious to her dismay. "Think how much more we can be for each other, Naomi. We'd make as great a team at home and as parents for Dora as we are at work."

She reached for his hand, squeezed it in a silent plea for him to stop. "If there was any chance I thought this would work, I would have made the first move, Malcolm. You would make the perfect husband for some incredibly lucky woman, like you once did for Zoe. But it won't be me. I love you, but I'll never be in love with you. And oh, God…I so hope this won't be a problem between us."

His expression reminded her of Andreas's earlier today. Disappointed but understanding, and not a little self-deprecating. Then he covered the hand gripping his. "How can it be a problem? We're friends, with or without anything more developing. And that's the difference between us, I guess. I am not in love with you, either, but I don't think I'll ever be in love again, not after Zoe. I thought my feelings for you might be enough. But you're probably right and they aren't." Suddenly his smile widened. "Hey, did you know we might have a far bigger thing happening than this contract?"

Relieved he'd let it go this easily, and apparently with no hard feelings, she said, "What could be bigger than that?"

"Andreas Sarantos. He called yesterday and said he'd come in tomorrow to 'settle things.' I don't want to be overly optimistic, but I really think he'll finally put his financing magic behind SUN Developments"

Andreas hadn't told her about this. Just as she hadn't told Malcolm about what had been going on with him. But with Andreas no longer keeping their living arrangements a secret, she hated for her partner to find out from someone else.

So she told him everything. At least the part about Petros's will and Dora, and their moving in with Andreas.

Malcolm listened in total astonishment, then finally whistled. "That's quite a radical change. How are you handling this?"

"It's been smooth," she lied. "Andreas makes everything so once he puts his mind to it."

"And you say Dora's taken to him."

"Dora adores him."

Malcolm's gaze became considering. "Is he the reason you didn't even consider my suggestion?"

"It's not because of him, no."

"Meaning he didn't make a move, but that doesn't stop you from being unable to consider anyone else, huh?"

Finding no more reason to deny this, at least to Malcolm, who was being so understanding, she nodded.

He leaned forward, his expression serious. "This has been going on with you all along, hasn't it? From way back when we first met Andreas?" She again nodded. "And him? I can't believe he hasn't snapped you up, especially now."

"I hate to use the cliché…but it's complicated."

Malcolm sighed. "I just bet it is."

After a moment of silence, she said, "Is it okay if we get going?"

Not that she wanted to return to where Andreas and his killer friendliness awaited her, but this confrontation, as wonderful as Malcolm was being, had left her drained.

"Sure."

After settling the bill, Malcolm courteously led her out of the restaurant.

As they waited for the valet to bring her car over, he turned to her with a frown. "You know, I'm no longer sure I want Andreas to take us on."

That stunned her. She grasped her partner's arm. "You're not letting what I told you influence you, are you? My personal situation has nothing to do with doing business with him."

"I actually think they're closely related. It all ties in to my faith in his judgment. An hour ago he was the guy who mines gold out of dross. Now he's the dolt who can't see the rare gem he literally has under his nose."

Her heart suddenly lifting at her friend's morale boost, she laughed. "Thank you, Malcolm."

"Maybe I'll keep our appointment only to find out what's wrong with him, and give him a piece of my mind."

"Oh, no, please don't even mention me. And don't you dare think of passing up this opportunity." She held his eyes until he nodded. "And, Malcolm…I'm sorry again if I disappointed you."

He waved her apology away. "You never disappoint me."

Overwhelmed by warmth for this man, she reached out to hug him. Malcolm hugged her back, before taking her arm with a grin and walking her to her car.

After closing her door, he leaned in the open window. "And, Naomi, relax, okay? We're good."

She nodded, profoundly grateful to have such a friend.

Then, waving to him with a broad smile, she drove away, her heart lighter than it had been in years.

By the time she entered Andreas's house, her heart was leaden again. It felt like going back to a prison cell every time she returned here.

She debated again if she should do something about it. Such as tell him how she felt. That she wanted him, and that if he still had any desire for her they should be together, and it wouldn't complicate being parents to Dora.

What always stopped her was her fear that she'd risk Dora's peace. For what would happen when Andreas had enough of her? Or wanted to replace her in his bed? Could she be certain that it wouldn't impact Dora?

Loki and Thor came rushing to welcome her, their presence, as always, a distraction from heartaches.

Carrying them both, she kissed and cooed to them as she walked to the family room, expecting to find Andreas working on his laptop. She braced herself for his now usual pleasantness.

Her smile faltered when she found him standing in the middle of the room, barefoot, his shirt pulled out of his pants and open, an empty shot glass carelessly in hand.

His body seemed relaxed, but it was the way his head was tilted, the way he watched her from beneath lowered eyebrows, and the total absence of his now accustomed smile that made her feel like a deer walking into a mountain lion's ambush.

Her steps faltered as she approached him, bringing his face into focus. Its stark lines seemed to be hewn from granite, and his eyes crackled like lightning.

"Anything wrong? Is Dora all right?" she whispered, even though she instinctively knew this wasn't about Dora.

Without relinquishing her gaze, he bent and placed the glass on the coffee table. "Put the cats down, Naomi."

It was only then she noticed she was hugging them tightly, as if to hide behind them, and they were squirming to get away. Cursing silently, she released them, and they jumped down and ran off to indignantly groom themselves.

She raised uncertain eyes to Andreas as he approached her, deepening her feeling of being stalked. Her hand rose to her throat, where she felt her heart had migrated, and his gaze singed it before moving to her lips, then her eyes, sending her heartbeat into a crazy spiral.

His voice was a predator's growl. "For forty-one nights I've held back, Naomi, kept my distance, given you something different. Now, no more."

He'd counted the nights since they'd last made love? "Andreas…"

All thought evaporated as his arm shot out. Next second she was slamming against his unyielding power. Then the world spun upside down as he…he…

Andreas had hauled her over his shoulder!

Her lungs emptied on a cry of shock, every nerve firing as his fingers sank into her buttocks and thighs. Her senses churned as he strode down the hallway, her world turning into a swirl of vertigo and overstimulation.

Then he was sweeping her from his shoulder and tumbling her onto a bed. His bed. Where she hadn't been sleeping every night of the last hellish month.

Before her heart could spill the next batch of chaotic beats, he was straddling her and pushing her jacket off, then pulling her blouse along with her bra over her head. He slid off her, only to sweep her skirt and panties down her trembling legs.

"Andreas…" That was all she could say. She said it over and over like an invocation.

"*Ne.* Moan my name like that, Naomi, whimper it, and when I'm riding you, scream it."

She would have screamed it right then if she had breath left in her. But all she could do was lie there, enervated, watching him push away and up to rid himself of his clothes with the same barely contained ferocity and haste. Then he fell back on top of her, like a starving predator over his willing prey.

He squashed her shuddering breasts beneath the hardness of his hair-roughed chest, rubbed against her until she keened and writhed to intensify the contact.

"This…this is what I've gone stark-raving insane for all those forty-one nights, Naomi. *This.*"

He bore down on her, grinding his huge, marble-smooth and hard erection into her mound. Her thighs fell wide apart and her back arched, begging for his total invasion.

He dragged her head back with a hand bunched in her hair as his lips latched on to hers. His roughly devouring kisses trailed down her cheeks, jaw and neck, drawing on her flesh, wrenching out every spark of desire from every blood cell, until she felt her very life force rushing into him. She tried to draw in a breath, but he lifted her off the bed, twisted her around and pinned her beneath him facedown, his hands beneath her cupping her breasts, his erection furrowing searing undulations between her buttocks.

With gush after gush of readiness flooding her core, she

undulated her hips against his hardness in a frenzy, eliciting a rumble of savage triumph from deep in his chest. *"Agápi mou, ne, ne.* Show me. Show me how much you need me."

And she did. She turned her head, blindly reaching for his lips, squirming beneath him, in heat. He caught her lower lip in a growling bite, sucked and pulled on it until it swelled, until she sobbed. Every part of her was disintegrating with the need to take him inside her. He anchored her with a bite where her neck flowed into her shoulder, and slipped one hand beneath her, probing her molten flesh until he took her over the edge. She screamed his name in a soul-searing climax.

As she was still in the throes, and with one hand still stimulating her, he crammed a pillow beneath her hips, spread her wide, then drove his erection all the way inside her drenched, clenching tightness.

Pleasure detonated from every inch of flesh that yielded to his red-hot thickness and length. Unleashed now, he powered into her, growling words of lust in English and Greek as he ravaged her mouth with scorching kisses, while his thrusting manhood drove her to mindlessness.

Ecstasy reverberated inside her with each thrust, each word, like the rushing and receding of a tide gone mad. It all gathered, swelling to its zenith like a tidal wave before the devastating crash.

Before it did, Andreas left her body and swept her around, his bulk and hands splaying her thighs wide in ferocious urgency.

Then he plunged inside her all the way again, this time finding what he was seeking, the gate to her innermost core, lodging into her womb. "Now, *agápi mou.* Come all over me...*now.*"

And she did, the coil of maddening need snapping, lashing through her, over and over again. She screamed, bucked beneath him with each blow of release that pummeled her.

He rode her harder through the storm, causing the shock waves to expand, to raze her, to wring her around his girth in contractions so violent they fractured her breaths, strangled her shrieks. She writhed in an agony of ecstasy, crushed herself against him, around him, inside and out, as if she'd assimilate him and dissolve around him.

In the depths of delirium, she heard him roar his release, felt his seed splash against her over-sensitized flesh, causing another wave to crash down on her, shattering her completely with the brutality of sensations.

It could have been minutes or hours before she lurched back to awareness. She found him spread beneath her, still hard and pulsating inside her, setting off mini quakes that kept her in a state of continuous orgasm.

He was regarding her with the same predatory intensity as before. As soon as she met his eyes he pressed her tight to his length and said, "Call Malcolm and put him out of his misery."

The gruff words interrupted her renewed swooning, made her jerk back. "What?"

Andreas looked positively menacing as he rumbled, "He asked you to marry him, didn't he?"

She pushed against him. "How do you know that?"

He let her put distance between them, reluctantly leaving her body. "He said something when I called him that made me realize he was going to make a move. He made it, didn't he?"

"And I told him it wouldn't work." Her heart started to thud painfully as she struggled to a sitting position. "Does this have anything to do with you hauling me off to your bed, literally? You were making sure I would say no to him?"

Andreas gathered her against his hot, hard body once more, his eyes so possessive she felt he was already invading her again. "I was damned if I was going to take it slow anymore, only for you to settle into considering me a friend, leaving you wide open for another man to make a move on you."

She struggled out of his arms, tumbling deeper into an abyss from the heights, which his possession had catapulted her to. "Well, he made it and I declined, so you didn't have to go to the effort of sabotaging him."

"I would have carried you off to my bed sooner or later. I have him to thank for making it tonight."

"Now you have. Hope you're satisfied."

Andreas trapped her beneath him again, ending her struggle, his eyes crackling with hunger. "I'm nowhere near satisfied. After all this deprivation I'll need a steady and intensive diet of you before I begin to remember what satisfaction feels like."

This felt real. But where had that passion been those forty-one nights he'd counted so accurately?

"I thought you no longer wanted to take me up on my offer."

"Of unlimited sex? I certainly don't. And I don't want to remarry you, either."

The words fell on her heart like a mallet.

She'd already known he didn't. But hearing him say it, and after what had just happened between them...

"I want to *marry* you. The first time doesn't count."

She gaped at him, her heart forgetting to beat.

"I've been trying to prove to you it would work between us this time, that I can be there for you and Dorothea in a family setting. I struggled to keep sex out of it to make it a real test for me, to prove it to myself as much as to you. But I guess we both know now where my limits are."

All this had been a test? He'd been demonstrating to himself before he did to her that he could be a family man?

Apprehension melting, she reached out a trembling hand to smooth the tension from his face. "I wish you had reached your limits way before now. Not that I didn't love exploring other sides to you, finding out about them even as you found them out about yourself."

Anxious eagerness flared in his eyes. "You did?"

She pulled him down, planted a tremulous kiss on that knotted brow. "Oh, I certainly did."

He groaned as his arms tightened around her. "I want you to forget everything that happened between us before."

She pushed away, allowing indulgence to enter her eyes and caress at last. "But there were so many memorable events."

"Toss them out. I'll give you new ones, as frequent as your voluptuous delight of a body can withstand."

That sounded like a dream come true.

Or it would have, if he'd said he loved her.

But he wanted her, and he wanted to give everything to Dora, and to the family they'd form around her. Whether their relationship or his emotions for her ever deepened beyond that, remained to be seen. But Naomi had been ready to settle for far, far less with him.

So she'd be marrying him again knowing she felt more for him than he did for her, but this time she had a hope the emotions he'd spent a lifetime suppressing would blossom enough that he'd love her back one day.

Until then, she'd take whatever she could with him and with Dora, the two pieces that made her heart, and the glue that held together her soul, her world.

He'd started making love to her again, but before he joined them together, he paused above her, tremors of tension traversing his great body as he groaned, "You haven't said yes, *agápi mou*."

She drew him inside her, gave herself over to him completely and cried out, "Yes, Andreas, *yes*."

Eleven

Announcing their impending marriage to Hannah and to Andreas's family was more emotional than anything she'd expected. To say everyone was delighted would be the understatement of the decade. But everyone also said they'd been certain this was coming. Seemed they'd all known things only Naomi had been oblivious to.

Then Andreas insisted on having the wedding on Crete, and as soon as possible, setting everything on hyperdrive, with Naomi finding herself in a situation she'd never experienced—becoming part of a large family.

Not that it was only she and Dora who were being engulfed and assimilated into the Sarantos family. Andreas was experiencing his family, whom he'd purposely alienated himself from since childhood, for the first time, too. And it was heart-wrenchingly poignant watching him sinking into their warmth and reciprocating it.

But it was Andreas himself who made her feel giddy with delight and hope for the future. Each day that passed he was becoming the man she'd sensed he could be all these years beneath the reticence and distance. He was opening up to her more every day, making a concerted effort to be there for her in every way. He was going all out to give her everything he hadn't given her in the past, and so many things she hadn't even known to hope for.

They'd arrived in Crete three weeks ago. And this time, Andreas had left it up to her to pick the house that would be their home for when they were in his homeland. He'd insisted she was the one who knew real estate, and that even without her expertise, he would have given her carte blanche to choose whatever house she wanted. He had given her the same with his whole life, anyway.

Though she wasn't about to take advantage of that total offer, she was touched beyond expression that he'd made it. She sometimes wanted to tell him to take it easy on her. It wasn't advisable to make her love him more than she already did.

But she'd eagerly taken him up on his offer to pick their home. There'd been one specific villa she'd dreamed of sharing with him from the moment she'd seen it.

It was in the Réthymno region, Crete's smallest prefecture. It was an area synonymous with gorgeous mountainscapes and beaches, legendary caves, historic monasteries and monuments, traditional mountain villages and luxurious holiday resorts. She'd been captured by the essence of mythical Crete in this remote and self-sufficient region from the first time she'd set foot in it.

The villa, which had felt like home the first time Andreas had set foot in it with her, was dominated at its back by the Lefká Ori, what the impressive White Mountains were called locally. Overlooking the crystalline waters of the Sea of Crete, it was nestled on a glorious stretch of white-gold beach. It was big enough to accommodate all the family who would come visiting, yet secluded enough for the two of them to forget an outside world existed.

And today, an hour from now, at the magical sunset hour, they would have their wedding there.

It would be nothing elaborate, since they couldn't even

think of it with their recent losses. Just a relatively small ceremony with their family and close friends present, where they'd exchange their vows. Their first vows.

"You better be ready." Caliope walked into the room where Naomi was dressing. Andreas's sister was starting to waddle in her eighth month, her turquoise chiffon brides-maid dress reflecting the color of her eyes and the waters surrounding the villa.

Accompanying her, Selene smirked at Naomi as she helped Caliope into a seat. She was wearing a similar dress, albeit one that hugged her trim figure.

"Andreas seems about to start tossing everyone in that gorgeous infinity pool you're having the ceremony around," Selene explained.

Naomi blinked, her heart starting to hammer. "Why? What's wrong?"

Caliope chuckled. "You don't get that you've unleashed the volcano that seethed beneath the ice, do you? The man is sizzling to make you his wife again…or for real, accord-ing to him. Aristedes sent us to fetch you ahead of time, as Andreas is working himself into a lather with all sorts of anxieties."

Her gut knotted. "What anxieties?"

Selene waved dismissively. "Just those that plague every breath of those who love too much."

Caliope and Selene thought Andreas loved her? Like their men loved them? It was so easy to think he did, with everything he did for her. Not that he'd said the words.

But she didn't need those anymore. She had far more than she'd ever dreamed she would. And it was all be-cause of him.

She took one last look at herself in the mirror, her heart turning in her chest at the sight of the radiant bride look-ing back at her. Andreas had gotten her the most luxurious wedding gown she'd ever laid eyes on, a dream of snow-white chiffon, satin and lace that hugged her figure, rip-ened her every curve. Every cultural influence that made up Crete was represented in its materials, cut and embel-lishments. The gown made her feel like the heroine of an ancient Greek fairy tale, a mortal about to join her life with the god who'd chosen her for his mate.

Caliope sighed. "You look beyond perfect, Naomi, a golden goddess, like Andreas always calls you."

Selene chuckled, then she echoed what Naomi had just thought. "Now hurry before your mate's wrath befalls the mere mortals awaiting your celestial ceremony."

A giggle overpowered Naomi as she gathered her cour-age and ran out, feeling she was rushing to meet her destiny.

As she walked through the open, sun-drenched spaces of their new home, their trio was joined by the other brides-maids—all of Andreas's sisters and oldest nieces, and Hannah's three daughters and her oldest granddaughters. Hannah herself was waiting for them outside with Dora.

With every step, it felt as if Naomi was forging deeper into a tranquil paradise. Her bridal procession stepped out onto the elevated open-air deck leading to the infinity pool, its glittering aquamarine waters segueing seamlessly into those of the sea. The sun was turning flame-orange and speeding on an intercept course with the horizon.

The combination of such pristine nature and lavish human design was breathtaking. When they were alone here, it felt as if they were the only man and woman on earth.

Right now, dozens of people were around, all dressed in colors complementing the setting, their faces painted in smiles. But Naomi could barely feel their presence. There was only one person in her awareness. Andreas. The man she'd loved from the first moment and would love till her last breath.

With his collar-length hair blowing in the balmy breeze,

every strand reflecting a different hue of the sun, he wore a white-on-white suit with an open-necked shirt and a gold rose in his lapel. He stood there, waiting to be one with her, in a pristine new beginning, every inch the Greek god that had come down to earth to choose a mortal for his bride. Naomi could only wonder again how it could possibly be her.

He suddenly broke away from the group of men he stood among—Aristedes, her partners and Selene's brothers—and strode toward her in an unrehearsed move. Naomi found herself breaking from her own companions and running to meet him halfway. Then she was in his strong arms, swept up and whirled around and around.

Laughing, tears flowing, she clung to his neck as he carried her back to the priest, who was in full Cretan garb. The ceremony, in both English and Greek, began with Andreas clasping her to his heart. She couldn't have dreamed of a better place to be for these life-changing moments.

As soon as they'd exchanged their rings and vows, and before the priest instructed him to kiss the bride, Andreas was devouring her and she was giving in to his passion, just as she'd so long ago surrendered all of her heart and soul to him.

Suddenly, something pulled her out of the dream world of his possession. Cries of surprise, ones she doubted were in response to his passionate display.

Andreas raised his head, too, and they both turned to the source of the excitement. It was Dora. Standing in front of Hannah, whose face was streaming in tears.

Dora was *standing*.

Then she took her first step.

In unspoken agreement, Naomi and Andreas ran toward her, both going down on their knees, their arms outstretched, their voices raised in ragged encouragement, for her to come bless their new union and complete the circle of their newly forged family.

To the thunderous cheering of all present, the determined darling—Nadine's and Petros's baby, and now hers and Andreas's in every way—kept going, putting one chubby leg unsteadily in front of the other, until she reached them and threw herself into Andreas's arms with a piercing squeal of triumph.

Then Naomi found Dora in her arms and both of them in Andreas's embrace, kissed and cosseted and claimed.

Naomi clung to Dora, to Andreas, wept with joy and prayed that she'd always be blessed with both of them, to love and to live for, for the rest of her life.

"This is not a Cretan wedding ritual…it's a cretin one."

Andreas's growl was met by generalized laughter, from his brother and the few guests who remained after the reception. He deeply regretted succumbing to the custom of keeping the groom away from the bride while she "prepared" herself for him.

He'd thought it would be a few minutes when he'd agreed to the harebrained idea. Aristedes had just informed him it would be one more hour.

Then his brother had the temerity to add, "Waiting will only intensify your desire. And besides, we haven't gotten a chance to exchange two sentences in the last several weeks."

"And you think the time to rectify that is on my wedding night? Are you nuts, Aristedes?" Andreas glared at him, then at Selene's brothers, the Louvardis trio who'd been ribbing the hell out of him in their oblivious bachelordom.

He heaved up to his feet, and they all followed suit, to try to make him sit down.

"Stand aside, all of you, and no one needs to get hurt."

More laughter met his threat, with everyone teasing him about his eagerness.

If only they knew he wasn't joking.

If he didn't get to Naomi at once, it might turn ugly.

After a lifetime of total control, ever since everything inside him had been unleashed, he no longer knew the man that had emerged from that self-imposed prison. He was still getting to know this new being, tentatively testing his triggers, and wary about provoking his boundless emotions and bottomless needs. And those had been dangerously provoked since he'd last seen Naomi.

It was unreasoning, the panic he felt every time she was out of his sight now. What he felt for her, and for Dorothea, was so acute at times, so agonizing, he sometimes wished for the days when everything inside him had been under airtight containment, and he could control how much he let out. He now knew the difference between his obsession with Naomi when his emotions had been stifled, and now, when nothing was held back anymore.

Now he left his companions behind and homed in on her vibe through this house that had already become his home, because she'd chosen it, because she and Dorothea were in it.

He burst into their room, found her lying on her side on the bed, an arm thrown over one of the bouquets he'd flooded the whole house with. She lurched around, her gaze as feverish as he knew his must be. So it was the same with her, as if they'd been breathing barely enough oxygen to survive. Now they got to gulp down all they needed to live, to soar.

He came down on his knees at the foot of the bed. Her smooth legs, which had grown honey-tanned under his agonized eyes these last weeks, were exposed as the traditional Cretan white wedding gown that made her look like an angel and a goddess in one rode up to her thighs.

The beast roaring inside him wanted to drag her, slam her into his flesh, overpower and invade and brand her.

And he'd done that, so many times before, to their mutual explosive ecstasy. But now…now it was different. Now they'd entered a new realm. He wanted to show her all the special things she'd unearthed inside him. He wanted to cherish her.

She gasped as he slipped her shoes off, and tried to turn to him fully. He stopped her with a gentle hand at the small of her back. She subsided with a whimpering exhalation, watched him with her plump bottom lip caught in her white teeth as he prowled forward on all fours, advancing over her, kissing and suckling his way from the soles of her feet, up her legs, her thighs, her buttocks and back, her nape. All the while, he unraveled ribbons, undid hooks and caressed the dress off her mind-blowing body. She lay beneath him, quaking and moaning at each touch, until he traced the lines of her shuddering profile with his lips. The moment he reached her mouth, she cried out, twisted on her back, surged up to cling to his lips in a desperate, soul-wrenching kiss.

Lowering her to the bed, he pulled back to take in her nakedness. No fantasy had conjured the beauty that had held his libido hostage from their first time together.

"*Monadikos, agápi mou*…unique."

And she was. Her beauty eclipsed that of the hundreds of white, cream and gold roses he'd filled their bedroom with.

Needing to worship her, to curb his hunger, tame it into tenderness, he found his hands were shaking as he undressed under her wide-eyed gaze and breathless encouragement.

Then he was all over her again, tracing the satin of her skin from toes to cheeks, tasting and kneading and nibbling, strumming every tremor out of her body.

Finally rising above her, he reveled in the sight, scent and sounds of her surrender, every shudder and moan pulverizing his intentions to be infinitely slow and gentle. Blood thundered in his head, in his loins, tearing the tatters of control from his grasp in a riptide.

Then she took it all out of his hands, hers sweeping over his back and buttocks in silent demand, their power absolute.

He surrendered, came between her shaking thighs, pressed her shuddering breasts beneath his aching chest. Then she conquered him, irrevocably.

Against his forehead, her lips prayed a litany of his name, and she clasped him to her body as if she couldn't believe he was there. Poignancy swamped him, choked him. He had to prove to her that he would always be there, was hers forever.

He rose on his knees, cupped her head, her buttocks, tilted one for his kiss, the other for his penetration. He bathed the head of his erection in the hot, moist silk of her luxurious welcome, absorbed her cries of pleasure, drinking in her pleas to take her, fill her.

Succumbed to the mercilessness of their need, he drew back to watch her eyes as he started to sink into her. Her flesh fluttered around his advance, hot and tight almost beyond endurance.

Her fingers dug into his shoulders, forcing him to stroke deeper into her. She cried out, a sharp sound of exultation that tore a growl of pride out of him.

She never took her eyes off his, letting him see every sensation ripping through her, her honeyed complexion brightening with her rising pleasure, burning up the dark gold she lay on.

"*Panémorfi*...gorgeous beyond description *agápi mou*," he said, his voice a ragged rasp. "The masters would have paid in blood to capture your beauty for eternity. And the way you feel inside...madness, magnificence."

She sobbed, thrashed her head, her hair rioting around her shoulders, a thousand shades of gold gleaming against the dark sheets. "It's you who's beautiful beyond words... you who feels magnificent...inside me. Give me all of you, *agápi mou*. Take all of me...."

Hearing the Greek words trembling on her lips was such a surprise, he almost keeled over her. She'd never said "my love" to him in any language.

He rose on extended arms, surveyed her feverishly. He'd always known there'd been need on her side. But without the trust, the certainty, he'd known that love hadn't been possible, not the way he'd seen it with his siblings. Was Naomi developing a new dimension to her emotions? Or was this endearment only fueled by pleasure and the maddening need for release?

Not that it mattered. She'd pledged to be with him, let him be with her and Dorothea, forever. He'd take what she could give when she could give it. Need could become love.

Now she needed fulfillment. And he'd give her all she could ever need.

Feeding her hunger for more of him, he thrust deeply inside her, watching in receding sanity as she accepted all of him, wild, abandoned. Then she was weeping as she sought his lips, her mouth and tongue dueling with his as her core throbbed around his invasion, demanding he take her harder, faster. He had to obey her.

His rhythm quickened. Plunging became pounding until her cries rose to a shriek that ripped through him. She arched up, coming around him in a climax so intense it shredded her screams, wrenched at his shaft. The knowledge that he was fulfilling her tore his own release from his recesses.

With a prayer that his seed would one day take root in her womb and create a miracle like Dorothea, he jetted inside her, prolonging her orgasm. One detonation after another of ecstasy rocked him, and her, locked them in a closed circuit of over-stimulation, dissolved them into one.

When it felt as if his heart would never restart, the tumult gave way to the warmth and weakness of satiation. He felt her melt beneath him, satisfaction and awe glowing on her face.

"Ómorfi gynaíka mou," he rumbled as he twisted, bringing her on top while maintaining their merging.

She opened her lips over his heart. What she said almost ripped it out of his ribs. *"Ómorfi sýzygó mou."*

He lurched with surprise, squeezed her tighter to him. "You understood."

She nodded, planting kisses all over his chest. "I know more Greek than you realize."

He raised her head, gazed into her heavenly, drugged with pleasure eyes, his heart booming. That she'd learned Greek, no doubt for him, at least enough to understand his words, that she'd answered his proclamation, calling him her beautiful husband, had delight bursting inside him. Resurging desire, too, since she'd purred the words in that new voice she now used with him, breathless, aware, overcome.

She rose a bit, her hair draping over his chest like a sheath of spun gold. She gave him such a smile, no inhibitions, satiated, yet insatiable. "Now that you've given me tenderness, it's time you ravaged me."

He crushed her to him, hunger raging again as if he hadn't just found total satisfaction inside her. "Your wish is my command, always. You can consider this just the appetizer, to get you ready for the main courses I have planned for the rest of the night."

"Oh, yes, yes, please…" she moaned her eager surrender, her face blazing at his promise, her body blossoming under his, undulating in a renewed dance of sinuous demand and submission.

"I will please you. I live to please and pleasure you."
Gathering her in his arms, he rose from the bed.

Then with her clasped to his heart he walked out through
the now deserted house to the pool where they'd joined their
lives. All the way there, she caressed and kissed him, clung
to him as if she was a part of him.

And for the rest of the night, he took her, gave himself
to her, with every exercise of possession and ecstasy deepening her sensual enslavement. And his.

It was dawn by the time Andreas had finished fulfilling his pledge, giving Naomi a wedding night that had
surpassed even their most explosive times together. Every
touch, every breath, had been pure ecstasy.

Now she lay nestled against his side, knowing for the
first time what perfection felt like.

But was it possible for everything to be so perfect?

And remain so?

Life had taught her that any measure of happiness had
to exact a terrible price.

What would be the price of all this bliss? And when
would fate demand its payment?

Twelve

Waking up in bed with Andreas, after making love deep into the night, and lying there with him, entwined, savoring the echoes of passion, building up to another plunge, all the while *talking,* had become Naomi's new addiction.

But that was only one of the delights that abounded in their lives now. A favorite one was not remembering where they were when she opened her eyes every morning, what with the way they commuted between Crete and New York.

It kept everything breathlessly exciting and was the best of all possible worlds. And as if they'd always done this, they'd thrown themselves into their shared life, mixing being passionate newlyweds with being Dora's parents, and active members of "their" family with running their businesses. Keeping that exhilarating balance was possible only because of the other's input and support. At least Naomi hoped she was as vital in making all that possible for Andreas as he was for her.

He did insist that he was discovering himself right along with her, and that the discoveries were all thanks to her. She truly hoped she was helping him mine the treasures inside him. She had no doubt she'd keep finding more in his depths, and more reasons to love him. She now believed all the heartache had been a tiny price for the privilege of finding him, of recognizing his truth even against all evidence, and of ending up having what she now had with him.

He raised his head from nuzzling her neck, running a hand heavy with possession and satisfaction down her back, his eyes eloquent with both as they met hers.

They'd been talking about Dora's first birthday party and how wonderfully everything had come together, and jokingly planning her second one. Or at least Naomi had been joking. She wouldn't put it past him to be talking seriously.

He sighed with pleasure as he sifted his fingers through her hair. "But I guess we can't make solid plans now, since by the time she's two, she'll probably have her own demands for her party."

Naomi chuckled. "I was right! You *were* serious!"

He squeezed her to his length, his leg driving in sensuous playfulness between hers. "Yes, laugh at the man who's been hurled from one extreme to the other."

Her hands luxuriated in the depths of his hair, just as her legs did in rubbing his between them. "I only do since you seem to enjoy the excruciating change so much."

"And how. And excruciating change is right." As he rose up on one elbow, a serious cast came over his face. "I still remember exactly how it felt at the time, yet I can't believe I ever feared having a child."

Her heart convulsed at the memory of the confrontation that had ended her hope of being with him in the past.

She ran her hand down his hard cheek, wanting to absorb any recriminations he might have. "That fear was just you being responsible, when you suspected you might have inherited your father's coldheartedness. Though if you didn't have I Kyría's ax hanging over your head, that fear should have made you realize you were nothing like him. Callous people don't fear their potential damage to others."

"I wasn't about to test whether I would turn out to be

my father or not, not with a child's life on the line." An-dreas shook his head, as if in wonderment. "Then fate de-livered me Dorothea."

The magnitude of emotion he transmitted in those words felt like an earthquake shaking through Naomi.

She took refuge in voicing something she'd been won-dering about. "You never call her Dora."

His lips melted with the profound fondness he reserved only for Dora. "It's the way I've thought of her from the first moment. That little magical creature from a realm I never dreamed I could enter." Suddenly, he frowned, as if hit by an idea he'd never considered. "But I'll call her Dora if you prefer."

Naomi cupped his face in urgent hands, wiping away the frown. "Oh, no, I actually love it that you have your own name for her. I think she knows it, too, and it's part of the special bond that has developed between you. Something that's only yours and no one else's, not even mine."

"I hope you're right, on her side. On mine, something inexplicable happened inside me from the first moment I saw her. Even when I was unequipped at the time to real-ize what it was. Everything that Petros meant to me was mingled with her own delightful cuteness and the way she reached out to me with her curiosity and acceptance. I think she instinctively recognized my involvement and just went ahead and claimed me. I felt overwhelmed by the need to protect her, but my fear of myself was so long entrenched I couldn't trust what I was experiencing, and I had to be certain it was real."

"It didn't take you long to become certain."

"I was irrevocably involved after that first evening, then the first day in our Manhattan Beach house. But I was still not certain how I'd react in the long run, on a constant basis, if she became a major part of my daily life. But after that month, I became certain. What I felt from the start was real, and it will only become more profound with time. There is absolutely nothing I wouldn't do for her, and I can't imagine I could ever love anything as much as I love our precious Dorothea."

Not even a child of our own?

It had been too soon to bring up even the idea of one, with everything they'd had to achieve during the last two months to create their shared life. Naomi had inserted an IUD the day after she'd gone to his suite and had intended to keep it in place until they made a decision when to have more babies. She'd had no doubt their time would come.

But now doubts were insidiously creeping in. What if Andreas wanted Dora because she'd already existed? What if she was so special to him he wouldn't want another child?

Naomi debated whether to vocalize her worries. Then he started to make love to her again and every mental process stopped, his passion and the pleasure he gave her short-circuiting them.

But afterward, when she was outside his field of influence, doubts returned with a vengeance.

She was beyond delighted that he loved Dora as if she was his own. Delighted for him and for Dora. But knowing that he'd felt that fiercely for Dora from the beginning unsettled her. It took her back to thinking she'd been incidental to all this. Especially since there was one more thing she couldn't escape. That he hadn't been anywhere near this vocal about how he felt for *her*.

What if he was this wonderful to her only because of his determination to give Dora the best life? What if all his actions were fueled by the bottomless paternal reserves he'd discovered within himself?

But even if that was true, what could she do about it? She had entered this marriage, again, knowing she felt more for him than he'd ever feel for her.

"Stop it."

She had to hiss the self-admonition out loud to abort the spiral of malignant thoughts.

She *wouldn't* fret and invent heartaches. She *would* be endlessly grateful for the blessing of having him and Dora in her life.

Two weeks later, they were back in New York, and she'd been clinging to her decision, had been letting their full lives together sweep her on an unstoppable tide.

But in spite of all her efforts, vague dreads weighed down her every waking and sleeping moment. Until the worst of it had manifested last night.

Andreas had had to shake her awake, to drag her from the depths of a nightmare where he and Dora had kept receding, with her running and screaming after them, until they disappeared.

By the time he'd managed to snatch her from the dream's tentacles, she'd been sobbing and shaking, had remained inconsolable in spite of all his efforts to soothe her. She hadn't told him what she'd dreamed about.

For it hadn't felt like a dream, but a premonition.

He'd refused to leave her to go to work, until she'd told him she was going out herself. When he'd insisted on accompanying her, she'd assured him that an ob-gyn office wasn't the place for him. Still, she'd had to pretend she was fully over her night terror, and swear her doctor visit was only a checkup, before Andreas had relented. Nevertheless, he'd promised he'd be home when she returned.

She'd always had difficult periods when she was troubled. But after she'd given birth to Dora, things had become so much better. Until lately. It had to be something *that* unbearable for her to go to Dr. Summers. Naomi didn't want to see the woman—Nadine's obstetrician and also hers during her pregnancy—for all the memories she'd bring back. She had even gone to a different doctor for her IUD.

Now she was wondering if the device was behind her unusually painful period, forcing her to seek the expertise of the doctor who knew her and her history.

An hour later, Miriam Summers grinned at her after she concluded her exam and drew some blood for tests.

"Everything is in order, with the IUD at least."

Jumping up to adjust her clothes, Naomi followed her out to her office. "At least? What else isn't in order?"

The woman waved. "Nothing, really. You just have congestion in the pelvic area, and I think this is what's causing the pain and heaviness."

"Could it be psychological?"

Miriam chuckled. "Actually, it's very physiological. It's a classic sign of sustained and unrelieved arousal. You and your husband don't have to abstain from sex in all forms while you have your period, you know."

"Oh. *Oh*."

Andreas had been all for alternative methods, but it had been she who'd refused, afraid it might be unappealing for him.

At her silence, Miriam rushed to add, "I haven't seen you or Nadine since Dora was born, so I have no idea what's been going on with your lives. I mentioned a husband because I noticed the wedding band, and I hope I wasn't out of line."

Naomi stared at her. How could she have forgotten this? Miriam Summers had no idea her sister was dead.

The woman groaned. "Seems every time I open my mouth I make it worse. What did I say wrong now?"

"Nothing, nothing…" Then, after taking a moment to collect herself, she told her about Nadine.

The doctor was evidently shocked. The silence that reigned over her elegant office became more oppressive by the second.

Then Miriam spoke again, hushed and heavy. "I can't

tell you how terribly sorry I am, Naomi. Nadine was one of my favorite patients, and it isn't every day I see a relationship like the one you two had. I am so sorry for your loss, but…"

She stopped, seemed to be struggling with something huge.

"But…but what, Doctor?"

"I think now that both Nadine and Petros are dead, you should know the truth."

The truth.

The truth. *The truth*.

The words reverberated inside Naomi's head as she walked New York's streets aimlessly.

The truth about Dora. And about Nadine.

Nadine had had no viable eggs. But Petros had loved her too much, had known how bereft she'd feel if she couldn't have that child she'd wanted more than anything in life. He'd begged Dr. Summers not to tell her about her total infertility, but to find an egg donor and let Nadine think the baby was hers.

Dora wasn't what remained to Naomi of Nadine. Wasn't related to her in any way.

What would happen when Andreas realized she had no claim to Dora, the baby who'd become the daughter he loved above all else, when he'd never once intimated he might want another one with her?

Then, as always when suspicions started, they spiraled from terrible to insupportable.

Maybe he'd known all along. Maybe he was now adopting Dora, but wouldn't make Naomi her mother officially. Maybe he wouldn't so it would be mess-free when he eventually had enough of her, and she eventually exited their lives. Maybe he'd only needed her because she'd been his path to Dora, married her because he wasn't certain Dora would grow attached to him without her help, without the security of her presence, and in the normalcy of a family life that only marriage could provide. But Dora was now more attached to him than to Naomi. Maybe now her use to him was over.

Logic said that if Andreas intended to end her presence in Dora's life one day, he'd do it while she was young enough to forget Naomi without repercussions to her psyche. Like she had forgotten Nadine and Petros as if they'd never been.

Now Naomi could see only two possibilities.

Either Andreas didn't know, and when he did, he'd still want to include her in their lives forever, if only for Dora's sake. Or the worst scenario was true, and she'd exit their lives in the not too distant future. She had no reason to think there'd be a third possibility.

Andreas didn't love her.

In his new vocal emotionalism, he would have said something if he did.

But he hadn't.

Somehow, she made her way to the house that no longer felt like home. Entering it, she felt as she had the first time she'd come here, like a guest reluctantly stepping into a place where she didn't belong, and might never return.

His presence deluged her even before she saw him exiting his study and striding toward her, his expression anxious.

He caught her to him, swept her off the ground in a tight embrace, before withdrawing to bestow kisses all over her face. "I was just about to go out looking for you!"

She forced her limbs to remain steady as she pushed out of his arms. She'd lived with uncertainty for far too long. Now all she needed was to know. Once and for all.

He was reaching for her again when she stopped him. By two words. *"I know."*

If she'd had any doubts, they evaporated in the heat of what flared in his eyes. Admission.

He'd known, too. All along.

Her nightmare, her premonition was coming true.

Both he and Dora had never belonged to her, but now belonged together. They would need her less every day, would recede until they vanished completely.

And she couldn't wait for this to happen slowly. If she was to die, she'd rather it was in one brutal blow.

"Naomi…"

She talked over him, her voice that of a drone. "Now that I know I am not related to Dora, I realize why Petros didn't even mention me in his will. He only wanted me to take care of his daughter until you stepped in. And now you have, and my role in her life is over."

"How can you say that? Dorothea needs you. She—"

Naomi again interrupted. "I know you'd go to any lengths to give her everything you think she needs. But she now has you. She loves you, and she'll forget me in no time once I'm gone."

"*Theos*, Naomi, *ne*…"

"I will tell Hannah everything, ask her to stay on with you if you want her. Then I will leave. This time, don't draw things out thinking I'll change my mind. I won't."

Andreas watched Naomi walk away, déjà vu pummeling him.

But it didn't feel like the past all over again. It felt a thousand times worse.

When she'd walked away before she'd looked wrecked. This time she looked…cold. As if there was nothing left inside her. As if the moment she'd found out that Dorothea wasn't her sister's child, she'd stopped caring. About her… and about him.

This was like nothing he'd feared when he'd hidden the truth from her from the start.

He'd been unable to take away her comfort in believing she had a physical part of her sister still alive and growing under her eyes and in her arms. The baby she considered her daughter, having given birth to her, and having raised her with her sister, then alone.

But was it possible she didn't love Dorothea as if she was her own? That all her feelings toward her had only been an extension of her love for Nadine, and therefore gone the moment that connection was shattered in her mind?

And what about him? He'd thought she…felt something real and intense for him. He'd thought she'd come to depend on him as he'd come to depend on her for his very breath.

Had he been mistaken, too, about what they shared?

He wanted to storm after her, tell her he wasn't letting her go this time. But how could he hope to keep her, if she didn't love Dorothea?

If she'd never loved him?

"Are you sure this is about what it seems to be about?"

Andreas stared at Aristedes. Nothing his brother or Caliope had said in so far had made any sense.

In an unprecedented approach, knowing true desperation for the first time in his life, Andreas had reached out for their counsel, before he lost his mind irrevocably.

After he'd told them the little he knew, they'd asked him a hundred questions. This last one didn't make more sense than any before it.

"What I mean is," Aristedes elaborated, "Are you sure this is about Dora? As big a shock as it is for Naomi to discover the child isn't Nadine's biologically, I don't see how it would cause such a drastic reaction on its own."

Caliope nodded. "Knowing what I know about Naomi, this sounds like it was the last straw."

"What last straw?" Andreas barked, his nerves snapping. "Everything was perfect. Up till…"

He suddenly remembered that nightmare she'd had. Those terrible moments she'd writhed in his arms in her sleep, and wept in such agony and desperation.

He related the incident, which had shaken him to his core, and which had only been eclipsed by the much bigger blow of what had happened a few hours later.

"But that was a nightmare! It couldn't have anything to do with what happened."

Caliope pursed her lips. "Maybe it wasn't a nightmare but a manifestation of all her fears and doubts and uncertainties from the past. They might have never been resolved, and they got the best of her while she slept."

"You mean her past with me? But the past has nothing to do with the present. I was a different man then. Or…do you mean that whatever emotional injury I caused her in the past has never healed, and it's why she couldn't love me now?"

Aristedes shook his head. "From what she told me, and from what I observed of her with you, I believe the past is to blame, but not in the way you think. It's actually because you didn't really change your ways in the present."

"What *are* you talking about? She was just telling me how I've changed from one extreme to the other."

"You have, where reaching out and taking what you need from others is concerned. But what about reaching out with your emotions? Have you told her how you feel about her? *Do* you feel anything for *her*, Naomi herself, beyond her being the third piece in this family unit you've become so dependent on and believe you can't live without?"

"So you think I turned from being passively self-centered and self-serving to actively, aggressively so?" Andreas seethed. "I had feelings for only her, even when I thought I had none. I always loved her, and now I do more than I thought possible. I worship her and I certainly can't live without her. As *her* and her alone."

Aristedes and Caliope exchanged a patient glance that had him on the verge of tearing the place down.

Before he did, Aristedes turned to him. "Have you told *her* that?"

"Of course I—"

He stopped abruptly, the breath knocked out of him at the enormity of the realization.

He hadn't.

His head spinning, he choked out, "I kept showing her..." He stopped, his protest clogging in his throat.

"You mean you never made a declaration like the one you just made to us?" Caliope prodded.

He squeezed his eyes shut. "No."

"Not once? Nothing close? In the past or now?"

He could only shake his head, feeling as if he was suffocating.

Caliope squared her shoulders. "Okay then, here's what I think she thinks, what led to what she did today. She always loved you, but you never reciprocated, beyond physically. Then you came back, but the only emotional involvement you exhibited was with Dora. Naomi thinks that you married her to provide Dora with a family. From her viewpoint, you never loved her, and whatever you think you've been doing to demonstrate your love hasn't shown her you love her for herself. The longer you made no emotional declaration to her personally, the more it left her feeling unvalued and unloved, and worst of all, convenient. With the blow of finding out she had no claim to Dora, she must be feeling unneeded, too, totally cut adrift. Once she believed her main value to you is convenience, it was only one step further to think it would one day end. By walking away now, she's saving herself more pain later on, and saving Dora an eventual injury, too."

This all sounded plausible, if only because every word cut him down to his recesses. He'd been so involved in his plans, in showing Naomi his feelings in his own way, he hadn't stopped to think if it was a way she'd understand.

But there was one reality he had to face now. Why he hadn't made an unequivocal confession of his feelings.

He'd felt it would be the ultimate vulnerability. That after he'd said the words, he'd lose his power totally, expose his every weakness. Life had taught him never to do that. And because he'd withheld that last bit of trust from her, he'd lost her.

He grabbed his hair in vicious hands, his groan wrenched from his gut. "I can't lose her. I *can't*."

Caliope rushed to put her arm around him. "You don't have to. Just go tell her what you just told us."

"The time for words is past, Caliope." Aristedes shook his head, his eyes solemn as he met his. "Naomi loves you with every fiber of her being, Andreas. It killed her, being with you in the past while she thought you didn't share that same depth of involvement. It remains her doubt and heart-ache now. It was why she left you once, and why she left you again. All she ever wanted was your love. If you can't *prove* that she has it, has always had it, that you would love her forever, no matter what, and above everything and *everyone*...then you *will* lose her."

Next morning, Andreas was standing in front of Naomi's apartment, bracing for another struggle.

She made it all unnecessary when she opened the door.

The moment he saw her he knew that every word Aristedes and Caliope had said was true. Naomi loved him with everything in her. It was why she looked as if everything in her had been extinguished.

Instead of such love being in his favor, it might be why he wouldn't be able to win her back. This time, she had to have absolute certainty of the depth of his equal emotions. If the evidence he'd brought wasn't enough…

No. He wouldn't consider that possibility.

Though everything in him clamored for her, he had to give her all he had first, before he could hope she'd reclaim him.

Brushing past her, he closed the door behind him, then turned to her. "Do you believe that I love Dorothea, Naomi?"

After a moment of apparent surprise, she nodded. "I do. I think your feelings are even more intense because they came after a lifetime of holding back."

"You already believe I'd do anything for her. But do you realize I'd rather die than give her up?"

Her face seized, her throat worked. She nodded again.

And he presented her with the papers. "This revokes any right I have to Dorothea in your favor. You can now apply to become her sole parent."

Silence. Nothing but silence as she stared at the papers in her hands, then up at him.

"This is my proof to you, *agápi mou*, that Dorothea has nothing to do with us, with why I wanted to marry you. You know I wanted you from the first moment I laid eyes on you, but what you don't know, what I never told you, is that I loved you just as long. I have never been able to articulate my emotions, have even been scared to. I thought it was safer for me to show you, and I've been trying to since I came back. I have so much to learn about how to express my love for you, since it's so huge, so encompassing, I get lost inside it. Though I suspect nothing I could do would ever convey the magnitude of what I feel for you. You are everything to me, Naomi, and I have no life without you."

When she continued to stare at him, her astonishment total, a terrible doubt hit him. "Wasn't that why you left? Because you suspected my motives for being with you?

Or did you leave because you no longer love me? Have I killed your feelings for me? Or did you never love me…?"

He suddenly found himself wrapped in her arms so tight his choking breath left him completely. His agitated lips were stilled beneath her trembling ones, tears wetting them, though he didn't know whether they came from his eyes or hers or both.

She studded his face with kisses as she clung harder and harder to him. "I've always, always loved you and will always, always love you. Oh, Andreas, my darling, *s'agapo*…"

Before tension could turn to elation, it resurged on one more paramount dread. "What about Dorothea?"

Naomi withdrew, her face gripped in remembered pain as tears rained down her cheeks. "It almost killed me to walk away from her. But I thought I'd have to give her up one day, and it was better for her if I did it now rather than later."

Andreas crushed Naomi in arms that trembled with too much love, relief and gratitude. "And now, *agápi mou*? Will you take us both back? Will you let me worship you for the rest of my days? Will you be my wife and my lover, the owner of my heart and life? Will you be Dorothea's mother and the pillar of her existence? This precious baby who was made by Petros and Nadine's love, and given life by yours, and will now grow up among us, and among our family, and be treasured for the rest of our lives?"

And he received her answering pledge, which she gave with the whole of her body and soul, giving him all of herself for his safekeeping.

He wallowed in her kisses and confessions, feeling blessed beyond measure. "Naomi, *s'agapo*, I love you, love you so…"

Her phone rang somewhere deep in her apartment. They ignored it. For the first three times. Then, suddenly, they were both running for it, struck by the same fear at once. It could be Hannah...Dora...

It wasn't. From what Naomi said as she answered, Andreas realized it was a doctor. The one she'd gone to see yesterday?

As she listened to the person on the other end, Naomi's face went slack, then she swayed.

Cursing, his fright soaring, Andreas swept her up in his arms as she ended the call, took her to the couch and knelt on the floor before her, grasping her hands. "What is it, *agápi mou?*"

"I—I went in for an exam, and...and..." She drew in a huge breath. "I'm pregnant."

It was his turn to stare. And stare.

Then he exclaimed, "But you had your period!"

She was almost panting now. "It's a false period. It happens. Especially since I have an IUD. The doctor missed it because it is so early, no more than two weeks, but the blood work was conclusive."

Naomi gulped down a breath as she stopped, looking stunned, and something else. Worried?

He squeezed her hands as they shook in his. "Are you worried? About having another baby so soon?"

She shook her head. "Actually, it's about you. You love Dora so much, I was wondering if you could want another—"

His lips stopped her trembling words in a feverish kiss. "I want, Naomi, I *want*. I want another baby made of our love. I want two or three or as many as you want and can have. I want anything and everything...with you."

Withdrawing to read the absolute truth of his words in his eyes, she cried a sound of such relief and delight as she surged to bury her streaming face in his chest.

Then she raised adoring, tear-filled eyes to his. "And I want anything and everything with you, my love, for the rest of my life."

As tears he'd never known surged from his soul, he pledged to her, "Never again will I let you feel alone, or be without me or without my love. I will spend my life showing you how you reanimated my heart and gave me everything worth living for, how you blessed my life, and saved it."

* * * * *

"Instinctively, I want to kiss you. But I've had that particular instinct for a long time now, and I'm not sure I should trust it."

Danielle smiled. "You should trust it."

His hands moved to her face, cradling it gently in his palms. "What about my other instincts?"

"You have other instincts?"

"To toss you down on the grass and ravish you in the moonlight."

Want and need instantly cascaded through her, robbing her of her breath. She wished it didn't sound so tempting. There were a million complicated reasons to keep her distance from Travis, even if her own desires were screaming at her to ignore them.

She came up on her toes to meet him. "Let's take it one instinct at a time."

* * *

The Last Cowboy Standing
is part of the Colorado Cattle Barons series from
USA TODAY bestselling author Barbara Dunlop!

THE LAST
COWBOY STANDING

BY
BARBARA DUNLOP

Published in Great Britain 2014
by Mills & Boon, an imprint of Harlequin (UK) Limited,
Eton House, 18-24 Paradise Road, Richmond, Surrey, TW9 1SR

© 2014 Barbara Dunlop

ISBN: 978 0 263 91465 8

51-0514

Harlequin (UK) Limited's policy is to use papers that are natural, renewable and recyclable products and made from wood grown in sustainable forests. The logging and manufacturing processes conform to the legal environmental regulations of the country of origin.

Printed and bound in Spain
by Blackprint CPI, Barcelona

Barbara Dunlop writes romantic stories while curled up in a log cabin in Canada's far north, where bears outnumber people and it snows six months of the year. Fortunately she has a brawny husband and two teenage children to haul firewood and clear the driveway while she sips cocoa and muses about her upcoming chapters. Barbara loves to hear from readers. You can contact her through her website, www.barbaradunlop.com.

To my mother, with love.

One

Travis Jacobs could do anything for eight seconds. At least, that's what he told himself every time he climbed up the side of a bull chute. Tonight's Vegas crowd was loud and enthusiastic, their attention centered on the current rider being bucked around the arena by Devil's Draw.

Putting the other cowboys in the competition from his mind, he looked at Esquire below him, checking for any sign of agitation. Then he rolled his cuffs up a couple of turns, pulled his brown Stetson low and tugged a worn, leather glove onto his right hand.

The crowd groaned in sympathy a mere second before the horn sounded, telling Travis that Buckwheat Dawson had come off the bull. Up next, Travis swung his leg over the chute rail and drew a bracing breath. While Karl Schmitty held the rope, he adjusted the rigging and wrapped his hand. Wasting no time, he slid up square on the bull and gave a sharp nod to the gate operator.

The chute opened, and all four of Esquire's feet instantly left the ground. The Brahma shot out into the arena then straight up in the air under the bright lights. The crowd roared its pleasure as the black bull twisted left, hind feet reaching high, while Travis leaned back, spurred, his arm up, muscles pumped, fighting for all he was worth to keep himself square on the animal's back. Esquire turned right, twisting beneath Travis, shaking him as if he was a bothersome gnat. Three seconds turned to four. Travis's hand burned against the rope, and his wrist felt like it was about to dislocate. The strain sent a branching iron along his spine, but he also felt completely and totally alive. For a brief space of time, life was reduced to its essence. Nothing mattered but the battle between Travis and the bull.

Esquire made an abrupt left turn, nearly unseating Travis, but he kept his form. His hat flew off into the dust. The blaring music and the roar of the crowd disappeared, obliterated by the pulse of blood pumping past his ears.

The horn sounded just before Esquire made one final leap, unseating Travis, sending him catapulting through the air. Travis summersaulted, grazing the bull's left horn, quickly twisting his body to avoid hitting the ground head-on. His shoulder came down first, with his back taking the brunt of the impact. As the air whooshed out of his lungs, a face in the crowd danced before his eyes.

Danielle? What the heck was Danielle doing in Vegas?

Then Esquire's menacing form filled his vision, and he leaped to his feet. Corey Samson, one of the bullfighters, jumped between them, distracting the animal while Travis sprinted to the fence.

Glancing back, he realized Danielle had to be a figment of his imagination. The crowd was nowhere near close enough for him to recognize a particular face. He heaved himself over the top of the fence and jumped to the ground on the other side.

"Nice one." Buckwheat clapped him good-naturedly on the back.

"Hey, Travis," Corey yelled from inside the arena.

Travis turned to see Corey toss him his hat. He caught the Stetson in midair, and Corey gave him a thumbs-up.

"Ninety-one point three," the announcer cried into the sound system.

The crowd roared louder, while lasers and colored spotlights circled the arena, the music coming up once more. Travis was the night's last rider, meaning he'd just won ten thousand dollars.

He stuffed his hat on his head and vaulted back over the fence onto the thick dirt, waving to the crowd and accepting the congratulations of the clowns and cowboys.

"You have *got* to go pro," Corey shouted in his ear.

"Just blowin' off some steam," Travis responded, keeping his grin firmly in place for the spectators, knowing he'd be projected onto the Jumbotron.

His older brother, Seth, had recently been married, and he'd committed his next three years to working on the Lyndon Valley railway project. Responsibility for the family's Colorado cattle ranch now rested completely on Travis's shoulders. Faced with that looming reality, he'd discovered he had a few wild oats left to sow.

"You could make a lot of money on the circuit," said Corey.

Travis let himself fantasize for a minute about going on the road as a professional bull rider. The image was tantalizing—to be footloose and fancy free, no cattle to tend, no ranch hands, no bills, no responsibilities. He'd ride a couple of times a week, hit the clubs, meet friendly women. There were no bleak, dusty, hick towns on this particular rodeo circuit. It was all bright lights and five-star hotels.

For a moment, he resented the lost opportunity. But he forcibly swallowed his own frustration. If he'd wanted to be a bull rider, he should have spoken up before now. While his brother and sisters were all choosing their own life paths, Travis should have said something about leaving the ranch. But it was too late. He was the last Jacobs cowboy, and somebody had to run the place.

A small crowd had gathered in the middle of the arena to celebrate his win. He unzipped his flak jacket to circulate a little air. Then he accepted the prize buckle and the check from the event manager and gave a final wave of his hat to the crowd.

Mind still mulling what might have been, he turned and fell into step beside Corey, their boots puffing up dust as they moved toward the gate.

"How long have you been on the road?" he found himself asking the bullfighter.

"Nearly ten years now," Corey responded. "Started when I was seventeen."

"You ever get tired of it?"

"What's to get tired? The excitement? The adventure? The women?"

Travis stuffed the check in his shirt pocket. "You know what I mean."

"Yeah, I know. When I get tired of the wheels turning, I go back to the folks' place in New Mexico for a while."

"Ever tempted to stay there?" Travis was trying to reassure himself that life on the road got old, that all men eventually wanted a real home.

Corey shook his head. "Nope. Though, last trip home, there was this pretty red-haired gal living down the road."

Travis chuckled at the yearning expression on Corey's face. "I take it she's calling you back to New Mexico?"

"Not yet, but likely soon. She's got some kind of a bullfighter fantasy going on inside that head of hers, and she's decided I'm the fire she wants to play with."

Travis burst out laughing.

Corey grinned and cocked an eyebrow.

"No pretty women calling me back to my hometown." There was nothing calling to Travis except cattle and horses.

Though, for some reason, his thoughts moved back to Danielle. But she wasn't from his hometown, and she sure wasn't any young innocent. She was twenty-eight, only a year younger than Travis. She was a graduate of Harvard Law, a practicing lawyer and probably the smartest, most sophisticated woman he'd ever met. She also flat out refused to give him the time of day.

"Think of that as another reason to go on the road," Corey countered.

"I'm on the road right now," said Travis. There wasn't a reason in the world he couldn't be footloose for the next few days.

He'd earned it, and he had a check in his pocket just itching to get spent.

"That you are." Corey clapped him on the back. "Let's hit the clubs and show off that new buckle of yours. I bet there are dozens of gorgeous ladies out there just dying to hear how you rode the bull a full eight seconds, and how I saved your life in the arena."

"Is that how you're going to play it? That you saved my life?"

"Damn straight," said Corey.

There were two men in the world Danielle Marin wanted to avoid. Unfortunately, both of them had turned up in Vegas.

She was attending an international law conference, so she'd been on alert for Randal Kleinfeld. It seemed likely the wunderkind D.C. attorney would show up for a lecture by his university mentor Stan Sterling. But Travis Jacobs had come out of left field, literally.

She'd been blindsided when the announcer called his name at the bull riding show, then mesmerized when the bucking bull burst from the chute. Travis made it look effortless, as if he'd been born on the back of a Brahma. That he'd won should have come as no surprise to her. When it came to all things ranching and rough stock, Travis was a master. Stone-faced and rugged, tough and no-nonsense, he was the absolute antithesis of the smooth-talking, urbane Randal.

Show over, and back at the conference hotel with her friends, Danielle couldn't help but ponder the differences between the two men. Travis sticking in her mind, she took a bracing swallow of her vodka martini.

"That's the spirit, Dani," called Astra Lindy from across the table, raising her cosmo in a mock toast.

"I told you it would be fun," said Nadine Beckman as she accepted a frozen Bellini from their waitress.

The four women were less than a mile from the bull riding arena, relaxing in the lobby lounge. The temperature was mid-seventies, a light breeze blowing in from the hotel pool and the gardens.

"It was a blast," Odette Gray agreed with an enthusiastic nod. "Cowboys have the sexiest butts." She'd gone with a light beer.

The other two women laughed. Danielle smiled, keeping her expression lighthearted, even as she called up a mental image of Travis walking away. It simply wasn't fair. How could so much sexiness be wrapped up in such an exasperating man? And what kind of character flaw made her want him?

She took another healthy sip of her drink, regretting that she'd let her three friends talk her into the bull riding excursion. It had seemed like a harmless diversion after a full day of conference topics like Comparative Legal Systems and Cross Border Taxation. And it should have been a harmless diversion. Who could have predicted that Travis Jacobs would choose this week to leave Lyndon Valley and show up in Vegas?

"I'd do a cowboy," Nadine brazenly declared.

"In a heartbeat," Odette agreed.

"Up close, they're dusty and crude," Danielle pointed out, speaking to herself as much as to the other women. "They talk slow, use short sentences, very small words."

"Crude can be sexy," said Nadine. "And the dust washes off."

Sadly, deep down in her secret heart of hearts, Danielle agreed. She'd once seen Travis after he'd cleaned up. The result had made her gasp for breath, and put her libido into overdrive.

"Dani knows cowboys," said Astra. "She spends a lot of time in Colorado."

"I wouldn't call it a *lot* of time," Danielle corrected.

Truth was, she avoided Lyndon Valley as much as possible. The Jacobs spread was right next to the Terrell ranch. And Caleb Terrell was one of her major clients. He lived in Lyndon Valley only part-time, so she could usually arrange to put in her hours for Active Equipment at his Chicago head office or at her own law office on the Chicago River.

"Caleb's a cowboy," said Astra. "He doesn't use small words."

"I was generalizing," Danielle admitted.

On a night like tonight, she needed to take every opportunity to remind herself there was a world of difference between her and Travis Jacobs. She was closer to Randal in background, values, temperament and, of course, profession.

She'd dated Randal in law school, breaking up with him at graduation when he secured a prime internship in D.C. and she had accepted the offer in Chicago. He'd wanted to stay together, but she knew it wouldn't work out. Long-distance relationships never did. Plus, she hadn't been convinced he was *the one*. He was close, and she couldn't exactly say what was missing. But her instincts had told her to end it.

Randal had not been happy with the split. Not that he had anything to complain about the way things turned out. He was rising fast on the D.C. legal scene. The firm he worked for, Nester and Hedley, had clients that included senators, congressmen and captains of international industry. Danielle's Chicago job was bush-league by comparison.

Which made it strange that a partner from Nester and Hedley had contacted her last week, making her an offer that was all but impossible to refuse. She could only assume Randal had a hand in it, and she didn't know whether to thank him or berate him.

The job would give her a chance to build toward an equity partnership in a prestigious, cutting-edge firm. Any lawyer would jump at that. But she didn't want to be beholden to Randal. And she didn't want to date him again. Maybe she was being ridiculously conceited, but she couldn't help but wonder if that would turn out to be part of the package.

"Good evening, ladies," drawled a male voice.

She glanced up to see a vaguely familiar man in a black cowboy hat, a blue-and-green Western shirt and faded blue jeans. A split second later, she caught sight of Travis slightly behind him, worn Stetson low on his brow, face tanned brown, a challenging glint in his cobalt eyes.

She was honestly too tired for this.

"Are you from the rodeo?" asked Nadine, glancing from one to the other.

"We are," the stranger answered.

Astra pointed to Travis. "He's the guy who won, isn't he?"

"Are you a bull rider, too?" Nadine chirped to the other man.

"I'm a bullfighter."

"So, one of the clowns?" she asked.

"There's a big difference between a clown and a bullfighter, ma'am. For example." He jabbed this thumb toward Travis. "I saved this guy's life tonight."

"I saw that," Odette put in knowingly.

"Nice buckle." Nadine had turned her attention and her brilliant smile to Travis. She reached out and touched the shiny, gold and silver prize at his waist.

Danielle couldn't help but roll her eyes at the bling. Really? He had to wear it?

"This is Travis Jacobs," the stranger introduced, removing his hat. "He's tonight's bull riding champion. And I'm Corey Samson, bullfighter extraordinaire."

"Did he really save your life?" Odette asked Travis on a note of awe. Danielle knew the question was more about flirting than any true amazement at Corey's feat.

Corey looked to Travis and waited.

"He most certainly did," Travis acknowledged staunchly. "Bullfighters are highly skilled, highly trained, and among the bravest men on the planet."

The word *wingman* flitted through Danielle's brain. Travis was trying to help his friend pick up Odette.

Nadine turned to her. "That wasn't short sentences and small words."

Travis's challenging gaze turned on Danielle. It was clear he remembered her using that particular phrase in the past.

"It was a generalization," she repeated, refusing to break eye contact with him.

"That's very impressive," Odette told Corey with an almost comical flutter of her eyelashes.

"Danielle is continuously unequivocal in her elevated specifications for interactive discourse," said Travis, keeping his expression completely neutral.

"How does he know your name?" Astrid immediately demanded.

"We met in Colorado," said Travis.

"Briefly," Danielle pointed out.

"Dance?" Corey asked Odette.

"Love to." She giggled as she came to her feet.

"Dance?" Travis asked Danielle.

"Too busy with my drink," she responded airily, lifting her long-stemmed glass.

"I'll dance with you," Nadine chimed in with obvious enthusiasm, holding out a hand.

"Ma'am," Travis answered her, gallantly tipping his hat, taking her hand and helping her to her feet.

"You know a real live bull riding champion?" Astrid asked Danielle as the two couples left the covered deck for the dance floor inside, and Danielle concentrated on *not* looking at Travis's rear end.

"He's not a champion." Danielle went ahead and finished off the martini. "He only does it as a hobby."

"He's pretty good."

"That's what happens when you spend your entire life on a ranch in Lyndon Valley."

Astrid seemed confused by Danielle's tone. "You hold that against him?"

"What I hold against him is that he's annoying and incredibly full of himself. To hear him talk, differentiating between a Hereford and a Black Angus is the only knowledge relevant to mankind."

Astrid was obviously fighting a grin. "Did you mix the two up?"

Danielle sighed. "They do look a lot alike."

Astrid chuckled.

"He mocks me," Danielle elaborated. "All the time, on every

level. And we only ever see each other at the ranch, so I'm always out of my element, and he has the advantage."

"You're a Harvard graduate."

"I *know*."

"You shouldn't let him get to you."

"I don't."

"I can tell."

Danielle regrouped. "It's just that his frame of reference is so different than mine."

"And that ticks you off."

"What ticks me off, is that he's such a snob about it. I'm intelligent. I'm hard-working. People respect me, even other cowboys. Caleb and Reed are perfectly fine with me."

Astrid nodded toward the dance floor. "Looks like he's getting along fine with Nadine."

Danielle couldn't help a reflexive glance at the couple as they danced together. "Nadine has probably been blinded by the shine off that enormous belt buckle."

"She always was attracted to winners."

Danielle couldn't help but take note of Travis's hand on the small of Nadine's back, her touch on his shoulder, the animated smile on his face, and the way she was chattering on to him. He twirled her around, and she laughed as he pulled her back, holding her even closer against him as they swayed to the music.

Danielle couldn't seem to stop a reflexive shimmer of sexual awareness from flashing through her belly. She pictured herself dancing with Travis. Then abruptly shook the image away.

"What's that?" asked Astrid.

"What?"

"You're blushing," Astrid accused.

"I am not."

"You got the hots for the bull rider."

"Not even a little bit."

"I think a little bit. I think more than a little bit."

"I'm ignoring it," Danielle declared, lifting her martini glass only to find it empty. She glanced around for the waitress. "I'm using intellect and reason to counteract inappropriate infatuation."

"You should dance with him," said Astrid.

"Not on your life."

"What happens in Vegas stays in Vegas."

"I'm sure not doing anything tonight that I have to leave in Vegas."

"I'm talking about dancing. What is it you have in mind?"

"Absolutely nothing."

She and Travis had come close to...well, close to *something* a couple of years back when he'd rescued her from a derelict barn. He'd mostly been amused, and she'd mostly been angry. But after they got back to his ranch house, and she'd showered and borrowed one of his sister's robes, there'd been a moment, a very long moment, when he'd look like he wanted to kiss her.

Her desire for that kiss had been so strong that it frightened her. She'd reacted defensively, uttering some patently untrue and hurtful remark. It had worked. He'd backed off. But it had also made him angry, and their relationship had never recovered.

"I see your drink is empty," Travis couldn't help saying to Danielle as he escorted Nadine to their table. He raised his brow in a question.

"That's your cue to dance with him." The woman called Astrid nudged Danielle with her elbow.

It was her cue to dance with him. Although he fully expected her to shoot him down, he had to take the chance. Danielle was in front of him, and he wanted to touch her. It was as simple as that.

Nadine dropped into her chair at the table, crossing her shapely legs and taking a drink of something frozen and orange. "Go for it, Danielle," she breathed. "The band's great."

Danielle shook her head. "I'm not—" But then she stopped. Her eyes went wide, and she focused on a spot behind his shoulder. "Sure." She rose to her feet. "Why not?"

Travis glanced behind him, finding a smartly dressed man

in his late twenties. He was clean-shaven. His light brown hair was slicked back, slightly shiny, neat around the ears. He wore an expensive, pin-striped suit, with a white dress shirt and a purple tie. The handkerchief in his pocket matched the tie, and his gaze was intent on Danielle.

"Dani," he opened with a dazzling, white smile.

"Sorry, Randal," she spoke breezily, linking her arm with Travis's. "Just about to dance." She all but dragged Travis toward the dance floor.

"What was that?" Travis asked, as he turned her into his arms.

"What was what?" she asked, all wide-eyed innocence.

"What was up with the guy back there?" He settled a hand on the small of her back.

"Nothing." She took a breath, placed her hand on his shoulder and stepped into the smooth jazz music.

She felt so good in his arms that he almost let her get away with it. The dance floor was crowded. The breeze from the open window ruffled her hair. Man, she was beautiful.

But he was too curious to let it drop. "You were about to turn me down. Don't pretend you weren't. Then that guy showed up, and you changed your mind."

Danielle gave her short, brown hair a little toss. It was soft and trendy, long across her eyes, wispy at her neck. "I didn't expect to see you in Vegas."

The longer he held her in his arms, the less he cared about the other guy. "Is that your way of telling me he's none of my business?"

"He *is* none of your business. But that's my way of telling you I don't want to talk about him."

"Okay by me."

"Thank you." There was an edge of sarcasm to her voice.

Travis was used to that. "I didn't expect to see you in Vegas, either."

"I'm attending an international law conference."

"Interesting?"

"It is if you like international law."

"Not exactly my forte."

"That's true, isn't it?"

"Why are you smiling?"

"Because, you're in my world now, cowboy."

He didn't exactly know what she meant by that. But he wasn't sure he wanted to pursue it, either, since it would likely mean they'd end up arguing. The way he saw it, Vegas was as much his world as hers.

"You saw me ride?" he asked instead.

"The girls dragged me along." She paused. "Bull riding is not exactly my sport of choice."

He wasn't about to take offense. He'd have been shocked speechless if she'd confessed to a secret love of bull riding. "Where were you sitting?"

She pulled back to look at him, her gaze quizzical. "Why?"

He wanted to know if he could have possibly seen her after his fall, but he wasn't about to explain that to her. "I wondered if you had a good view."

"Fourth row, across from the chutes."

"Good seats." He could have glimpsed her on the way down, maybe filed her image away in his subconscious and brought it up when he hit the dirt. It was possible.

She frowned. "I'm not sure being closer makes it any better."

"Are you trying to pick a fight?"

She hesitated almost imperceptibly. "We never seem to have to try."

Travis's skin prickled in warning, and he glanced around the room, catching the glare of the man who'd approached Danielle at the table. "Who *is* that guy?"

"I thought we'd moved on."

They might have moved on, but the other man obviously hadn't.

"Are you dating him or something?" Travis asked.

"No."

"No to dating him, or no to *or something*."

She drew her arms from him. "This was a bad idea. I'm going back to the table now."

"He's waiting for you."

She reflexively turned her head, but Travis stopped her with a gentle palm on her cheek. "Don't look."

She stilled.

"He's staring daggers into me. If I'm gonna have to fight, you'd better warn me now."

She gave a weary smile and a small shake of her head. "Nobody's fighting."

Travis gathered her back into his arms, and she picked up the rhythm again. His body gave a subconscious sigh, and he drew her closer this time, her chest brushing his, thighs meeting as they moved. She was exactly the right size, exactly the right shape. She fit perfectly into his arms.

"I'm pretty sure I can take him," he mused, breathing in the fresh fragrance of her hair.

"His name is Randal Kleinfeld. I knew him in law school."

"In the biblical sense?"

She tipped her head back, dark eyes chastising him. "You are insufferably rude, you know that?"

Travis might be rude, but Randal was intensely possessive. Not that Travis blamed him. Even he could see that Danielle was a gem, a beautiful, sensuous, fiery gem of a woman. And for the right man, there'd be no looking back.

"Did you date him, Danielle?"

"It's business, Travis. He wants to talk to me about a job. With his firm. They've made me an offer to move to D.C."

Travis didn't like the sound of that. If she switched firms, she would also switch clients. She might never come back to Lyndon Valley on business with Caleb.

He tried to tell himself it didn't matter. They'd seen each other maybe a dozen times in the past two years. They were barely acquaintances. Mostly they fought. There was certainly nothing personal between them

Still, he found himself bracing for her answer as he posed the question. "Are you going to take it?"

"I don't know. That's why I don't want to talk to him. I don't need any pressure while I make up my mind."

Travis glanced at Randal again, taking in his clenched fists and the dark scowl that furrowed his aristocratic brow. It was patently obvious that he was after more than just a business relationship with Danielle. And Travis realized he had no way to stop him.

Not that he wanted to stop him. Danielle's personal life, in D.C. or anywhere else, was none of his business. He hoped it wasn't Randal's business. He hadn't seen much of the guy, but what he'd seen, he didn't like.

Thankfully Randal didn't have the upper hand, at least not at the moment anyway. Right now, Travis was the guy who had her in his arms, while Randal was the guy on the sidelines. He deliberately eased their bodies farther away from the crowd and splayed his hand across the small of her back, thinking he liked it this way.

Two

The next morning, Danielle told herself that Travis's dancing her to the exit and spiriting her to the hotel elevator to get her away from Randal was no big deal. She didn't owe him any grand thank-you. She'd expressed her appreciation last night, and he'd been polite about it. It was done, over. It had accomplished its objective.

She didn't need to contact him again. In fact, it was better if she didn't contact him again. Their dancing last night had confirmed her secret fear. His body was as fit, as rock-hard and as sinewy as she'd fantasized.

He was tall and broad. His chin was square, nose just imperfect enough to be masculine. His blue eyes sparkled with what she swore had to be hidden secrets. And even fresh out of the bull riding arena, he smelled fantastic. She supposed he'd probably showered. But it wasn't any shampoo or cologne she'd reacted to last night. It was pure, male pheromones that had pushed up her pulse and made her skin tingle in anticipation of his touch.

When he'd pressed their bodies together, a rush of pure arousal had flooded her system. Through the back of her thin, satin tank top, she'd felt the individual calluses on his fingertips. Her breasts had brushed his denim shirt, teasing her nipples, making them embarrassingly hard. Under her own hands, she'd felt the solid strength of his shoulders, the shift of his muscles, and she'd longed to touch every inch of him.

Dancing with Travis was like secretly watching an erotic movie, or spending a week's pay at the spa or eating chocolate cupcakes with gobs of buttercream icing. You knew you shouldn't, but sometimes a woman couldn't help herself.

Now, she made her way to the Sinatra Room to attend a panel on emerging market tariff relief. There was a refreshment stand in the south lobby, and she'd left herself time to pick up a cup of coffee and a muffin. She was thankful that she'd stopped after one martini last night. For a few minutes there, she'd been tempted to order another.

"There you are, Dani," came Randal's friendly voice. "I don't know how I missed you last night."

"Good morning, Randal." She quickened her pace.

"Are you going to the tariff panel?"

She was tempted to say no so he wouldn't join her. But it was an important panel. And if he saw her there later, it would just be embarrassing.

"I am," she answered. "Just got to grab a coffee first." She veered off to the right.

"Coffee sounds great." He kept pace. "I'll buy. So, how've you been? How are things in Chicago?"

"Good," Danielle replied. "Business is brisk."

"You got the letter from Nester and Hedley?"

"I did."

They joined the long line snaking out of the small coffee shop.

"Nice offer?" he pressed.

"Did you have something to do with that?"

Randal held up his palms in a gesture of innocence. "I wish I had that kind of clout."

She checked his expression, not sure whether she was buying it or not. "You didn't bring me to the partners' attention?"

"I did not. I think they were impressed by the Schneider Pistole merger."

Danielle still wasn't convinced. "And how did they know about Schneider and Pistole?"

"Everybody knows about Schneider and Pistole. You successfully navigated some very protectionist waters. Bookmakers were giving it seven to one against."

"Very funny."

The line moved ahead, and they squeezed to one side to let departing patrons get past. The aromas of icing and cinnamon teased Danielle's senses. She'd told herself to go with a whole grain, fruit muffin. But the sweet confection was tempting.

Randal's attention went to the menu board near the ceiling. "I was saying to Laura just last week—"

"Is Laura one of the partners?" Danielle found it hard to believe he'd had nothing to do with the offer.

"Laura's my girlfriend."

"You have a girlfriend?"

"Don't sound so surprised."

"I thought…I mean…" Danielle didn't quite know where to go with this. She'd assumed he wanted to rekindle things with her. Had her ego led her that far astray?

"I'm a young, decently intelligent, decently looking man with a bright professional future."

"Of course you are." But the declaration sounded artificial even to her own ears.

Randal chuckled. "You should come to D.C., Danielle. It's where all the action is."

"There's a lot going on in Chicago, too."

They came to the counter.

"Why do I get the feeling you've maxed out there?" He looked to the clerk. "Two large coffees, one with cream and sugar, one black." Then he raised his brow to Danielle. "That still right?"

She nodded. She still sweetened and softened her coffee.

"I'll take a blueberry bran muffin," she told the young woman.

"Same for me," said Randal, reaching for his wallet.

"You don't have to buy."

"You wouldn't say that if you saw the number of zeros on my bonus check."

The clerk grinned brightly at his joke as she rang in their order, obviously aware that she was serving a good-looking, successful guy.

"That explains the Fendi suit," said Danielle.

"Come and work with me. The salary they quoted is only the beginning."

"I'm thinking about it," she admitted, accepting one of the cardboard cups, and balancing the muffin in her other hand.

"Good." His smile went wide.

There was a momentary, overly friendly glint in his eye that gave her pause. But she quickly squelched her suspicion. The man had a girlfriend. The idea that he was still pining over her after all these years was ridiculous.

Still, as they started to walk away, he touched her elbow, and something familiar moved up her spine. She shook off the ridiculous reaction, stepping to one side. It was over between them. He had another girlfriend. And she was absolutely *not* one of those women who took another look at her ex as soon as he was taken by somebody else.

She took a nibble of the dense, molasses-based muffin as she navigated her way through the milling crowd. As she moved into the big lobby, a movement flashed at the corner of her eye. She turned her head and scanned the cavernous space. Suddenly, her gaze caught and held, a sensual awareness washing through her in earnest.

She swallowed.

Travis was leaning indolently against a marble pillar. He should have looked out of place in a plaid Western shirt and faded blue jeans amidst a sea of dark, designer suits, but he didn't. Somehow, the lawyers looked out of place around him.

"How's the muffin?" asked Randal, his voice startling her.

"Mmm. Good." She gave an appreciative nod.

Randal glanced at his watch, making a right turn toward the meeting room. "We'd better hurry."

"I guess." She wondered why Travis was here so early in the morning. In fact, why was he here at all? Last night, he'd told her he was staying at the Blonde Desert just off the Strip.

She half expected him to approach them. But he didn't. Just stood here, watching, a half smile on his face.

"Dani?" Randal prompted, stopping a half step ahead.

For some reason his voice was starting to grate.

"I'm coming," she answered, peering at Travis a moment longer.

Then she determinedly went ahead, setting a course for the panel discussion, determined to ignore Travis's presence, but fully aware of his form in her peripheral vision.

She wondered if he had a cell phone. If she knew the number, she could send him a text and ask him what he was doing in the hotel. It occurred to her that Caleb likely knew. She could text Caleb and ask him for Travis's cell. Would that be weird?

"Over there," said Randal, as they moved with the flow of the crowd through a set of double doors.

Astrid was waving at them from a classroom style table, on the aisle, halfway up the room. Seats were filling fast, and the panel participants were taking their places at the front of the room. Danielle parked her shoulder bag under the table and took the seat next to Astrid. She draped her purse over the back of the chair, while Randal sat down next to her. Odette and Nadine arrived, and they squished one more chair into the table, pushing Randal's shoulder against Danielle's.

"Just like old times," he joked in her ear, harkening back to their days in law school.

Astrid leaned forward, looking across Danielle to answer Randal. "At least we don't have to write the bar exam this time."

Randal gave her an easy smile.

The moderator spoke into the microphone, asking people to get settled, and the rest of the audience quickly took their seats.

Though the speakers were well-versed in their specialties, and the debate was lively, Danielle couldn't get her mind off

Travis, wondering if he was still in the lobby, and what had brought him there in the first place.

Two hours in, when one of the audience members wandered off on an arcane point of law to do with protocols for the functioning of supranational tribunals, she gave in and slipped from her seat. Randal looked surprised and none too pleased at having to move his seat to let her pass. She took her purse but left her shoulder bag, letting everyone think she was going to the ladies' room.

She'd be right back. The odds that Travis was still out there were overwhelmingly small.

But, there he was.

One of the uniformed women had stepped out from behind the now-empty conference check-in desk and was talking and laughing with him. His gaze lifted, and he caught sight of Danielle. She stopped, not exactly sure what to do. She could still pretend she was going to the ladies' room, avoid even acknowledging him.

He didn't move, and neither did she.

Finally, she decided this was ridiculous. She wanted to know what he was doing here, and she'd go and ask him. She started across the mostly empty space, occupied only by hotel and conference staff, and the odd delegate who, like her, had stepped temporarily out of their session.

Her heels clicked on the marble floor. She was conscious of every step. Travis's face was impassive, but he kept watching as she grew closer.

"Sounds good," he said to the young, blonde woman. "I'll talk to you later."

Then he nodded to Danielle. "Hi there."

The woman watched over her shoulder with obvious curiosity as she moved back to the long registration table.

"What are you doing here?" Danielle asked without preamble.

"I was getting a coffee, but then Melanie and I started chatting."

Danielle cast a reflexive glance to the woman who wasn't even hiding her interest. "I meant, what are you doing at this hotel? You said you were at the Blonde Desert."

"When the Emperor Plaza found out I was a bull riding champion, they comped a suite."

"Did you flash your belt buckle?"

He grinned. "Never thought of that."

"How did they know?"

Travis nodded toward the closed door of the meeting room. "He in there with you?"

"You mean Randal?"

"You still think it's just business?"

"Absolutely." More than ever. In fact, she was embarrassed now that she'd ever thought it might be something else.

Travis cracked a mocking half smile.

"What?"

"For such a smart woman, you're really not a very smart woman."

"Yeah? Well, for such a dumb cowboy, you really are a dumb cowboy."

If she'd hoped to get a rise out of him, it didn't work. His expression never faltered.

"You're reading way too much into this," she told him, glancing guiltily toward the meeting room, thinking she needed to get back there and catch the end of the session.

"No, I'm not," said Travis.

She decided to put a stop to the debate. "He's got a girlfriend back in D.C."

"Not a very good one."

Danielle folded her arms across her chest. "Now, that's just absurd. You don't know a single thing about her." Danielle didn't even know her name.

"I know he's thinking about cheating on her."

"You're clairvoyant as well as a bull rider?"

"You don't need to be clairvoyant to read lust in somebody's expression."

Danielle's thoughts faltered, taking her down a worrisome pathway. "Was it me?"

"That he's lusting after?"

"No. I mean, did I say something, or do something to make it look like I was interested in him?"

Travis rocked back ever so slightly. "*Are* you interested in him?"

"No. I mean, I don't think so. But I could be one of those women."

"One of what women?"

"The ones who don't want a guy, but don't want any other woman to have him, either. I mean, maybe when I heard he had a girlfriend, I subconsciously started getting jealous."

"You're not one of those women."

"How do you know for sure? I might be." What an incredibly distasteful character trait.

"It's not you. It's him. He sends out possessive vibes for about a hundred yards."

"We haven't seen each other in four years."

"Doesn't matter," Travis confidently drawled.

The sound of applause drifted through the walls. Seconds later, four sets of double doors opened across the lobby, people spilling out in a steady stream. She guessed that answered whether or not she was going to catch the end of the session.

"Here he comes," said Travis.

Danielle followed the trajectory of his gaze.

"Straight for you."

"He's got my bag."

"A convenient excuse."

"A gentlemanly act."

Travis coughed out a laugh.

"You just can't believe you might have it wrong," she challenged.

"He'll ask you to lunch," Travis predicted. "And when you tell him you're having lunch with me, it'll kill him. He'll say or do something to put me in my place. He'll be absolutely compelled to point out the cultural differences between you and me, and how he's the better man."

"I'm not going for lunch with you."

"Mark my words," said Travis as Randal arrived.

"You left your bag behind," said Randal, sparing a fleeting glance in Travis's direction.

"Thank you," Danielle offered, feeling a smug sense of satisfaction.

"Travis Jacobs," Travis introduced himself, holding out his hand.

Randal seemed to hesitate for a split second. "Randal Kleinfeld." He shook hands. "I went to Harvard with Danielle."

"So, I hear," said Travis.

Randal turned his attention back to Danielle. "So, what would you like to do for lunch?"

She could all but hear Travis's mocking thoughts, feel him daring her to test his theory. If she did, she'd be stuck going to lunch with him. If she didn't, he'd probably never let her live it down. But when Randal didn't try to put Travis in his place the way Travis had predicted, Danielle would feel as if she'd won something, too.

It was worth a lunch with Travis, she decided.

"I'm so sorry," she told Randal. "But Travis and I have just made lunch plans."

Randal's attention darted briefly to Travis. His eyes narrowed as if he was none too happy. But when he spoke to Danielle, his expression smoothed out again.

"I thought you might like to hear about the rest of the tariff Q and A." Randal smiled, and his gaze slid to Travis again. "We could contrast tripartite arrangements pertaining to intraregional trade distortions versus the harmonization of partner states."

"We're going to contrast the black bulls with the white ones," Travis said with a straight face.

Danielle thought it was a stretch for Travis to take Randal's words as a slight, but she nearly laughed at the comeback.

"I can make some introductions to people at the firm," Randal pushed on. "You should use the break time to your advantage."

"Sorry," said Danielle. "But I already have plans."

Randal hit Travis with a disparaging look. "You're going to take advantage of her good manners?"

"I was going to pay for the lunch," said Travis.

"That's not the point."

Danielle reached out to where Randal held her bag. "Thanks for bringing this. I'll probably see you later on in the day?"

Before Randal could react, Travis removed the bag from his grasp.

"Jacque Alanis Signature Room?" Travis asked her in a clear voice, naming the most exclusive and expensive restaurant on the Strip. Then he took her arm and deftly turned her for the main entrance.

"You're the one who's throwing down the gauntlet," she accused as they moved out of earshot.

"If his motives are pure, he'll have no interest in which restaurant we choose."

"We're going to contrast the black and white *bulls?*"

"He tossed out all that technical language for my benefit."

"Lawyers always talk that way."

"You don't."

Danielle tried to decide if he was right. "I do when I'm with other lawyers."

"You don't do it to belittle other people in a conversation."

She thought about that. "Sometimes I do it to you."

He seemed to ponder the comment as they walked out the doors of the main entrance. "Sometimes I deserve it."

Danielle gaped at him in astonishment, as he gave a hand signal to a doorman.

Within moments, a long, white limousine was pulling to the curb, and the porter held open the back door.

"You have got to be kidding," she told Travis.

"He's still watching. I want to make this good."

Danielle didn't believe that for one minute. "By now, Randal's gone to lunch with someone else."

"No, he hasn't." Travis guided her forward with a hand on the small of her back. "And the more I look like a rival, the faster he'll tip his hand, and prove me right. He's still after you."

She put her hand on the open car door. "This is going to cost you a fortune."

"You're talking to a man with bull riding prize money in his jeans."

"You're going to spend it all just to make a point?"

"Might as well spend it on you." His blue eyes were fixed and determined.

She gave an unconcerned shrug, answering as she slid into the car. "Fine. I've got nothing against the Jacque Alanis Signature Room."

Travis grinned and slipped the doorman a bill before following her inside. The door shut behind him, and his phone began to ring. He reached into the breast pocket of his Western shirt.

"I think the Signature Room requires a jacket," said Danielle.

He gazed at his phone display. "In the absence of a jacket, they require a good tip." He gave her an eyebrow waggle. "It's Vegas, baby. You mind if I take this? It's Caleb."

Danielle felt her eyes widen. She wondered how Caleb could have known she was with Travis. Then she remembered Caleb and Travis were close friends. Then she realized she was making a colossal mistake by accepting his invitation to lunch. This was Travis, her archenemy from Lyndon Valley. Why had she let her guard down?

"Hey, Caleb," he said into the phone.

Then he paused and listened, brow furrowing in concern.

The driver put the limo into gear and pulled ahead.

"Is everybody okay with that?" he asked.

Danielle didn't want to be nosey, but she couldn't help think something was wrong back at the Jacobses' ranch.

"No. If that's what he wants, then it seems like a good solution." Travis paused again. "Yeah. Sure. I'll get it done."

The limo pulled into the busy street, and Danielle hung on to a handle as they bumped from the hotel driveway. The Signature Room was only half a mile away, but traffic was busy.

Travis's gaze went to Danielle, a conspiratorial smile growing on his face. "She's here? Really?"

She held her breath, not exactly sure why she wanted Caleb kept in the dark, but quite certain that she did.

"I'll watch for her," said Travis. "Thursday, it is. See you then."

He ended the call. Then he grinned at her. "Caleb just informed me you were in Vegas."

Danielle struggled to frame the right words. She didn't want to offend Travis, but she didn't want anybody getting the wrong idea, either.

"Relax," he drawled. "I'm not going to kiss and tell."

Her guilt turned to irritation. "Nobody's kissing anyone."

"It's an expression."

Her own phone chimed.

He glanced to her purse. "Go for it. I did."

"Thanks." She popped the snap and reached inside, extracting the slim phone. It was Caleb.

She pressed the answer button, watching Travis as she spoke. "Hi, Caleb."

Travis's brows shot up. Then he grinned, shaking his head.

"How's the conference?" Caleb asked.

"Interesting, so far," said Danielle, thinking it was interesting, and on more than one level. "It's going very well," she added.

"Good. Glad to hear it. Listen, I'm going to be in Vegas on Thursday."

Danielle shot a reflexive and accusatory glare at Travis. He could have mentioned that fact.

"You're coming to Vegas," she said to both men.

"We're going to hold Alex Cable's bachelor party there. You remember he's marrying Mandy's cousin Lisa?"

"I do," Danielle confirmed.

Caleb's wife, Mandy, had only recently discovered Lisa was her cousin. Lisa was Mayor Seth Jacobs's Chief of Staff, and Danielle had worked with her on permitting for the Lyndon Valley railway. Alex also had a family connection. He was Mandy's brother-in-law Zach's partner in DFB Brewing Company.

"We were going to hold it at the brewery, but they ran into a problem with some renovations, so we're moving to plan B. Hey, you'll never guess who else is in Vegas this weekend."

"Who?" she asked, her voice going slightly high pitched as guilt contracted her stomach.

"Travis. He's going to plan everything, and we'll fly in Thursday afternoon. I'd like to meet with you about the Columbia accounting firm and a couple of other things if you can still be there."

"Sure," said Danielle. "No problem." She had planned to fly back to Chicago on Tuesday, but Action Equipment was a very important client. She'd meet Caleb whenever and wherever he needed.

"He's bull riding," said Caleb.

"Travis?"

"Mandy saw where he won yesterday."

"Good for him," said Danielle.

"You're at the Emperor Plaza?"

"I am," she admitted.

"I'll see if Travis can get our rooms there."

"Good idea."

"Perfect. Talk to you Thursday."

"Bye, Caleb." She pushed the end button, letting her hand drop into her lap.

Travis's phone rang.

"That'll be Caleb," she told him fatalistically. "He wants you to get them rooms at the Emperor Plaza."

Travis grinned. "Hi, Caleb."

The limo took a wide turn, and Danielle hung on again. It then came to a smooth stop in front of the restaurant entrance.

"Sure," said Travis. "I'll send the particulars as soon as I have them. You want strippers?"

Danielle shot him a glower of disapproval.

Travis chuckled into the phone. "Yeah, that's what I thought. I wouldn't want to tangle with her either."

The driver pulled opened the limo door, letting sunshine and warm air flood in. The noise from other traffic and the sidewalk crowds displaced the relative quiet of the limo.

"Gotta go," said Travis. "I've got a hot lunch date."

"Very funny," Danielle muttered as she shifted to the door.

"Ma'am," said the driver, holding out his hand.

She accepted the offer of assistance, smoothing her skirt as she stepped onto the sidewalk. Travis climbed out, her bag in his hand.

He paid the driver. Then he generously tipped the maître d', and they were quickly shown to a table on the second-floor patio. They had a sun umbrella above them, flower boxes decorating the rail beside them, and a panoramic fountain display across the street. The white tablecloth billowed slightly in the breeze, held down by a low, floral centerpiece and an abundant setting of fine china, crystal and silver.

It was warm, and Danielle shrugged out of her gray blazer. The waiter offered to hang it up, and laid a linen napkin across her lap.

She glanced at her watch to see it was coming up on noon. "I need to get back by one-thirty."

"No problem," said Travis, accepting a slim, leather-bound menu from the waiter.

The man handed Danielle a menu, while a second waiter filled their glasses with distilled water. The traffic noise and stereo music wafted up to them, along with laughter and a few yelps from the crowds below as the fountains danced higher. It was only noon, but many youthful tourists were already in the party spirit.

"Tell me you were joking about the strippers," said Danielle, focusing her attention across the table.

"I was joking about the strippers."

"That didn't sound sincere."

"If Alex wanted strippers, I'd get him strippers."

"Would you want them at your bachelor party?"

"Nope." There wasn't the slightest hesitation in his answer.

"Are you humoring me?"

"No."

"Are you sure?"

The Travis she'd observed over the past two years was ribald and rowdy. She could easily picture him whooping it up at a bachelor party.

He sat forward, resting his forearms on the table and fixing his gaze on her. "If I was getting married, I expect I'd be seeing a gorgeous woman naked on a regular basis. I wouldn't have the slightest interest in anyone else."

Danielle had to give him points for that. "Good answer."

"Thank you. I'm not without experience."

"Seeing naked women?" she joked.

"Falling in love."

That answer threw her. "You're in love?"

Travis was in a relationship? What had she missed? And why had a knot suddenly formed in her stomach?

"I watched Caleb, Reed, Seth and Alex all fall head over heels in love. I think I know what to expect."

"But you're not in love yourself?"

"Not yet." His expression turned reflective. "But if it happens, I know I'll recognize the signs."

The knot in her stomach relaxed.

"Your turn," he told her, his inquiring tone putting her on alert. "Ever been in love?"

Unsure how much she wanted to disclose to Travis, she bought herself a moment, reaching for two of the flowers in the centerpiece, switching their places to fix the balance.

"I've dated men I liked," she allowed. "Some, I liked very much. But love?" She shook her head. "I probably wouldn't know the signs if they bit me on the backside."

"I can tell you the signs," Travis offered easily. "Or I can bite you on the backside. Your choice."

A rush of unexpected arousal raised the temperature on her skin.

Travis grinned. "You're blushing."

"I'm embarrassed. You're far too crude."

"No." He waggled his brows. "I'm exactly the right amount of crude."

Danielle couldn't help remembering Nadine's brazen comments. Crude could be sexy. Crude could be very, very sexy.

Three

When Travis spotted Danielle across the lobby that evening, he knew his hunch had paid off. Randal was with her, as he'd expected. They were part of a larger group that included her friends Astra, Nadine and Odette, obviously gathering together before leaving for a function.

She was dressed in a black cocktail dress. He wouldn't call it basic. It was off the shoulder, with a lace trimmed neckline that sparkled with inset jewels. The hammered satin molded to her breasts, fitting her waist, and flowed smoothly down to midthigh. She wore delicate diamond earrings, and a thin, diamond choker.

Her shoes were silver, barely there, with long, thin heels that made him want to peel them off and toss them in the corner of his hotel room.

Randal clearly felt the same way. The man was practically salivating as he gazed at her shapely legs. Danielle was slender, very much suited to elegant clothes. But, with big, brown eyes and full, red lips, she looked sophisticated one minute, innocent the next. A man didn't know whether to protect her or ravish her. Travis wanted to do both.

While the group chatted, he made his way closer. He'd picked up a suit in one of the hotel shops. It was basic, charcoal-gray, with a white shirt and silver striped tie. His hair was trimmed neat, his face clean-shaven. The only thing that differentiated him from the lawyers in the room was a pair of polished, black cowboy boots.

"Travis," Nadine sang out, motioning him over. "Look, Danielle. It's Travis."

Danielle spotted him, and her round eyes went wider still. It might have been the shock of having him show up unexpectedly, but he hoped it was surprise at how well he'd cleaned up.

He'd made her at least an hour late for her workshops this afternoon. He should have felt guilty about that, but he didn't. They hadn't made any plans to see each other again. But he'd guessed that whatever evening shindig was being put on by the conference would start in the lobby.

Nadine skipped over and gave him a friendly hug. She was dressed in deep purple with lots of sequins.

She pulled back. "You look terrific."

"Thanks." He made a show of taking in her dress and her dangling earrings. "You look very beautiful yourself."

She gave a delighted grin at the compliment.

His gaze moved to Danielle, catching Randal's scowl on the way by, and experiencing a thrill of satisfaction.

"Good evening, Danielle."

"Travis," she acknowledged evenly, an unspoken question in her eyes. She likely wanted to know what on earth he was doing.

"Nice to see you again, Randal." He nodded to the man. "Astra, Odette." His gaze paused on a thin, expensively dressed, older woman, standing next to a man who looked to be her husband.

"Claude and Catherine Hedley," Danielle introduced. "This is Travis Jacobs. Travis is from Lyndon Valley, Colorado. He's a friend of Caleb Terrell, Active Equipment, one of my major clients."

Catherine Hedley gave a warm smile. "So nice to meet you, Mr. Jacobs. Are you attending the conference?"

Travis stepped forward to gently shake the older woman's hand. "Please, call me Travis. I'm not a lawyer, ma'am."

Randal piped up. "He's a bull rider."

Claude Hedley looked surprised by the revelation.

"I'm a rancher, sir." Travis held out his hand to Claude. "Our spread is next door to Caleb's in Lyndon Valley."

"And he won first prize last night," Odette put in helpfully.

"Caleb diversified into Active Equipment many years ago," Danielle elaborated, obviously trying to make up for the social gaffe of being acquainted with a bull rider. "While the Jacobs family has gone into politics, the arts in New York, and a fast-growing international brewing company."

"The brewery is my brother-in-law," said Travis, unwilling to push the spin too far. "I just take care of the cattle."

Claude Hedley shook his hand. "Call me Claude. It sounds like your family is up and coming."

"His sister is Katrina Jacobs," said Astra. "The ballet dancer."

Travis glanced at her in surprise.

"I've got internet," said Astra.

"Danielle, your friend should join us for the reception," Catherine Hedley put in. Then she looked to Travis. "We're touring the Van Ostram Botanical Gardens."

Randal obviously couldn't hold his tongue. "I'm sure Travis has plans with the rodeo crowd."

"As a matter of fact," said Travis, glancing at his watch. "I just had a meeting postponed."

"That settles it," said Catherine with another smile. "You know, I do believe I've seen your sister dance."

"She's been with the Liberty Ballet for several years now."

"That makes sense, then."

"We can catch the limos out front," Claude offered, stretching out an arm to invite them to proceed.

Randal swiftly sidled up to Danielle. They were slightly ahead of Travis as the group began to move.

"What are you doing?" Randal hissed at her in clear annoyance.

"What do you expect me to do?"

"Get rid of him."

"How would you suggest I do that?"

Travis couldn't tell whether Danielle thought getting rid of him was a good idea or not. It didn't really matter, since he wasn't going anywhere except with her. Randal might be able to snow Danielle about his intentions, but Travis was on to him, and he was going to force the man to show his hand.

"You need their support," said Randal.

"They've already made me an offer," Danielle countered.

"Getting through the door is only the first step."

"Catherine invited him, not me."

"Everything the man says and does tonight will reflect on you."

Travis bit his tongue. He was tempted to tell Randal he'd do his level best not to spit and swear in front of the Hedleys. But he didn't want Randal to know he could overhear.

The group was forced to split up, taking two of the black Escalade SUVs. Randal jockeyed hard, but ended up with the Hedleys and Odette, where he politely, if reluctantly, offered to clamber into the third-row seat.

Travis intended to do the same in the other vehicle, but Nadine insisted that she, Astrid and Danielle could fit in the middle seat, and Travis should ride up front. The driver slanted a covetous glance at the three beautiful women in his rearview mirror and gave Travis a discrete thumbs-up as they pulled away.

When Astrid expressed a desire for breath mints, Travis asked the driver to stop and hopped out to buy them for her. He took enough time to be certain the Hedleys' group would have headed into the reception by the time the second Escalade arrived at the gardens.

Travis tipped the driver and helped each of the women out of the vehicle. The trees at the entrance were lit with tiny white lights. Glowing orange lanterns illuminated a stone walkway, while colored spots gave a fantasy aura to the leafy plants and flowering gardens.

Danielle moved up beside him as they passed a glowing, purple pond. "What exactly are you doing?"

Travis considered a range of answers and decided to be honest. "I'm making him stark raving mad."

"Why? I'm sure you had far better things to do tonight than hang out with a bunch of stuffy lawyers."

"You're not a stuffy lawyer."

"You know what I mean."

"He's going to show his hand, Danielle. He can't stand the competition, and he's going to make a pass at you. And then you'll know."

"Know what?"

Travis counted off on his fingers. "That he's willing to cheat on his girlfriend. That this was never about a job. That he wants you back in his life, back in his bed."

She went silent for a long moment. "It's not true."

"Yes, it is."

"Why do you even care?"

The question stopped Travis. It took him a minute to collect his thoughts. "I care because he's lying to you."

They walked a bit farther in silence, beneath a canopy of oaks, green, red and blue spots glowing up their trunks.

Finally, she drew an audible breath. "What you're doing doesn't make sense, Travis."

"Why does it have to make sense?" Even as he said the words, he knew she was right. He had absolutely no reason to meddle in her life.

"Everything has to make some kind of sense," she countered.

"Maybe to a lawyer. But cowboys operate on instinct."

She paused at the bottom of the stairs that led up to the pavilion, turning to face him. Astrid and Nadine were several yards ahead.

"And, what's your instinct telling you?" she asked.

He gazed down at her. His instinct was telling him to kiss her, and kiss her hard. But he couldn't do that here. Not that he could do it anywhere.

"It's telling me he's no good for you, Danielle. He's no good for you, and I'm the only guy around to stop him."

"I am a grown woman, Travis. I can stop him all by myself."

Travis smiled at that. In many ways it was true. But his way was faster, and he didn't like the odds that she'd end up getting hurt. "He's too sneaky, and you're too kind."

"What do you mean I'm kind? I fight with you *all* the time."

"It's safe for you to fight with me."

She tilted her pretty head sideways, and he couldn't help but think it was the perfect angle to kiss. "Your instincts telling you that, too?" she asked tartly.

"Yep. And they're infallible." He offered her his arm to walk up the staircase.

Inside the reception, Danielle left Travis to his own devises. She quickly found herself swept up in a whirlwind of introductions and conversations with the who's who of Nester and Hedley. It seemed they were interested in her South American experience. Brazil and Columbia were rising on everyone's trade radar in D.C., and their expertise was weak for the region. They saw an opportunity to get in early on this new wave, and they wanted Danielle to head up an entire division.

It was a genuine, exciting offer that didn't appear to have anything to do with Randal. In fact, she'd barely seen him since they arrived. The senior partners seemed to know her entire professional history, even details of Caleb's Active Equipment activities and challenges in Columbia.

It was close to eleven when, throat raw from talking over the music, and feet sore from her high shoes, she pushed her way up to a bar stool and asked the bartender for a soda and lime.

"He's watching you," came Travis's deep voice from behind her left ear. He took the stool next to her.

"He's barely said a word to me all night long. Honestly, the only person creeping me out here, is you."

"He's known where you were every second."

She angled toward him. "First, I don't believe you. Second, I've been talking with his bosses. They're the ones who have his attention, not me."

Travis reached for a handful of the snack mix on the bar. "Keep telling yourself that."

"I will, thank you very much."

The waiter set her drink down in front of her and looked to Travis for his order.

"Are you hungry?" Travis asked her. "Those little crab puffs and cheese squares didn't do it for me."

"I'm not leaving yet."

"I'll take a beer," Travis said to the waiter. "Whatever you've got on tap."

"It's by the bottle, sir."

Danielle couldn't help but grin as she stirred the ice in her soda and lime.

"Anything from DFB?"

"Mountain Red?"

"Sounds great."

The waiter turned to the glass-fronted refrigerator.

"This isn't a honky-tonk," Danielle pointed out.

"Are my country roots showing?"

She realized how snobby she sounded. "An honest mistake. No big deal."

The waiter returned with an open bottle of Mountain Red and a chilled pilsner glass. Travis handed him a tip, and Danielle realized she was the one who lacked class.

"How's it going?" Travis asked her as he tipped the glass and poured in the amber liquid. It foamed slightly at the top of the flared glass.

"They seem serious," she answered, gazing at the bubbles in her own drink. "They know a lot about me."

"Yeah? All good?"

She smiled to herself. "They think it's good. They know what I did for Active Equipment and a few others, and they want me to head up a South American division."

She couldn't help replaying the conversations in her mind. If Claude Hedley was to be believed, she'd be on the cutting edge of a global wave of interest. The earning potential would be massive, and she'd be in a position to set her own priorities and parameters.

"You going to take it?" asked Travis.

"I'm thinking about it," she answered honestly. Then it suddenly occurred to her she was talking to a close friend of Caleb's.

She quickly turned to take in his expression. "But…uh…"

He caught on quick. "You don't want me to tell Caleb."

Her hand went reflexively to his forearm. "I'd never ask you to lie. But it would be better for me if you didn't mention it to him right away."

He took a reflective drink of his beer. "Your secret's safe with me."

"Thank you. I'm sorry to put you in that position."

"I know you didn't do it on purpose."

"I really didn't think this through." Where had her common sense been yesterday when she'd mentioned this to Travis.

"Unusual for you?" he asked.

"Very."

"He's coming over."

"Who?"

"Randal. Who else." Travis's gaze went down. "You're touching me, and he feels threatened. He's about to stake his territory."

She immediately realized she hadn't taken her hand from Travis's arm. Then she realized his arm was warm, hot actually under her fingertips. He was solid, strong and alive. She didn't want to pull away.

"Don't panic," Travis muttered in an undertone. "But I'm going to touch your hair."

"Wha—"

Before she could finish the word, he gently brushed the back of his knuckles along her cheek, smoothing her hair back over her ear.

She froze, every nerve ending in her body focusing on the

gentle touch. Pings of awareness and desire shot out, sending signals of desire to every corner of her body.

"Dani," boomed Randal's voice. He wrapped a hearty arm around her shoulders and gave her a pat. "It looked like things went well?"

Travis's hand fell away. "Hello, Randal."

"Oh, Travis." Randal pretended he'd just noticed him. "How're you holding up here?"

"Managing just fine," Travis responded.

Randal turned his attention back to Danielle. "What did they say? More importantly, what did *you* say?"

"She hasn't made up her mind yet," Travis put in.

Randal sent him a glare. "I asked Dani."

"Well, *Dani* told me first."

"Travis," Danielle warned.

He was entitled to whatever theory he concocted, but that didn't give him the right to pick a fight.

Randal drew back his shoulders, lifting his chin. "She did, did she?"

"They offered me a South American division," she quickly told Randal.

"That's great." His shoulders relaxed. "I'm going to head up Europe, starting in September. We'd be at exactly the same level, on the partners' floor. I don't have to tell you, that's an impressive way to enter the firm."

"You don't have to tell me," Danielle agreed.

"The expense account is unlimited. The benefits are top-drawer, and the work is some of the most intellectually stimulating—"

"Randal?" she interrupted.

"Yes?"

"I've been listening to the sales pitch all night."

Travis stifled a chuckle.

Randal's attention immediately flew to him. "You got something to add here?"

"Not a thing," said Travis, polishing off his beer. "You're doing just fine all by yourself."

Randal glared a moment longer, but then something caught his attention across the room. "There's old man Nester." He squeezed Danielle's shoulder, lowering his voice to a conspiratorial level. "Give me three minutes to break into the conversation, then come over and join us."

He walked away.

Travis looked at Danielle, and she stared back.

"Well?" he asked.

She was all schmoozed out. Her feet were swelling. Her makeup was about to crack. And the last thing she wanted to do was humor the wheezy, narcissistic Edger Nester through what she'd heard tended to be half-hour-long discourses on the flaws in judicial procedure. If she took the job, she'd have to put up with it. But she wasn't there yet.

"I'm out of here," she told Travis.

His hand went immediately to her elbow, helping her down from the high stool, before turning them to a nearby side exit.

They came out into the gardens, quiet in the late hour. The breeze had picked up, cooling the air, and Travis quickly shrugged out of his suit jacket, draping it around her shoulders. They started down a winding flagstone walkway.

"That was a quick decision," he noted.

"I've only met Mr. Nester once, but I've heard tales of his boring orations, and I'm tired." She reached down and peeled off her sandals, moving to the soft grass at the side of the path. "My feet are killing me."

"You want me to carry you?" he offered.

She shook her head, though the thought of being held in his arms gave her a shiver of excitement. "This is nice." She curled her toes into the dense blades of grass.

He took up a slow pace, along the edge of a narrow brook, in the general direction of a purple lighted pond, leaving the music and laughter behind them. "If you resign, what will happen in Chicago?"

"You mean, what will happen to Active Equipment?"

"And your other clients."

"They'll be assigned to other lawyers."

"Does that worry you?"

"I'd feel guilty," she admitted, switching her sandals to the other hand. "But I'm not the only lawyer in the world. My firm has many other people who are perfectly capable of servicing my clients."

"So, there's nothing unique about you?"

She smiled at that. "I'd like to think there was. I'd like to think I was irreplaceable. But that would be a little conceited, right?"

His voice was low, sounding almost annoyed. "Some people *do* have to stay where they're needed."

"Do you think I'm letting Caleb down?"

"I wasn't talking about you."

She paused, tilting her head to peer up at him. "Who?"

He stopped walking, seeming to hesitate for a long moment, as the babble of the brook rose around them, the scent of the flowers sweetened the air. "I was talking about me."

"You're leaving Lyndon Valley?" She could hardly believe it. In her mind, Travis *was* Lyndon Valley. While the Terrells and the other Jacobs siblings might come and go from the ranches, Travis was the stalwart, always there, always available, always taking care of anything and everything.

He shook his head. "My point was, I *can't* leave Lyndon Valley. The ranch needs me."

"And you need the ranch." She thought she understood.

"Something like that." There was an edge to his voice.

"You think I'm abandoning the people who count on me."

It was hardly the same situation. Just because she'd gone to law school and started in a particular job, didn't mean she had to stay there forever.

"If you were abandoning them. If they told you, you were abandoning them. If you knew it would hurt them, would you stay?"

"That's a hypothetical situation." She'd like to think she'd done some good work for Caleb and the others over the years. But she'd hardly cripple anyone's business if she moved on.

"Hypothetically speaking, and I'm not going to hold you to it, if you knew it would hurt them, would you leave anyway?"

She searched his expression. "What are you getting at, Travis?"

He gazed at the lighted trees. "Responsibility, I guess—the kind of responsibility that paints a man into a corner and limits his choices."

She stepped forward, still not pinning down where he was going with this. "You're getting very philosophical on me, cowboy."

He gave a self-conscious smile. "Just trying to help you make a decision."

"You want me to stay in Chicago."

"I want you to understand the true details of your options."

A door banged shut on the pavilion, and several voices rose in the garden.

"He wouldn't come looking for me," Danielle said, more to herself than to Travis.

"Oh, yes, he would." Travis snagged her hand, striding across the sloped grass, tugging her toward a dark corner where they'd be screened from the path.

She had to trot to keep up.

They made their way behind a hedge, beyond the orange glow of the walkway lanterns, to a secluded corner where blue light filtered weakly through the maple leaves. Her mind went back over his words. He'd said it limited a man's choices, not a woman's choices, not a person's choices.

He abruptly stopped, and she nearly ran into him.

"Your feet okay?" he asked, turning.

"Travis, do you *want* to leave the ranch?"

"No."

She pondered a second longer. "But you resent that you can't. Or, wait a minute, you resent that you don't have the choice."

This time he hesitated before answering.

"You should tell them," she said.

"Tell them what?"

"That you—"

"That Katrina can't be a ballerina?" Travis spoke right over her, annoyance in his tone. "That Seth should give up being mayor? That Mandy can't be in Chicago with Caleb? Or that Abigail should force Zach to sell his brewery?"

Danielle definitely saw his point. It didn't make it fair, but she understood how he must feel.

"We're the fifth generation," he told her.

"That's a lot on your shoulders."

"They're broad shoulders."

Her gaze strayed. "Yes, they are."

"You won't say anything to Caleb."

"And mess with your self-righteous sense of nobility?"

"I'm not self-righteous."

She gazed up into his eyes. He was taller when her feet were bare. Taller, stronger, magnificent.

"You are noble," she whispered, finding herself shifting closer to him.

"I'm practical."

"You operate on instinct," she reminded him, tilting her chin, moistening her lips, wondering if she could possibly be more obvious.

"I do," he breathed.

"So, instinctively…"

His hands bracketed her hips, easing her against him. "Instinctively, I want to kiss you."

She smiled.

"But I've had that particular instinct for a long time now, and I'm not sure I should trust it."

"You should trust it."

His hands moved to her face, cradling it gently in his palms. "What about my other instincts?"

"You have other instincts?"

"To toss you down on the grass and ravish you in the moonlight."

Want and need instantly cascaded through her, weakening her knees and robbing her of her breath. She wished it didn't sound so tempting. There were a million complicated reasons to keep her distance from Travis, even if her own desires were screaming at her to ignore them.

She came up on her toes to meet him. "Let's take it one instinct at a time."

"Yes, ma'am." His lips came down on hers, warm and firm, fueled with purpose and expectation.

One arm went around her waist, the other bracing the back of her head. She dropped her sandals and clung to his shoulders. Then she ran her hands through his hair, pressing her body against his, parting her lips and inviting the sweep of his tongue.

His kiss deepened, and she clung tighter, letting the sweep of arousal and desire flood through her. Leaves clattered above them. A blue glow surrounded them. The grass was cool on her feet, while Travis's hot palm moved its way down her cheek, to her neck, to the bare shoulder revealed by her dress.

He stopped there, fingertips caressing against her skin.

He broke the kiss and pulled back, breathing deeply.

She had to blink the world back into focus.

"We have to stop now." His tone was slightly ragged.

"I know." She understood that they were playing with fire.

He stepped determinedly back, letting his hold drop away from her, putting space between them.

When he spoke again, his deep voice rumbled through her. "I guess that was inevitable."

"Kissing me?"

He held her gaze in the dim light. "Well, that, too. But I was thinking it was inevitable that kissing you would be fantastic."

Fantastic? She loved that word. Her skin glowed. Her lips tingled. Every inch of her body felt the sensual impact of Travis.

Still, *fantastic* didn't quite do it justice.

Four

"*That* was fantastic," Travis shouted to Corey as he clambered out of the dusty dune buggy in the parking lot of Desert High Rentals. He peeled off his crash helmet, calling again. "I think we've found a winner."

Corey gave him the thumbs-up as he stepped away from his own tube-style, open-air vehicle. It had once been red, but now was plastered with dirt and debris from their twenty-mile race across the desert.

"It's a toss-up between this and paintball," said Corey.

The two men started toward the compact, white-painted building and the chain-link compound that held neat rows of rental dune buggies.

"I was trying to figure out if we'd have time to do both," Travis added.

When Travis had called Corey this morning, Corey had quickly agreed to help out. So, they'd spent the day testing activities for the upcoming bachelor party.

Hot air ballooning had been a bust—too sedentary. Sky diving was another option, but they couldn't count on everyone buying into that. They'd looked into bus and boat tours, and even gambling, but Travis was pretty sure thrills and adrenaline was the way to go.

A keg of beer, spicy, fried junk food and the Colorado Rockies game on the big screen at the Emperor Plaza's Ace High

Lounge was a given. Travis had booked it for the private party Friday night.

"How early will these guys be willing to get up?" Corey asked.

"They're mostly cowboys. But I guess it depends on how it goes Thursday night—whether things stay down to a dull roar. Caleb's pilot is flying everybody in around four."

Thursday would be informal. They'd stop by a bar or two along the Strip, maybe play a little poker.

"Book paintball for the morning," said Corey. "If they get blasted the night before, they can bloody well cowboy up."

Travis grinned. Better to have too much planned than too little.

"Paintball, it is," agreed Travis. "Followed by dune buggy racing in the afternoon, and then Ace High for the night."

"The guys can all crawl to their rooms from there."

"We should have been party planners," said Travis as he set his helmet down on the counter, in the shade of the porch at the rental building.

"Party planners don't get the girls," Corey responded.

"How'd it go out there?" asked the rotund, fifty-something clerk as he set his magazine down and stood to meet them.

"Great," Travis replied. "It's a very exciting course. We're looking to bring a group back with us on Friday afternoon."

The man pulled a clipboard down from a hook on the wall and rustled up a pen from a drawer beneath the counter. "How many in your group?"

"About thirty. Better make it thirty-five to be safe."

The man's bushy brows went up. "Thirty guys? Do they each need their own buggy?"

"I'd plan on that," said Travis.

The man stepped away, opening a back door to shout outside. "Micky. Can you do thirty-five for Friday afternoon?"

The response was muffled.

"Well, call the parts store. Get them to overnight freight."

Another muffled response.

Travis glanced at Corey, who made a show of crossing his fingers. "We don't want to go with the river boat tour."

"Not unless they can guarantee models in bikinis."

"And that zip line seemed pretty lame."

Travis agreed. Though it sounded exciting to soar suspended hundreds of feet above the ground, in reality, it had been more like an amusement park ride. You had no control over anything that happened. You just hung there and watched the scenery go by.

The dune buggy man turned back to them. "We can cover you." He made a notation on his clipboard. "If this is a corporate event, you better check your insurance." He handed Travis a written brochure.

Travis glanced at it without reading. "If it's a private event?"

The man gave a gap-toothed grin. "Better buy yourself some event insurance. This ain't covered under your regular homeowner's policy."

"Then I guess it's a corporate event," said Travis. "Can we bring a credit card with us Friday?"

"Sure thing." The man glanced at today's rental agreement. "Mr. Jacobs."

Travis reached out to shake the man's hand. "Thanks for your help."

With a nod, Corey slid his helmet across the counter, and they turned to step off the low porch.

"There's a place called South Rim, partway back on the highway," said Corey as they crossed the asphalt parking lot under the scorching sun. "It's pretty laid-back, burgers and steaks. About a dozen beers on tap. Might work for lunch on Friday. You want to check it out?"

"Sure," Travis agreed, pressing the unlock button on his rented SUV. "I could absolutely go for a beer."

It was nearly five o'clock, and his other option was going back to the hotel. If he went back to the hotel, he was sure he'd go against his better judgment and start hunting around for Danielle.

It had been a mistake to kiss her last night. He knew it then, and he knew it now. But a man could only take so much. And being alone in the dark with a beautiful, desirable woman, who scoffed at the right moments, laughed at the right moments and gazed up at him with huge, dark bedroom eyes, well, kissing her had been inevitable.

He levered into the driver's seat and started the engine, peeling out of the parking lot and onto the road.

He'd relived the kiss about a thousand times already. Then he'd thought about doing it again, thought about doing even more, then he'd pulled himself ruthlessly back. Danielle was Danielle, the same woman he'd fought with for months. She had a professional relationship with his brother-in-law Caleb, another one with his sister Katrina for the Sasha Terrell Fund.

Nothing had changed between them. He'd found Danielle sexy as soon as he'd met her. She found him coarse and unrefined. She didn't like his sense of humor, thought his perspective was limited, thought he was and always would be a hick cowboy from backwater Colorado.

It was all true, and no amount of sexual attraction was going to change any of that. Which meant nothing more could happen between them.

He smacked a hand down on the steering wheel in frustration.

"What?" Corey turned to look.

"Nothing."

"You don't want to go to the South Rim?"

"The South Rim is fine. I'm hungry, and I'm damn sure thirsty."

"Well, okay, then."

Brimming with pent-up energy, Travis ignored the double line on the highway, pulling out to pass a semi as they wound up a hill. A pickup suddenly crested the rise, and he slammed the brakes, dumping his speed and pulling back behind the tractor trailer. Both the semi and the pickup driver leaned on their horns.

Corey gripped the handrail on the ceiling of the SUV. "Well. That was exciting."

"They need more passing lanes," Travis grumbled.

"We should have let you take another lap on the dune buggy." Corey sat back. "Work whatever the heck it is out of your system."

Travis knew what he needed to work this out of his system, and no motor vehicle could help him. He found his mouth flexing in a wry smirk. What he needed, he couldn't have.

"What?" Corey asked again.

The double lines ended, replaced by a single, broken line, and he ducked out to check for oncoming traffic. This time he could definitely make it. He stepped on the accelerator.

"I think whiskey's my best bet," he called to Corey as the engine revved higher.

"That sounds like girl trouble to me," Corey called back, hand gripping the handle again.

"It is girl trouble," Travis admitted.

"Back home?"

"In Vegas." He pulled back into the right lane, backing off and letting his speed drop down again.

"You've only been here two days."

"I work fast."

"Parking lot's coming up on your right. Past the motel and the park. The green sign."

Travis slowed, flipping on his signal light, and pulling to the shoulder so he wouldn't slow the semi down as it built up speed on the downhill grade.

The South Rim was a long, low brown building, perched on the side of a canyon. The floorboards on the deck squeaked under their boots as they made their way to an oversized, red door. Travis opened it to reveal a dim room with a polished, red wood bar, heavy tables and comfortable looking leather chairs, all surrounding three well-kept pool tables.

On the far side, glass doors led out to a deck that overlooked the canyon. The deck was dotted with low, planked tables and

Adirondack chairs, turned toward the view. Vintage rock music gave a muted backdrop from overhead speakers, while the smell of grilling burgers hung in the air.

"Go ahead and grab a table," called a thirty-something woman from behind the bar. She was wearing a white blouse over a pair of black slacks, with her hair pulled back in a neat ponytail.

A dozen of the thirty or so tables were occupied, and a few people sat out on the deck. Two men shot a game at one of the pool tables. It was obviously an adult crowd, and conversation seemed cheerful and relaxed.

"You want to shoot a game?" asked Corey as he ambled toward a table.

"Sure." Travis dropped his hat on a chair and rolled up the sleeves of his white-and-gray checked shirt.

Realizing how much sand and dust had clung to him from the dune buggy ride, he headed for the men's room to take off a layer. Looking at himself in the mirror, he couldn't help but be impressed that none of the staff had turned their noses up as he and Corey walked in.

By the time he got back to the table, the waitress had produced glasses of ice water and a couple of menus. Travis ordered a beer and selected a pool cue.

"Hi there," came a soft female voice as a blond woman sauntered over to him. At a nearby table, a brunette closely watched the exchange.

"I'm Sandy," she introduced.

"Travis," he returned. "Nice to meet you."

The men's room door banged shut behind Corey. Then a smile lit his face as he approached the pool table.

"Corey," he introduced himself to the woman, holding out his broad hand.

"Sandy," she repeated. Then she turned to look at the brunette. "My friend is Linda."

"You gals from around here?" asked Corey.

She grinned. "We 'gals' are from California. San Diego. You?"

"I'm a bullfighter on the pro bull riding circuit."

"You're one of those guys with a red cape and a tight, gold-tassel-covered jacket?"

Travis coughed out a laugh at the image.

"That's in Spain, not in Nevada. I'm the guy in blue jeans who saves the cowboy's ass when the rangy brahma bull bucks him off and threatens to gore him or trample him." He gestured to Travis. "Guys like him. I saved his life on Saturday night."

Sandy looked to Travis. "That true?"

"It's true," Travis affirmed as he racked up the balls.

Linda rose from the table and wandered over. "You're a bull rider?" she asked Travis.

"I'm a rancher. Eight ball?" he asked Corey.

The waitress returned with Travis's beer, and Corey ordered one for himself. "Eight ball it is," he said to Travis. "So, what do you women do in San Diego?"

"We're caterers, mostly weddings, but corporate parties, too."

"Isn't that a coincidence." Corey took the break, hitting the racked balls hard and sending them shooting across the table. None went into a pocket. "We're planning a party right now."

"What kind of a party?" she asked.

"Bachelor party," said Corey.

"So, you'll be down on the Strip?"

"Part of the time," said Corey.

Travis called solids and took his first shot, putting away the six ball.

Corey gave a groan at the nice shot. "We're also doing paint-ball and dune buggy racing."

Travis couldn't help but hope Corey didn't mention their plans for lunch here. The women seemed nice enough, but this party wasn't going to be about pickups.

"Is one of you the groom?" asked Linda.

Corey grinned as he shook his head. "We're the party planners."

"The groom is a friend," said Travis. This time he sank the four.

"Am I being hustled?" asked Corey with obvious good humor.

"Does the groom live in Vegas?" asked Sandy.

"Colorado," answered Corey.

Travis missed the three, and Corey chalked his cue.

Sandy moved away from Corey, bringing her closer to Travis.

"So, Mr. Bull Riding Rancher, are you—"

"Would you like to order lunch?" The waitress's question interrupted.

Relieved, Travis turned his attention to the woman. "I'll take a cheeseburger."

"Same here," called Corey as he lined up on the ten ball. He pulled back his cue and made a perfect shot.

"Who's hustling who?" Travis joked, moving from the pool table to their dining table to take a drink of his beer.

He hadn't wanted Sandy to finish her purring question. He wasn't in the mood to flirt. His mind kept slipping to Danielle, wondering where she was, if Randal was with her, if he'd made a move on her.

Corey sank two balls in rapid succession. Then he missed, leaving a promising-looking table for Travis.

Conversation between Corey and the two women swirled around him, with the occasional burst of laughter. Travis worked his way through the rest of the solids, earning cheers from the women as he made a particularly tricky bank shot to sink the seven.

He easily finished up the eight ball to take the game.

"I guess you're buying lunch," he said to Corey as the waitress arrived with their burgers.

"You're the one with the good payday," Corey countered. "And I did—"

"I know. I know," Travis cut in. "You saved my life."

Travis returned his pool cue to the rack.

"Nice meeting you," he said to Sandy and Linda as he headed to sit down.

Corey obviously picked up on Travis's thinking. He also said goodbye, rather than asking the women to join them.

They hesitated slightly, but then returned to their own table.

"What the hell?" asked Corey as he swung into his chair across from Travis.

"I just want to eat." Travis stuffed a fry into his mouth then took another swallow of beer.

Corey frowned as he lifted his high-stacked burger. "After I did such a great job of chatting them up for you."

"They weren't really my type."

"Beautiful, friendly and built isn't your type?"

It was Travis's turn to frown. "Charming," he mocked.

"I think you'd better tell me a little more about this Vegas woman trouble. It's obviously cramping your style. Which wouldn't bother me much, except that it's blowing back on me."

"There's nothing to tell."

"Uh-huh." Corey's tone was clearly skeptical.

"She's hot, but she's off-limits."

"She's married?"

"Not married. There's a professional relationship to maneuver around. Two of them, actually."

"Can you fix them?"

"Nope."

"Then my advice to you is move on."

"That's what I'm doing."

Well, he'd move on as soon as he opened Danielle's eyes about Randal's motives. Travis losing didn't mean Randal got to win.

The conference's windup golf tournament had finished, with Randal taking fourth place. Danielle suspected he could have done better, but he'd once confided in her that winning outright was a bad strategy for a young lawyer. In his estimation, it was better to be strongly competitive, but to let the senior people prevail, at least for a while.

The final dinner was in full swing, a gourmet buffet set up in the gardens of the hotel, the aromas of sage and rosemary from the steamer trays mingling with vanilla and cinnamon at the dessert display. White linen covered tables were illuminated by floodlights and torches.

At one of the many bars set up around the perimeter of the lawn, Danielle accepted another "superior court" drink. It was a special recipe invented by the hotel's chief bartender for the conference. It was a surprisingly delicious concoction of fruit juices, crushed ice, tequila and liquors. It was the final night of the conference. She planned to take advantage of the pool deck in the morning while her colleagues all flew home, so a little indulgence in liquor tonight suited her just fine.

"Thank you, Caleb," she muttered under her breath, toasting him in absentia. If he hadn't requested a meeting on Thursday, she wouldn't be in line for an impromptu mini vacation tomorrow.

Randal separated himself from the crowd, coming up beside her. "You didn't golf?" he opened.

He'd changed into suit and tie since the tournament ended, and now looked urbane and confident with a three-olive martini in one hand.

"That's because my golfing is not going to impress anyone."

"Nobody cares how well you golf at these things."

"Also," she elaborated, "I don't particularly like golf."

She sipped the frozen drink through a straw, while her lightweight dress rustled against her thighs in the night breeze.

"It's a great way to build relationships. Everybody who is anybody is out on the links at something like this."

"I was happier chatting with Astra."

Randal polished off the martini, exchanging the empty glass for a fresh drink as a waiter passed, taking an immediate sip. "Astra won't get you a partnership. Besides, you can chat with Astra any old time."

"She lives in New York." It wasn't very often the two women got the chance to see each other in person.

Randal frowned. "That's not what these things are for."

"You do realize that you care more about schmoozing and corporate climbing than most people."

"I care more than you do," Randal acknowledged. "But I don't care more than most people. Honestly, Dani, sometimes you are so naive."

"Naive? Are you serious?" She'd been called a lot of things in her lifetime, but never naive.

He took another sip of his drink, prompting her to do the same. The superior courts tasted best when they were ice-cold.

"You seem content to stand by and let people blow past you."

"What people?" she challenged.

He made an expansive gesture with one arm. "These people. All people. Well, all lawyers." He moved forward, dramatically lowering his voice, and she realized he must have had a few martinis before he got here. "You have a brilliant mind, Dani." His gaze focused on the neckline of her black-and-blue dress. "You have the whole package." He looked her in the eyes again. "But you seem singularly intent on wasting it."

She was starting to get annoyed. "I'm not wasting anything." She'd spent five years developing her knowledge of international law.

"When you hesitate. When Nester and Hedley make you a sweetheart of an offer, and you hesitate, do you know how that looks?"

"Like I'm prudent and conscientious?"

"Like you're indecisive and ungrateful."

"*Ungrateful?* Excuse me?"

His voice rose a little. "They're the top law firm in D.C., probably the most prestigious in the country."

"It's still a big decision," Danielle found herself feeling defensive. This time, she took a calming sip of her drink. Taste had nothing to do with it.

"What's to decide?" he demanded.

She listed off on her fingers. "To leave my firm. To leave my city. To leave my friends."

"You'll make new friends."

"I have some very good friends."

"Male friends?"

BARBARA DUNLOP   63

She frowned. "Some. What difference does it make?"

Randal shrugged and polished off his drink. "That sounds like it might be a boyfriend."

She pressed her lips together, thinking it was probably time to end the conversation.

"Is that what it is, Dani? You won't come to D.C. because of some guy you're sleeping with?"

"That's none of your business," Travis's voice interrupted as he loomed up next to Randal.

Randal twisted around to face him, his jaw clamping down. "This is a private party."

"Hello, Travis." Danielle couldn't help but feel grateful for his arrival.

"Hello, Danielle."

Randal's gaze darted from one to the other, settling on Travis. "How did you get in here?"

Travis kept his gaze on Danielle. "I flashed my belt buckle."

She couldn't help but grin.

"Everything okay?" Travis asked her.

Randal angled his body toward Travis. "That's none of *your* business."

"I'm fine," Danielle quickly put in, at the same time willing Travis to stay put. She had no desire to return to her conversation with Randal.

"Are you hungry?" Travis asked, seeming to read her mind. "Can I get you a fresh drink?"

"We're having a private conversation here," Randal firmly stated.

Travis's gaze slowly moved to Randal. "Yeah?"

"Yeah."

"Well, maybe you want to do that in a less public place."

Randal turned to Danielle. "Let's go."

She didn't know how to react. She didn't want to be rude to Randal, but she certainly didn't want to leave the party with him.

"Aren't there more people you need to see?" she asked, glancing around. Surely Randal wouldn't give up an opportunity to schmooze.

"There's something I need to ask you." There was a determination in his eyes.

"Right now?"

"Right now." He reached for her hand, twining his fingers around hers.

She automatically pulled back, and his hand came with hers.

Travis stepped forward, tone hard, words deliberate. "Let her go."

Randal held his ground, glaring at Travis. Both men were still and silent for what seemed like a full minute.

Finally, Randal let go of her hand.

He turned to Danielle. "I'd like to speak with you."

"Let's do it later." She wasn't afraid of Randal, but his behavior bordered on the bizarre.

He stared at her for another long moment.

"Fine," he ground out. "Later."

With a withering look at Travis, he turned to stalk away.

"That was weird," she couldn't help commenting.

"You okay?"

"Perfectly fine." She shook off her feelings. "You?"

Travis grinned. "I've been to plenty of parties that ended in fights."

She shook her head at the ridiculous notion. "You weren't going to fight."

"He wasn't going to fight. I would have."

"You're incorrigible."

"Just from a different part of the country than him."

"What are you doing here?"

Randal had been right on that count, this was a private party, only the conference delegates had been invited. She doubted very much that flashing a bull riding belt buckle would have got Travis past security.

"Hedley invited me. Probably thanks to your exaggeration of my family's artistic and political success."

"That's how you play the game." She glanced down and noticed her drink glass was empty.

Travis noticed, too, and took it from her, quickly flagging down a passing waiter and handing it off.

"Thanks," she told him.

"Would you like another?" he asked.

"I think I will. Thanks to Caleb, I don't have to go to work in the morning."

"I was hoping to find you here," said Travis as they moved toward a nearby bar. "I need your advice on something,"

"You mean you didn't come to the party to mingle with lawyers and judges?" Out of the corner of her eye, she caught sight of Randal.

He was talking to one of the conference presenters. He glanced up, and their gazes met. She quickly looked away.

"As appealing as that sounds..." said Travis.

Danielle smiled at his sarcasm.

"I'm going to have to sign a contract on Thursday. I'm sure it'll be a simple matter for you, but I need to make sure I understand the liability."

She tried to switch to her lawyer brain, and quickly realized she was a little tipsy. "What kind of a contract?"

"Dune buggy racing."

She rested her hand on the bar and turned to peer at him. "Excuse me?"

"For the bachelor party. Thirty or so guys are all going dune buggy racing. Either me, or the ranch, or maybe Active Equipment, needs to pay the bill and make sure our insurance covers the liability." He switched his attention to the approaching bartender. "Can you give us two of those tall, frothy, orange things."

"You probably want to ask me tomorrow instead," said Danielle. "I've already had a couple of drinks, so I can't guarantee the quality of my advice."

He smiled at her. "Tomorrow's fine."

The bartender set the drinks on the bar top, and Travis handed him a tip.

"So, do you believe me now?" Travis asked as they turned away, heading in the general direction of the fountain pool.

"Believe you about what?"

"About Randal's motives."

"No," she answered with confidence.

Nothing had changed.

"He tried to hold your hand," Travis pointed out.

"He tried to get me away from you."

Travis took a sip of the drink and grimaced. Then he held it up to the light, inspecting it. "Really? *This* is what you're drinking."

"Cowboy up," she told him, using an expression she'd borrowed from Caleb.

"I think I'd rather come off a bucking bull."

"Wimp," she muttered.

"And why do you think he was so hell-bent on getting me away from you?" Travis asked.

"I don't know if you've noticed." They came to an empty bench facing the gardens, and she sat down. "But Randal doesn't like you much. And you're not helping matters by being so sarcastic all the time."

Travis sat down at the other end of the bench. "I don't know if *you've* noticed, but I'm not trying to make friends with Randal."

"Really?" she drawled with exaggerated sarcasm.

"I'm the competition, and he knows it."

"Oh, get over yourself."

"I kissed you, and he didn't."

"I used to date him, Travis." As soon as the words left her mouth, she regretted them.

Travis shifted on the bench. "I mean lately."

"Okay, no," she backpedaled. "He hasn't kissed me lately. Not in five years, as a matter of fact."

Travis took another, tentative sip of the drink, turning up his nose again. "Whereas, I kissed you last night. And he can tell it by my swagger."

"That's crazy." She tried for a haughty tone, but her words came out breathy as memories of the kiss bloomed in her mind.

Her body's reaction was nearly as strong as it had been in the garden, making her grateful to be in the middle of a crowd. Since, it was frighteningly tempting to do it again.

"What do you think he wanted to talk about?" Travis asked.

She pulled herself back from the unbidden fantasy. "He thinks I'm insulting Nester and Hedley by not snapping up their offer. He believes, and he's right, that they're the most prestigious law firm in D.C., and people would crawl over broken glass for the chance they're giving me."

"Doesn't mean it's right for you."

"Doesn't mean it's wrong."

Travis seemed to give that some thought. "Did he have anything to do with you getting the offer?"

"He says not." She took another drink.

"He also said he has a serious girlfriend."

"We have no evidence to suggest otherwise."

"Oh, yes, we do."

She pinned him with a dubious stare. "You are by far the most clairvoyant cowboy I have ever met."

"Doesn't take a mind reader to see what that guy's thinking."

Before she could respond, a neatly dressed waiter appeared in front of them. "Kobe beef sliders?" he asked, holding a silver tray out to Danielle.

"Yes, please," she answered, realizing she was hungry. She helped herself to a cocktail napkin and one of the mini burgers.

Travis took two.

"If I don't eat something soon," said Danielle. "You'll have to pour me into bed."

The waiter quirked an amused smile as he backed away, and she realized how the words sounded.

She glanced at Travis. "I didn't mean…"

He grinned at her embarrassment. "I know what you meant."

A second waiter arrived, this one carrying a tray of champagne. At his offer, Danielle held up her half-full superior court and shook her head.

"Any chance I can exchange this for a beer?" Travis asked.

"Of course, sir." The waiter took his drink.

"Anything from DFB," said Travis.

"I'll be right back."

"You're very loyal," Danielle couldn't help but note as the waiter disappeared.

"Zach makes very good beer."

"Lots of companies make very good beer."

"Lots of companies aren't co-owned by my brother-in-law and the man who's engaged to my cousin."

"Unusually loyal," said Danielle, biting into the burger.

"And you're not?" asked Travis. "Don't they make lawyers take some kind of an oath?"

"That's confidentiality. And that's a professional relationship, not something lifelong like family."

Travis's tone turned curious. "What about your family?"

"What about them?"

"Are you close? You must be loyal to them." He examined one of the tiny burgers, biting off half.

"Loyal? Of course. Close? Well, we're not exactly that kind of family."

"What kind of family are you?"

"Just me and my parents."

"Are they lawyers?"

"They have law degrees, but they're corporate executives in New York City. Dad works in Midtown for a transportation conglomerate. Mom's downtown at an international fashion chain."

"Do you see them often?"

"Not really. We're not a, you know, Sunday dinner in the suburbs, confide your deepest secrets kind of family. We're all pretty self-sufficient."

He looked curious. "What does self-sufficient mean?"

She pondered how to elaborate. "You know how some mothers want their daughters to find a good man, get married and give them grandchildren?"

"I do," he nodded.

"My mother wasn't like that. She always told me not to count on a man to take care of me. It was vital that I educate myself, develop a good career. And if, *if* I decided to one day get married, it should be an equal partnership, with an iron-clad prenup to protect me when it all fell apart."

"That's not very romantic."

"Maybe not, but it is very practical." Danielle took another bite of the burger. "This is delicious."

"I was thinking cynical."

"Not delicious?" she joked.

"So, what would your mother think about Randal?"

"That I ought to be doubly careful with the prenup, since he's a smart attorney."

Travis smiled at that. "Maybe you should marry a dumb cowboy instead."

"Sure." She kept her tone deliberately light, memories of their kiss still doing a number on her hormones. "Know any?"

Travis laughed. "Was that an actual compliment?"

For a second she was puzzled.

"You don't think I'm dumb?" he prompted.

"I never thought you were dumb."

"Sure you did."

"I thought you were annoying."

"Your beer, sir." The waiter approached. "DFB C Mountain Ale."

"Perfect," said Travis, accepting the tall glass. "Thanks."

The waiter nodded and withdrew.

"Do you still think I'm annoying?" Travis asked, taking a swig.

"Sometimes," she admitted. Though those times were getting fewer and farther between. The Travis she was coming to know in Vegas wasn't like the one she remembered in Lyndon Valley.

"I'll try to do better," he offered.

"And here I thought you were *trying* to be annoying."

He gave a sheepish shrug. "Sometimes, I am. But only because I thought you were a snob."

"I'm not a snob," she told him with conviction. "I'm self-sufficient."

He thought about that for a moment. "I'm sorry about your family. They don't sound like much fun."

"They've been my family for a long time. I'm used to them." Though, for some reason, she found his sympathy touching.

His blue eyes were soft in the dim light, his expression uncharacteristically caring. He was handsome. He was sexy. He was smarter than she'd expected. And now he seemed genuinely compassionate.

She could feel herself being pulled to a very dangerous place. She struggled to remember all the reasons he irked her. He was a sarcastic, smart-ass, dusty, sweaty, tough-as-nails cowboy, who didn't have any use for big-city lawyers. He might kiss her, but he was never going to respect her as a person. If she let this thing go any further, she was definitely going to get hurt. Travis, on the other hand, would saunter away unscathed.

She forced herself to glance at her watch. "I think I'll call it a night."

"Had enough of lawyers?"

"Had one too many drinks." She rose to her feet. "These things are giving me a headache."

Travis rose with her. "Do you want me to walk you to the elevators?"

She quickly shook her head. "I'll be fine."

The last thing she was going to do was give herself a chance for second thoughts. She was walking away from Travis, his deep blue eyes, his strong, broad shoulders and his sexy smile, right this second. And she wasn't looking back.

Five

Danielle made her way along a fieldstone walkway that was illuminated by yellow-toned pot lights, past the lush gardens, the overhanging oak trees, and across a small footbridge that covered a babbling brook. She passed a few guests coming the other way, while the noise of the conference party gradually faded away behind her.

"Had enough?" Randal's voice unexpectedly broke the quiet as he came up beside her on the narrow path.

"Getting tired," she told him, deciding it was best to simply ignore their tiff from earlier.

"It was a good conference," he offered.

"Interesting discussions," she agreed. "I'm not sure I concur with the direction the country seems to be taking on tariffs for emerging economies."

"You have to remove the exemption at some point," Randal countered. "Or you risk flooding the market and compromising domestic manufacturing."

"Maybe," she allowed. "But you also risk protectionism on the other side. Then again, I'm a little drunk, and so are you. This might not be the best time to make any sweeping policy decisions."

Randal laughed at that, sounding more like his old self, and she found herself relaxing.

"So, have you decided?" he asked.

"About moving to D.C.?"

"Yes, about moving to D.C. What else is there for you to decide?"

Whether or not to sleep with Travis was the first thing that came to Danielle's mind. But as quickly as the thought formed, she squelched it. She wasn't going to go there. There were less than two days until they went their separate ways, possibly for good. Once she was back in Chicago, and especially if she left there for D.C., she was certain these feelings would disappear.

"Danielle?" Randal prompted.

"I told them I'd let them know in a week."

He was silent, but she could feel his disapproval.

"It's the best I can do," she offered into the silence.

It was a great offer, but it was also a very big decision. Caleb Terrell wasn't the only client she'd miss working with. There were another half dozen that she'd represented for years. Their holdings were complex and interesting, and she liked to think she was a pivotal piece of their international successes so far.

"You're overthinking," said Randal, his voice tight.

The path widened out to a small, dim courtyard. A waterfall splashed at one side.

She stopped. She wasn't overthinking. She was thinking exactly the right amount, given the magnitude of the decision. And she wished he'd back off and let her do it.

"We can't keep having this same argument," she told him.

He gave her an easy smile. "We're lawyers. That's what we do."

"Well, I'm tired of doing it."

"Danielle." With a gentle hand on her shoulder, he urged her to one side of the courtyard.

She drew a deep sigh, but went along because she wanted to get this over with and get back to her room.

"Say whatever you need to say," she told him. "And then I'm going to bed."

His expression faltered for a second. But then it smoothed out. "Danielle." He took her hands in his.

She glanced down, uncomfortable with the intimacy of the gesture.

"I'm afraid if you leave here without deciding, you'll go back, get comfortable in Chicago, and you won't do what's best for you."

She raised her brows, looking at his face. "And you think you know what's best for me?"

"I know you pretty well," he countered.

"You once knew me pretty well," she corrected.

"I still do. People don't change that much." He paused, and his expression turned intense. "You and me…"

She was getting a bad feeling here. "You and me, what?"

His hands squeezed hers. "I can't help but wonder if we made a mistake. Moving to different cities, breaking things off, we never really—"

"Wait a minute." She tugged her hands from his. "You said you had a girlfriend."

"I do." He nodded rapidly. "I do. But, well, I'm not exactly sure where that's going."

"Don't do this, Randal. I'm not—"

He put an index finger across her lips. "Shh."

She was too shocked by his touch to react.

"Let it happen," he told her.

To her horror, he leaned in, tilting his head, closing his eyes, clearly intending to kiss her.

"Randal!" she squealed, quickly jumping back.

His eyes popped open and he stumbled.

"What do you think you're doing?" she demanded.

He rubbed his hand along her arm. "I'm showing you what can be."

"It can't be. It's not going to be."

"You can't possibly know that. We had something great once. If you take this job, if you come to D.C., we'll have a second chance."

She shook her head, moving farther back, and his hand dropped from her arm. "I'm not looking for a relationship, Randal."

"I'm not talking about two kids, a dog and a white picket

fence. We can be good for each other. I can be great for your career."

She didn't deny that. Randal was a very successful lawyer, well respected in D.C. and across the country.

He stepped forward, expression softening, tone cajoling. "I'm not asking for a decision right this minute."

"I'm not going to mislead you, Randal. Yours isn't a direction I'm going in right now."

His features tightened. "So, *that* you can decide right here and right now?"

"Yes." She was positive she didn't want to rekindle something with Randal, surprisingly positive, in fact.

He frowned in annoyance. "It's him, isn't it?"

"Him, who? There is no him."

"The bull rider." There was venom in his tone. "You've got the hots for the bull rider."

"That's none of your business."

"That means yes."

She stepped away. "Good night, Randal."

"Danielle." His tone turned sweet as he took a step toward her.

"Don't." She held up her palms to stop him, continuing to walk backward. "You've had too much to drink. At least I hope you've had too much to drink. This isn't like you."

"Dani."

"No." She turned on her heel, walking swiftly down the path toward the hotel lobby.

There, she turned abruptly into the ladies' room, letting the door close behind her and dropping into a padded, French provincial chair in the entry area. She'd hide here for as long as it took, hours if necessary. But she wasn't going to risk running into Randal again.

Her mother had been right. And if it wasn't so late, Danielle might have been tempted to pick up a phone and tell her so. A woman couldn't trust any man to look out for her best interest. Men would always look out for their own.

* * *

Back-to-back with his paintball team member Reed Terrell, Travis gasped for breath. They were crouched behind a wooden barrier, having sprinted away from the "enemy." Both men were decked out in protective gear, and each held a paintball rifle filled with yellow balls. They'd split into three teams, blue, red and yellow. He and Reed were the last of the yellow team to still be "alive."

"How many do you think are out there?" Reed asked.

"Alex for sure on blue."

Reed coughed out a deep laugh. "Nobody wants to kill the groom."

Travis gripped his weapon. "I've got no problem killing the groom. But I think Caleb's still alive on red, and maybe Seth, too."

"I'll take out your brother, if you want to take out mine."

"I got Zach on the other side of the hill. So, I don't think there's anyone else besides Alex left on blue."

Something clanged against metal, and both men stilled.

"The shed," said Travis.

Reed peeked over the top of the wooden wall. "If we're fast, we can make the trench and follow it down to the hay bales."

"I'm fast," said Travis. "But you're more power than agility."

"You go first. I'll cover you, and maybe you'll get a shot."

"Unless he's inside the shed."

"Or maybe on the roof." Reed reached out and tapped Travis's shoulder, silently pointing upward.

Travis saw it, too. A slight movement at the peak of the roof. "Seth," he said.

"You sure?"

"Oh, yeah. He had that twisted gray thing on his helmet."

Reed peeked up again. "You can see from here?"

"Just a glimpse. But it's him."

Three rapid-fire shots echoed through the air, paintballs smacking against the wooden wall.

"They've found us," said Travis.

"Go for the trench."

Travis nodded. "On three."

Reed counted off. When he got to three, Travis sprinted out of their cover while Reed shot over his head.

He dove into the trench, quickly checking himself for paint splatters. He was unscathed.

He looked back and gave Reed a thumbs-up. Reed pointed toward the hill, and Travis quickly looked over, spotting Caleb. It took him a second to realize that Caleb was creeping up on Alex. He quickly signaled Reed to hold.

Caleb made it, stood up and fired once at Alex, hitting him in the back. Travis took three shots, hitting Caleb with two of them. Caleb turned in shock before going down on one knee. Travis quickly turned his attention to Seth.

It was obvious Seth knew somebody was in the trench, but he couldn't see Travis. He did, however, have a chance at hitting Reed. Travis bounced a shot off the near side of the roof and shouted for Reed to run. He shot again and again, hearing Reed's footsteps behind him.

Reed plunged into the trench beside him, breathing hard.

"Took out Caleb," said Travis.

"I saw that. Just Seth left?"

"I think so."

"I can almost taste the free beer," laughed Reed.

"He's got the high ground," Travis pointed out.

"Yeah, but he's practically a city slicker these days. And there are two of us. If we split up, the best he's going to do is take out one. Yellow team still wins."

"Good plan," Travis agreed.

"You go north along the hay bales," said Reed. "When you get to the far end, I'll run south over the field."

"That's suicide."

"Only if the city slicker can still shoot."

Travis grinned at the idea of Seth going soft. He couldn't imagine that ever happening.

"You're fastest," said Reed. "By the time he takes me out, you'll be around the end with a clear shot."

"Make sure you stay alive for at least twenty seconds."

"Will do," Reed said with a nod, adjusting his safety goggles.

"Good luck," said Travis.

"You, too."

Travis stealthily maneuvered his way along the trench, popping up behind the hay bales, then hugging them, crouched low, in an effort to get closer to the shed. When he came to the end of the bales, he turned to signal Reed.

With a mighty yell, Reed jumped up out of the trench, dodging and weaving his way across the field, firing at the roof of the shed.

As soon as Seth started to shoot at Reed, Travis burst out from cover, sprinting as fast as he could around the end of the shed. He spotted Seth, stopped, breathed, put the rifle to his shoulder and squeezed off a careful shot.

He hit Seth square in the back, forcing a grunt and a cuss word from his lips. Travis grinned, while Reed whooped. The rest of the players cheered and whistled from the hillside.

While Seth made his way to the ladder, Reed appeared around the wall of the shed, grinning from ear to ear, holding up his arms and turning around to show Travis he hadn't been shot.

"City slicker jokes coming up," he gloated.

Travis held out his hand, giving Reed a firm shake. "Thanks, partner."

"Good shot," said Reed.

"He's a lot bigger than a gopher."

Reed laughed.

Seth hopped to the ground from the ladder and started toward them.

"Good day to be me," Reed joked.

"For the free beer?" Travis asked.

"And someone soft to sleep with. I'm the only one who brought his wife along."

"Katrina is here?" The revelation surprised Travis. He hadn't expected his sister to come along on a guys' weekend.

"When Caleb said he was meeting with Danielle, Katrina decided they should do some shopping."

"They're *together?*" Travis wasn't sure why the thought bothered him.

Reed looked at him strangely. "Yeah. Why? That a problem?"

"No, no. It's no problem."

Danielle and Katrina. Would Danielle mention their kiss? If she did, would Katrina tell Caleb? Would the whole valley end up knowing? Did he care?

"Travis?" asked Reed.

"Huh?"

"You fighting with Danielle again?"

"What fighting? We barely saw each other. She was hanging out with all those lawyers, and I was riding bulls and planning a bachelor party." He scoffed out a laugh. "Fighting. As if. We'd have to have been in the same room for more than a few minutes to be fighting."

"Travis?" Reed repeated.

"Yeah?" Travis struggled hard not to feel like a deer in the headlights.

"What the hell's wrong with you?"

Katrina gazed fondly at the high-heeled, leopard-print pumps on her dainty feet. "I really don't need to buy another pair."

"Did you need to buy the last pair?" Danielle teased, gazing at the jeweled, gold sandals on her own feet.

Her freshly polished, glittering green-and-gold toenails peeked saucily up at her. It was an odd color, but Katrina had talked her into it during their pedicures. Now Danielle kind of liked it. And it certainly went with the shoes.

"I didn't actually need the last dozen pair," said Katrina, coming to her feet and moving to the mirror in the shoe store.

The saleswoman stood discreetly by, waiting to see if they needed assistance.

"They're gorgeous," said Danielle.

"They'd be great with jeans."

"Walk around on yours," Katrina urged.

Danielle stood. The shoes were surprisingly comfortable.

Katrina's enthusiasm ramped up. "We should go dancing tonight."

"Your husband is going to be busy at a kegger."

"Then tomorrow night," said Katrina. "We should stay an extra day."

"I can't," said Danielle. She'd already stretched out the trip way further than she'd planned.

"Sure, you can." Katrina waved away her refusal. "The Sasha Terrell Fund and Active Equipment are both very important clients."

"True enough," Danielle was forced to agree.

"If we want you to stay in Vegas to discuss, I don't know, spending strategies, you have to stay."

Danielle came to a stop in front of the mirror next to Katrina. *"Spending strategies?"*

"Yeah, you know, what to do with all our money and stuff."

"These really are killer shoes," said Danielle.

"That settles it. We're staying to dance."

"And Reed is going to agree to this?"

Katrina's lips curved into a suggestive smile. "I can get Reed to agree to anything."

"That's as much detail as I want to know."

Katrina gave a delighted laugh. "We're going to need dresses, something outrageously sparkly and short. The kind that make men's jaws drop open."

Danielle couldn't help but picture Travis's jaw dropping open. She tried to stop herself from thinking about him, but Katrina's carefree exuberance was infectious. It wasn't like anybody could read her mind. If she wanted to fantasize about gyrating on a dance floor in a short, sparkly dress and killer gold shoes in front of Travis, it was nobody's business but her own.

They bought the shoes. Then they made the rounds of some high-end dress shops, each laughing their way through about forty dresses. In the end, Katrina went with a mauve-and-white sheath, with a sparkling bodice and subtle, purple flowers on the skirt, saying that Reed liked her with a bit of color.

For Danielle, there was no choice but gold. She found a strapless party dress, with a glittering, tight bodice that fanned into a short, three layered, crinoline skirt, scattered with gold sequins. It was by far the sexiest thing she'd ever owned. She might have chickened out, but Katrina was very persuasive.

Purchases in hand, Katrina marched them straight to the nearest hotel, easily finding an available limo.

"Now, we're going to do something exciting," said Katrina as they pulled out from the entrance.

"This hasn't been exciting so far?"

It was one of Danielle's most indulgent days ever.

"Not yet," said Katrina with a secretive grin.

"I'm getting hungry." Danielle glanced at her watch, noticing it was after six.

"I have an appointment," said Katrina. Then she leaned forward to call to the driver. "Abyss Photo Studio, please."

"You need pictures?" Danielle wondered if they were for Katrina's dancing career.

"I need pictures," Katrina confirmed.

"In Vegas?" Surely, she got her publicity shots taken in New York.

"It's a special photographer that I heard about."

A few blocks down, they left the strip and pulled into a small parking lot in front of a neat, nondescript building.

"Would you like me to wait, ma'am?"

"That would be great," said Katrina, sliding forward to hand the man her credit card. "That way we can leave all the bags here. We might be an hour or more."

"Not a problem."

"An hour?" asked Danielle. "How many pictures do you need?"

"Quite a few." Katrina took back her card and bounced out of the limo.

Danielle followed. "These are for work?"

"Not work," said Katrina as she opened the shop door. "For Reed. He has a birthday coming up."

"Oh," Danielle responded politely as she followed her inside. But she was thinking Reed must have hundreds of pictures of Katrina.

Then she glanced around the opulent reception area, taking in the sample pictures on the walls. *"Ohhh,"* she repeated. Now, she got it.

The portraits displayed were sensual, sexy, some of them downright erotic.

She followed Katrina to one of three private reception desks. "I guess Reed's going to be one happy birthday boy."

"I hope so," said Katrina. "What he really wants is a baby."

Danielle couldn't help but be surprised. "You're thinking about getting pregnant?"

"Not right now. Maybe in a couple of years."

"Would you have to give up dancing?"

"I'll want to retire from the stage eventually, maybe do choreography, or something else behind the scenes. When your husband donates ten million dollars to your ballet company, you can pretty much have any job you want."

"Is that the trick to unfettered employability?" Danielle joked. She'd been helping Reed and Katrina manage the Sasha Terrell Fund, named after Reed's mother, for nearly two years now.

Katrina gave her an answering smile. Then she sat down in an armchair in front of a neatly dressed, friendly looking woman. "Katrina Terrell. I have an appointment."

Danielle took the chair beside her.

The woman smiled brightly at both of them. "Will we be taking your pictures together?"

Katrina drew back in obvious confusion. Then she glanced at Danielle and her eyes danced with amusement. "Oh, no, we're just friends."

Danielle stifled a grin. "I'm only here for moral support."

The woman was obviously embarrassed. "I'm so sorry. I misunderstood."

Katrina waved the apology away. "No problem. If I was going to have a girlfriend, it would be Danielle."

Danielle's grin grew wider. "Thanks. I think."

Katrina twisted her body, giving Danielle a considering look. "You know…"

"I don't think Reed would let me date you," Danielle gamely carried on the joke.

"That's not what I was thinking."

"Good to hear."

"I was thinking you should get some pictures done, too." Katrina quickly turned back to the woman. "Do you have time to give us each a photo shoot?"

Danielle felt her jaw go lax. "I'm not—"

"Certainly," the woman agreed, typing into her computer. "We can manage that."

"Oh, no," Danielle stated with conviction.

"Oh, yes," said Katrina, nodding happily.

"I don't even have a boyfriend."

"You will someday. Save them. Put them away."

"I'm not dressing up like a floozy. What if they end up on the internet?"

"There's no chance of that," said the woman. "We give you a glossy copy of your favorite shots, and you keep the original memory card. We don't keep a single record here."

"Come on," Katrina cajoled. "It'll be a blast."

"I'm way too shy," Danielle protested.

"You are not. Besides, they can be romantic. They don't have to be naughty."

"This is ridiculous," said Danielle.

Maybe if she had someone to surprise. Maybe if she had…

Her brain flashed an image of Travis, but she determinedly shook it away.

"You're not getting any younger," said Katrina.

"Excuse me?"

"You'll have a boyfriend again. Of course you'll have a boy-friend again. And probably soon. And if it's not soon, and if you're getting kind of old and wrinkly, I bet he'll want to see pictures of you when you were young and hot."

"I'm not getting old that fast." Then again, would she want to do this when she was older? Not that she was saying she wanted to do it now.

"When are you going to have a chance like this again?" asked Katrina.

"Our photographers are the top of their field," noted the woman behind the desk. "The pictures can be very tasteful. You pick the costumes yourself. And each customer can choose four pieces of lingerie that are yours to keep. We have the latest and most luxurious lines."

"My treat," said Katrina, handing the woman her credit card.

"Really, I can't," said Danielle.

The woman accepted the credit card. "We have an extraordinarily high level of customer satisfaction."

"Ring it through," urged Katrina.

"Do you have anything in flannel?" asked Danielle.

"No, but we have some full-length, satin nighties. I tell you what," said the woman, swiping Katrina's card. "If you're not completely satisfied, we'll destroy the memory card and I'll refund Mrs. Terrell's money."

Danielle couldn't quite find an argument for that, and she found herself agreeing.

In the end, she had an astonishingly good time. They started with a makeup artist and a hairdresser, before moving into the clothing store.

The studio provided complimentary champagne, which they drank while joking their way through lacy baby-dolls, slips and camisoles. Katrina braved a low-cut, black push-up bra and a pair of tiny panties. In the end, Danielle threw caution to the wind and modeled a magenta teddy, with gold, satin trim and mesh cut-outs across her middle. She paired it with black stockings and her new jeweled shoes.

"We have *got* to find you a boyfriend," said Katrina as they gazed at the photo proofs, selecting ten for immediate printout.

Danielle hesitated over one of the magenta teddy pictures. She was turned slightly to one side, her hair looking soft and sexy, her eyes bright, smile provocative, the angle hinting at the curve of her hip and her behind.

Katrina nudged her in the arm. "Don't be so shy. The camera loves you. I sometimes wear less than that when I dance."

"You're the one the camera loves," said Danielle, switching her attention to the pictures of Katrina. There was a reason audiences adored her as a prima ballerina.

"We're both pretty hot."

Though Danielle might be reluctant to admit it, she was surprisingly happy with the pictures. The photographer had known just how to capture her best looks. The lighting was soft, and her skin seemed to glow.

Katrina took over the mouse and dragged the magenta teddy shot into Danielle's print basket. "There, that's ten."

"I can't believe that's me," Danielle admitted.

"Well, I sure can." Katrina straightened. "Let's go find ourselves some dinner."

The photographer packaged their prints and handed each of them their memory cards. Danielle secured everything in her shoulder bag, and they headed back to the limo.

After a fabulous dinner, and a late night of girl talk with Katrina, the limo driver pulled up to the front doors of the Emperor Plaza.

"Don't worry about the bags, ma'am," the driver instructed as he helped Katrina out of the car.

"Welcome back," greeted a uniformed porter, smiling at both women. "We'll be happy to deliver your packages."

"Room thirty-four sixteen," said Katrina.

"And your name, ma'am?"

"Katrina Terrell." She pointed. "Those five are mine. The others can go to Danielle Marin's room."

"Eighteen twenty-two," Danielle added.

"We'll take care of it. Have a good night, ladies."

They thanked the limo driver and made their way into the brightly lit lobby.

"They're in the Ace High Lounge," said Katrina.

"Who?"

"Reed and the rest of the guys."

"You're not going near that place, are you?" Danielle had no desire to go anywhere near a bachelor party at midnight.

"It's my husband, my brother-in-law and two brothers."

"And thirty-five other men."

"Who won't dare look at us sideways."

"What do you mean us?"

"Come on." Katrina studied a brass sign. She pointed down a hallway. "This way."

"I'm tired," Danielle protested. She was. "I want to go to bed."

Katrina linked her arm and tugged her forward. "Too bad. You have to come and keep me company."

"Who says?"

"I say. And I just paid for your sexy pictures."

"I thought we agreed never to speak of them again." Danielle wanted to get them safely locked away as soon as possible. She was beginning to worry about carrying them through airport security. What if someone searched her luggage? How embarrassing would that be?

Katrina laughed, still tugging her along the hallway. "Your secret's safe with me. Come on. You owe me."

"I paid for dinner," Danielle pointed out, but she gave up and kept walking.

"Aren't you at all curious?"

"About what men do at bachelor parties?" asked Danielle. "I honestly don't want to know."

"Maybe someone jumped out of a cake."

"I hope not. That's so eighties."

"I'm sure they kept it tasteful."

"Travis did the planning."

"Good point. This might be more exciting than I thought. Here we are."

Danielle hesitated. If it turned out there were strippers in there, it was going to be mortifiying.

Before they could pull on the door, it opened from the inside, loud music thumping from the depths of the dim room. Caleb appeared, jerking back in obvious surprise at the sight of them.

"Katrina. Danielle." He gave a wide grin. "What are you guys doing here?" It was subtle, but his speech was measured, as if he was being careful to properly enunciate his words.

The door swung shut behind him.

"Having a good party?" asked Katrina.

"Fantastic," he responded. "You want me to get Reed?"

"We want to find out what's going on inside," said Katrina.

"No, we don't," said Danielle.

"You always were the smart one," Caleb said to Danielle.

"Thank you."

"What's going on in there?" asked Katrina.

"We're drinking DFB beer and watching a game."

"Are you drunk?" asked Katrina.

"I am not."

"Is Reed drunk?"

"Reed doesn't get drunk."

The door opened again, bashing into Caleb's shoulder and sending him stumbling.

This time, it was Travis who appeared.

"Danielle," he grinned heartily. "You're back."

"We've been shopping," said Katrina.

"So, I heard, baby sister."

"And out for dinner," she continued.

Danielle held her breath, fearing Katrina might mention the pictures. But the door opened again, and Reed joined them.

He zeroed in on Katrina. "Hey, sweetheart." He moved to stand next to her, putting a hand on the small of her back and giving her a quick kiss on the temple. "Did you have a good time?"

"It was great. I got you a birthday present."

Danielle stilled, bracing herself. She couldn't help a fleeting glance at Travis, and found herself shifting from one foot to the other.

"What did you get me?" asked Reed.

"Oh, no," Katrina teased, waggling a finger. "Not until your birthday."

"Yeah?" he growled on a challenging note.

"Yeah," she responded saucily.

"We'll see about that." He looped an arm around her shoulders. "Good night, boys," he called to Travis and Caleb, as he steered her down the hall.

Their departure spurred Danielle to action. "I'll say goodnight as well," she told Caleb, glancing briefly to Travis as she backed away.

"We can talk tomorrow," said Caleb.

The words brought Danielle to a halt. "Were you looking for me today?"

She and Caleb had met briefly when he arrived Thursday night. But she'd understood he was going to be busy all day. At least that's what Katrina told her. Now she realized she'd never actually checked with Caleb.

Caleb shook his head. "I'd have called you. Tomorrow's fine."

"Okay," Danielle nodded, relieved. "I'll be there."

"I'm done, too," said Travis, breaking away from his brother, and coming up next to Danielle.

Her stomach gave an involuntary quiver of excitement.

Caleb glanced back at the closed door. "Yeah," he agreed. "I think the party's winding down." He started forward.

Reed and Katrina were far ahead in the lobby, disappearing around the central fountain.

"Thanks for entertaining Katrina," said Caleb. "I know Reed appreciates it."

Danielle gave a short laugh. "Katrina entertained me. I feel like I've been playing hooky all day long."

"You put in way too many hours," said Caleb.

"A lot of lawyers put in more hours than I do."

She couldn't help thinking about Randal and the others at Nester and Hedley. How hard did they work? What was the pace like in D.C.?

"I'm in the north tower," said Caleb, pointing to an elevator sign, and turning toward the hallway. "'Night."

"Good night," Danielle called after him.

She and Travis walked a few feet in silence.

"I'm west," she told him.

"I know."

She remembered he'd walked her to the elevators that first night.

"How was the bachelor day?" she asked.

"No insurance claims from the dune buggy races," he said, reminding her of the policy she'd reviewed for him yesterday.

"That's good news. Who won?"

"Alex."

Danielle gave him a suspicious look. "The groom? Was the fix in?"

"Maybe a little. Reed and I rocked at paintball. We took it for the yellow team."

Danielle couldn't help but smile at the pride in his voice. "First the bull riding, and now paintball. There's just no stopping you, is there?"

"No, ma'am, there is not." There was a wry note in his voice, as he reached out to press the call button for the west tower elevators.

Two older women joined them waiting.

"You don't need to wait for the car," said Danielle.

"My suite's up there, too."

Six

The middle elevator car pinged, the red up arrow lighting. Three men strode with them into the elevator, along with the two older ladies. Danielle pressed eighteen and moved into a corner, while Travis pressed thirty-four, the top floor, and shifted to stand beside her.

One of the three men took a lingering, visual tour of her white slacks and blue tank top. She ignored him, but Travis stepped in front of her, lifting his chin and folding his arms across his chest.

She couldn't help but smile at the gesture. For some reason it sent a shot of warmth through her chest. It was gentlemanly, she told herself, kind of sweetly old-fashioned.

The men filed out on the fourteenth floor, and she stepped out from behind Travis, smiling and shaking her head. "You didn't have to—" As she moved farther, her shoulder bag snagged on the elevator rail, jerking out of her hand, clattering upside down to the floor.

Danielle swore. Travis turned at the sound. And the two older ladies stared at the items bouncing on the floor.

Travis crouched to help, while Danielle scooped up her wallet and cell phone, snagged a makeup bag, her keys and a hand mirror. She stuffed them into the open bag, checking the floor to make sure nothing more embarrassing had slipped out.

Then she realized Travis had gone still. She twisted her neck to look at him, freezing in horror when she saw the envelope in his hands. Her boudoir photos had fallen halfway out, and he was staring, eyes wide, at the magenta teddy photo on the top of the stack.

He rose, silently sliding the photos back into the envelope and refolding the flap.

Danielle couldn't speak. She couldn't look at him. The embarrassing shot scuttled through her brain. It was her worst nightmare come true.

He handed her the envelope as the elevator pinged on the eighteenth floor. But, before she could exit, his hand wrapped around her upper arm.

The women glanced at her in puzzlement.

His grip wasn't tight. She could have easily pulled away, darted for the door, escaped and left town, finding a way to never, ever face him again.

But she didn't. She complied with his unspoken request.

The door slid shut, and the elevator rose.

While they moved, Danielle turned hot, then cold, then hot again.

The doors opened on twenty-three, and the two women got off. Travis kept hold of her arm. He stayed silent until the doors had shut completely.

When he spoke, his voice was guttural. "Tell me they're not for Randal."

The question surprised her so much, she forgot to answer.

"Tell me," he repeated with an edge of desperation.

"They're not for Randal," she quickly told him. "They're not for anybody. They were a lark, a silly, stupid idea that I regret already."

He nodded sharply. His hand slipped from her arm. "Okay."

That was it? One word? What did he mean?

The elevator pinged on thirty-four, the doors opening yet again.

Travis crossed the car. He pressed eighteen again then moved through the doorway.

Danielle's knees went weak with relief, or maybe it was disappointment. She couldn't quite pinpoint which.

But then he stopped. The doors started to shut, but he stuck his arm out to block them. He turned fully around, gaze intense, seeming to drink in the sight of her and swallow it whole.

"I've tried so damn hard to ignore this," he rasped.

Heat and desire washed over her again. She told herself to shut up. She told herself to stay still and let it pass.

"So have I," she confessed in a small voice.

He didn't move. He waited.

Her stomach contracted. Her blood pounded in her ears. She struggled to suck in oxygen.

Stay put, her logical brain ordered.

There was absolutely no mistaking the hunger in his expression. His eyes were dark, his jaw clenched tight. His entire body seemed poised to pounce.

If she moved, she was done for. They were done for. If she took one step toward him, she'd be in his bed in minutes. And nothing would ever be the same between them again.

She moved one foot, and then the other. In seconds, she was out the door and into the hallway.

He turned beside her, released the door, silently took her hand in his and made his way along the short hallway.

Neither spoke as he swiped his key card in the double doors at the end. One door swung open, soft music greeting them, warm air, thick carpets, soft lighting, scented oil wafting through a richly appointed living room.

They walked inside, and the door clicked shut behind them. Astonishingly, her trepidation disappeared. Her uncertainty and fear vanished. She knew she was right where she wanted to be. She was alone with Travis at last, and all the reasons to keep her distance seemed to evaporate into thin air.

He turned to face her, his own expression relaxing. He smiled gently, blue eyes softening in the dim light. He smoothed back her hair. And with the opposite hand, he twined their fingers together.

"You are so incredibly beautiful," he whispered.

"How did this happen?" she breathed, wondering if this might be a dream.

"My guess is good genes and healthy living."

She couldn't help but smile.

His own smile faded, his gaze zeroing in on her lips, his hand moving to cradle her cheek.

"I'm about to kiss you," he warned.

"I'm about to kiss you back."

"You promise?"

"I promise."

He leaned in, voice deep and low. "This is going to be fun."

Her laughter was quickly lost in the touch of his lips. They were smooth, firm and hot. He smelled of male musk, tasted of smoky scotch whiskey. He deepened the kiss, and she welcomed him in.

He wrapped his arm around the small of her back, pulling her against him. Her bag dropped to the floor as she reveled in the heat of his steel hard thighs. She wrapped her arms around his neck, letting her head fall back, drinking in the magic of his kiss and letting waves of passion wash through her.

His thumb slipped beneath the hem of her tank top, stroking the bare skin of her back, tracing the small bumps of her spine, first up and then down.

Feeling her way, she flicked open the buttons of his shirt, sliding her palms along his washboard stomach and the definition of his chest, eliciting a groan from deep in his throat. She found a small scar near his left nipple, tracing the ridge with her fingertip. She eased back from his kiss, dipping her head to kiss the scar. Then she kissed a path to his shoulder, pushing off his shirt.

He shrugged out of it, finding her lips, kissing her deeply as his hands skimmed her bare skin and cupped her breasts through her lacy bra. He groaned again and scooped her into his strong arms. She clung to him, still kissing as he carried her across the suite, through a set of double doors, and into a massive bedroom with a four-poster bed.

The room was lit softly by a bedside lamp. The French doors were propped open, sheer curtains billowing in the warm breeze.

He set her on her feet. Then he peeled off her tank top, pulling it over her raised arms, tossing it on a nearby chair while his gaze feasted on her snowy white bra.

"You get more beautiful by the second."

She splayed her hands across his tanned chest. "So do you." She found the scar again. "Bull?" she asked.

"Don't remember."

"Seriously?"

"I've got a few of them. Does it bother you?"

"Not at all. They make you seem rugged and sexy."

He gave a playful grin. "I am rugged and sexy."

"That you are," she agreed. Then, feeling bold, she reached back and released her bra, letting it fall away. "I'm not exactly rugged."

He drank in the sight of her bare breasts. "I'd hate it if you were. You're soft and sexy, exactly how you're supposed to be."

She watched as his tanned, callused hand closed over her breast. His palm was warm, but her nipple beaded hard in reaction.

He curled an arm around her waist again, drawing her close.

"Soft," he whispered as his lips came down on hers.

She inhaled his scent, drank in his taste, tangled her tongue with his. He felt so incredibly good pressed against her. She gave her passion free rein, letting the rest of the world fall away.

He seemed content to kiss her forever. But the heat was building inside her, and she was impatient to feel all of him. She slipped her hand between their bodies, popping the button on the top of his jeans.

He copied her move, releasing her button.

She slid down his zipper.

He sucked in a breath, and did the same.

She pulled back and smiled. Stepping away, she kicked off her shoes and shimmied out of her jeans.

He did the same, standing in black boxers, staring at her skimpy, white lace panties.

She hooked her thumbs into the thin strip of fabric.

He snagged his waistband.

"Shall we count to three?" she joked.

"Three." He stripped down his boxers, kicking them across the floor.

She waited, just to see what he'd do.

He crossed the small space and drew her into his arms. His hands skimmed down her back, cupping her buttocks while he kissed her neck. His magical lips made their way to her shoulder, across her chest. Then with excruciating slowness drew one nipple into his hot mouth.

She groaned with pleasure, scraping her fingernails across his thick hair. He moved to the other, and she gripped his shoulders to steady herself. A craving pushed its way through her bloodstream, peaking her nipples and pooling in her lower belly.

She gasped his name.

He instantly scooped her up, lifting her to lay her on the soft, satin bed. He reached for her panties, drawing them slowly down the length of her legs. Then he rose above her, all sinew, strength and power. It was by far the sexiest moment of her life.

Without hesitating, she eased her legs apart.

"More beautiful by the second," he rasped, bending lower to kiss the inside of her knee.

As he worked his way up, she couldn't hold still, twitching then squirming, then gasping and arching off the bed as he reached home. He kept going, kissing her belly, making her quiver as he reached her breasts, then her neck, then finally her mouth.

She slid her hands down his back, over his buttocks, around to grasp him, reveling in the hot texture and her own anticipation.

"You in a hurry?" he rasped in her ear.

"Yes," she hissed. "Yes, yes, yes."

He reached for the bed stand, producing a condom.

In moments, he was above her again, kissing her deeply, kneading her bottom, adjusting her thighs, pressing against her, slipping inside her, deeper and deeper. He felt so incredibly good.

She groaned in satisfaction, tipping her hips, wrapping her legs around him. His tongue stroked the inside of her mouth. Her hands gripped his back, tighter and tighter. Desire coiled in her belly, while his long strokes and satisfying rhythm spiraled her higher and higher.

The room grew hotter, and moisture beaded across her body. Traffic sounds blended to a roar in her ears, while the breeze teased her damp, sensitized skin. Then time and space disappeared, nothing existing except the pulse of Travis and the primal urge of her own body to reach for the pinnacle of release.

Color glowed to life inside her brain, shooting sparks of light along her synapses while pleasure built along her limbs, curling her toes and drawing moans of intense desire from her deep in her chest. Travis echoed the sounds, increasing his pace, his breathing speeding up, his heart thumping strong against her chest.

Then, her body roared and her world convulsed, and she cried out his name while waves of pure pleasure raced through her body. His kiss deepened, and he grasped her tightly to him while his own body shuddered with completion.

She spent long minutes drawing in deep breaths, her chest moving up and down. He shifted his weight, easing partway off, one leg staying over hers, his hand splayed across her stomach. The ornate, white pine posts of the bed came into focus, then the paintings on the wall, mounted above a cream-colored sofa and two peach armchairs.

She pushed her damp hair back from her forehead and stretched the kinks out of her legs. "Probably a good thing we didn't know that."

He kissed the tip of her shoulder. "Didn't know what?"

She turned to look at him, not feeling remotely coy or shy.

"How it would be between us. We might not have waited two years."

Comprehension dawned in his eyes, and his mouth crooked in a wry smile. "I might not have waited two minutes."

The first thing to enter Travis's sleep-filled brain was the scent of wild flowers. His thoughts wafted to Lyndon Valley, the springtime colors, the rolling hills. But then he felt the satin skin of Danielle's stomach, warm and soft under his rough fingertips. He heard her breathing and realized the scent was her shampoo.

This was better than home, so much better than home.

He blinked his eyes open to gaze at her delicate profile. Her hair was mussed from sleep, her eye makeup slightly smeared, her cheeks flushed, and her dark lips parted.

She'd stayed.

He smiled at the knowledge that she'd slept in his arms.

"You're awake early," came her husky voice.

"So are you," he whispered in return.

"You woke me up."

"I didn't mean to."

"You moved your leg."

"I didn't mean to do that, either." He'd have stayed perfectly still for hours if it kept her in his arms.

She stifled a yawn with the back of her hand, opening her dark fringed, coffee-brown eyes to look at him. "What time is it?"

"I don't know. Maybe seven."

She shifted up on one elbow, the drape of the white sheet covering her rounded breasts. "Do you have to get up?"

"Not yet. You?"

She shook her head. "I need to meet with Caleb, but my flight's not until noon." Then her expression faltered, and she sat up, bringing the sheet with her. "Unless you want me to have to get up. I can't tell, was that a question or a hint?"

He reached out to slide an arm around her waist, tugging

her back toward him. "It was definitely a question. And I was absolutely hoping you'd say no."

He stretched up to meet her, kissing her lips.

He'd meant it to be playful, but the kiss quickly deepened to sensual. She kissed him back, and it turned very serious. Arousal instantly snaked its way through his body. He eased back on the pillow, drawing her against his bare chest.

His hands stroked down her back, reminding himself of every inch of her. She stretched out, laying on top of him, limbs entwining with his, her soft breasts pressing against his chest. His arms wrapped themselves around her, holding her close, losing himself in the magic of her taste, scent and texture.

She drew back, smiling. "Good morning."

"Good morning," he responded, trying to gauge if he was taking things too fast.

"I forgot to tell you something."

Disappointment slid through him. "You have to go?"

"No. Not that." She pushed up so that she was sitting, straddling his hips.

He liked that position, liked it a lot, even though the moist contact of her body made it difficult to concentrate on anything she might say. He struggled not to fix his gaze on her beautiful breasts. They were round, pert, beautifully pink-tipped, and exactly the right size for his palm.

"Randal tried to kiss me."

Travis's attention flew to her face.

"He *what?*"

"He tried to kiss me. After the windup reception."

"Did you let him?"

Though Travis knew leaping from the bed to slam a fist into Randal's face was stupid—for one thing, Randal was back in D.C.—he desperately wanted to injure the man.

"No, I didn't let him," Danielle responded tartly.

Travis felt marginally better. "What happened?"

"He tried to talk me into accepting the job in D.C. He said he didn't know where things were going with his girlfriend. And this would give us a second chance."

Travis battled hard against the anger and frustration building inside him. He wasn't angry with Danielle. It wasn't her fault Randal had no morals. Still, his tone came out harsher than he'd intended. "Do you want a second chance?"

She glanced down at their naked bodies. "Do I *look* like I want a second chance with Randal?"

Good point. She was in Travis's bed, naked, and Randal was halfway across the country. Some of his anger dissipated.

"What I'm saying here, is that you were right, and I was wrong. I misjudged Randal. I'm owning up to that."

Travis's hands reflexively reached forward, bracketing her hips, hoping he'd heard what he thought he'd heard. "What did you just say?"

"You want me to repeat it?"

His body felt lighter, a smile tugging at his lips. "Yeah."

"Okay, Travis Jacobs. You were right, and I was wrong."

"Will you marry me?"

The second the words were out, a wave of emotion cascaded through his body. He wasn't sure whether it was horror, shock or longing. He did know it had been a dumb thing to say, even as a joke.

Luckily, Danielle laughed. "Sorry, Travis. But your ego is going to have to make it through life without my constant reinforcement."

He gave an exaggerated sigh of disappointment.

"So, what are you going to do?" he asked.

She sobered. "I'm still thinking about it. If I go to D.C., Randal might be a hassle for a while. But he'll eventually get the message."

Travis hoped that was the case. He hated the thought that Randal might somehow change her mind.

"It's a fantastic opportunity," she told him wistfully.

Travis found his focus going to his hands. They were callused and scarred, tanned dark against her creamy, soft skin. There was no better metaphor for the distance between them.

He might want her. He certainly wanted her badly at the moment. But the divide between them was huge. He was a coarse, backwoods cowboy, who made a living with his hands. She was a gorgeous, sophisticated woman, brilliant enough to take on the best in the world and win.

Unexpectedly, her fingertips touched against his stomach. "What about you?" she asked.

He didn't understand the question, so he made a joke. "Nobody offered me a job in D.C."

"Have you ever thought about what you want to do?"

"I'm a Colorado rancher."

"I know that. But you hinted that night at the party that you might have broader aspirations. Your brother and sisters all expanded their horizons."

Travis tried not to be offended by her phrasing. "Corey thinks I should go pro on the bull riding circuit."

"Wow." She squeezed her hands around his waist. "That'll challenge your intellect."

His jaw tensed. "We can't all be geniuses."

"I'm sorry," she offered.

"Sorry that I'm not a genius?"

She smacked his hip with her open palm. "Sorry that you're such a grouch."

He gave her a suggestive wag of his brow. "Want to do that again?"

She tossed her short hair. "You're trying to distract me."

"I'm glad you're catching on."

"You don't want to talk about it, do you?"

He pulled into a sitting position, bringing his face in front of hers. "Talking is definitely *not* what I want to do right now."

She looped her arms over his shoulders. "What is it you want to do, cowboy?"

He lifted his brow again. "Can I see the rest of your pictures?"

The question clearly took her by surprise. "I'm burning those damn pictures."

He smoothed back her hair, tone cajoling. "Oh, don't do that. Lock them away if you want to, but don't destroy them."

"It was a foolish idea to have them taken. I'm not the kind of woman who takes naughty pictures."

He slipped his hands up her hips, along her waistline and over the sides of her breasts. He cradled her face. "I happen to like the Danielle who takes naughty pictures."

She hissed in a tight breath. "What happens in Vegas, should definitely stay there."

He gave her a brief, gentle kiss, telling himself to keep a rein on his passion. Whatever they did next, was up to her.

"What else do you want to happen in Vegas?" he asked.

Her shoulders relaxed. "We're going to do it again, aren't we?"

He kissed his way along her shoulder. "Doing it again has my vote."

"You're incorrigible."

He smiled at that.

"Then again, I seem to be incorrigible too."

"That's a fair division of incorrigibility," he noted.

Her arms tightened around his neck, and her soft body melted against him. "You are an exceedingly sexy, handsome, exciting man."

"And you are the woman of my dreams." He kissed her deeply, giving his burgeoning passion free rein and letting his hands roam.

She moaned against his mouth, her nipples beading against his chest, heat and moisture gathering where their bodies met. Her kisses were the sweetest thing in the world. And her soft, smooth body seemed custom-designed for his.

Once again, he let the world disappear, immersing himself in Danielle, determined this time to make their lovemaking last for hours.

Wrapped in a fluffy, white, hotel bathrobe and curled up in a padded lounger on Travis's hotel suite balcony, Danielle sipped a strong cup of coffee. She was fresh from the shower, and the midmorning air was cool against her scalp.

Travis appeared in the open doorway clutching a mug of coffee. A pair of navy sweats rode low on his hips. His chest was bare. He was now clean-shaven, and his hair was also damp. She tried not to stare, but she couldn't help marveling at his rugged sex appeal. She'd spent half of last night and most of this morning making love with him, but she'd jump into bed again if he so much as crooked his little finger.

There had to be something wrong with her.

Her phone pinged and vibrated on the small, metal table next to her lounger.

"The real world?" Travis asked, moving to the second lounger.

"Seems like." She smiled at him, reaching for the phone.

He eased his body into the lounger, lifting his bare feet while the sun rays gleamed against his tanned chest.

Gaze hopelessly glued to his sinewy body, Danielle pressed the answer button and put her phone to her ear.

"Hello?"

"Hey, Danielle. It's Caleb."

"Morning, Caleb." She met Travis's eyes.

"Are you up and around?"

"I just showered," she answered.

Travis grinned at the way she used the truth.

"I'm meeting Reed and Katrina for breakfast in the Garden Café. Can you join us?"

"Of course." She guiltily reminded herself she was supposed to be here on business.

"Twenty minutes?"

"I'll be there."

"Great." Caleb signed off.

She let her phone drop into her lap. "Duty calls," she told Travis, trying not to feel dejected by the need for such an abrupt departure.

Their interlude was never going to be anything but temporary. It was over, and that was that. She'd have to go directly from breakfast to the airport, and she might not see Travis again for months. If she took the job in D.C., months might turn into forever.

For a split second the thought of never seeing Travis again made her panic.

His phone chimed, and he scooped it from the table as she stood up.

"Yeah?" He paused. "Hey, Caleb."

She stilled, locking gazes with Travis.

"Breakfast?" he asked into the phone. "Sure. When?"

There was another pause. "I'll be there," he said and hung up.

Danielle hesitated. She felt a ridiculous sense of relief that she didn't have to walk away from Travis this very minute. But they were going to breakfast with his friends and family. They likely wouldn't have a chance to say a personal goodbye. She wasn't sure what to do.

Travis stood. His expression was serious as he moved the few steps to stand in front of her.

"Kiss me goodbye?" he asked, gently sliding his hand around the back of her neck.

"I don't know what to say," she confessed. It seemed to be suddenly ending so fast.

"I don't, either," he told her, easing forward.

His free arm went around her waist, pressing her to his body. His lips touched hers, gently, softly, far too fleetingly.

He drew back, voice a whisper. "You surprised me, Danielle Marin."

"You surprised me right back," she admitted. In a few short days, Travis had turned her opinion of him on its ear.

"Are we going to leave this all in Vegas?" he asked.

"I don't see that we have any choice." But an unexplainable pain pressed into the center of her chest.

"You're right," he sighed.

Then he placed a soft kiss at her hairline, then his lips moved against her skin as he spoke. "When I wave an impersonal goodbye to you in the lobby later on? Know that what I really mean is this."

He bent his head, tilting sideways, kissing her long and hard and deep.

It ended far too soon.

"I'll mean that, too," she managed.

"Okay." He nodded and took a step back. "Okay."

She put a steadying hand on the doorjamb, ordering herself to move back inside the suite. "I'll go down to my room and change."

"I'll meet you in the café."

"In the café," she agreed, allowing herself a long, final look.

Seven

Caleb was alone when Danielle approached the table. It was large and round, set in one corner of the second floor patio, overlooking the pool.

"'Morning," Caleb greeted, rising and pulling out the chair next to him.

"How are you feeling?" She couldn't help remembering how jovial he'd been at the end of the party last night.

"None the worse for wear. Did you have fun with Katrina?"

Shopping and dinner with Katrina seemed like a long time ago. "We had a great time."

"Good. The bachelor party went well. But I think Alex is getting pretty sick of all this guy stuff and about ready to get married now."

Danielle laughed at that as she sat down.

"I had a call from a Pantara executive last week," said Caleb, taking his own seat.

"Pantara Tractors?" Danielle named a huge, European equipment supplier, headquartered in Germany.

Caleb nodded. "They're interested in a merger."

The announcement surprised her, since Pantara was nearly twice the size of Active Equipment. "With you?" she confirmed.

"Yes, with me."

"They want to merge or buy you out?" She certainly wouldn't recommend Caleb sell to the competition.

"Merge. I'd remain CEO, with a voting majority, and we'd create a new class of preferred shares."

She sat back in her chair, puzzled at the apparent generosity of the offer. "Why?"

"That's what I need *you* to find out."

"So, there really was a legitimate reason for me to stay in Vegas."

He gave a mock expression of astonishment. "Of course there was a legitimate reason. What made you think there wasn't?"

"Well, I haven't done much work since you got here."

"That's about to change."

"'Morning," came Travis's gravelly voice.

She reflexively glanced up, and a wave of familiar warmth flowed through her body at the sight of him. "'Morning," she responded, her tone more husky than she'd intended.

Travis, on the other hand, kept his expression perfectly impassive as he gave her a passing smile. She felt half-dejected, half-impressed.

"Hungover?" Caleb asked him.

"Me?" Travis took a chair across the round table. "I was pacing myself. Zach's the one we should worry about."

Danielle couldn't help wishing Travis could sit next to her, but she understood why he couldn't.

"Zach's been a party animal all his life," said Caleb. "He'll be fine."

"Have you ordered?" asked Travis.

"Nope," Caleb answered. "I was just talking to Danielle about being my point person for the Pantara merger."

"Is that going to work out for her?" Travis snagged Danielle's gaze, and she realized he had to be wondering about the impact of the Nester and Hedley offer.

She could tell by his expression that he thought she should tell Caleb about her possible job change. And he was absolutely right about that. She owed it to Caleb to be honest. If she might not be around for the Pantara deal, he needed to know now.

"Caleb?" She angled her body to face him.

"Hmm?" He'd picked up a leather-bound menu.

"Before we discuss Pantara."

"We don't have to do it over breakfast and bore everyone."

But she wasn't going to let herself off the hook. "You need to know I've received an offer to join a new firm, Nester and Hedley in D.C."

Caleb lowered the menu, and looked over at her with those piercing, blue eyes. "Is it a good offer?"

"Yes," she admitted. "It's a very good offer. They're the top, international law firm in the country. It would open up a lot of doors for me, give me a chance to work on issues of enormous significance."

He set the menu down and gave her his full focus. "Are you going to take it?"

"I don't know," she answered honestly.

"When will you know?"

"I told them a week."

"So you might stay with Milburn and Associates?" he pressed.

She struggled not to glance at Travis. "I might stay."

"Can I ask you one more question?"

"Sure."

"Are you looking to find a way to leave Chicago, or did this come at you out of the blue."

"Out of the blue," said Danielle. "That's part of the problem. I like Chicago. I like my clients. And, don't take this as me buttering you up, I like working with Active Equipment. You're a big part of the pull for me to stay put."

Again, she fought not to look at Travis. It had nothing to do with him, she assured herself. Even if she was the kind of person to make a decision based on a man, Vegas with Travis had been just that, Vegas with Travis. It wasn't about to translate into the real world.

"Then let's talk Pantara anyway. You can hitch a ride on the jet today and give us some extra time."

"Are you sure?" It was going to be a very complex project. If she left in a few weeks, her work could all turn out to be a waste of time.

"'Morning, all" Katrina called as she and Reed approached

the table. She hopped into the chair next to Danielle, and Reed sat next to her. "What did we miss?"

"Danielle's going to catch a ride home with us this afternoon," said Caleb.

"We're not going home this afternoon," said Katrina. "And neither is Danielle."

Caleb lifted a questioning glance to Reed.

"We're going dancing," Katrina piped in. "You should have told him," she said to Danielle. "We bought great new dresses yesterday, and we have to give them a test run."

Reed gave his brother a helpless shrug. "I'm not about to tell my wife she can't dance."

Danielle jumped in. "If Caleb needs me to—"

"Never mind." Caleb waved off her protest with exaggerated resignation.

"But—"

"We'll catch a commercial flight tomorrow," said Reed.

"I can't stay and dance." Danielle turned to Katrina. "I'm really sorry. I'd love to stay, but I've missed too much work already." If she wasn't careful, Nester and Hedley would be her only option, because Milburn and Associates would be letting her go for nonperformance.

"You can stay if it's billable hours," said Caleb.

Danielle turned sharply. "Oh, no you don't." She wasn't about to let Caleb pay her to stay an extra day in Vegas.

But he ignored her, extracting his cell phone from his shirt pocket. "Danielle, I seriously need to talk to you about Pantara. This is business." He pressed a button and lifted the phone to his ear.

"That's a ridiculous stretch," said Danielle.

Caleb simply waved her off.

"Hey, sweetheart," he said into the phone. Then he paused. "It was terrific. Listen, do you want to go dancing tonight?

He smiled as he listened to whatever Mandy was saying at the other end of the line. "With your sister and my brother, who else? And Danielle's coming, too." Another pause. "No, here. You can come to Vegas."

His grin widened. "Absolutely. Yeah. I'll talk to you in a few hours." He hung up.

"I'll stick around," Travis offered.

Both Caleb and Reed looked over at him in surprise.

He shrugged. "I'm the only single guy you've got, and somebody has to dance with Danielle."

Both Caleb and Reed nodded, seeming to agree that it made perfect sense.

Travis's deep blue eyes shifted to Danielle's, and she felt a wash of decadent longing radiate from her core.

"Hey, Zach." Caleb's sudden call across the restaurant startled her.

Katrina nudged her arm. "What?"

Danielle turned to Katrina in confusion. "Huh?"

"Is something wrong?" Katrina whispered. "You've got a funny look on your face."

"Everything's fine." It was better than fine. Which was very bad. Danielle shouldn't be this happy about spending an extra evening with Travis.

"What's up?" asked Zach as he made his way closer to the table.

"The five of us are staying here 'till tomorrow," said Caleb. "Can you let the pilot know to bring Mandy back? She'll be at the airport in Lyndon."

"Sure thing," said Zach, taking the chair between Reed and Travis.

Travis sat back, looking smug and eminently satisfied.

"What's that?" Katrina asked Travis.

"What's what?" He gazed levelly at his sister.

"You look...I don't know." She turned to Reed. "Did I miss something? Did you guys have strippers last night?"

"Of course not," said Reed.

"We did not," Zach confirmed.

"Then why does Travis look so happy?"

"I'm not happy," said Travis.

But it was obviously a lie. Danielle could only hope she wasn't giving off the same kind of glow. And, if she was, that nobody put two and two together.

Travis and Caleb had stayed back to pay the limo driver, allowing Reed, Katrina, Danielle and Mandy to go on ahead along the Strip. Katrina was on Reed's arm, wearing something white and silky, with a little bit of purple. She looked fresh and young as she always did. Mandy, who had just arrived on the Active Equipment jet, was in basic black. It was tough to get his middle sister out of her blue jeans and into a dress at all. She rarely wore anything very fancy.

And then there was Danielle. Her dress was strapless, tight, gold and sparkling across her body, then fanning into a short, stiff, multi-layered skirt, scattered with gold sequins that winked under the lights. Her legs were long and shapely, ending in strappy gold sandals. She outshone every woman on the block.

"My brother's attracting a lot of attention," Caleb joked.

It was true. As people passed Reed and the three women, they craned their necks, clearly wondering who he was to warrant three gorgeous dates.

"At least he makes a good bodyguard," said Travis, thinking he'd better not let Danielle wander around alone tonight. He'd have to stick close to her side to keep the wolves at bay. Which he was totally willing, no, make that eager, to do.

"Hey," Caleb interrupted his thoughts, an accusation in his tone.

"What?" Travis glanced around, trying to figure out what was wrong.

"I can see the way you're lookin' at my lawyer."

"It's the same way every other guy is looking at your lawyer," Travis quickly retorted.

"They're not dancing with her."

"Too bad for them."

"I'm serious, Travis. You can't be messin' with Danielle. She's too important to Active Equipment for you to make her mad."

"I'm fifteen feet away from her."

"Promise me you won't try anything."

"Don't be ridiculous," Travis scoffed.

"I'm not being ridiculous. I want your word on that."

Travis shot Caleb an exasperated look. "Why are you being so paranoid?"

"Because you're not promising me anything."

"We aren't ten-year-old girls. I'm not going to pinky swear."

"Travis," Caleb intoned. "Why are you being deliberately vague about this?"

"Because it's none of your business."

"It is my business, exactly. How is it not my business?"

"We're consenting adults."

"You're not—" Caleb stopped short, voice going low. "*What* did you do?"

"I'm not going to answer that. Besides, Danielle getting ticked off at me is not your biggest risk. Your biggest risk is her dream job in D.C."

It was clear that answer got Caleb thinking.

Travis took advantage. "If I was you, I'd be convincing her that the Pantara project is worth her giving up D.C."

"The Pantara project *is* worth her giving up D.C."

"You've got nearly a week to play with." Travis felt guilty about what he was doing here, but not guilty enough to stop. "Bring her back to Lyndon Valley for a few days and convince her."

Caleb focused on Travis again, sizing him up. "You want me to bring Danielle back to Lyndon Valley?"

"You know Nester and Hedley will be working on her. You know Randal will be trying to convince her to take the D.C. job. Hell, he might even head for Chicago and track her down in person."

"Who's Randal?"

"A guy from Nester and Hedley."

"Just a guy?" Caleb probed.

"Just a guy."

They started walking again.

"And you'll be okay with that?" asked Caleb. "With Danielle spending a few days in Lyndon Valley."

Travis shrugged, trying to look unconcerned, as if he couldn't care less one way or the other. "Sure."

Throbbing music rose in volume as they neared the Aster Club's entrance. Voices also rose from the long line of patrons and carried across the sidewalk.

If Danielle was in Lyndon Valley, he reasoned, she was away from Randal. She was also with Travis. Not that he expected her to give him the time of day back home. She'd been pretty clear that this was a Vegas thing only. Still, better she was with him than somewhere she might fall into Randal's clutches.

Caleb's tone turned even more serious. "What's going on, Travis?"

"Why does something have to be going on? Danielle's been to Lyndon Valley lots of times before."

"And you always fight with her there. And now you're dancing with her?"

"Take a look at that." Travis nodded to where Reed had walked boldly up to the VIP entrance.

The bouncer unclipped the velvet rope and gestured them forward.

"I guess three gorgeous women will do that for you," said Caleb quickly picking up the pace to catch up.

Travis did the same.

The bouncer put the flat of his hand on Caleb's chest.

"We're with them," Caleb explained. "Mandy, honey?" he called.

Mandy turned. "That's my husband," she called back to the bouncer, but the man seemed unimpressed.

"I won Bull Mania Saturday night," Travis offered.

The man's eyes narrowed, then his expression changed to a welcoming smile. "I recognize you. Come on in."

Caleb gaped at him. "You have got to be kidding."

"Works ever better if I bring along the belt buckle."

"That's sad."

"You think that's sad. Let me tell you about my complimentary hotel suite."

Caleb gave a baffled shake of his head as they made their way through the entry hall.

Inside the Aster Club, Travis beelined for Danielle. He could already see the interested looks from other men, and he wasn't leaving her alone for a second.

He wrapped an arm around her waist. "You want to dance first or drink first?"

Her lips curved into a dazzling smile. "Dance."

"Okay." He led her through the crowds and into the bright colored light.

He didn't see where Caleb or Reed had gone, and he didn't particularly care. He twirled Danielle, laughing, into his arms. The music was loud and vibrant. There was no point in trying to talk, so they simply danced.

She was light in his arms, sensitive to his lead. She was fun to dance with, but as they moved through the songs, their spins and dips decreased, while their holds became longer and more frequent. On the fourth song, the DJ slowed things down, and Travis pulled her close, settling her against his chest.

He inhaled the fresh fragrance of her hair, felt her curves nestle into him, and tipped his head toward her bare shoulders. If Caleb caught sight of him and Danielle, there wouldn't be a doubt left in his mind what was going on. But Travis didn't care. His time with Danielle was going to be limited one way or the other, and he was going to make the most of what he had.

As the song wound down, she tilted her head back. It was hard for him to resist kissing her.

"I'm getting thirsty," she told him.

"This way, then." He linked her arm in his, maneuvering their way off the crowded dance floor.

They cleared the light show, traversed the length of the bar, finding a quieter corner with soft furniture, low tables and muted lighting. They chose a section of a curved, bench sofa in an empty grouping, each sitting on one side of a curve, knees close together.

A white shirted waiter immediately arrived. "Can I get you a drink?"

"Mojito for me," said Danielle.

"I'll take the same," said Travis.

Danielle raised her brows. "You're sure you want to trust my taste in drinks?"

"I figure you've got to get it right sometime."

She looked to the waiter. "Bring him a beer. Anything from DFB."

The waiter glanced to him for confirmation.

"Aren't you bossy."

"I am." She sat back on the sofa.

"I'll take the beer," Travis confirmed. "I like your dress," he told Danielle as the waiter walked away.

Sitting down, she looked even better if that was possible. The dress accentuated her perfect breasts, showed off the indent of her slender waist, emphasized her creamy, smooth shoulders and her graceful neck. And those legs. If he could have designed a perfect pair of legs, they would be Danielle's.

"Thanks," she smiled, picking up the mini menu in the center of the table. "You hungry?"

"I'd eat. What do you feel like?"

"Something spicy." She let the menu fall open in her hands.

"There you are," came Katrina's breathy voice.

Travis's sister plunked down into one of the rounded chairs across the table from Danielle. Reed took one look at the size of its mate, and moved to the end of the sofa instead.

"Any interest in a Thai platter?" asked Danielle.

"I'd go for that," said Katrina. "And Reed'll eat anything."

"This is true," Reed agreed easily. "Living in New York, I've discovered I have an international palette."

"That's a very gracious way of putting it," said Travis.

The waiter arrived, and Katrina immediately pointed to the mojito. "I'll take one of those."

"Is that DFB?" Reed asked, pointing to Travis's beer.

"C Mountain Ale," said Travis as he accepted it.

"Sounds good to me," said Reed.

"We'd like the Thai platter," Travis told the waiter. "And bring us some of the barbecue sliders as well."

Danielle nudged his knee. "You can take the cowboy off the range?" she asked him, tone lightly teasing.

"I guess I'm not as international as Reed." Their gazes met and locked, and it took him a moment to break it.

"Hey, all." It was Mandy's voice this time. She was followed by Caleb who stopped the waiter to place their drink order.

Mandy took the chair next to Katrina, and Caleb took the one around the end of the table from her.

"At least Alex and Zach made it home from the bachelor party," said Mandy.

"They've got the most to do," said Reed.

Alex was marrying the Jacobses' cousin Lisa, while their brother-in-law Zach was his best man. Zach and Alex had started DFB brewery together years ago, only recently moving it to Lyndon Valley.

"The rest of you will have to come home eventually," said Mandy.

"Tomorrow, for sure," said Caleb. Then he glanced at Katrina. "Right?"

"Sadly, yes," she agreed. "But Danielle and I had to have a chance to show off our dresses."

Mandy glanced to Danielle. "I can sure tell Katrina helped you pick that out."

Danielle frowned as she glanced down. "It's not exactly my usual style, is it?"

Travis couldn't help jumping in. "Just because she's a lawyer, doesn't mean she's staid."

He received surprised looks from his sisters.

"Who said she was staid?" asked Katrina.

"We love Danielle," Mandy put in staunchly. "You should stop picking on her, Travis."

Caleb coughed in obvious amusement.

"What is wrong with you?" Mandy asked her husband. "Do you have a problem with Danielle's sense of style?"

"Of course not," said Caleb. "I trust Danielle's sense of everything. I'm hoping to send her to Europe."

Mandy's tone changed to one of eagerness. "We're going to Europe?"

"Danielle's going to Europe. Why? You want to go, too?"

Mandy gave an eager nod. "Maybe for a few days?"

Travis felt Danielle shift beside him. He could guess what she was thinking. If she took the job in D.C., she wouldn't be going anywhere for Active Equipment. He silently thanked his brother-in-law for making her choice perhaps a little more complicated.

"Have you made a decision about D.C. yet?" Travis asked Danielle.

It was nine in the morning, and he was shaving at one of the bathroom sinks in his suite while she applied a layer of mascara at its twin.

"I have five days left," she reminded him, holding her eyes wide for a moment so that her makeup wouldn't smear.

They were hurrying to meet the others in the lobby for the trip to the airport. She'd picked up her suitcase on the way to his suite last night. When they got back from the club, there'd seemed no point in her being coy about wanting to spend their final night together.

"You must be leaning one way or the other." He used a towel to wipe the excess shaving cream from his neck.

"I'm leaning toward putting the decision off as long as possible." She wanted to do both. It was impossible, of course, but that was what she wanted.

Travis turned to look at her profile. "You know he's going to lobby you to come to D.C."

She gazed at his reflection in the mirror as she applied some lip gloss. "Are you lobbying me on Caleb's behalf?"

"I'm not on my brother-in-law's payroll."

"Then, why are you asking?"

"Because Randal will lobby you," Travis told her with conviction. "And he's got his own agenda."

"Is this an I-told-you-so lecture? Because I already conceded to you on that point."

"This is a 'his agenda is not in your best interest' lecture."

She tucked her lip gloss and mascara back in her makeup bag, running a comb through her now dry hair. She really didn't want to have this conversation with Travis. He might be a macho, overprotective cowboy, but her life was hers, and she could take very good care of herself.

"I'm a big girl, Travis. And I'm reasonably intelligent."

He looked surprised, his face reflecting in the mirror. "I didn't mean to insult you."

She found herself growing impatient. "You're not insulting me. You're crowding me." She pivoted to face him. "I just spent the last two days in *your* bed, not in his."

"And I bet he knows it."

"So what?"

"So, it'll make him want you even more."

"Really? Truly? That's what you want to say to me this morning? That by sleeping with me, you've somehow made Randal more attracted to me? As if I couldn't do that all on my own."

"Whoa." Travis drew back.

"No, you whoa, cowboy." She lifted her makeup bag, deciding to make a swift exit. "You're a fun guy, and a good lover, but we're about to go back to our real lives, so you can stop fretting about what I'm going to do next."

He went silent for a beat. "Caleb will be upset if you leave."

She shook her head, forcing down the reflexive guilt she felt for even thinking about taking the D.C. job. "No, Travis. You don't get to use Caleb or Reed or Katrina against me. This is my life, and one weekend with me does not give you the right to interfere."

"I'm not interfering."

She headed for the bathroom door. "This is my decision."

He followed, and they emerged into the airy, opulent bedroom. "Of course it's your decision. I never said it wasn't."

Her suitcase was sitting on the mussed up bed, and she tossed in the makeup case and zipped it shut. "You're as bad as Randal."

"I'm nothing like Randal."

"Then let me figure this out on my own."

"I am."

"Good." She stepped into her shoes, glancing at her watch. "We're out of time."

"Yeah." His voice sounded hollow. He stared at her a moment longer then lifted the suitcase from the bed, moving toward the living room.

She slung her purse over her shoulder and followed him out.

"You want to go down first?" he asked her.

"Sure."

She met his eyes. She didn't want to fight. But she felt the need to protect herself from him encroaching on her life after they left Vegas. The interlude had been exciting, mind-blowing, completely unforgettable. But it had to end, and it had to end right here.

"I don't know what to say," he admitted.

"I think you want to say goodbye."

A muscle flexed near his right eye, but he didn't answer.

"Goodbye, Travis," she offered.

"Don't you dare try to shake my hand."

Before she could react, he drew her tight into his arms.

"Goodbye, Danielle," he whispered against her ear. "You call me if you—"

"Don't," she interrupted, pulling back.

"—ever need anything," he finished.

"I'm not going to need anything," she denied. She'd gotten along perfectly well, some might say extraordinarily well, in her life before he came along.

He gave a nod of acceptance. "Good luck with your decision. Somebody's going to be incredibly lucky to get you."

For some reason the compliment made her uncomfortable. She tried to make light of it. "Only until I make my first big mistake."

"You don't make mistakes, Danielle."

"Oh, yes I do. And I will. And when I do, well…"

She stopped. She realized she was rattling on, postponing that moment when she'd have to walk out his door.

"I have to go." She gave him a fleeting kiss on the mouth, then broke eye contact and extended the handle of her suitcase, tipping it onto its wheels.

Travis hesitated, but then he moved to open the suite door.

"I'll see you down there."

"Thanks," she nodded without looking at him and forced herself to walk through the door.

Shoulders squared, head held high, she quickly moved along the length of the hallway to the elevators. She didn't hear Travis close the door behind her, but she didn't look back. She rounded the corner, pressed the call button, and told herself to buck up.

Her future was square in front of her. Randal's unwelcome attention notwithstanding, D.C. was an excellent move for her to make. Caleb could find another lawyer. There were hundreds of other good lawyers in Chicago. Six months from now, Active Equipment wouldn't even miss her. Heck, they probably wouldn't miss her six weeks from now. She'd make sure her replacement was totally up to speed.

The elevator door opened silently in front of her.

Somebody else could manage the merger. Somebody else could go to Europe. And she'd never see Travis again.

The elevator started downward, it left her stomach behind.

Eight

On the plane ride back to Lyndon Valley, Caleb had asked Danielle to stay and work with him on the Pantara merger from their ranch for a few days. It seemed Mandy's favorite mare had fallen sick, and she didn't want to leave Lyndon Valley right away.

Danielle understood Caleb's desire to be near his wife, but she was anxious to get back to Chicago. Beyond the emotional complication of being so near to Travis, she needed to spend some time in her own office. She wanted to ponder what she'd be giving up by moving to D.C., maybe clean up her files, put herself in a position to make the move—if she decided she wanted to make the move.

But Caleb was her client, so she'd agreed to stay. She put her energy toward making contacts in Germany and working with international stock exchange listings. She struggled hard not to think about Travis being just down the road, tried not to wonder what he was doing, alternately hoping he would call and then being glad he hadn't. She'd been at the Terrell Ranch for a day and a half, and she hadn't had any contact at all with him. Not that she was paying attention. Talking to him would truly be a bad idea. Seeing him would be even worse.

Footsteps sounded in the hall, and Caleb appeared in the entry of the small office on the second floor of the ranch house.

"It's nearly six," he informed her.

"That's two in the morning in Germany. They'll be back at

the office in six hours." She was polishing a memo to have in Pantara's inbox when they arrived in the morning.

"All the more reason for you to stop working."

Danielle clicked open the attachment on an email. "I've got some German case law I wanted to go over on foreign owner-ship in strategic industry sectors."

Caleb moved into the room. "Anyone ever tell you you're a workaholic."

She glanced up at him, blinking in mock astonishment. "I'm sorry. *You're* accusing *me* of being a workaholic?"

"I'm a business owner," said Caleb. "I'm supposed to work 24/7."

"I'm billing you for all these hours," she informed him, scan-ning the index page of the document she'd just opened.

"I'm responsible for keeping you from working yourself to death."

"It's barely six o'clock, Caleb." When she was in Chicago, she rarely left the office before seven. And here, she didn't need to commute through traffic. She scrolled down to the executive summary of the paper.

"What time are you getting up?" he asked.

She hadn't decided yet, but likely around four. It was always a challenge to operate across overseas time zones.

"Mandy's putting burgers on the grill."

"Could she save one for me?"

"Travis is here."

Danielle's attention shot to Caleb. She swallowed, struggling to keep her expression neutral.

"I invited him up for a burger."

"That's nice."

It was obviously going to happen eventually. The Terrells and Jacobses were lifelong friends. She knew from spending time on the ranch in the past that they dropped into each other's places all the time. Travis was Mandy's brother. Of course he'd want to spend time with her while she was in Lyndon Valley.

Caleb cocked his head toward the door. "Let's go."

She glanced back at the computer screen. "I wanted to go through—"

"You have to eat."

She supposed that was true. But if she scanned the executive summary right now, she could come back later and zero in on the salient points. Plus, it would give her a few minutes to prepare herself for seeing Travis again.

"I'll be right down," she told Caleb.

"You're coming with me now."

"You don't trust me?"

"I trust you to get your nose buried in that paper and forget all about eating, sleeping and everything else."

Danielle knew she wasn't about to forget about Travis. He was downstairs, merely one floor below her. How should she act? What should she say?

"Danielle?"

"I'm coming," she capitulated, hitting the save button.

She'd treat him as a friend—no, as an acquaintance. She wouldn't fight with him, like she usually did. But she wouldn't say or do anything to allude to their fling, either. She'd be polite but distant, professional.

She rose from the desk chair and followed Caleb out of the office. They made their way to the end of the hall and down the staircase to the farmhouse living room. Voices came through the kitchen, the smell of barbecue smoke on the evening air. Mandy and Travis were obviously on the deck.

"Wine?" asked Caleb as they rounded the corner.

"Absolutely," she answered, just as she caught sight of Travis.

She stopped dead at the sight. He was laughing with Mandy, stance relaxed and easy, a bottle of beer in one hand. Dressed in a faded denim shirt and a worn pair of jeans, he looked completely at home against the backdrop of the mountains and the Lyndon River below. Her heart did a triple beat inside her chest.

"It's a merlot," said Caleb.

"Huh?" She gave herself a mental shake.

Caleb held up a bottle of red. "Merlot."

"Sounds great," she managed.

He snagged a wine glass from a shelf.

Mandy caught sight of her.

"Hey, Danielle," she called, grinning as she waved the spatula.

Travis swiveled his head, and their eyes met. A wave of energy passed through the air between them. Danielle felt it from the roots of her hair to the tips of her toes.

"Here you go," said Caleb, holding out the glass of wine.

"Thanks." She accepted the glass and took a big swallow.

"Thirsty?" asked Caleb.

"Very." She forcibly dragged her gaze from Travis.

Caleb turned to round the kitchen's island and head out the double doors.

Danielle forced herself to follow, telling herself to be professional. She could do this.

"Hello, Travis," she offered brightly. "Nice to see you again."

There was a brief moment of confusion in his eyes. "Hello, Danielle."

"How are things at the ranch?" she asked, choosing a deck chair near the rail to get herself off her wobbly legs.

"Same old, same old," he answered, pulling a chair from the dining table to face her. "Cattle, horses, broken water pumps."

"Were you able to fix it?" she asked.

"Ask him about the accounting software," Mandy suggested.

"The water pump was no problem," Travis answered.

"With Amanda gone, we tried to streamline the books," Mandy put in. "The new computer system is going to be the death of him."

Travis turned to peer at his sister. "I didn't sign up to do paperwork."

"Dail-E Entries?" asked Danielle.

"That's the one," answered Mandy.

"How did you know?" asked Travis.

"It's the most popular. If you take the tutorial, it's pretty straightforward."

"Travis, follow the instructions?" Mandy mocked.

Caleb laughed.

Travis frowned. "I don't have time to learn from a cartoon dog that talks to me like I'm a five-year-old. I've got real work to do."

"So, you tried the tutorial?" Danielle asked, struggling not to be amused by his obvious frustration.

"I made it through lesson three. Then I went outside and branded some steers instead."

Danielle grinned, feeling more relaxed. She sipped at the tasty merlot.

"You should go down give him a hand," Mandy said to Danielle. "You could probably show him how to work the system in a fraction of the time it would take to do the tutorials."

So much for relaxed. The last thing she needed was to be alone with Travis. "I'm pretty busy with Pantara."

"I can spare you for a few hours," Caleb offered easily.

Danielle looked to Travis, meeting his deep blue eyes. The energy vortex was pulling her in again.

"It'd be a big help," he said, expression perfectly neutral.

She had no idea whether he wanted to get her alone, or whether he truly wanted help with his accounting software. Either way, she'd look churlish if she refused.

"Sure," she offered, slugging back the last of her wine, kicking herself for having opened her mouth in the first place. "I can give him a hand."

Travis wanted to get this right. He didn't want to overstep, but he didn't want to pretend nothing had happened in Vegas either. Last night, Danielle had been polite but distant. Sure, Mandy and Caleb had been there the whole time, but she hadn't let on for a second that there'd ever been anything between them.

This morning, she was coming down to the Jacobses' ranch. He'd worked for a few hours, then he'd stopped to shower and shave, not wanting to offend her while they were working in close quarters. The ranch office was tiny, little more than a converted storage closet off the living room. It had a small desk and chair, a file cabinet and a computer. Travis had pulled in a stool for himself, so they'd both be able to sit down.

There was a knock on the front door. His chest tightened, knowing it had to be Danielle. Nobody else would bother with that formality.

He popped a mint in his mouth, reflexively straightened his shirt, glanced around the cluttered room, then headed across the living room to the entry foyer. Jackets, boots, hats and gloves littered a row of hooks and a bank of cubbyholes. He'd never given a moment's thought to the mess, but now he wondered what the utilitarian house looked like to Danielle.

She probably lived in a sleek, modern apartment. Maybe she had white, leather furniture and chrome fixtures. She probably had a cleaning lady who dusted her fine art and kept exotic plants looking lush and green. The only things Travis grew were oats and sweet grass.

He swung open the door.

"I'm only here to help with the software," she announced, expression stern, her eyes dark and serious.

She wore a pair of designer jeans, brown fashion boots and a dark blazer over a silver blouse. Her short hair had lifted in the breeze, but ended up chic rather than messy. She carried a big shoulder purse that was saddle bag brown. Somehow, she managed to look both city and country at the same time.

"Software is my current problem," he responded, stepping to one side and gesturing her in.

Not that he didn't plan to have other problems in the future—chief among them, an overpowering urge to pull her back into his arms. For now, he wished he could to erase this formality between them, get back to the intimacy they'd shared in Vegas. Those nights they were in his hotel suite, he'd felt closer to her than he'd ever been with a woman.

She stepped over the threshold. "Point me to your office."

He did. "Through that door."

She gave a nod and started walking.

"Can I get you anything?" he called to her back. "Coffee? Juice?"

She didn't bother turning as she answered. "Coffee would be good. Does your computer have a password?"

"Wrangler."

That time, she turned. "Seriously?"

He shrugged. "It seemed appropriate, easy for everyone to remember."

"We should talk security sometime."

"Sure. What do you want in your coffee?"

"Black," she responded.

He couldn't help but grin.

"What?"

"I was just trying to decide if you were more city or country. Black coffee is a good start."

Her gaze narrowed. "Is black coffee city or country?"

"Country, ma'am."

"I don't know about that."

"If you'd asked for a caramel, chocolate mocha with whipped cream, I'd have gone the other way."

"Aren't you the biased, judgmental cowboy?"

He just grinned, turning for the kitchen. "Log-on name is *Jacobs,*" he called over his shoulder.

"Of course it is. You probably also have a welcome mat for hackers."

There was a pot of hot coffee in the kitchen, so Travis was quickly back in the office with a stoneware mug in each hand. Danielle had taken the chair, and he set the blue mug down on the desk beside her. Then he perched himself on the stool over her left shoulder.

"This is the main menu." She pointed with her mouse.

"I got that much," he responded, taking a sip of the hot brew.

"On a daily basis, you'll need the top three items, entering payable, entering receivables, and printing checks. These next three are reports, including a balance sheet. And the rest are for setting up master files, doing audits and occasional trouble shooting."

She turned to look up at him. "So far, so good?"

"I understand the main menu," he responded, thinking she was beautiful. She smelled amazing. He could only hope he'd be able to drag his attention from her long enough to learn the other elements of the software.

"Glad to hear it." She turned back.

"Double click on payables, and it opens up a date entry screen." She demonstrated as she spoke.

The screen that came up in front of them showed about twenty fields, everything from vendor name to shipping date.

"Do you have a vendor master file set up?"

"No."

"Seriously?" She closed the screen.

"Sorry," he felt compelled to offer.

She heaved a sigh. "This is going to take longer than I thought."

As far as Travis was concerned, that was good news. He liked having her here. The longer it took, the better his chances of—

He stopped himself. His chances of what? He didn't want to seduce her. Not that he wouldn't give his eye teeth to sleep with her again, but that wasn't why he wanted her to stay.

He just wanted to be with her, he realized. Hear her voice, talk with her, joke with her, argue with her, find out what she was thinking about the D.C. job and about a hundred other things.

"Travis?" Her tone was sharp, and she smacked him on the knee.

He realized she'd been talking just then, and he hadn't heard a word. "What?"

"I said I'm going to show you how to create a vendor master file. You build it tonight, and I'll come back in the morning."

Oh, that didn't sound good. "How does that work?" he asked, mind searching for a way to make her stay. Ten minutes in her company simply wasn't going to do it for him. He'd been look-ing forward to seeing her all night long.

"Here." She clicked the mouse through a couple of menus. "You need to enter all of your supplier's tombstone informa-tion, and the system will assign them a five-digit number. That's your vendor ID."

"I type with two fingers," he lied. "There's no way I can enter all that stuff tonight."

She closed her eyes for a long moment. "You have got to be kidding me."

"No, ma'am."

"You do realize I have a whole other job."

"Yes, I do." But he couldn't seem to bring himself to care about that at the moment.

"And you do realize your brother-in-law is paying several hundred dollars an hour for me to type for you?"

"He offered," Travis defended, silently thanking Caleb for setting this whole thing up.

"So, I have to type in all of your vendors before we can even start."

Travis gave a shrug of innocence.

"Do you at least have a list of their names and contact in-formation?"

"Maybe." He stood up and maneuvered his way to the cabi-net. "I know they each have their own file folder."

"Give me strength," Danielle breathed from behind him.

Travis opened the drawer, pulling the first file. "Should I read them out to you?"

"If that's the best we can do, that's the best we can do."

"Acme Feed and Supply," he began. "Seventeen twenty-two, Rosedale Road."

Danielle's fingers clicked on the computer keys while Travis worked his way through the files.

At Streamline Irrigation Equipment, she finally agreed to break for lunch.

They left the office and worked together in the kitchen, making stacked sandwiches on rye bread, with turkey, cheese, to-matoes and cucumbers. Travis retrieved a pitcher of iced tea from the fridge, and they perched on stools around the island breakfast bar.

"This is a big job for one person, isn't it?" she opened before biting down on her sandwich.

"Running the ranch?" he asked, surprised that her mind might have gone to that.

She nodded.

"It is," he agreed.

He knew he'd have to find himself some additional help of some kind. But he hadn't quite wrapped his head around what that might be. The place had gone from a family of six, exclud-ing Katrina, with a wide variety of skill sets, down to only him in less than two years.

"Do you think Seth might come back and help you?"

"Not anytime soon. The railway project is going to take at least a couple of years."

"Maybe you should find yourself a wife," she suggested.

He frowned as he bit into his own sandwich. If he had a wife, he couldn't sleep with Danielle anymore.

"Someone who can rope and ride and cook and type," she continued. "I'm sure there are plenty of nice ranch girls in Colo-rado who know their way around a personal computer."

"Maybe I can take out an ad and collect resumes," he of-fered dryly.

"You could fill out an online dating profile. Just be specific about what you want."

"Is that how you're planning to do it?"

She sucked something from the tip of her thumb. "I don't need a man."

"Right, I forgot. Self-sufficiency is your mantra."

He didn't know why he was getting annoyed, but he was. He should be happy that she wasn't interested in a serious relation-ship. That should leave Randal out in the cold.

"It is," she agreed. "And I don't have a ranch to run. My

condo is pretty low maintenance. No livestock or irrigation equipment." She grinned into her sandwich. "Good thing. It's probably against the zoning bylaws anyway."

"What makes you so cheerful?" he couldn't help asking.

A few minutes ago, she'd been clearly frustrated at having to spend so much time helping him. Now, talking about marrying him off, all of a sudden she was bubbly and joking.

"You're complaining because I'm too happy?"

"I don't know why you want to see me married in such a hurry."

"I was only suggesting it as a means to divide the workload."

"Yeah, well if I marry some Colorado ranch girl, I'm going to have to sleep with her."

"That's the generally accepted convention. Though, legally speaking, it doesn't necessarily nullify the marriage if you don't."

He couldn't seem to help the annoyance churning its way through his stomach. "Legally speaking?"

"Yes."

Their gazes met and held.

"I'm guessing she'll expect it," he noted.

"I'm guessing she will."

"And if I don't want to?" he asked softly.

"Then, you'll probably have some explaining to do."

The room went silent between them. The only woman he wanted to sleep with was Danielle. Did she know that? Could she guess that?

"I've missed you," he told her.

"Don't."

He reached for her hand, taking it in his own. "You want me to pretend I didn't miss you?" He was tired of tiptoeing around his feelings, of measuring his every word.

She looked him straight in the eyes. "Yes."

For some reason, her answer amused him. "Do you also want me to pretend I'm not attracted to you?"

"That would be helpful."

"Why?"

"All the regular reasons."

"There are regular reasons? What are the regular reasons?"

She thought about it for a moment. "For starters, because I'm me, and you're you." She stretched her arm around the kitchen. "You have to take care of all this. Which is good, which is great. But I'm only going to be here for a couple more days. After that…" She paused. "After that, I have to…" She pulled her hand from his.

Travis's chest tightened. "You're going to take it aren't you."

At first she didn't answer.

A cold feeling of dread moved through his stomach. "Danielle?"

"Yes," she whispered. "I'm going to take it. I have to take it." Her voice grew stronger. "It's a once-in-a-lifetime opportunity to do exactly what I want to do with my career."

"And Randal?"

Her eyes narrowed. "What about Randal?"

"He's going to be there."

Her tone went tight. "And?"

Travis couldn't seem to stop himself. "And, you know he wants you. He's not going to give up."

The thought of Randal seeing her every day, having an open field to charm her and convince her. It might take him weeks or months, but eventually, he might succeed. They'd been an item once before.

"I can handle Randal," said Danielle.

"Can you?" Travis demanded. "Can you really?

Her face flushed. "What kind of a question is that?"

"You didn't do so well *handling him* in Vegas. You didn't see it coming. You wouldn't even believe me until it was almost too late."

"Almost too late for *what*?"

"He tried to kiss you."

She came to her feet. "And I stopped him."

"Do you think that settles it?"

"It settles it in my mind."

"Not in his. He's regrouping, re-strategizing. He's going to come at you all over again with a new game plan." Travis couldn't let this happen. With every fiber of his being, he knew he couldn't let this happen.

Her eyes went dark with anger, and her jaw clenched down tight. "That's got nothing to do with you."

He knew that was true, but he didn't care. "You can't go to D.C."

She was silent for a long while. Then she shook her head. "Watch me." She turned on her heel and walked out.

Danielle's heart was pounding and her hands were still shaking as she brought the car to a halt in front of the Terrell ranch house. Travis's questions had made her angry. His demands had infuriated her. Her career was none of his business. Randal was none of his business. None of this was any of his business.

She rammed the gearshift into Park and turned the key.

The idea that she couldn't manage Randal was ridiculous. It was insulting. Yes, sure, Travis had seen it coming before she had. But Danielle was the one Randal tried to kiss. She was the one who'd held him off. She'd told him no. She'd set down the ground rules. She was absolutely and completely capable of taking care of herself in D.C.

She exited the car, slamming the door harder than necessary. Then she stalked her way to the porch.

She'd slept with Travis twice. Big deal. They'd promised to leave it in Vegas. Well, she'd left it all in Vegas. As far as she was concerned, he was Caleb's neighbor, Katrina's brother, nothing more, nothing less.

She entered the ranch house, closing the door firmly behind her.

Okay, so maybe she still had the hots for him. Maybe she missed him. Maybe she couldn't stop dreaming about him. Again, big deal. Nobody got everything they wanted in life.

"Danielle?" came Katrina's voice.

"I'm back," Danielle called out, struggling to keep the anger out of her voice.

"What's wrong?" Katrina appeared in the entry hall. "You sound upset. You look—" Katrina peered at her. "What the heck?"

Danielle knew she couldn't brush it off completely. "I had a fight with Travis," she confessed, bracing herself for the worst.

"Is that all?" asked Katrina, expression neutralizing. "You fight with him all the time."

"Yes," Danielle agreed. "I do." A little bit of the tension left her stomach.

Maybe this was a good thing. Fighting with Travis was certainly more normal than sleeping with him. Although, their fights hadn't used to upset her this much. Then again, their fights had never been this personal before. Maybe she could look at this as a step back to their old relationship. It was worth a try.

"Did you get the software up and running?" asked Katrina.

"Partway," Danielle answered. "We ran out of time," she lied.

"I think Caleb will be glad to have you back." Katrina moved toward the living room, and Danielle went with her.

"Is something wrong?"

Katrina glanced at the stairs. "Judging by the language I'm hearing. Yes."

"Uh-oh." Danielle headed for the staircase.

"So, you'll finish tomorrow?" called Katrina.

"Pantara?" Were they done? Could she go back to Chicago now? That would be great news. She'd love to put Lyndon Valley in her rearview mirror.

Katrina looked at her as if she'd lost her mind. "The accounting software. Will you finish with Travis tomorrow?"

It was on the tip of Danielle's tongue to announce that she'd already finished with Travis. But that would only provoke questions.

"I think he'll be fine on his own now," she answered instead.

"That's great," said Katrina.

A string of swearwords echoed down the stairs.

Danielle glanced up. "Oh, that doesn't sound good."

"I've been afraid to investigate," Katrina confessed.

Danielle couldn't help hoping it was Pantara. Then again, she hoped it was a problem she could solve. She paused, realizing she would have to solve it in only three days.

She was almost out of time. Very soon, she'd have to tell Caleb her decision.

She mounted the stairs.

When she peeped into the office, Caleb had his phone to his ear. He motioned her forward.

"That's not good enough, Stan." Caleb paused. "Tell them no way in hell. Tell them we've got an ironclad contract. There is no loophole. And tell them to source the raw materials out of Brazil if they have to and pay the extra freight."

Danielle could tell he was talking to Stan Buchannan, the president of their South American division.

She sat down to wait for him to finish.

"Yeah," Caleb said gruffly. "Call me after." He hung up the phone.

"Trouble?" she asked, relieved to be back on familiar ground.

"I need you to go through the Greystoke contract. They want to backorder us on steel."

Danielle sat up straight. "They can't do that."

"That's exactly what I said." He gave a sheepish grin. "Well, I said a few other things, too."

"Won't that shut down the Columbia plant?" She moved to the computer desk, typing her log-in and password to the Active Equipment server.

"It sure will," said Caleb.

"It's all in Annex P," she spoke as she typed. "You'll be able to sue them into bankruptcy."

"I don't want to sue anyone. I want my production lines to keep running."

"You think threats will help?"

"I think they need to know exactly the consequences if they mess with me."

"On it, boss."

"That's what I like to hear."

Katrina appeared in the doorway. "Has the storm subsided?"

"For now," said Caleb, coming to his feet. "Sorry you had to hear all that."

"Danielle, I just talked to Travis."

Danielle's fingers faltered on the computer keys.

"He says he does need you to come back tomorrow. Something about finishing the vendor master file and looking at the payables system?"

"He'll be able to figure it out," said Danielle, blindly scrolling her way through the contract.

Katrina hesitated. "I know you were arguing, but maybe you should call him directly. There seems to be some confusion."

"Maybe later," said Danielle. "I need to get through this for Caleb right away."

"Sure," Katrina replied.

There was a moment of silence, before Danielle heard her walk back down the hall.

Thankfully, her vision cleared, and she was able to find Annex P.

"What's the confusion?" asked Caleb, moving up behind her.

Danielle swallowed. "I don't know. He's stubborn."

"No kidding."

"It's all there in the instructions."

Caleb paused. "What was the argument about?"

Danielle was losing her concentration again.

"Same old, same old," she offered airily. "But I really need to focus here."

"I know what happened between you two in Vegas."

Mortification washed through her. She spoke before she could stop herself. "Travis *told* you?"

"I guessed. He didn't deny it. And now, neither are you."

She shook her head at her own foolishness. She should have pretended she didn't know what Caleb was talking about.

"It was nothing," she told him now. "It's nothing. It was nothing, and it's over."

"Okay." Caleb's voice was calm and kind.

In her peripheral vision, she saw him sit down. "So, what was the argument about?"

Danielle knew it was time to tell him the truth. She turned to face him, screwing up her courage.

"I'm sorry."

"You have absolutely nothing to be sorry about. You're an adult, and—"

"Oh, no. Not that." She felt her face heat. "Travis is angry because I told him I was taking the D.C. job." Nervousness gripped her stomach. "I'm sorry about that, Caleb. The opportunity is just too good to turn down."

He smiled understandingly. "It's your decision, Danielle."

"I hate that I'm leaving you," she confessed. "I love working with Active Equipment. And this new project with Pantara. It's going to be huge, Caleb. You know that, don't you?"

He nodded. "I know it's going to be huge. I'd truly love to have you there with me."

For a second, Danielle was afraid she might tear up. She could barely speak. "I'm sorry."

"And I'm sorry Travis upset you. Your decisions are yours alone. He's got to respect that."

"That's what I told him."

"Good for you."

Caleb was such an understanding man, such an incredibly professional business owner, her behavior with Travis in Vegas suddenly seemed worse than ever. She felt like she had to explain.

"Travis and me," she began.

But Caleb shook his head. "Is none of my business."

"But I was there working for you. And he's your brother-in-law. And—"

"Stop talking, Danielle."

She pressed her lips together.

"My advice?" he asked.

She was a little afraid to hear it. "Sure."

"Go back tomorrow and talk to him."

Before Caleb was even finished speaking, she was shaking her head. "You don't understand."

"I understand that you're upset, and that's not good. Knowing Travis, he said something stupid. But he's a hothead, he blows up fast and cools down faster. I'm betting he wants to make it better."

She swallowed convulsively, tears threatening once more. "It's not that simple."

It wasn't just that she was angry with Travis. She was afraid of her own emotions. She didn't want to leave him. In his kitchen this afternoon, she'd come dangerously close to making a career decision based on a man. She couldn't do that, *wouldn't* do that. The thing between her and Travis was tenuous and fleeting. The Nester and Hedley offer was concrete. It would last. She couldn't afford to make an illogical decision that would affect the rest of her life.

Caleb gazed at her for a long moment. "Okay. You're right. You know what's best for you. You do whatever you want."

She gave a rapid nod. "Thank you."

"I am sorry to lose you," he told her. "But I'm genuinely happy that you have this opportunity."

"You're an incredible man, Caleb Terrell." She meant it with all her heart.

Nine

Caleb marched into Travis's living room, smacking his hands down on the back of a brown, leather armchair in obvious anger. "What in the hell did you do to her?"

Travis came to his feet. "Huh?" He did a double take of Caleb's icy expression. "You mean Danielle?"

"*Yes,* I mean Danielle."

"I didn't do a thing to her. She got ticked off and left."

"She was practically in tears. Do you have any idea what it takes to make Danielle cry?"

Guilt clenched Travis's stomach. Not that he'd done anything wrong. Randal was the bad guy here. Travis was trying to help. "I told her the truth," he defended.

"What truth?"

"The truth about Randal Kleinfeld. Did she tell you she's taking the D.C. job?"

Caleb gave a sharp nod.

Travis felt his nostrils flare. "It's a mistake. A big mistake. This whole thing has been orchestrated by Randal Kleinfeld, and he's trying to get back with her. I warned her in Vegas, but she wouldn't listen. Oh, sure, later, when he showed his true colors, she admitted I was right. But does she remember that now? No. She thinks he'll back off. She thinks she can handle him. But he's pond-scum. He'll hurt her. And she can't be around him."

Caleb's expression had moderated. "Is that what you told her?"

"Not in so many words. I reminded her that he had ulterior motives."

Caleb moved around the armchair and sat down.

Travis followed suit on the sofa across from him.

"Did you try to talk her out of it?" he asked.

Caleb shook his head. "It's her choice, her career. I can't hold her back."

"You wouldn't be holding her back," Travis pointed out. "You'd be saving her from a big mistake."

"It's a hugely prestigious law firm," said Caleb.

"One in which Randal is well and thoroughly entrenched. What do you think will happen if she refuses to date him? He'll get revenge. He'll try to undermine and discredit her. And he's the one with the contacts and relationships in D.C., not her."

"And if she does date him?" Caleb asked.

Travis felt his blood pressure go up a notch. The thought of Danielle in Randal's arms made him want to put his fist through a wall.

"That'll make it even worse," he told Caleb. "He'll trap her, and her entire world will be tangled up with that jerk."

Caleb was silent for a moment. "It's still her decision."

Travis gazed at his brother-in-law, grappling inside his head. He shouldn't say what he was about to say, but he had to say it.

He spoke softly. "You can stop her."

Caleb immediately refused. "No, I can't. And even if I could, I won't. I'm not going to guilt-trip her into staying with Milburn and Associates."

"Not Milburn and Associates." Travis had a better idea. "Active Equipment."

Caleb drew sharply back. "We're not a law firm."

Travis drummed his fingertips on the arm of the sofa, composing his arguments. "But you could use a staff lawyer. I've heard enough about the business to guess you could use Danielle full-time. Pantara and South America alone would keep her busy." He paused. "Make her an offer. Make it a good one. Keep her for yourself."

The grandfather clock ticked off seconds in the corner of the room. Travis could feel his heart beating in his chest. His body temperature rose a degree, and sweat began to form on his skin while he waited for Caleb's answer.

It was a full minute before Caleb spoke. "What's going on here, Travis?"

Travis knew he had to be honest with Caleb. "Randal can't have her. I can't let that happen."

"You want to keep her in Lyndon Valley."

"Yes."

"You want to keep her with you?"

Travis swallowed. He didn't understand why, and he didn't know how, but every instinct he possessed told him to keep her close and protect her. "Yes."

Caleb's hand rose to his chin, and his eyes took on a far-away look.

"What happened to all the fighting?" he finally asked.

"We still fight," Travis admitted.

Caleb seemed to digest that. "See, trouble is, I'm not convinced you're not Active Equipment's very own Randal."

Travis nearly came out of his seat. "I'm not some pretentious fake. I'm not going to hurt Danielle. I am *nothing* like him."

"Can you swear to me you're looking out for her best interests?"

"Yes."

"That you're not going to hurt her?"

"Yes."

"You nearly made her cry already."

Travis did come to his feet. "That was over Randal. He's the only thing we fight about now. I like Danielle. I don't want her hurt. I don't want her stuck in D.C. with a scheming shyster who's out to get her." He drew a breath. "You know you want to keep her, Caleb. This is a perfect solution. It might not be exactly what she'd planned, but she could have a fantastic career with you. Active Equipment is going to be a global conglomerate. You're going to need people you trust. She's been with you since the beginning."

Caleb stood. "Seth isn't the only Jacobs who should have gone into politics."

"I'm not spinning you a story," Travis said with complete conviction.

"If you are, you're doing one heck of a good job."

Travis clamped his jaw to keep himself from overselling the idea. He realized he cared more about Caleb's decision in this than he'd cared about anything in his life.

The silence stretched.

"I can offer," said Caleb.

A powerful rush of relief thudded through Travis.

"But I doubt she'll say yes."

"Convince her," said Travis with mounting enthusiasm.

"I'll lay out the facts, but that's all I can do."

"Offer a high salary, a good title, maybe vice president. Give her a bonus structure. Make sure you include dental. You've got dental at Active Equipment, right?"

"You want to take over on this?"

"No, no." Once again, Travis forced himself to stop talking.

"She'd be a valuable executive, and I have no problem making her a top offer. But I'm not a D.C. law firm, and that may be a deal breaker."

Travis forced himself to recognize the truth in Caleb's words. Danielle might not take the offer. There was nothing to indicate she'd even consider being a corporate lawyer. Truth was, there might not be a single thing he could do to keep her out of D.C.

Danielle's bag was packed and waiting by the front door. She was in the office, putting the initial Pantara files in order for Caleb and whoever took her place. She needed to get back to Chicago today and give her notice in person before she called Nester and Hedley to accept their offer.

She'd transferred all of the attachments from her email account to Caleb's computer. She'd taken copies of her Pantara emails, and she'd filed all of her legal research by country. From what she could see so far, Pantara had some financial challenges, but nothing critical. What they seemed to be looking for from the merger was access to Active Equipment's customer base. It was becoming well known across international markets that Active Equipment was supplying superior products and top-notch after sales service to its clients in construction, resource extraction and heavy industry.

Satisfied that everything was well under control, Danielle closed her email box, shut down the file program, and rose from her desk chair. She lifted her bag, slipped it over her shoulder, and took a last look around the room.

It was a quirky, little office with a sloped ceiling and a small window overlooking the hay barn, the fields and mountains beyond. Danielle couldn't help but smile at the thought that she was likely the only lawyer at Milburn and Associates who had a view of cattle from her office window.

Crossing to the window, she experienced a bit of nostalgia, realizing she'd never see this particular view again. Though she and Caleb had formed a quasi-personal relationship over the years, she was under no illusion that they'd see each other socially.

She'd certainly never see Travis again. The thought brought a familiar ache to her chest. She knew it was crazy to feel this way, and she'd spent most of last night fighting it. She wasn't going to miss him, at least not long term. Theirs wasn't that kind of a relationship. Theirs wasn't a relationship at all.

Still, she was sorry they'd fought yesterday. In fact, when she woke up this morning, she'd been half tempted to go to him and apologize. He might have been belligerent and meddlesome, but she hadn't needed to lash out at him. He didn't know Randal the way she did. Randal wasn't going to be a problem.

In fact, after the few nights with Travis, she wouldn't be looking twice at Randal ever again. She knew the difference now between mediocre physical intimacy and true lovemaking. Travis had made love to her, and she'd never again settle for less.

"Danielle?" came Caleb's voice.

She turned to face him, banishing her melancholy thoughts

and squaring her shoulders. Her decision was made, and it was time to move forward.

"Everything's filed," she told him. "It should be easy for someone else to take over." She moved toward him, determined to make this a professional, succinct goodbye. "But call me if you need anything, anything at all."

"Do you have a minute to talk?" he asked, his expression quite serious.

She paused. "Yes. Is something wrong?"

He gestured to the desk chair. "Nothing's wrong."

"Good." She hesitantly sat down, perching on the edge.

He braced his butt against a side table. "I'd like to make you an offer."

She waited a moment, trying to figure out where he was going. "An offer for what?"

"A job."

"You mean keep you as a client?" She had to be honest with him. "That'll depend on Nester and Hedley. But I'm not sure Active Equipment will fit in with my new portfolio. Of course, the firm overall would be thrilled to have you come over. But you might not be assigned to me."

"I wasn't talking about Nester and Hedley."

"Oh." Then she was stumped.

"I want you to work for Active Equipment. Full-time. As a corporate attorney. Your title will be Vice President of International Affairs."

Danielle slumped back in the chair, blinking at Caleb in confusion. "Uh, could you repeat that?"

"Vice President of International Affairs."

"I don't understand."

He cocked his head sideways and smiled. "I don't want to lose you. You know as well as I do how far we've come, how much potential we have going forward. I need smart people around me that I can trust. You're an incredibly smart person, and I know I can trust you. Money won't be a problem, you can name your price. And we have dental."

Danielle gave a helpless laugh. "Dental?"

"Does that sweeten the pot for you?"

"I still don't understand." She'd never thought of any career path other than a law firm. She didn't understand what Caleb meant by Vice President of International Affairs.

"You'd be doing all the things you do for Active Equipment already, plus, well plus whatever else you want to do. I know you, Danielle. I can point you in a general direction, and you'll figure out how to help me." He braced his hands on either side of the table. "You said yourself you weren't looking to leave Chicago, that the Nester and Hedley offer had come out of the blue. Well, here's another out of the blue offer for you. I hope it's something you'll consider."

She didn't have the first idea of how to respond. She loved working with Caleb, with Active Equipment. She was certain they had a huge future ahead of them. But to abandon her entire career plan, to take a complete left turn like that? How could a person make that decision?

"I'm already packed," she told him, realizing how silly it sounded even as the words came out. Who cared about an over-night bag down in his foyer?

"Do you have any questions?"

"I don't know. My brain seems to have shut down."

Caleb laughed. "I'm torn between telling you to go away and think about it and giving you a thorough sales pitch right here and now."

"I have a flight booked to Chicago," she pointed out, glancing at her watch.

"I have an airplane," he countered.

Her mind ticked through the possibilities. She could stay in Chicago, take on a whole, new exciting venture, and she wouldn't have Randal to worry about. She wouldn't be the new person on the totem pole. She'd have flexibility, autonomy. The sky was the limit for Active Equipment. And, *and,* if she did want to move to a law firm at some point in the future, a vice president position at an international conglomerate would look very good on her resume.

And then there was Travis. She'd be in Chicago, but she'd

still have her connection to Lyndon Valley. She was certain she'd be back, possibly often. Intellectually, she knew that was probably a bad thing. But emotionally, she wasn't ready to let him go. If she said yes to Caleb, she'd get to see Travis again.

For a second, she heard her mother's voice inside her head, warning her to never, never, *ever* make a career decision based on a man. But she shoved it away. It was a good job offer. It was a great job offer. Travis was incidental. She'd make certain he stayed incidental.

"I feel like I should negotiate something," she told Caleb.

A grin stretched across his face. "There's nothing to negotiate. Just tell me what it'll take."

"You're just going to hand me a vice presidency, on a silver platter?"

"You've earned it."

"I'm not sure about that."

"Well, I'm sure about that. And I'm the one who counts."

Danielle grinned.

Caleb came to his feet. "What do you say?"

She rose. "I think you've just made me an offer I can't refuse."

Caleb stuck out his square, callused hand. "That was my plan."

She reached out to shake it.

His expression was warm, his tone deep and sincere. "Welcome aboard, Danielle."

It took Danielle a week to clear things up at Milburn and Associates. She would have stayed longer, but they were clearly annoyed with her for leaving, doubly annoyed at losing Active Equipment as a client, and things in the office were tense. By midmorning Friday, she was walking out the door. By noon, she was on the corporate jet winging her way back to Lyndon City to meet Caleb.

She struggled not to think about Travis, but the closer they got to Lyndon Valley, the more he was on her mind. She hadn't spoken to him since their fight, and she couldn't help but wonder how he'd reacted to the news that she'd be working for his brother instead of going to D.C. He hadn't wanted her to take the job in D.C., but that didn't mean he wanted her underfoot, either.

Part of her wanted to avoid him. The other part wanted to get the first meeting over with as soon as possible. At least once she saw him she'd know where things stood. Whatever it was, she promised herself she could handle it. She'd have to handle it. She'd closed all the other career doors in her life, and her professional future was with Active Equipment. She was absolutely determined to succeed.

Caleb met her at the small airport, stowing her suitcase into the canopy of the pickup truck.

"Glad to have you with us," he offered, opening the passenger door.

She smiled, genuinely happy. Now that she was here, everything felt right. She grasped the door handle and hauled herself into the cab, smoothing her short skirt beneath her on the plaid-covered bench seat.

"Nester and Hedley would have sent a limo," she couldn't help but tease.

"We'd break an axle in the potholes," he retorted, clearly not the least bit offended or apologetic.

"I can see I'm going to have to adjust my standards."

"I don't think you'll have any trouble." He closed the door to round the hood.

She glanced down at her straight, black skirt, the white blouse and the blazer that she'd worn out of habit. If Caleb was going to need her in Lyndon Valley very often, she'd have to rethink the wardrobe.

"I may have to invest in a pair of plain ol' blue jeans," she told him as he opened the driver's door.

"Co-op's open 'till nine."

Danielle laughed. "That would be a first."

"Twenty bucks a pair. You can buy two."

She could buy five. Her blazer alone had cost four hundred dollars.

"But not today," said Caleb, slamming the door and hitting the key to start the engine.

"What's today?"

"Rehearsal dinner tonight."

"Rehearsal dinner?" Then it dawned on her. "Lisa and Alex's wedding?"

"Is tomorrow." Caleb confirmed as he pulled the shifter into reverse and backed out of the gravel parking spot.

She glanced at her watch. It was after two. "Do you have time to take me all the way to the ranch?" She didn't understand how he was going to make it back for the dinner.

"We're not going to the ranch."

"A hotel?"

That wasn't a problem. She could set up shop in a hotel room for the weekend. Maybe she would shop around for some more casual clothes.

"We're staying at the mayor's mansion."

"What do you mean 'we'?" Danielle wasn't involved in the wedding.

"Everyone's there for the weekend."

Everyone would most certainly include Travis. Danielle's mouth went dry. "You can drop me off at a hotel."

"What?"

"Caleb, I don't want to be in the way." And she didn't want to see Travis.

She'd thought she did. She'd thought the best thing was to get it over with. But she'd changed her mind. She wanted to put it off as long as possible. She very much feared he was holding a grudge. While she couldn't stop thinking about how much she liked him.

"You're not going to be in the way," said Caleb. "The place is huge."

"Square footage isn't my worry. This is a very special occasion for your family."

"They're pretty excited," Caleb agreed as he slowed down, entering the city limits.

"They'll be too busy to worry about me."

He sent her an arched look. "What makes you think they're going to worry about you? They'll park you in a bedroom, and you'll blend with the crowd. Katrina can't wait to see you."

Danielle gave an involuntary smile at the thought of hanging out with Katrina again.

"Fine," she agreed. She'd simply make sure she stayed out of everyone's path, especially Travis's.

"You say that as if you had a choice."

Danielle twisted her body to give him a mock scowl. "Are you going to be some kind of autocratic boss?"

He glanced at her. "You have a problem with that?"

She huffed a little. "You might find yourself with a rebellious employee."

His lips stretched into a grin. "I can live with that."

He flipped on his signal and pulled into the palatial driveway of the mayor's mansion.

The lawns were fine trimmed, as were the hedges. The building itself was three stories high. A huge front porch greeted them, with white pillars and an ornate rail.

Danielle took a deep breath, steeling her nerves.

Her next meeting with Travis was likely only moments away.

Travis watched from an archway leading to the great room while Katrina squealed and gave Danielle a tight hug. Then it was Lisa's turn, then Mandy and finally Abigail. His arms felt ridiculously empty and she hadn't even looked his way.

"You're coming to the dinner, right?" Lisa asked her. "And to the wedding."

Danielle glanced momentarily to Caleb then back to Lisa. "I'm... Uh... No. I have work to do. But it's very kind of you to ask."

"Don't be silly." Lisa grabbed her hands. "You have to come."

"Absolutely, she'll come," Katrina put in. "It's a wedding.

And there's no way we're leaving you here all by yourself while we go out and party tonight."

Danielle shook her head. "I really can't intrude. It's your family."

"You're family now."

"I'm an employee," Danielle corrected. "Just because I happen to be here working—"

"Don't insult us," said Mandy.

Danielle turned to her in obvious astonishment.

"Caleb thinks of you as much more than an employee. We all do."

"But—"

"Please come," said Lisa in a cajoling voice. "It would make me happy to have you there. And I'm the bride. You can't say no to the bride."

Danielle glanced to Caleb again, clearly uncertain about what to do.

"I don't need you to work on anything tonight," he told her with conviction.

"I don't have anything suitable to wear to a wedding," she protested, gesturing to her rather severe suit. "It's all like this."

"We'll go shopping," Katrina piped up.

"You've got work to do, young lady," Abigail reminded her. "Decorating committee. All of us."

Katrina gave a pretty pout.

Travis stepped forward. "I'll take her shopping."

The five women, along with Caleb, swung their gazes toward him.

"You?" asked Katrina in obvious astonishment. "Going dress shopping?"

"I'm not decorating," he pointed out. He didn't give a damn what errand got him alone with Danielle, so long as he got there.

He looked at her, struggling to keep his tone and expression neutral. "What do you say? Make the bride happy?"

"I'm—"

"I suppose you could drive her to the mall," Katrina put in.

"But you have to send me a picture of each dress so I can help choose."

"You don't trust my taste?" Travis asked her.

"Why on earth would I trust your taste?"

"I'll send photos," Travis promised, making a show of looking at his watch. "But we'd better get going."

Before Danielle had a chance to protest, he paced across the room and took her arm, gently turning her and urging her toward the front door.

Caleb shot him a knowing smirk as he passed by, but Travis ignored him.

"Rehearsal at six. Dinner's at seven," Lisa called from behind.

Travis gave them all a wave over his head. "We'll be back in plenty of time."

Then he pushed open the front door, and suddenly he and Danielle were alone. He had no idea what to say.

"What just happened?" she asked, glancing over her shoulder in confusion as they walked toward the wide staircase.

"You've been bamboozled by the Jacobs family."

"But why?"

He shrugged, pulling his truck keys out of his pocket. "Lisa wants you at the wedding. Really, Danielle, there was no chance they'd leave you home alone tonight."

"I offered to stay at a hotel."

Her words gave him a little jolt. He didn't want her at a hotel. He wanted her here, with him, where he could talk to her, look at her, listen to her breathe. He realized he had it bad for her, but he couldn't fight it. All he'd done for the past week was miss her. If he hadn't known she was coming back to work for Caleb, he might have gone stark raving mad.

He opened the pickup door for her, offering his hand to help her up to the seat. "Nobody wants you to stay at a hotel."

She ignored his hand and hoisted herself up to the seat. "I feel like an interloper."

"You're not an interloper. So stop worrying."

With her settled, he moved to the driver's seat. It was only a couple of miles to the Springroad Mall. He knew Abigail's favorite store was Blooms.

Once on the road, the silence settled between them, and he could feel the tension ramping up. Danielle tugged her skirt an inch down her thigh. Then she smoothed back her hair then tapped her fingertips against her knee.

Travis turned on the radio, filling the cab with a country ballad about lost love. He immediately wished he hadn't done it.

"It ought to be sunny for the wedding tomorrow," he noted out of desperation.

She didn't respond.

"They're having the wedding in the garden." He paused. "Reception in the mansion."

"I'm sorry," she blurted out.

He was confused. "About the wedding?"

"No. About the last time we spoke. I shouldn't have stormed out on you. You were out of line, and I was angry, but I could have handled it better."

He was so surprised by her unexpected words, that he didn't know what to say.

She was silent, then she adjusted her seat belt. Then she moved her sun visor.

He finally came up with, "I didn't expect you to apologize."

"I kind of expected you would."

Okay, that was even more surprising. "Me? What for?"

He'd only stated the facts.

"What for?" Her voice went a notch higher. "For meddling in my life."

"That wasn't meddling. That was warning you about someone who was operating against you."

"I told you I could deal with Randal."

"You don't have to deal with him anymore." And *that* was thanks to Travis. Though he'd never let on.

"I know that. But, I could have. And I would have. And you need to keep your opinions to yourself."

Travis thought about it for a moment. "I don't really see that happening."

She pressed her lips together. "At least keep your opinions about *my* life to yourself."

He shook his head. "Seems unlikely."

"Am I going to have to avoid you?"

"Personally, I'd suggest you get used to hearing my opinions. It'll be a whole lot easier than avoiding me."

"Travis," she protested.

"I mean, take a look at us now." He swung the truck into the parking lot of the Springroad Mall. "You're in town fifteen minutes, and already we're together.

"That's your fault," she accused.

"It is," he agreed. He'd shamelessly manipulated himself into this position. "But it shows you how easily it's going to happen."

He brought the truck to a halt, and they both climbed out of the vehicle.

"I thought things might have changed," she told him as they crossed the parking lot.

"What things?"

"You and me. Our relationship."

Her words took him by surprise. Did the woman have amnesia? "I'd say our relationship has changed a whole lot."

"Not fundamentally."

"Yes, fundamentally."

"You're still the same. I'm still the same. We can't seem to help from rubbing each other the wrong way."

It was on the tip of his tongue to make a joke about all the times when they'd rubbed each other exactly the *right* way. But he kept silent.

"Let's find you a dress," he said instead, nodding to a large purple sign on the side of the mall. "Abigail seems to like Blooms."

"I'm sure it's fine," said Danielle, sounding like she was heading for the executioner.

He opened the glass door. "You might want to work up a little enthusiasm. It's an important wedding, and I'm buying."

"Oh, no, you're not."

"I got you into this."

"Caleb got me into this. I asked him to drop me off at a hotel."

"Everyone would have been disappointed if he'd done that."

Travis included himself in everyone. Even now, sparring with her, frustrating her, on the receiving end of nothing but her annoyance, he was incredibly glad she was here. He realized he'd rather be arguing with Danielle than doing anything else with any other woman.

She gave an exaggerated sigh. "I wouldn't have been disappointed."

He nudged her shoulder. "Cowboy up. This isn't the end of the world."

"Cowboy up? I'm dress shopping here."

"It's a versatile metaphor. It means quit whining and get 'er done."

"I know what it means."

They passed through the big doorway to Blooms, and she stopped in front of a display of dresses.

"So, are you going to do it?" he asked.

She squared her shoulders, reaching for a simple, gray cocktail dress. "I'm going to do it. I'll buy myself a dress, say happy things to the bride and groom and cheerfully chat my way through dinner."

"It's a tough life," Travis deadpanned.

"Shut up."

"I don't think Katrina is going to like the gray." He extracted his phone from his jeans pocket and turned on the camera. He wasn't crazy about gray, either. He hoped he could talk Danielle into something sexier.

Ten

Danielle pulled the curtain shut on the changing cubical, and hung three dresses on the hooks placed around it, dropping her purse on the chair. She hadn't been crazy about the gray dress, either. She might have mixed emotions about attending Lisa's wedding. But if she was going to be there, she wanted to help celebrate, not bring anyone down with such a somber color.

She stripped out of her suit and pulled on a knee-length, aqua party dress. It had cap sleeves and multi-layered, gauze skirt. It was pretty, but seemed a bit young and frivolous for the occasion.

"Let's see," came Travis's voice through the curtain.

"I don't like it," she called back.

"I need to take a picture."

Danielle rolled her eyes in the mirror.

"Katrina's texting me," he said.

Danielle decided it was easier to humor Katrina than fight with her. "Fine." She drew back the curtain.

"Come out," Travis instructed.

Danielle took a few steps forward.

He raised the camera and snapped a shot. "Turn around."

She felt incredibly self-conscious under his scrutiny. "This is ridiculous."

"Tell that to Katrina."

Danielle reluctantly turned around. She posed for only a moment, then she retreated back into the changing room.

She didn't like having Travis stare at her. Okay, actually she did like having Travis stare at her. And that was the problem. There was nothing about a fashion show that ought to have been sexy, but she was getting aroused anyway. It was embarrassing.

She switched to the next dress, determined to get this over with as quickly as possible. The silk fabric was soft against her skin. It draped over one shoulder, with a wide, sash belt. She'd forgotten to remove her bra, so she had to take off the dress and try again.

"Ready?" called Travis.

Standing there in nothing but her panties, Danielle's chest tightened, and her skin flushed in reaction to the mere sound of his voice.

"Just a sec," she called out a little breathlessly.

She pulled the moss-green silk over her near naked body, reaching around to zip up the back. When she turned, she nearly groaned in despair. Her nipples had hardened and were clearly visible through the fabric. There was no way she was leaving this room.

"Danielle?" he called.

"It's definitely a no-go."

"Let's see."

"Not this one."

"Come on. Katrina is waiting. She gave a thumb's down to the blue one."

"No kidding." Danielle glanced back into the mirror. Okay. Her body had calmed down a little. She could risk it.

She pulled back the curtain, walking out on the carpet.

"Not bad," said Travis.

"Really? You're a fashion critic, too?"

He snapped a picture. "I know what I like on women."

"What you like on women has no bearing on my decision here."

He swirled his finger, indicating she should turn around. 'Probably a good thing. If I had my way, you'd be—"

"Don't you dare say something indecent." She turned back.

He grinned unrepentantly. Then his gaze dropped to her breasts and stayed there.

Uh-oh.

"Next," she quickly stated, whirling to get back into the changing room.

The third dress was a muted, Carolina blue. It was rich satin, with a strapless, tucked, crisscross bodice. Tiny crystals at the waist and neckline gave a muted sparkle, while the full skirt draped softly over a subtle crinoline, ending just above her knees.

"Katrina says no again," Travis called.

"Your sister has good taste," Danielle called back.

She craned her neck to look at the back of the dress, straightening the neckline, then she took in the side view. It wasn't bad at all. She'd have to pick up some dangling earrings, but her neutral pumps would work with it.

She opened the curtain and stepped out.

Travis stood still and stared.

"What do you think?" She pirouetted.

He stepped closer then closer still, until he was almost touching her. She caught her breath.

"You're going to dance with me, right?"

"That's not an option."

"Oh, yes, it is."

"Travis."

His broad hand covered hers. "Listen, we can pretend all day long, but there's something between us. And it's not going away. Dancing with you is the very least I want to do."

His blue eyes were intense while they held her gaze. His hand was warm on hers, his scent surrounding her, reminding her of things she'd hoped to forget. But she remembered in vivid detail, and her pulse leaped, her humming arousal gathered strength.

"I'll dance with you," she told him.

He smiled, and his hand tightened around hers.

"But that's all I'm promising."

"That's all I'm asking."

She hesitated for a moment. "You like the dress?"

His voice went husky. "I like the dress. I like what's inside the dress. I'm going to love the whole package when we're dancing together."

"Travis," she sighed this time. She knew she should make him stop flirting, but her protest was only halfhearted.

"I'm very glad you're not in D.C."

She grabbed the opportunity to tone things down. "I think it's going to work out with Caleb."

Travis opened his mouth, but then closed it again without speaking.

"You should take a picture for Katrina," Danielle prompted

"I don't really care what she says."

"I thought we were humoring her."

"Okay." He took a step back. "Smile."

Danielle turned and paused for a second picture. Then she made her way back into the change room.

"I'm going to need some earrings," she called as she finished putting her own clothes back on.

"Katrina likes it," came Travis's response.

"That's good."

Danielle slung her purse over her shoulder and hung the dress over her arm, sliding back the curtain to exit.

"Do you mind if we look for earrings?" she asked him.

"Not at all. You want me to carry that?"

"You don't have to be my assistant." Danielle had never met a man eager to trail after a woman in a dress shop lugging around her purchases.

"I'm a gentleman." He removed the sparkly dress from her arm and draped it over his own.

"You're not at all insecure about your masculinity, are you?"

"You can't get more macho than bull riding."

She glanced around at the dozens of shoppers. "Nobody here knows you ride bulls."

"We're in Lyndon City, Danielle. Everybody here knows I ride bulls."

"So, the real test is if you're willing to follow me around shopping in Chicago."

"Bring it on, sweetheart."

Her heart skipped a beat at the endearment. Luckily, she didn't need to respond, because they'd arrived at the jewelry section of the store. She quickly veered away from him, zeroing in on an earring display.

She moved her way past the studs and hoops. She needed something with a drop. When she came to the right section, she concentrated on the display beneath the glass, refusing to look back at Travis.

A pair quickly caught her eye. They were white gold, in a twisted vine pattern, decorated with white sapphires and aquamarines. She asked the clerk to see them and held them up to her ears in front of a small mirror on the countertop. They were perfect.

"Find something?" asked Travis from a few counters away.

"I did."

"You're pretty fast at this."

"You go shopping with a lot of women, do you?" she asked as she moved toward him.

"Occasionally. I do have three sisters. Though, Mandy's in and out in about thirty seconds."

"You find something for yourself?" Danielle teased, glancing down at the display. To her surprise, it was diamond rings.

He pointed. "That one looks like Lisa's. She went with colored diamonds. Mandy's is classic, a solitaire. Katrina's is really modern." He pointed to a platinum, nonsymmetric swirl with varying sizes of diamonds decorating it. "Reed bought it at some fancy store in New York. I can't even imagine the price tag."

"Are you doing a study of engagement rings?"

"Just thinking about the differences between the Jacobs women. Abigail has an heirloom ring from Craig Mountain Castle."

"That sounds nice."

He studied the display case in silence for a moment.

"Do you have a favorite?" she asked him.

"Favorite sister?"

She nudged him with her elbow. "Ring."

He shook his head. "You?"

They all looked beautiful to her. "I've never given it a lot of thought. My family's focus was more on the prenup than anything else."

Travis chuckled.

"I think," she ventured in all honesty. "The ring's a bit irrelevant. I'd be a lot more interested in the man presenting it."

"Good answer."

The clerk appeared in front of them. "Can I help you with something?"

Danielle and Travis glanced rather guiltily at one another, both obviously realizing how this looked.

"Un, no," she quickly answered. "We have a friend who's getting married."

It wasn't really much of an explanation, but she quickly rattled on. "I'm ready to pay, if you could direct me..."

"Right over here," she pointed to a nearby register. "I'll be happy to ring those through for you."

Danielle ducked her head and quickly followed the middle-aged woman. What was the matter with her? She needed to put up barriers against Travis, not engage in cozy chats over diamond rings of all things.

There were a whole lot of people at the rehearsal in the garden of the mayor's mansion. Danielle stood off to one side, trying to stay in the background. She had been introduced to the Jacobses' parents, Hugo and Maureen. Lisa was the daughter of Maureen's deceased sister Nicole. Nicole had run away from home as a teenager, and the family had only recently learned of her daughter's existence.

Danielle had met Abigail Jacobs on several occasions. Her

husband, Zach, had grown up with the groom, Alex, in a home for orphaned boys. She was also already acquainted with Niki Gerrard, Caleb and Reed's half sister. Niki had recently married Washington, D.C. mover and shaker Sawyer Layton. The two now spent as much time as they could on their own ranch in Lyndon Valley.

Abigail was the matron of honor, while Zach served as best man. Katrina and Mandy were bridesmaids. Two of Alex's longtime friends from DFB Brewery were standing up as groomsmen. Danielle couldn't immediately remember their names. Nor could she remember the names of their girlfriends. Seth, as mayor, was officiating, right now directing operations for the rehearsal. His new wife, Darby, was clearly pivotal in the organization of the event.

"You okay?" Travis's voice so close startled her.

"I'm fine," she answered.

"You look worried."

"I'm just trying to keep everyone straight."

"I could write up a cheat sheet."

"That would be nice. Did I ever mention I'm an only child? When I get married, *if* I get married, there will be approximately six people in attendance."

"I doubt that."

But Danielle gave a decisive nod. "There'll be no need at all for a cheat sheet."

"Wait until you see all this tomorrow."

"I'm dreading it."

"Don't be modest. You're in crowds all the time. Look at the conference in Vegas. I've seen you work a room."

"With lawyers," she protested. "I can talk business all day long, but put me in a family setting." She gave a shiver. "I pretty much panic."

"I'm a lowly cowboy, and I braved your lawyers' Van Ostram Gardens for you."

"Lowly cowboy, *huh*," she mocked. "You fit in anywhere."

"So do you."

Seth called out to Darby, who gave a saucy answer while moving the bridesmaids into position for the mock procession. Everyone erupted in laughter.

"Holidays at my house were sedate and boring," said Danielle. "Nobody teased, nobody joked. We dressed impeccably, and discussed meritorious topics of international interest, while staff served fine French cuisine."

"Sounds horrifying," Travis remarked.

"My point is that my upbringing was very different from yours, and this massive family thing is intimidating."

"Holidays at our house were bedlam and chaos."

"I bet you loved it."

"I loved it," he agreed.

A sense of emptiness overshadowed Danielle's feelings.

Hugo was giving Lisa away, putting her hand in Alex's, who gazed down at her with love and longing. She tried to imagine her own father walking her down the aisle, shaking the hand of her soon to be husband. The picture didn't work.

He'd probably wax on about the archaic convention of a woman passing from her father's care to her husband's. Danielle could take care of herself, she didn't need to count on any man. By the way, did she need him to look over her prenup?

A spurt of laughter erupted from her.

"What?" asked Travis.

"Nothing. Will you really help me?"

"Help you what?"

"Navigate your family tonight?"

There was a very slight pause before he answered.

"Yeah." His voice was husky, and the back of his hand brushed lightly against hers.

A spurt of desire in her abdomen was followed by a warm glow moving up her arm. She almost curled her hand into his palm, stopping herself just in time.

"That's a wrap," called Seth. "I think we've got it under control."

His wife, Darby, whispered something in his ear.

He grinned and immediately wrapped an arm around her, giving her a kiss on the temple.

"The cars will be waiting out front," he called to everyone else.

Chatting happily, the crowd started along the concrete pathway to the back of the mansion.

"Big breath," Travis whispered to Danielle as they both moved to follow.

They traveled in the same car, and Travis sat next to her at one of five round tables set up in the private, second-story room of the Riverfront Grill. It had an expansive view of the Lyndon River, looking west over the Rockies, and they were just in time for a gorgeous sunset.

Caleb and Mandy, along with Katrina and Reed, had joined them at the table. Alex and Lisa sat with Zach and Abigail at the head table, along with Hugo and Maureen. Danielle noticed that Maureen stuck fast to Lisa, taking every opportunity to hug her or smooth her hair. Both women glowed, seeming delighted in each other's company.

As Katrina chatted happily about the wedding cake, the flowers and the decorations they'd put up at the mansion during the afternoon, Danielle began to relax. Katrina raved about Danielle's dress, sharing the pictures with Mandy, and teasing Travis about being a shopping companion. Caleb and Reed stepped in as well, but Travis took it all in stride.

They were interrupted by the clinking of a knife against a glass. The room went silent, as Hugo rose to his feet.

Though he'd suffered a stroke many months back, he was now fully recovered. He looked strong and sure standing in front of his family.

"This is the time," he opened in a clear voice, "a toast would traditionally be given by the father of the bride." He looked to Lisa and smiled lovingly. "As you all know, these are special circumstances."

He paused and cleared his throat. "What I'm about to say to you, I've discussed at length with your mother, with my wife Maureen."

Maureen reached up from her chair and took his hand, gripping it tight.

"I spoke with Lisa this morning. She and Alex have asked me to tell you this." Hugo paused again, clearly bracing himself.

Everyone in the room had gone still and silent.

"As you all know, we learned of Lisa, your cousin's, existence only recently. Her mother Nicole was an amazing young woman, who we miss and mourn every day. What you don't know, is for a short time, many, many years ago, Maureen and I grew apart in our marriage. We separated, even considered divorce."

Danielle felt Travis stiffen beside her. She glanced at his profile, seeing his jaw tighten and his eyes go hard.

"During that time, I had a short-lived relationship with Nicole. It ended amicably. She moved on, and I thought it was merely a blip on the radar of our lives." Hugo reached for a glass of water and took a drink.

Maureen reached up with her other hand, wrapping them both around his. Lisa was blinking rapidly, while Alex had placed an arm around her.

Danielle, along with everyone else in the room could guess where this was going. She reflexively reached for Travis's hand. It was cold against hers, but she held on.

"Seth, Travis, Abigail, Mandy, Katrina." Hugo named each of his children individually. "Lisa is not just your cousin. She is your sister."

It was Hugo's turn to blink, but he couldn't quite contain his emotion, and a single tear streaked down his wrinkled face. He turned to the wedding couple. "And so, as the father of the bride, it is my proud and incredible honor to congratulate Alex, and tell you, Lisa, that I love you very much, that Maureen and I both loved your mother, and we could not be more delighted to have you as part of our family." He raised his glass. "To the beautiful bride."

There was only stunned silence, and then applause filled the room. Katrina squealed and jumped to her feet, rushing to Lisa to hug her tight. Mandy followed after her.

Maureen came to her feet and hugged Hugo, the two embracing for a long time.

Travis didn't move. He looked as if he'd been sucker punched.

Danielle leaned in, pressing herself against his shoulder. "Go," she whispered. "Lisa needs you right now."

Travis turned to stare blankly at Danielle.

"Go," she repeated, giving him a small shake. "Tell your sister you love her. Anything else can wait."

He seemed to rouse himself. Then he nodded his agreement.

He rose from his chair and strode determinedly to the head table. His eyes were warm, and his smile was genuine as he spoke to Lisa. He hugged her to his chest, then he shook Alex's hand. That he didn't speak to his father seemed lost in the general chaos surrounding the family.

"Looks like the women are taking it better than Travis and Seth," Caleb muttered.

Danielle scanned the room for Seth and realized Caleb was right. Seth was hugging his mother. Over her shoulder, his expression went tight and accusatory for the fleeting second that he met his father's eyes.

Danielle quickly switched her attention to Caleb. "I shouldn't be here." It wasn't right that she was witnessing this intimate family moment.

"Travis wants you here," said Caleb, causing Reed to send him a confused look.

"He wanted to dance with me," said Danielle. "He had no idea this was going to happen."

"It's good that you're here," Caleb insisted.

Katrina returned to the table, wrapping her arms around Reed's neck. "Isn't it wonderful?"

"It's a surprise," Reed responded.

"A good surprise. A *great* surprise."

"Well, well, well," said Mandy as she took her seat next to Caleb.

"People are complicated," said Caleb, lifting her hand and kissing her knuckles.

Travis plunked down. "Is *that* the word we're using?"

The tension was clear in his tone, and Mandy and Katrina both gaped at him.

"I think it's the right word," Danielle quickly put in. "Life doesn't come in a neat package with a bow on top."

He gave her a hard look. "That doesn't mean it—"

She grasped his shoulder, pulling up to kiss him hard on the lips. He stilled in what had to be shock. She pulled back a mere inch from his face.

"Shut up," she whispered harshly for his ears alone. "Don't hurt your sisters. Don't upset your family. Just shut up right now."

He didn't answer, but he leaned in and kissed her again, this time longer, and he was obviously no longer shocked.

They drew apart to amazed stares of everyone at the table.

"Danielle and I dated in Vegas," Travis told them all, his tone back to normal. "So, you might want to get used to her kissing me."

"You dated in Vegas?" asked Katrina.

"We had lunch," said Danielle. "You know we danced that night. I wouldn't exactly call it—"

"Dating," said Travis with finality, and he looped an arm around her shoulders.

"Well, well, well," Mandy repeated.

Reed stepped in, reaching for one of two bottles in the center of the table. "I think I should pour the wine."

"Excellent idea," said Caleb.

Danielle swiftly lifted her glass and held it out. She had no idea what was going to happen next, but a little wine sure couldn't hurt the situation.

Seth joined Travis where he'd parked himself against the wall, gazing through the window at the lights on the river walk below.

Seth copied his posture, leaning back, staring out the window. "You as ticked at him as I am?"

"Yeah. For a minute there I wanted to string him up."

"He cheated on our mother," said Seth, downing a final swallow of whiskey.

Travis wished he had one himself. "She didn't deserve that."

"They *were* separated, I suppose."

"Do you have any memory of that?" Travis asked his brother. "I don't remember any fights, any trouble. Did it all just go away?"

"I have a vague recollection of yelling, of Mom telling him to leave, crying. She was hugging you, and Abigail was in the bassinet. I think I picked her up and brought her to Mom."

Seth tried to take another drink, but the glass was empty. "Weird, huh? That memory shimmering there all this time?"

"He shouldn't get off scot-free."

"It seems like Mom's forgiven him."

"She loves him," said Travis. His mother was kind, caring and pragmatic. Just because she'd given their father a break, doesn't mean he deserved it.

"We love him, too," Seth reminded his brother.

Travis wanted to argue the point. They loved the man they'd thought he was. This was a whole new side of him.

"What are you going to do?" he asked Seth instead.

"Nothin'. It was a long time ago, and it brought us Lisa. It's up to Mom to forgive him or not. And it seems like she has."

Travis thought about that. "With you and Darby. Would you ever, I mean even if you were fighting, would you cheat on her?"

Seth's gaze moved to Darby. "Not even with a gun to my head."

"Good to know." Somehow that reaffirmed Travis's faith in his gender. "Caleb and Reed, do you think? 'Cause I might have to kill them if they hurt our sisters."

Seth grinned. "Not a chance. Not Zach, either. Despite what you hear, bro, most men don't cheat. We marry the right person, and we stop wanting anyone else."

Travis's gaze fell on Danielle, laughing and talking with Katrina. He thought he understood what Seth meant. He wasn't married to Danielle, wasn't in love with her, but when she was around, the entire world disappeared. Other women were irrelevant.

"Thanks," he told his brother, straightening away from the wall.

"What are you going to do?" asked Seth.

"Nothin'," Travis tossed over his shoulder.

His brother was right. Their father and Nicole were the past. Lisa was the present.

He reached Danielle. "Hey."

She turned and smiled at him, and he felt its impact right to his toes.

"You want to walk?" he asked on impulse.

"Walk where?"

"Back to the mansion. We can cut across the park."

She glanced down at her shoes, which were heels but not too high. "Sure."

"See you guys back there," sang Katrina, taking her leave.

Travis slipped his hand over Danielle's, and they took the back exit, climbing down a narrow staircase to come out at the river walk.

"You okay?" she asked as they set a course along the bank, the sound of the river filling in the background.

"I'm okay. I talked to Seth."

"Did you talk to your dad?"

"Not yet. But I will. I don't like it. I'm not sure my mother should forgive him. But that's not my call to make."

"Really." She seemed surprised.

"What really?"

"I know you meddle. And I always heard you were a hot-head."

"I am a hothead."

"That was a sound, reasoned, rational decision."

"I have my moments."

"That, you do," she agreed as they walked.

"You're the hothead," he accused.

"I most certainly am not."

"You kissed me to shut me up. Was that reasoned and rational?"

"No, that was impulsive. But you were about to do something really stupid."

"Impulsive is another way of saying hothead."

"I notice you don't disagree on the stupid part."

He tugged her playfully against his arm, and she hop-skipped to keep her balance.

"I don't disagree on the stupid part," he told her.

"That's progress."

"Progress toward what?"

She shrugged her slim shoulders. "I don't know."

They walked in silence for a while, along the river, then across the park walkway. Travis kept her hand in his, glancing every once in a while at her profile, reminding himself how beautiful she was, how smart, how funny. He was content simply to be with her, and he wished the walk would never end.

Too soon, they arrived at the back gate of the mansion and its gardens.

"What now?" asked Danielle, taking in the arched wrought iron.

"I've got the combination," he told her, typing into the key pad. The lock clicked free, and he pulled the gate back wide enough to allow them to go through.

"Impressive," she said as she passed.

"You mock my bull riding, but this does it for you?"

"Bull riding is brute strength, no thinking required. This shows preplanning and intelligence."

"I've never met a foolish bull rider," Travis defended.

"I bet you've met a lot of bruised ones."

"True enough."

"Why would an intelligent man get on the back of a two-thousand-pound beast intent on doing him harm?"

"The adrenaline rush," answered Travis, pulling the gate back into place. "You can't beat it for a thrill."

She'd stopped to wait. So they were now facing each other in the dark garden.

"You like thrills, cowboy?"

He heard a sensual edge to the question, but he was sure it was his own imagination.

"I love thrills." He wanted to kiss her so badly, it was all he could do to hold back.

She was drop-dead gorgeous in the moonlight. Her hair was mussed, her lips dark, her eyes soft pools above beautifully flushed cheeks.

"I like safety and predictability," she countered.

He raised his fingertips to her chin. "That's too bad."

"Why?" she asked in a voice that had gone low.

"Because I'm not predictable, and I'm sure not safe."

His lips parted, but she didn't reply.

"I'm going to kiss you, Danielle," he warned.

"I know," she acknowledged.

"And I'm not going to stop."

Eleven

Danielle let herself mold against Travis's body, holding herself tight against his hard strength. She hadn't known until now just how much she'd missed him, how much she'd ached for his touch, his taste, his scent. There was nothing reasonable or rational about her emotions, but she felt as if she'd finally come home.

She kissed him deeply, instantly opening up to him as his tongue tangled with hers. His hand slipped its way down her back, cupping her buttocks, pulling her tight to the vee of his thighs. She twined her arms around his neck, stretching up to devour his kisses.

Her skin felt too tight, warm and restless. At the same time, desire swirled from the base of her belly to the tops of her thighs, circling, tightening every nerve ending it found. The breeze buffeted her ears, muting sounds and blocking out the world. There was only Travis, nothing but Travis.

Their kisses went on and on.

"I've missed you," Travis groaned against her mouth. "I've missed you so, so much."

"Don't let me go," she begged. She couldn't stand it if something broke them apart right now.

"I'm not letting you go."

He kissed her again, over and over, until both of them were breathless.

He drew his head back, kissed her once more, then drew his head back again.

"The gazebo?" He canted his head to the side.

She nodded her agreement.

He took her hand, and they rushed down a short pathway. It led to a cedar gazebo, octagonal in shape, a half wall bottom with screened window openings around the top. The night breeze and the scents of pine and asters wafted inside. A bench seat stretched along the walls, and Travis sat down.

He pulled her forward. She clambered up, straddling his lap. Her skirt rode up, but she couldn't have cared less. The closer she could get to him the better.

He tipped his head to kiss her. His thighs were warm against her bare legs, her knees braced on the smooth, cool, wooden bench. He looped his arms beneath her blazer, stroking her back through her thin blouse.

She shrugged out of the confining jacket and tossed it on the bench beside them. His broad hands cradled her ribcage as their kisses continued.

After long moments, she slowly straightened from him. She looked deep into his eyes, smiling with knowing anticipation. She tugged her blouse from the waistband of her skirt. Then, starting with the bottom button, she popped them free, one at a time.

His breathing was deep and even, his fingertips convulsing gently against her as he watched her progress. His gaze locked onto the seam of her blouse, eyes widening as she drew it open, revealing her lacy, white bra.

"Have I told you that you're gorgeous?" he rasped.

She slipped the blouse off her shoulders and tossed it on top of the blazer.

"You ain't seen nothing yet," she told him, reaching back to unhook her bra.

She didn't feel remotely self-conscious. She wanted him to see her. She wanted him to touch her. She wanted to make long, slow love with him tonight. Maybe she was being hotheaded and impulsive. But she couldn't bring herself to care.

She peeled off her bra, and he sucked in a tight breath.

"How did this happen?" he mumbled.

"I was born a girl."

"Thank goodness for that."

"You're overdressed," she prompted.

He lifted his gaze to hers. "Can I just sit here and stare at you?"

His words brought a smile to her lips. "For how long?"

"Forever."

"Sure," she told him, leaning down to kiss his mouth. "But we'll miss the wedding."

"What wedding?"

As she kissed him, she pushed off his jacket. It pooled on the bench behind him, and he freed his hands. She went to work on his tie, then the buttons of his shirt.

His hand closed over her breast, and she fumbled with a button, a moan escaping from her lips. His palm was warm, her breasts cold and the contrast was unbelievably arousing.

"I want you," she told him. "So very much."

"Oh, Danielle," he groaned. "I don't know how to be without you."

He ripped off his shirt, wrapping his arms tightly around her, drawing her bare breasts to his skin. He kissed her again, his mouth on hers, tongue delving.

A sense of urgency overtook her.

She got rid of the rest of her clothing and his in record-breaking time, and then, they were one.

His hands slipped up her skirt, cradling her hips, pressing her down then lifting her up, synchronizing her to the rhythm of his body. Warmth radiated from their joining. Pleasure skipped across her skin. She kissed him desperately, while her hands kneaded his shoulders, then his back, then his buttocks.

"Don't stop," she told him. "Keep going forever."

She wanted the sensation to go on and on. She was happy and safe. Travis's arms were strong around her. There was no yesterday, no tomorrow, nothing else mattered except the two of them together.

His thumbs slipped along her thighs, up to where their bodies joined. She gasped and jolted at the sensation, her head falling back and her toes curling in her shoes.

"Forever's not possible," he told her through gritted teeth.

"Now," she cried out. "Right… Now…"

He groaned his release, and her climax cascaded through her. Her body convulsed around his, as warmth bathed her skin in pleasure.

She went limp, falling against him, her head on his shoulder, unable to move.

He anchored her close, massaging her bare skin. Then he reached for his suit jacket and draped it around her, cradling her in the warm cocoon.

When she finally found the strength to raise her head, he touched his forehead to hers.

His tone was low, almost reverent. "You rock my world, Danielle Marin."

She drew back, blinking, making a show of gazing around the gazebo. "There's still a world out there?"

His chuckle was deep. "I wish there wasn't."

She met his eyes, unfathomably beautiful. Something shimmered and bloomed inside her chest, and for a split second she feared she might tear up.

He smoothed back her hair. "Will you date me now?"

She couldn't help but smile. "I guess I'd better date you now."

"For starters, do you want to be my date at a wedding? There's a bit of family drama in the background, and a crowd of hundreds, but otherwise it should be fun."

"I would love to be your date at a wedding. I've got a really great dress."

He sobered.

So did she.

Unable to help herself, she leaned forward and kissed his mouth, gently to start. Once, twice, three times.

His hands came up, palms cradling her face. His jacket fell away, and she leaned against him, got lost in his kisses, wrapping herself around him all over again.

"What *is* this?" she gasped when they finally came up for air.

He buried his fingers in her hair. "I have no idea. But it's getting stronger."

The wedding came off beautifully, a sunny, fall day with flowers still blooming in the garden beds. Danielle loved Lisa's strapless, A-line gown, of white chiffon. It had a sweetheart neckline, and the snug bodice was accented with sparkling beads. Her blond hair was pulled back in a causal knot, held there by a jeweled comb. She carried a small bouquet of white roses and purple iris. Alex looked incredibly handsome in a black suit with a crisp, white shirt, his purple tie matching her bouquet.

Danielle had sat next to Travis in one of the front rows, where he'd surreptitiously held her hand, stroking his thumb across her knuckles while the couple repeated their vows beneath a flower and white chiffon decorated arch.

Dinner was sumptuous and impressive. But as soon as the formality of the first waltz was complete, Travis claimed her hand and guided her onto the dance floor. A few dozen other couples joined them, and they were swallowed into the crowd.

As he drew her into his arms, Travis sighed heavily in her ear. "I've been waiting for this since you left me last night."

"It's a tough life," she gently mocked, parroting his words from yesterday.

"Tell me you missed me, too."

"I missed you, too," she admitted.

They'd said goodbye in the mansion's back foyer last night, each retiring to their respective rooms. She'd lain awake half the night thinking about him, missing his arms around her, wondering where she and Travis went from here.

"I *need* to sleep with you tonight," he told her now.

She eased back to admonish him. "Aren't you presumptuous." Even though she wanted exactly the same thing.

"No," he swiftly denied. "I mean, not that. I mean, yes that, but only if it's what you want. What I mean is *sleep,* literally. I want you in my arms all night long." He drew her back against him. "I've realized nothing else is good enough."

As much as she'd love to spend the night in Travis's bed, she felt compelled to inject some reality into the conversation. "I don't see how we manage that."

"Not here," he agreed.

"But we are here. And so is everybody else. One of the joys of that humongous family of yours."

"A hotel," he suggested.

"Oh, that's discreet."

"We could go back to the ranch."

"Wouldn't that seem a little odd, us leaving together on a two hour drive at midnight?"

"Maybe," he allowed, going silent.

"I feel like it's prom night," she muttered.

"Backseat of my car?" he offered on a lighter tone.

"I don't think it's going to work out tonight, Travis."

They might be able to get away for an hour or so, but there was no way they could disappear for the entire night.

"It has to work out," he insisted.

"There'll be lots of other nights," she reassured him.

He drew back. "Are you serious?"

Her stomach lurched in regret, her skin prickling with embarrassment. That was entirely the wrong thing to say. What was she *thinking*? She struggled to think of a way to turn the words into a joke, dial them back.

"Will you promise me lots of other nights," he asked her. "Because I can convince myself to give this one up, but only if I know there'll be others."

"Where is this going, Travis?" she forced herself to ask him. "What exactly do you want?"

"I want to spend time with you. It's as simple and as complicated as that."

Her entire body relaxed. "I want to spend time with you too."

"That's good." He pulled her close again, kissing her surreptitiously at her hairline. "That's very, very good."

The music drew to a close.

"Travis," came Maureen's cheerful voice as she sidled up to them. "Come dance with your mom."

"Love to, Mom," he answered warmly. "Don't go far," he whispered to Danielle as she drew away.

She nodded her agreement.

Her heart singing along with the music, she all but skipped off the dance floor. Dating Travis was complicated, but when they cut through to the heart of their attraction, it was also very simple. They liked each other, so they'd find a way.

She was thirsty, and so went in search of a bar.

The connected rooms of the mansion were crowded with guests, but the mood was joyful, and people smiled and nodded as she passed by. She was starting to recognize a few of the faces and feeling less like an outsider. She realized she was truly enjoying the evening.

A uniformed bartender greeted her as she approached one of several rollaway bars set up around the perimeter of the hall.

"Soda and lime," she requested.

"Coming right up." He deftly flipped a clean glass, filling it to the brim with ice.

While she waited, she heard Mandy's voice nearby. "Caleb hadn't even thought of it."

Danielle leaned back, craning her neck, catching a glimpse of the ice-blue, satin bridesmaid gown.

"So, it was Travis's idea?" came Katrina's voice. "Because that's sort of dangerous."

"I thought so, too," Mandy returned, as the bartender dropped a lime slice into the glass. "Caleb said that Travis was adamant he had to hire her."

The bartender filled the glass with soda water. "Here you are, ma'am." He handed it to her.

Mandy kept speaking. "Something about keeping her out of D.C."

Danielle stilled.

But Mandy wasn't finished. "She had a killer job offer there."

"What I don't get," said Katrina, "was how it's Travis's business at all. I mean, I get that he's attracted to her. But you know his track record. Why would he interfere in her career? And why would he drag Caleb into it?"

Danielle's stomach clamped down hard. She knew she had to announce herself. She had to tell the two women she could overhear. She forced herself to move back, to where she could see them.

"It's not at all like Travis," Mandy agreed. "But I think it worked out for—" Her gaze caught Danielle's, and her eyes grew huge. "Danielle," she sputtered.

Katrina whirled, her mouth forming an O of shock.

"I'm so sorry," Danielle quickly put in, hearing an edge of hysteria to her own voice. "I didn't mean to intrude. I just…" She gave a vague wave toward the bar. "I was…" She didn't know what to say. She didn't know what to do.

The only thing for certain was that Caleb had hired her as a favor to Travis. He didn't want a company lawyer. He didn't need her on his payroll. He'd been helping out a lifelong friend who wanted to sleep with her. And who'd decided he had some kind of a right to interfere in her life.

"I'm sorry," she quickly finished, turning to rush away.

"Danielle," Mandy called from behind her.

Danielle didn't look back. She plunked her full drink on the tray beside the bar and carried on through the front foyer, escaping outside to the fresh air.

She had a credit card in her handbag. She had some cash, a comb, a lipstick and a couple of tissues. It would do until she could have her other things delivered.

She trotted down the front stairs. The air was chilly against her bare arms, and through the thin dress, but that didn't matter. All that mattered right now is that she got away, away from Travis, away from Caleb, away from their families and her humiliation.

Her new job was a fraud. And she couldn't go back to the old one. She'd left Milburn and Associates on bad terms, and she'd turned down Nester and Hedley. She had absolutely no prospects. She honestly didn't know where she went from here.

A hotel first, she supposed. And then she'd need to update her resume. On the bright side—

Her breath caught and her chest tightened painfully. She couldn't seem to come up with a bright side.

The second Travis saw the expression on his sister Mandy's face, he knew something was wrong.

The song was ending, so he quickly excused himself from his mother, crossing the dance floor to meet Mandy. Katrina was hovering behind her.

"What?" He glanced from side to side, trying to identify the source of the problem.

"It's Danielle," Mandy blurted out.

Travis's stomach clenched hard. "Is she hurt?"

Mandy swiftly shook her head. "She's fine. She left."

His fear was replaced with confusion. "What? Why?"

"She overheard us. Well, me. She overheard me talking about her job at Active Equipment."

Travis still didn't understand. "She had *work* to do? Now?"

"No." Mandy drew a breath. "She heard me say you'd talked Caleb into hiring her."

Travis's world went still. Then a roaring sound started in his ears. "You didn't," he rasped.

"I'm so sorry," Mandy continued. "I think." She swallowed. "She might have heard me say you wanted to keep her out of D.C."

"Where'd she go?"

"Through the front door."

"When?" Travis demanded, his feet already moving toward the exit.

He didn't hear Mandy's answer. He elbowed his way through the colorful, laughing crowd. People spoke to him, but he didn't answer. The sounds and sights of the reception blended together, incomprehensible and meaningless. The only message that mattered was inside his head. He had to get to Danielle. He had to explain.

He burst through the big door, sprinting to the street, glancing one way and then the other.

He spotted her, half a block down, under a streetlamp, marching along in her blue dress and high heels, the crystals sparkling in the light.

"Danielle," he called.

Her shoulders stiffened, but she kept walking.

"Danielle," he repeated, breaking into a run. "Stop."

This time, there was no reaction. She completely ignored him.

His strides ate up the sidewalk, and he quickly caught her. "Danielle, please, let me explain."

She lifted her chin and increased her pace. "You don't have to explain a thing."

"Stop," he pleaded.

She stopped and turned on him. "No."

"Let me tell you what happened."

"I *know* what happened. You got Caleb to manipulate me. You couldn't keep me out of D.C. by yourself, so you made him do it for you. You are a self-centered, unbridled control freak."

"I am not a control freak, I—"

"Do you have *any* idea what you've done?" she demanded, eyes blazing under the light.

"I want what's best for you," he insisted, knowing it was entirely true.

"You don't get to decide what's best for me. Randal doesn't get to decide, and you don't get to decide."

"Randal's a selfish jerk."

She jabbed a finger against Travis's chest. "And you are exactly like him."

"I am *nothing* like him," Travis growled.

"Really?" she demanded. "He wanted to sleep with me, so he found me a job in D.C. You wanted to sleep with me, so you found me a job in Lyndon Valley. Tell me right now, what's the difference?"

The difference was that Travis wanted what was best for Danielle. Randal wanted what was best for Randal.

She didn't wait for him to answer. "The difference is, you're worse, Travis. Because you actually ruined my career. I have no job. I had two, count 'em *two* solid, viable, well-paying job opportunities, and you made me blow them both."

"You have a job at Active Equipment."

"Don't insult me. That's a sham."

Caleb's voice interrupted. "It's a real job, Danielle."

Her eyes darted past Travis to where Caleb had caught up to them on the sidewalk.

"Not you, too, Caleb," she rasped. "I trusted you. I thought we had—" Her voice broke.

Caleb stepped forward. "You *can* trust me."

"You can trust me, too," Travis felt compelled to put in. "I might have suggested—"

"Stop talking," Danielle ordered him in a stone-cold tone.

She looked at Caleb to include him as well. "Both of you stop talking. This is *my* life. You don't get to mess with it." She took a backward step away from them. "I'm leaving now."

Travis made to follow. "No."

Caleb grabbed his arm to stop him.

Travis struggled to shake off the grip. No way, no how was he letting Danielle leave like this.

"Take a car," Caleb told her, waving one of the sedans forward. "Take it to the Sunburst Hotel. Active Equipment has an account."

"I'll pay for my own hotel room," she snapped.

"Don't go," Travis barked. "Let's go someplace, let's talk."

She gazed up at him, or rather through him. "I never want to speak to you again."

The car pulled up, and she moved to the curb.

"Danielle," he pleaded, straining toward her.

Caleb's grip tightened. "Not now," he ordered in Travis's ear.

"I can't let her go."

She opened the back door of the sedan.

"You have to let her go."

As she climbed inside, Travis jerked free.

"For now," Caleb said to him. *"For now."*

Danielle slammed the door shut.

Travis swore.

"You'll talk to her tomorrow," Caleb offered.

Travis swore again.

"She'll be at the Sunburst." Caleb clasped him on the shoulder. "And you'll talk to her in the morning."

"I'm so sorry," Mandy said, surprising Travis with her presence. "I truly did not realize she could hear me."

He wanted to rail at his sister, demand to know what had happened, demand to know how she could have been so indiscreet. But he knew it wasn't her fault. It was his fault.

He wasn't anything like Randal. But right now Danielle had no way of knowing that.

"I have to talk to her," he said out loud. He didn't think he could wait until morning.

"And say what?" asked Mandy, moving a little closer to him.

He gazed down as his practical, pragmatic sister looked him square in the eyes. "And say what, big brother?"

He didn't understand the question.

"That you're in love with her?" Mandy asked.

Something shifted inside Travis, the possibility opening up like sunshine on an early spring morning.

In love with Danielle? How great would it be to be in love with Danielle? That would mean he could care for her, protect her. He could spend the rest of his life with her. They could live together, build a family like his siblings had done. He could grow old with Danielle by his side.

"Travis?" Mandy interrupted softly.

"She hates me," he found himself saying.

"She's only angry," Mandy countered.

Travis hoped that was true. She'd been angry with him before, and he'd been able to reason with her. Maybe he could do it again this time.

"I wasn't wrong, you know," he told his sister.

"Wrong about what?"

"To keep her out of D.C. To keep her with me instead of him."

"Maybe so," Mandy allowed. "But I'm not sure that should be your opening line."

Danielle gazed at the pink glow of the sun coming up over Lyndon City. She was curled up in an armchair, facing the picture window in her hotel room, wrapped in an oversized T-shirt. Checking in last night, she'd asked about buying something to sleep in and was given the shirt out of their storage room.

It wasn't until Danielle got to her room, that she realized it was left over from the mayor's race. The shirt was roomy, long, nearly down to her knees, and emblazoned across the front it said JACOBS HAS MY VOTE. Now, she hugged it to herself, blinking away tears, pondering the irony.

She'd fallen in love with Travis last night. She thought it must have happened while they were dancing. Then again, maybe it had happened at the rehearsal, or while they were shopping. Or maybe it had happened way back in Vegas.

She didn't really know, and it didn't really matter. She was in love with Travis, and he'd betrayed her. The worst part was that he didn't even understand what he'd done. He was so stubborn, so blind, so brazenly self-confident that it never occurred to him he could make a mistake.

If Travis saw the world a certain way, then that was the way of the world. If anyone disagreed, then they were misguided. That conviction gave him license to manipulate people and events. He'd wanted her in Lyndon Valley, so here she was, in Lyndon Valley.

Yet again, her mother was proven right. Men looked after their own interests. Women were on their own.

Should she have seen this coming? Should she have guessed the depths of Caleb's loyalty to Travis?

Mentally debating what she should or should not have known, was exhausting. She knew she ought to care about her career. But all she knew at the moment was that she missed Travis. She loved him. Or at least she had loved him. For a brief magical time last night, they seemed to have a shining future.

There was an abrupt knock on her hotel room door, and her nerves jolted to life. She gripped the arms of the chair, staying firmly in place, telling herself there wasn't anyone she wanted to see right now.

The knock came again, followed by Caleb's voice. "Danielle? I brought you some things from the mansion."

She was disappointed, and she hated herself for feeling that way. She'd wanted it to be Travis. Even in the midst of his outrageous behavior, she wanted it to be him. How could she allow herself to be so weak?

"Danielle?" Caleb called again.

She pushed herself up from the chair, gritting her teeth in determination. She would need to talk to Caleb at some point. And she did need to get her things. Better to get it over with now. Then she could make a reservation back to Chicago.

Bracing herself, she unlocked the door and pulled it open.

Her heart lurched in her chest when it was Travis standing in the hall.

They both stared at each other. He looked as exhausted as she felt.

"We need to talk," he opened softly.

She swallowed, struggling to find her voice. It was buried by heartbreak. "I don't think I can."

"Then just listen."

She shook her head in denial. "You can't do this to me, Travis."

"I want what's best for you. I always have."

A little bit of her strength returned. "You've truly convinced yourself of that, haven't you?"

"Can I come in?"

"No."

"We can't leave it like this."

"Where's your brother-in-law? Or should I say your partner in deceit?"

"He knows I need to talk to you."

"End justifies the means?" she mocked. "Yet again?"

"Let me explain. Hate me if you have to, but at least let me explain."

His beautiful, blue eyes were wide, and there was a vulnerability to his tone that wormed its way into her heart. She couldn't find it in herself to refuse.

Wordlessly, she stepped back, opening the door to him.

He immediately came in, closing the door, pressing his back against it.

For a minute, they both just stood there. His gaze flicked to her T-shirt, then to her bare legs below it. Something flared in her belly, and she hated herself for still desiring him.

"I couldn't let him have you," Travis began, his tone unguarded.

"That wasn't your choice to make."

Not that Randal had a single chance of winning her back, especially after she'd come to know Travis. Randal was nothing to her anymore.

"I was absolutely certain I was doing the right thing."

"You always are."

He nodded. "I knew you'd love working for Caleb. I knew Caleb would love having you there. It was a good fit. It was a win-win."

She found herself growing impatient. "Just admit it, Travis."

He jerked his head back. "Admit what?"

"Quit with the 'I did it for you' and 'I did it for Caleb.' Just admit you wanted to sleep with me, so you found a way to keep me around."

He pushed away from the door, taking a couple of paces into the room. "Is that what you think?"

"It's the truth."

He faced her square on. "That I wanted you around? Sure. That's the truth. But not so I could sleep with you."

"I was there, Travis, remember? I know what you wanted."

His expression softened. "Okay, yeah, I'd take you in my bed any day of the week."

Her stomach shimmered with desire again, and she fought the urge to throw herself into his arms. She wanted to kiss him. She wanted the night he'd promised her on the dance floor. Then she wanted a hundred more like it. She wanted Travis in her life every night and every day.

"I wanted you Danielle." His tone was husky. "I wanted everything about you. On some level." He coughed a harsh laugh. "I guess I already knew I was in love with you."

Her mind screeched to a halt.

"But I knew you wouldn't marry a cowboy," he continued.

Wait, what? What was that part about loving her?

"So," he told her. "I settled for the next best thing. I was wrong." He raked a hand through his hair. "I pretended I was right, because I wanted it so bad. And if you'd actually moved to D.C., I'd have had to move there too to keep an eye on Randal."

Her mind was still grappling with his declaration of love. He loved her? She wouldn't marry him? How did he know she wouldn't marry him?

"Travis—"

"I'm sorry, Danielle." He reached for her shoulders, his touch light, cradling them ever so gently. By contrast, his tone was harsh. "But he can't have you. I can *never* let him have you."

"Travis?"

"Yes?" he choked out, faced pained, expression taut.

"You should ask me to marry you."

He blinked in obvious bafflement, his jaw going lax.

"I want you to ask me to marry you."

His expression remained taut. "Okay," he started slowly. "Will you marry me, Danielle?"

"Yes."

"What?"

"I'll marry you."

He gaped at her. "Why?"

Her lips curved into a smile. "Because I'm in love with you." She pressed her palm to his chest, covering his heart as she stepped closer. "I love you, Travis."

"I'm a cowboy."

"I know."

"You're an intelligent, accomplished, world-class legal genius."

"So we both agree, I'm smart enough to know when I'm in love?"

His arms slipped around her back. "You love me?"

She moved into his arms, resting her body against his. "You better hope so, cowboy, since we're engaged."

"We're really engaged?"

"Unless you want to take back your proposal."

His hands moved to cradle her cheeks. "Not on your life. And you're not taking back your acceptance. We're engaged, Danielle Marin, and I'm going to marry you just as soon as we can get in front of an official. Can you be ready in an hour?"

"We're not in Vegas anymore. I don't think there's a chapel in the lobby."

"Seth will marry us. And he can expedite the license."

"You want to marry me today?"

"Yes. Absolutely. I don't want you to change your mind."

He leaned in to place a soft, lingering kiss on her lips and she basked in his gentleness and his solid strength.

"I'm not going to change my mind."

"I can't take that chance."

"Okay," she agreed on a whisper. "I'll marry you just as soon as you want."

"I love you, Danielle."

Her heart squeezed tight in her chest. "Travis, I love you so much."

He smoothed back her hair. "My family's already here. But, what about your family?"

Danielle wasn't so sure that was a good idea. "You want to argue with my mother about a prenup?"

"You want a prenup?"

"No. But she will."

He loosened his hold on her ever so slightly. "What do you want to do?"

"Elope? No frills, a simple ring, a simple ceremony. It's the outcome that matters to me, Travis, not the event."

He thought about it for a moment. "Can we tell my family before we go?"

"Sure. Maybe Katrina and Reed can come with us."

A smile grew on Travis's face. "We will need witnesses. Vegas?"

"On the deck at Jacque Alanis?"

"Katrina will make us go dancing."

"As long as you hold me close."

"I'll hold you close, Danielle," he vowed, enfolding her in his arms. "I'm going to hold you close forever."

* * * * *

A sneaky peek at next month...

Desire™

PASSIONATE AND DRAMATIC LOVE STORIES

My wish list for next month's titles...

In stores from 16th May 2014:

❏ The Texan's Forbidden Fiancée – Sara Orwig

& My Fair Billionaire – Elizabeth Bevarly

❏ Expecting the CEO's Child – Yvonne Lindsay

& Baby for Keeps – Janice Maynard

❏ A Bride for the Black Sheep Brother
  – Emily McKay

& A Sinful Seduction – Elizabeth Lane

2 stories in each book - only **£5.49!**

Available at WHSmith, Tesco, Asda, Eason, Amazon and Apple

Just can't wait?

0514/51

Special Offers

Every month we put together collections and longer reads written by your favourite authors.

Here are some of next month's highlights— and don't miss our fabulous discount online!

THE CHATSFIELD

Playboy's Lesson

MELANIE MILBURNE

On sale 6th June

3 in 1 GREAT VALUE

Out of HOURS *Office Affairs*

SARAH MAYBERRY NICOLA MARSH KATE HEWITT

On sale 6th June

MAISEY YATES

Married on Paper

On sale 6th June

Save 20%

on all Special Releases

Find out more at

www.millsandboon.co.uk/specialreleases

Visit us Online

0614/ST/MB471

Hot reads!

These 3-in-1s will certainly get you feeling hot under the collar with their desert locations, billionaire tycoons and playboy princes.

**Now available at
www.millsandboon.co.uk/offers**

Blaze is now *exclusive* to eBook!

FUN, SEXY AND *ALWAYS STEAMY*!

Our much-loved series about sassy heroines and irresistible heroes are now available exclusively as eBooks. So download yours today and expect sizzling adventures about modern love and lust.

Now available at www.millsandboon.co.uk/blaze

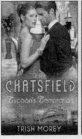   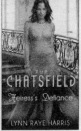

Join our *EXCLUSIVE* eBook club

FROM JUST £1.99 A MONTH!

Never miss a book again with our hassle-free eBook subscription.

★ Pick how many titles you want from each series with our flexible subscription

★ Your titles are delivered to your device on the first of every month

★ Zero risk, zero obligation!

There really is nothing standing in the way of you and your favourite books!

Start your eBook subscription today at www.millsandboon.co.uk/subscribe

Join the Mills & Boon Book Club

Subscribe to **Desire™** today for
3, 6 or 12 months and you could
save over £30!

We'll also treat you to these fabulous extras:

- 🌹 FREE L'Occitane gift set
  worth £10

- 🌹 FREE home delivery

- 🌹 Rewards scheme, exclusive
  offers…and much more!

Subscribe now and save over £30
www.millsandboon.co.uk/subscribeme

The World of Mills & Boon

There's a Mills & Boon® series that's perfect for you. There are ten different series to choose from and new titles every month, so whether you're looking for glamorous seduction, Regency rakes, homespun heroes or sizzling erotica, we'll give you plenty of inspiration for your next read.

By Request
Back by popular demand!
12 stories every month

Cherish™
Experience the ultimate rush of falling in love.
12 new stories every month

INTRIGUE...
A seductive combination of danger and desire...
7 new stories every month

Desire™
Passionate and dramatic love stories
6 new stories every month

nocturne™
An exhilarating underworld of dark desires
3 new stories every month

For exclusive member offers go to
millsandboon.co.uk/subscribe